Rescue!

Written by Marie Daley

Dedication

To: Dave and Patty from The Game Depot in Tempe, Arizona. They have always supported me from their warm hearts! They are two people who are truly dedicated to others and have rescued so many of us here in the Valley – even if in small ways!

Special Thanks to Tammy Pike for all her help!

The Adventures of Ryes and Garth

Tayna's Dawn

Winterhaven

Winds of Change

Striding Forth

Rescue!

Table of Contents

Concept art by Adam Mathison-Sward

This page intentionally left blank

Two Hearts Under the Stars

The stars wheeled overhead as Ardis and Sabin sat near the Phoenix fountain. The lights reflecting through the water of the underground pool up thought the glass-like panels that surrounded the fountain on two of the eight sides, making it seem a more magical tonight for Ardis, as they sat on a bench near the fountain. She smiled as her eyes met Sabin's.

"I can't believe it! Two Talents?" she breathed out, still stunned. "You're an amazing man, my dear husband!" Sabin grinned in pride as he shifted closer to her side and wrapped an arm around her waist, pulling her closer to him.

"It surprised me, to be truthful," he admitted, embarrassed. "I'm still trying to wrap my mind around it." She nestled into the warmth of his embrace, then reached up and began a long, passionate kiss. It wasn't often when they could get a few moments of escape like they had tonight! Katas and the cubs were staying at Ryes and Garth's overnight.

"And both our sons having Talent, too! They're going to be a true handful when they're grown," Sabin admitted with a sigh, once their lips parted.

"I'm hoping all our cubs will be Talented," Ardis said, her eyes dancing by the moons' light. She realized she was clutching at his tunic top, almost as if she was afraid to let go of him.

"Ardis, Love, you may not have Talent, but are extremely talented in your own way. Don't ever forget that! What is truly bothering you tonight?" he teased, knowing the answer and understanding why she'd insisted they come out here late tonight.

"You know," she breathed, trying to find her smile once more as she looked into his warm, wonderful eyes. "You left for a couple of weeks to return an evil man to his chief and then ended up gone for months! And when you did make it back home, you were barely able to do anything with that broken leg. I shudder to think what this trip out into what our Sleepers call, `The Dark,' will do to you, or if you'll truly make it back home!" The women they'd rescued out of the frozen tombs of Doran's valley were still leaning and adjusting back to what living actually meant. Their lives had started hundreds of years ago, and the changes left many uncertain.

Sabin sighed as he held her tightly in his arms, trying to figure out a good way to reassure her. Then inspiration hit and he opened up to her from within with his new Mind Voice Talent, as he still struggled to learn how, trying to recall what Raya showed him earlier today.

"Let me show you, truly show you, a few things," he gently teased, suddenly feeling she was unwilling to be this intimate with him. She saw he was puzzled by it, as she didn't understand it either. Finally, she relaxed and opened up to him, from within her heart, ready. He then showed her what both he and Dastin saw during the battle of the Talents with the southerners; the great city that Winterhaven is now destined to be, and he was now fully confident it would happen! They both marveled at the huge buildings, crowds of people, the shuttles riding on rails overhead and the bright light that came off the Windrose Stone, which wasn't mounted above them as yet. But it was their Phoenix fountain.

"There's a dome overhead?" Ardis noted, wondering why it was there. "Do our descendants become that unused to wonderful things like rain or snow?"

"I've no idea, but I've come to believe that we will both be very active in making sure Winterhaven evolves into a great city that might actually rival Hailys, in its own time. So, while I might be out in `The Dark,' my heart will be here with you at home," he assured her. He let the memory go of this wondrous Vision. "I never knew I could have a shared Vision that way," he admitted a bit chagrinned, understanding Ryes and Maren's shared Visions better now. He felt her warm-hearted humor.

"With Ryes powering things up, I can imagine a great many things can happen. She's gotten stronger and has more Talents to call upon, but somehow, I don't think she knows yet how to cover her own back. I don't fully trust our Sleepers, either. They used to plot to take over Winterhaven, but I believe that's died away. Is there anything I can do to help her, since you and Garth aren't going to be here for a few days?"

"Why not learn how to tap into her Talents and figure out how to use them, too? I know Bethy will grab onto her and pull up her Mind Voice and other Talents, and Ryes lets her. She'd let you, too, you know," he asserted. He felt her humor again.

"So, I can see how you're doing up there? That's an idea!" she returned, merrily. "She loves and trusts me and will let me do it, too! And I'll help watch after her."

"You two aren't going to let us get too far anymore," he replied, teasing again, and giving her an upwelling of his deep love for her.

"After all the trouble we had figuring out you guys were the ones for us, no way," she assured him. She returned her own deep love for him. Sabin then laughed as he opened his eyes, keeping his Talent up, and scooped her up in his arms.

"You are going to see exactly how much I love and care about you, my dear lady," he sent, as he stood up and headed back to their home. He'd be up in The Dark in a few days and could watch the stars all he wanted to, then.

This page intentionally left blank.

Haily's Starport

Early last spring, seven Matlowe villagers set out for the great ruins of Hailys, because Sabin was banished for six months for killing a cub-killer; it gave the Matlowe Village elders time to collect evidence of the dead man's guilt – one way or the other. It also allowed them to escape Maren's father, Korman, who'd been known to kill others in challenges. Garth wasn't going to ever let Korman get his claws on Ryes, and she didn't want him to get his claws on Garth! During their journey they found the Temple of Doran and her evil plans, but Ryes bested her in a Talent battle, which was partly a within contest of wills, as well as a physical assault. Afterwards, they discovered Hailys and a few treasures that could be gleaned from their past, even if most of the things found puzzled them. Garth beat Korman in a challenge in Hailys when he followed them there. After leaving Hailys, they found a deserted, human, research facility, which they named Winterhaven. Later, while Garth and Sabin were away to settle a peace treaty, Ryes called down a derelict, human, colony transport ship, the Star Quest, which came from Earth, and she and Maren saved what few humans remained onboard in suspension tubes. Since then, the two peoples, both starmen and humans, discovered they could meld; being of one heart in truth and later that they could actually interbreed. Now they wanted to build a secure future for them all! And it'd been foreseen they were destined to conquer the Snagospin, the dark enemy who destroyed Tayna over three-hundred years ago. Being planet-bound, they only need a way to reach them!

"Ah, come on Ryes, we just got back!" Sabin vehemently protested, as he sat in his office the next day. They'd arrived the evening before, having travelled several days to get back from the Caravaner Spring Gather, and the last thing he wanted was a trip out to Hailys tomorrow. They still had to get their things sorted out and clean again, after spending almost four weeks away. What he realized, more than anything in this moment, was he only wanted to enjoy being home with only "normal" concerns for a few days. She smiled impishly at this, then gave him a nod of her head in understanding, her green eyes meeting his orange-gold ones.

"All right, I'll ask Mitt if she minds, then. I know what you mean, though; a long trip does take it out of you!"

"It wasn't my imagination about Torr and Dodi being together? I thought Ardis was going to have a fit when they picked up Tobin last night. She was starting to get attached to him." Ryes nodded her head in regret. She'd seen the way she was bonding with the infant when they were out at the gather site.

"It was a shock for us, too. But Maren helped her to bring in her milk, so she could feed him naturally. He says he thinks it might be a little short of a year before Dodi's next season is upon her, so hopefully they'll have things worked out, one way or the other, by then. Dodi looked so happy and proud, but I feel sorry for Tobin, having this mother, then that mother, and now another one. I hope he'll be all right!"

"Me, too," he grunted. He still had his own sister's pregnancy to deal with, yet. Wait until their mother found out! He thought it'd be best to tell her the day before the formal announcement. He could imagine the screaming and yelling! Even so, he knew he was still glad to be home. Suddenly, he realized he was having a familiar feeling and reached out to grab Ryes' hand. He wanted it as strong and clear as possible, tapping her Booster.

There was a crowd gathered near the silent bulk of the Star Quest, all eyes cast upwards to the sky above. Coming down slowly, as if a leaf surrendering to a precarious breeze as it fell from a tree, was a starship. This one looked different, but like the Star Quest, it carried scaring upon its outer hull. Garth turned to him and smiled.

"Looks better than we thought," he commented.

"I thought it'd be larger," Ethan added, frowning at the sight. Luckily, it managed to set down near the Star Quest, well away from their new construction projects.

"Thanks, Ryes," Sabin said, as the Vision released him. She quirked an odd smile at him.

"Why...?" she stammered, not sure what she was even asking. It was as if the both of them stood there in fact, but not like the ones she and Maren shared.

"You do boost my Visions and I'll warn you right now, if I ever feel one coming on and you're close by, I'll be tapping into your abilities again. They're strong and clear when I'm in contact with you, which I've discovered through the last year being around you," he explained, grinning wolfishly.

"So good as to be of some service," she returned with a small bow and smile as she blushed, still a little unsettled. He chuckled at the expression on her face, bowing in return, amused he'd unsettled her again.

"Do you think Mitt could handle it?" he suddenly asked, wondering if he should go along with them, after all? "She is young and still learning her Talents," he added.

"I think she can, but the final decision is Garth's and I'm not breathing a word to Mitt, until he approves it. We'll see what he says. He may just wait until you're feeling centered once more," she ventured with a smile.

"Let me know what he says," he requested. She gave him a nod, then got up.

"Take a few minutes to walk about the apartment complex with Ardis, later. I think you'll like some of the innovations the crew's come up with," she suggested, teasing him.

"I think I will," he agreed, as she stepped over to the door. She turned to smile, then waved as she left. He turned back to his console and typed in a quick message to his wife.

"Sabin's tired and doesn't feel up to it, yet," Ryes explained to her husband, sitting in his office afterwards. She was still a little unsettled about being used by him, and the way he bragged about it.

"They just got back last night, after all. Have some mercy for him," he teased. "So, we'll delay your journey for a few days. What will it matter? The past just is... and will remain so written." She sighed, seeing he was right to a point.

"I was thinking of using either you, or Mitt to fill in. After all, you both have strong Talents," she countered, smiling sweetly.

"I still have to get used to the idea of actually having Talents," he returned, huffing at her reminder. "I forgot that now I could possibly try to go with you." He recalled that horrible, odd feeling he got whenever she Time Walked far back into the past, then realized that he felt better in the role of being her guide back; just in case she needed his help to reconnect. And he could count upon Sabin to make her mind him while journeying into the past.

"You haven't told anyone yet, have you?" she pressed, realizing it only now.

"Only Sabin, Torr, Maren and the elders," he replied, chuckling, realizing she knew him too well! "With what we found in the library in Matlowe, we may not need any further trips back into the far past," he ventured, hoping to dissuade her.

"I still have to save my great aunt. I've no idea from what, but how can I find out, if I don't go back to see?" she pressed, sure on this account. Her instincts were screaming at her that she had to accomplish this deed, if nothing else. "I'm starting to have nightmares of Hailys' destruction again. Somehow, I know this is tied in with my Great Aunt Adina." Garth didn't look happy with her, but realized she was right.

"One more explorative trip is all I'm allowing," he finally granted with a heavy sigh, hoping he wouldn't regret it. "I'd rather you wait until Sabin feels more up to the task, than risk Mitt. Her Talents may be strong, but has no true experience, yet," he said, then paused as he recalled hearing what she and Axel were discussing the other day in the shuttle hangar. "Actually, I think Axel has a better idea of how to use her Talents than she does. It's a good thing she's used to listening to him." Ryes huffed out a laugh, thinking it sounded true.

"So, did the new treaty work out all right?" she suddenly asked. It was one of the things he and Sabin were working on at the gather. Now that they had the wisdom and counselling of Dr. Cruthers and Rowan to add weight to their side, they were trying to renegotiate the treaty with the plain's tribes.

"Dara was impressed and is looking at our new draft. He'll have his counter proposal ready by the next gather. Kyma's also working on drafting a treaty with us, so we gave him an altered copy. He sees advantages to having close ties with Winterhaven. I'm only surprised he didn't try talking Mitt into accepting him for her mating later this summer," he admitted, chuckling.

"He sure spent enough time with her, up in the choppers," Ryes agreed with his observation. "But she's too hooked into Minn, to take anyone else's interest seriously. Did you catch that play Mason made for her, as if he were trying to win her back?" she asked. He shook his head no at this, wondering about it. "I'm only surprised she didn't leave boot prints across his back, as he practically threw himself before her feet. Poor Shadd. She was so embarrassed. I hope she's rethinking her choice of playmates, now."

"Torr and Dodi seem solid, so I don't think she'll have a chance of winning him back. It's nice to see Torr happy, again."

"That's true," Ryes admitted, smiling. She was glad they were doing well and hoped they'd stay together for a while, at least, still feeling uncomfortable about Tobin.

"I almost forgot," she hinted, smiling. "Sabin shared one of his Visions with me." Garth's eyes took on new interest, nodding for her to continue. "Actually, he started having the Vision and quickly grabbed my hand. Afterwards, he told me he tapped me because my Booster make his Visions stronger and clearer, and anytime he has another one when I'm near, he'll do it again. Talk about being used and abused!" she mockingly groaned in protest, smiling. Garth chuckled, then leaned forward and took his wife's hand into his own.

"Show it to me," he urged. She knew he'd want to see it and was ready for the request. She closed her eyes and opened up to him from within, showing him what they saw. After several long moments, they both dropped out of the link. "So at least one will make it for sure," he stated. "Though it does look pretty beat up."

"At least they get through," she insisted. "It looks like it sustained some kind of guidance damage, to be drifting down so crazily, and it's almost three-quarters of a size smaller than the Star Quest. I wonder how large the crew is?" she wondered aloud.

"Hopefully, all of them will make it," he breathed, then smiled for her. The message they received previously from Earth's military stated twelve ships were being sent out, seeking Tayna for help in breaking the Darken's blockade. "Anything else of importance?"

"No. Pretty slow day around here. Guess we all still need to recover from that gather. It's a good thing we've only committed to the Caravaner's Gather and the Great Spring Gather. I think that's more than enough fun, for now. But I can bet we'll be pressed to participate in the Great Fall Gather, too," she stated. "We're doing our preparations for the Great Spring Gather with the lessons we've learned from this last one, kept more in mind. We're also installing the call station over in Matlowe, and putting up a new column of the laws, which were supposed to be posted in the Village Square, later this week."

"Did they finish their analysis of the metal of the original column?"

"Yes. It's the same one used for the beams in the buildings in Hailys. It takes one truly hot fire to get that stuff to melt for molding. Phil thinks if we can duplicate their process, we'd have some great, lightweight metal for our shipbuilding ventures. I guess it's pretty tough stuff," she told him.

"I wonder if they used it for building their own ships, in the past?" he speculated, looking puzzled. "We've never tried to excavate the great crater, where the space port once stood, but if they did use such metal in their ships, they might still lie buried beneath the dirt and rubble!"

"I don't know. I could ask my Aunt Adina," she hinted, smiling mischievously.

"I already told you, you can go when Sabin's ready," he reminded her, huffing in exasperation. "I'll talk with him after lunch and see when he thinks the two of you should go."

"Sounds good to me. I'd better move and check on things in my office before lunch, myself. Gareth bit me this morning, looking like he meant it. I may be weaning them soon, since they're used to using the bottles and sippy cups now, anyway."

"He might be teething," Garth suggested, laughing at the look on her face.

"I'm not a teething ring, and that's my final decision," she replied, knowing it amused him.

"Whatever you think best, Sweet One," he told her. "See you for lunch," he promised, standing up as she stood. She smiled as he kissed her, then was quickly out the door. He sighed as he sat back down, turning back to his terminal.

"They were headed to the spaceport, so it only makes sense," Ryes asserted as Garth piloted the chopper toward Hailys. "They were going to leave for Kahmarr, never to return. Whatever happens has to be out there."

"Since you're the one leading this expedition, we'll head for the spaceport," he replied, giving in. He altered his course to take them to where the spaceport once stood. It was early in the morning, with the sun having just risen. The view from the chopper was breathtaking, as the reddish-yellow sunlight began to bring color to the swiftly passing world below them. The land west of Hailys was starting to border the plains, so there were fewer trees, but the grasses were tall and green with their new spring growth, waving in the light southerly breeze. Garth circled the area where he intended to land, making sure there'd be no untold surprises awaiting them, then lightly landed the aircraft.

"Wait," Garth cautioned Ryes as she reached for the door's release, having already unbuckled from the seat's harness. "Quincy, Monty, give it a quick look around," he ordered.

"I could do that with my Talent, or you can with yours," Ryes scolded, but he quietly met her eyes, making sure she was paying him attention, as the two men left the chopper out one of the rear doors.

"You're going to need every bit of energy you've got for this venture. Don't waste it in checking the area for predators. And I need practice to learn to understand what my Talent is telling me. This isn't the time. Let the gentlemen perform their duties, and learn a little patience," he advised, finally smiling for her. She gave him a nod of her head, understanding.

"Maybe I'd better go give them a hand?" Torr volunteered. "They've only hunted on a team before and may not know a predator's trace from a herd beast's."

"You have a point," Sabin agreed, smiling. "Why don't you and Gann double check them?" Garth gave them a nod of agreement, so both men exited, following in the humans' footsteps. After almost ten minutes, they heard the all-clear whistle. By then Garth had finished his shutdown procedure and was more ready for this, himself. Ryes had sat fidgeting nervously, worried over what she thought the emergency was, from which she had to save her great aunt.

"Let's go," Garth ordered, grabbing his backpack. Ryes grabbed hers as she jumped out the door into grasses, which came up to her knees. She was glad she wore her tall boots today! There was an unexpected pistol shot and she found herself flattened, burrowed into the grasses, glad of the cover and her reflexes.

"It's only a snake," Gann called out loudly, with a laugh. She stood back up to see him holding up a brown, three-foot long viper, whose head had been shot off. For some reason she couldn't name, she was glad it wasn't her viper. Garth looked disgusted, as his brother walked over and threw down the carcass near his feet.

"Warn us, next time," Sabin growled out. They gathered as a group and started walking toward the crater's edge, which lay only fifty feet away. Ryes noted the wildflowers and wild grains growing here, stopping to pick some as she went.

"Just can't leave the poor plants alone, can you?" Maren teased, as he saw her putting some of the wild grains into a collection bag she'd pulled out of her backpack. She smiled up at him, shaking her head as she shoved the bag back into her backpack.

"You never know what we'll find!" she told him. She started idly weaving the wildflowers into a wreath, as they walked.

"Let me guess, you're going to wear those?" Dr. Cruthers merrily questioned her, pointing to her wreath.

"I used to wear flowers in my hair all the time, when I was younger," she related with a wistful sigh. She looked to him, smiling.

"I grew out of it, but still like to do silly things like make wreaths, every now and then. I love the way these pink ones smell," she added, smiling as she picked more, inhaling their fragrance before adding them into her creation. Garth chuckled.

"On that particular rainy day, I recall finding one of your blue flowers, after you ran off," he told her, "I think I kept it for years." She blushed as she looked to him, meeting his eyes. Yes, she could well believe he'd do something like that.

"I guess I should get back into the habit," she teased, "At least you won't have to hold me down to get a flower anymore." Maren, Sabin and Torr laughed as Gann looked embarrassed. He recalled that day and taking his chance to help beat up the little outcast girl, who always had the best toys from off the caravans. He recalled that Garth held her down, but never struck her.

"Ryes, I'm so sorry for what I did to you when I was young and stupid," he apologized for his actions, as a thoughtless child. She saw this, and gave him a kindly look and nod of her head. She understood, appreciated it, and let it all go, once more.

"The past is only that," Maren told him, seeing Gann's distress. "She forgave us," he assured him, smiling. He sighed relief, seeing it in her clear, emerald-green eyes. Ethan looked interested, as if wondering what secret they shared?

Ryes and Garth reached the edge of the crater and stopped. It wasn't as deep, nor as wide as the one in the center of Hailys but was still impressive. A wide variety of grasses, brush and trees covered the ground, far below their feet. It was like an isolated garden, with the occasional metal beams sticking up as if some strange, leafless plants growing among the normal vegetation. Ryes itched to climb down to explore it, even if it looked like it'd be a difficult climb.

"Dr. Cruthers, did any of your earlier explorations determine if that death dust was used here, too?" she suddenly asked, turning to see him studying the scene below them. His eyes met hers, wondering why she needed such information now?

"We barely found this crater when we had to evacuate, so I don't believe any scans were done to determine if the danger exists here, or not. You're not planning on a trip down into the crater now, my dear?"

"Not now, but maybe at some time in the future," she replied, memories of some hazy dreams about it danced behind her eyes.

"Yeah, her pink flowers grow down there in abundance," Maren commented with mischief in his eyes as he looked at her. "Got to have plenty of those ones."

"Oh Maren, come on. I know that if I told you I was going to explore there, you'd be clamoring to come along," she stated, the look in her eyes daring him to refute her. He sighed as he finally nodded his head. She knew him, too well. Suddenly, Garth started looking around, tension in his stance. Then he relaxed as he realized none of

the trees in this area looked anything like the ones in their Vision.
Even the ones below weren't tall enough. It wasn't here, at least.

"Let's get you set up over there," Garth suggested, pointing
to some nearby trees. "The sooner you get started, the sooner we can
be on our way home." Ryes sighed, knowing he was right. She was
enjoying the time out but was sure he was thinking of the work he still
had to finish before the next gather.

The trees here gave off a wonderfully spicy scent, as their
branches hung low with their many blooms. Ryes and Torr spread out
a large groundsheet, after checking the area beneath first for any
lurking dangers. Next Ryes brought out her blanket, with Maren
helping her to unfold it. They placed it down over the groundsheet,
looking for all the world as if they were out for an early morning
picnic. As Ryes, Sabin and Maren sat down, yellow and white flower
petals began to drift downward on the breeze, falling lightly to the
ground. Ryes plucked a flower up from her lap, laughing happily.
Garth gave her a warning look; she sighed and tried to relax, so they
could get down to doing what they came all this way to finish. She
placed her wreath upon her head in a small show of defiance and the
other flower in her pocket. Ethan sat near her, pulling out his pipe
and filling it; a pair of drones buzzed overhead, recording everything.

"Be careful, my dear," he cautioned, feeling she needed the
warning. She smiled for him, giving him a nod of her head.

"Mind your time," Garth warned her. Sabin nodded his head
in agreement.

"I'll try," she replied. She took in a deep breath, releasing it
slowly. Flutter-wings were loose in her stomach, even if this was her
third trip. She closed her eyes, reaching down for her center, then
over for Sabin's hand. He clasped hers securely, their minds now
linked using her Mind Voice. Then she unleashed her Time Walking
Talent, casting them back through time.

There was that old, now familiar, wrenching sensation, which
caused her stomach to feel out of place. This shifting was far harder
to endure, than the shorter trips she was used to make to learn the
human base, before the Star Quest landed. The gold and green light
and torrent of rushing power threatened to engulf them. She held on
and searched for her Aunt Adina and Hadu-ramashan, her aunt's
guardian. If she could find them, she felt she'd be fine. This focus
gave her strength to resist the effects of the shift and save Sabin from
the worst of it, too. Finally, the shifting settled, and she opened her
eyes upon the bustling spaceport.

"This place is astounding," Sabin commented, as they stood
up and marveled at the view down upon the busy port around them.
They arrived sitting next to a great glass panel. Below them the port
was laid out. It was amazing!

There were many levels here with offices, shops, restaurants,
bars and places to rent rooms, declared by their bold, garish-like
signs, spread out through them and curving around the main, oval-
shaped pit, going both left and right from where they viewed it. There

were men and women clothed in brown, green and black uniforms, who looked to keep the peace, like the human police officers they'd seen in old human vids.

There were areas where the ships at the far end of the pit, stood ready for boarding, some with lines of people in the process. The ships looked to be of all sizes and shapes. There were ships to the one side where crates, barrels and boxes of various types were being unloaded onto carts and pulled off elsewhere, out of sight by small machines, which the humans would've called robots. Others were bringing cargo and baggage out to waiting ships, helping their crews to load them.

"Look," Sabin pointed out. There was a ship shaped as a great, gold ball, being clamped down and pulled out to the far end of the deeper pit area, where another was just landing and the clamps moving into place to take possession of the craft. Once the arriving ship was out of the way, the clamps were released, and the gold ship rose upwards at an astounding rate of speed. They both practically held their breaths, until it was out of sight, off into the bright, morning sky. It was soon followed by four other ships, in rapid succession.

"Amazing!" Ryes breathed, "and very different from the way the humans run their starports, from Dr. Cruthers' memories."

"Who said the humans always have the right way to do things? From what I understand, we were star explorers for several thousands of years before the humans journeyed out from their home world," he pressed, in an irritated response. She gave him a nod and a rueful smile in surrender at his rebuke, then turned back from the tremendous pit, to look to the bustling crowds behind them. She saw her Aunt Adina just getting off the shuttle, with Hadu making sure she was never crowded, even here. People gave way before him, with a hint of fear rimming their eyes. He was a predator walking among the herd, and they knew it.

"Aunt Adina!" Ryes called out, waving. She and Sabin quickly trotted toward them, smiling. They saw them and stopped to wait.

"My goodness dear, you are cutting it close. We only have an hour before we have to start boarding our ship out," she mildly scolded, still smiling. Ryes smiled in return, giving her a nod.

"I wanted to catch you at the port, before you left," she replied. "Is there time for a quick chat?"

"Hadu, please ask if the ship could be held for an extra fifteen minutes?" she requested, then turned to Ryes. "We will make a little time. Come over here," she gestured, as Hadu used his headset to make the request. He stayed with them and still alert to everything around them. "So, what news do you bring? I see you have given birth to your children, and now you both sport the same symbol on your clothing," she inquired politely, as they sat in a booth, like the one they used at the other end of the shuttle's line. She smiled at the flowers in her hair. Ryes sighed, nodding her head.

"We've been very busy, and I was studying the human legends and found this bird of fire, who rose from the ashes of destruction. I thought it suited our recreating our lives," she explained with a smile. "I've called down a human starship, with only a handful of the humans, who originally built the place we call Winterhaven, aboard. Their ship had been attacked by the Snagospin, the same people who attacked Hailys, and these few survived by being placed in a cold suspension. Shortly after that, I had my four cubs, with the youngest, Rhin, being a Booster. With the spring, we uncovered a hidden repository under Matlowe Village and a recording left by a Prince of Kahmarr telling us a little of what happened, shortly after the attack. We're just starting to fully understand the last of the message he left, now," she told her.

"A Prince? Which one?" Adina questioned, curious.

"Prince Callas of House Ladearis. He looks like an older version of my cousin, Maren. He said his Talent's Healing," she answered. "He did name Garth as his heir, as his wife was a strong Visionary and she saw us finding and opening what they left. The family name and legacy were passed down through his full-blooded sister, Isyiah of House Ladearis, who was here visiting with him. He said their library was filled with all that they could glean from Hailys, Pygoth and Montas, which were destroyed." Adina smiled, knowing she had no idea what her cousin looked like, but dismissed it as unimportant. The sister's name was familiar, but this was not the time to worry about it.

"Your son, Rhin, may be the one who is supposed to aid you, dear. Have you yet figured out how or what may be happening that you need to rescue us from?" she questioned.

"I fear that it's the attack upon Hailys, itself. I've been having horrible dreams about it, far different from the vision my mother showed me. And it's the only thing I can think of which Hadu wouldn't be able to handle," she asserted. Sabin nodded his head in agreement. Adina paused for a moment, within, feeling her truth, even if she wasn't here physically. It was that strong!

"What is a Talent of One? The Prince was talking about looking for her but was unable to find her. It must be a very strong Talent, for him to believe it'd be the only way to take out the Snagospin Talents," Sabin added, still wondering.

"A Talent of One?" she laughed lightly at this, breaking her inner stillness, shaking her head. "It is not one Talent, but all fourteen Talents born into one person. Your mother is a Talent of One, Ryes," she informed her, meeting her emerald-green eyes. "I only have Mind Voice and Earth Shaper, myself. It was the reason why it was so important I discover exactly what happened to your mother. Your grandfather, Tair of House Clenons, helped her escape an arranged marriage."

"It was the man she was supposed to marry, his family and their plans for her that terrified her, not the idea of marriage," Ryes assured her, smiling. "I spoke with her spirit." Adina sighed in relief.

"Yes, they are an ambitious bunch and I tried to warn Mada of this before she made the final arrangements," she stated, hiding her surprise about her casually speaking with Tyra's spirit; still, it gave her an odd twinge of pride. "Now will you accompany us, as we must try to reach our ship. We can talk along the way. I did message Mada about what you told me the last time, just before we boarded the last shuttle here. I got her reply a few minutes ago and she sounded amused. I am not sure if she believed my story," she related with a wry smile. "She must think I am experiencing some kind of hallucinations, brought about by all my stressful travels." She laughed lightly at this, as Ryes laughed in agreement. They stood and headed for a tube, which delivered people to various levels, within the concourse. The crowd was still heavy, and Ryes' aunt was unwilling to push things, with Ryes and Sabin being in spirit form, and vulnerable.

"Where's everyone going?" Sabin asked, not liking the press of travelers around them.

"Everywhere there is to go in the known worlds," Adina supplied with a warm smile. "I keep forgetting you do not have access to starships in your own time. Life must be very simple and dull."

"Simple sometimes, but never dull," Sabin returned with a smile. "Garth and I left for a few days to set up a peace treaty with the plainsmen and ended up gone for several months. Now that's a trip I wouldn't want to repeat. From now on, we travel by rovers and choppers," he assured her. She looked puzzled by his reference.

"He means by a ground convenience, which resembles a small shuttle on wheels, or land rover, as the humans call it. And a chopper is a propeller driven, vertical take-off and landing aircraft," Ryes explained. Hadu gave her a nod of his head, understanding her references. Aunt Adina had turned back to see if they could work their way in through the dense crowd.

Suddenly, there was a tremor which ran through the platform beneath their feet. People started screaming, not knowing what was happening. The wild motion stopped, and the crowd seemed to be holding its collective breath, waiting to see if it would be repeated. Ryes was hit by a sudden chill. This was just how her nightmares began!

"RUN FOR COVER! RUN AWAY FROM HAILYS!" Ryes yelled out, surprising those standing around her. She knew what was coming; there was no doubt in her mind. People behind them started running in every direction, in panic, as Hadu grabbed Adina and picked her up. He ran back for the area near the booths they just quit, with Ryes and Sabin right upon their heels. There was a tremendous sound of thunder, coming from behind them and the shaking was so bad that most everyone was thrown off their feet. The walls, themselves, suddenly cracked, shattering under the assault from above. Hadu kept running, heading for some doors, which were labeled to indicate an exit up to the surface. They gained the outer doors amid a panicked press of people, just as a terrifying ball of fire came rushing up behind them. They reached the doors, rushing through them, as Hadu pushed them closed on them, knowing they were in spirit form, trying to use the doors as a meager shield against the fire. They passed through, still right behind them. As the fire engulfed the doors, blowing them open again, Ryes turned.

"NO!" she cried out and the fireball stopped, exactly as the one did when the portal was rigged to kill those who tripped it in the wrong manner, in Matlowe. Not knowing where to direct the energy of this massive ball of flame, she directed it back upon itself, which extinguished this one, as well as a great swath of flames near it, but still fires burned freely outside, beyond the doors.

"Ryes! How did you do that? You are only Time Walking! You should not be able to do such a thing!" Aunt Adina cried from the safety of Hadu's arms. There were flames in the passage and stairs above them, so she quelled those too, but the gallery they just quit was quickly engulfed again, as Ryes turned to face her aunt, her eyes full of her own questions. Massive beams and other pieces of the building crashed down to crush many who weren't killed by the fire's embrace. Others were still running, blindly seeking safety, some toward them, passing them as they rushed toward the stairs upward, some away, appearing lost and desperate.

"I have no idea. Only that I can't let either of you die. Why shouldn't I be able to use my other Talents, if the essence that is me is here? But I think we'd best return. I spent too much energy doing that. I'll be back soon, I promise," she vowed. With this, she pulled Sabin and herself back to their own time, the wrenching feeling was so strong, it almost made her pass out. It had never been like this before! But she realized Garth's presence was ahead and went to him with joy in her heart at feeling his nearness. She felt her body around her as Maren was yelling something at her. She couldn't respond. It was all she could do to breathe! She was too cold and tired. She heard Sabin's voice and felt better that he sounded all right. Then there was the warm softness of the blanket wrapped around her, as her body shivered in reaction. Something was pressed to her lips, and she was being encouraged to swallow. It was hot and sweet, and she recalled it was something she liked to drink. But she sought the warm darkness of nothingness for a while, just feeling so tired and only wanting to rest in its velvety embrace and forget, for a moment, that horrifying destruction.

Sorrow's Release

Chapter 2

Adina stepped over and picked up a wreath of pink flowers, which had been upon Ryes' head. She was in utter shock. Never in all recorded time, had a Time Walker been able to extend his, or her, other Talents while in spirit form into the past! With the fires raging around them and the floor still shaking below her feet, Adina turned back to Hadu, showing him the wreath. The shock in his eyes showed her it wasn't her imagination, alone. Time Walking was a rare Talent, and she truly didn't know how often a Time Walker carried an additional Talent. Still Ryes' abilities were strong and very unique!

Finally, letting go her own, personal sorrow, and finding her center, she reached out with her Talent, sealing the way behind them with a wall of reinforced earth, to keep the fires and smoke back. There were none left alive on this level, stirring on the other side of the doors. Those trapped with her and Hadu looked to her for salvation. She didn't know if she had the energy but thought if she could create a clear way upwards, it might help them all escape this madness, which was threatening to engulf them. She realized Ryes and her son might truly be their only lifeline, after all. She put the flowered wreath upon her head, to show she believed.

"Finally," Maren breathed, looking down as Ryes opened her eyes, seeing she was back where she belonged, once more. She realized they were flying in the chopper. "How do you feel?" he pressed, needing to hear her voice.

"Exhausted," she assured him in a croaking voice, trying to find her smile. She was sure she quirked a small one at least. He suddenly hugged her to himself, almost crushing her with the strength in his arms.

"Don't you ever do that to us, again!" he scolded, his fear naked in his voice.

"I'll try not to, but I need to go back to save her, Maren, or she'll die!" Ryes told him, tears starting to flow. "I can't leave her to die like that! The whole city is being demolished around them!" She saw the look on his face and knew he was deeply torn inside.

"She's awake?" Ethan asked, joyful to see her responding at last. Ryes caught his warm smile and tried to smile for him too.

"We didn't get many answers; we were rudely interrupted," Ryes told him, trying to let go of her sudden, deep heartache. She saw Garth glance back; the look in his eyes almost started her crying again. She closed her eyes with a sigh and just rested in Maren's arms. She had new problems to unravel and somehow, she had to come up with a way to save her great aunt, Hadu, and as many of those poor, trapped people as she could. She drifted off to a regular sleep, long before they reached Winterhaven.

"I know it seems silly to you, but I'm checking everyone in Winterhaven," Ryes told Gann as he reluctantly stood before her, now at the head of the line, of a long line of people. Most of the others had been cleared to continue with their day, but a handful were talking with Mitt and Raya quietly off to one side. Surprisingly two humans were among them, Scott, and Max. Talents were what the humans call psi abilities, which allowed one, who had the gifts, the tools to reach out into the physical world with their will and effect changes around them. The starmen have fourteen distinct Talents. They are Mind Voice, Empath, Healer, Visionary, Dreamer, Manipulator, Catalyst, Booster, Inner Sight, Time Walker, Fire Shaper, Water Shaper, Storm Caller and Earth Shaper. And while the humans have several in common with the starmen, like Mind Voice, Visionary and Empath they have five other, distinct Talents of their own. They are Electrokenisis, Psi-shield and Blade, Sixth Sense, Telekinesis and Chameleon. The starmen have been breeding Talents for uncounted generations, while the humans for only a few hundred to a thousand years – depending upon whom you asked.

"I don't have a Talent. I would've known by now," Gann protested. She looked straight into his eyes.

"Sit," she ordered in a low voice, having reached her limit with such protests. She wanted to get this all done! He sighed, gave in and did as she bid, realizing he wasn't being given a choice today. "Thank you," she added, as she calmed herself, "now close your eyes and relax. I promise this won't take long." He gave her a nod and tried to comply, but he truly wasn't in a mood to relax right now. She took his hand and once she saw his eyes were closed, so closed her own and opened up from within.

Gann was as tall as his littermate, Garth, and well-muscled as him, but as Garth had honey-colored eyes, his were a dark brown. She trusted Gann in many ways; having gotten to know him well with the close association between the brothers. She found that she usually gave his counsel more weight because he was so like his brother. Because of this, she reached out to him to explain, first.

"Did Garth tell you?" she asked directly, before they began. She felt his puzzlement very clearly. It ignited her own humor, having guessed as much, knowing her husband. "I found he has two Talents and since Mitt has two Talents and there's latent abilities sleeping in all our cubs, I thought you of all people here in Winterhaven would surely have Talent, too," she explained.

"So, because so many other members of my family have Talent, you believe I do too? Why haven't I seen signs of this before?" he asserted, his heart full of doubts. Her mirth filled their contact again.

"Garth didn't know he had Talent until I found it at the caravaner's gather. Let me take a look," she pressed. He gave in and tried to relax. She delved within him seeking out the small orb of extra energy deep within his being, and found she wasn't disappointed. The glowing energy of his sleeping Talent was right where she expected to find it.

"Oh my..." he stated, startled by its existence.

"I'm going to release it and I need you to take control of the Talent. You have to tell it YOU control it; it doesn't control you. I'm here for you, but this is your life, don't let it take it from you," she warned. She felt his reluctance now, which didn't surprise her at all.

"Can't we let it sleep?" he pressed, excited, and panicked at the same time.

"In time it will open on its own, at least I'm here with you to help. I know you can do it! Garth conquered his very quickly and you've got the willpower to do this and to spare." She felt his reluctant agreement after a moment's consideration. So, she released it and backed out of the way, but remained in contact, and urged him to take down his Talent and make it his own, but she was with him too. He struggled as he was awash with power within, not sure what to do with it. It confused him and he was panicking. Ryes was trying to encourage him, then Mitt joined them.

"Come on, Gann, you used to put me in my place all the time and if you can handle me and Karr, this is nothing," she urged with humor coloring her inner voice. Her spirit and energy gave him the courage to fight the torrent and make it bend to his will, at last. Both women enfolded him within with love and joy at his triumph.

"I did it," he sent in return, pride in his mental tones.

"You sure did," Mitt encouraged, "and it looks like you have Mind Voice like I do now, with another one. Ryes, have you looked at our parents, or Myron, yet?"

"They're due to be checked today," she promised, "and Gann you have Empath, as your second Talent. Thanks, Mitt," she added, relieved she joined them, having been the right goad for him.

"I realized you two were taking too long," she happily admitted, "so thought I'd better check it out... just in case. I'm glad I could help." There was pride in her heart, which they both felt clearly.

"Thanks, Mitt," Gann sent, now able to "speak" more clearly within their commune. "Garth has two Talents? I remember you saying he could use his when we were at Hailys, but didn't understand what you meant then. What does he have?" he pressed, wondering and amazed.

"Garth has two?" Mitt threw in, surprised, "I knew the Empath, from when we fought those southern Talents, but what else?"

"He never told either of you?" she asked, mentally sighing. "He has Flame Shaper and Empath. I thought he would've told you both by now. I awakened his Talents when we were at the caravaner's gather."

"I haven't seen him practicing," Mitt commented. Ryes humor filled their inner commune.

"I keep reminding him he needs practice, too," she replied.

"We'll make sure he takes the time, since I know we're going to have to practice our Talents, too," Gann promised, responding with his mental laugh. Mitt put in her agreement.

"Your sister and Raya can help you learn how to best use your new Talents," Ryes advised, then gently let both siblings go. They opened their eyes and Gann blinked for a moment, as if trying to get a new feel for himself. Mitt jumped to her feet and put her arms around his neck while laughing, giving him a kiss on the cheek. He laughed as he hugged her, then stood up.

"Come with me and you can talk with Raya about your Talents," she urged. She took his hand and pulled him across to the tables she and Raya set up, so they could get started. Ryes sighed. So far Scott and Max were the only humans with Talents, but she hoped for more. They needed all the Talents they could find! She turned to see Sadie was next and smiled at her with welcoming warmth.

"So, how did the Talent hunt go today?" Garth asked at dinner, as he sat down next to his dear wife. She was spooning food into Rhin's mouth, but as soon as she got his food in, she turned her head for a moment and cast him a merry smile.

"I have two Talents," Gann told him flat out, then set his tray down hard on the table, across from Garth, interrupting what Ryes was going to say. It was so hard it rattled the plate and silverware, and wildly sloshed his tea; being harder than he'd meant, but he kept his gaze steady. Garth did a surprised chuckled as he turned toward him and gave him a nod.

"So, what do you have?" he asked, as his brother sat down, appearing agitated.

"So, what do you have?" Gann countered with a pointed laugh. Garth blushed and gave him another nod.

"Fair enough. She told you?" he asked, not glancing over to his wife, as he heard her laughing lightly. He wasn't sure if it was something one of the cubs was doing, or his being put on the spot. Perhaps both?

"She told both of us," Mitt stated, as she set her own tray down, with a harsh laugh. "When were you planning upon telling us? Or don't your siblings count anymore?" she pressed. He shook his head, blushing a deeper gold.

"You're both very important to me," he protested, "we've been so busy the last few days."

"Ha!" Ryes put in with a teasing laugh. "You need to take more time for our family and our greater family," she added, meeting his eyes with the truth in her own. He nodded in surrender.

"Alright, I now have Fire Shaper and Empath and before you ask, yes, I need to start taking some time to learn how to use them," he admitted to his siblings. "So, what do you have now, Gann?" he asked, smiling once more.

"I have Mind Voice but also Empath, so we can help each other practice our Talents as a team," he suggested with a sigh. "It's been a while since we've practiced anything together." Old regrets were clearly heard in his voice.

"After dinner, how about the three of us go to my office and just talk," Garth suggested, realizing Ryes was right.

"Let's use the time to practice our Mind Voice Talents too," Mitt threw in as an idea. He gave her a nod, as Sabin, who heard the last of their conversation, smiled in understanding. Ryes had found his Mind Voice, which he'd been using for some time now, and never knew. He'd need to practice it with others, too. But not when Garth was getting some time with his brother and sister.

"How come you're not coming out for the hunt?" Ardis asked, puzzled, as she caught up to Ryes in her office. "You love the forest!"

"Someone's got to stay behind and keep things going here," Ryes quickly replied, knowing it sounded thin, even to her own ears. She met her eyes, wishing she could explain it all, but the words refused to come to her lips. She couldn't bear to deal with death right now. Not after Hailys of the past... It was as if the stink of the fires and death were still around her, and she, too, had no escape!

"We need your guidance," she prompted, trying to think of a way to get her out of the office. Ryes hadn't stepped outside of Winterhaven in days. She found that she'd even left Honey's care to others, which was unheard of! "Just that little bit you did from the last time on that recording, let me know it'll take me years to get that good."

"And I thought I was pretty clumsy and out of practice," she replied, with a tight smile, "but I truly can't go. Garth piled all this work on me, and I've got to get it done before our Founder's Day celebration and the next gather. Maybe next hunt?" she offered guiltily. Ardis looked disappointed, but gave her a nod and a smile, not willing to push it just yet, then paused by the doorway, turning back.

"Next time, and I'm holding you to it!" she vowed. Ryes smiled a more genuine smile and nodded her head to this.

"I will," she assured her. Ardis felt better, as she turned to leave, still trying to figure out what was truly wrong now, then paused, looking back inside again.

"I'll tell you everything that happens," she promised. Ryes gave a nod, then she left, leaving her door open, just as she found it. Ryes turned back to her terminal, her mind still searching for a way to rescue her aunt, without endangering Rhin.

"Hey, aren't you going to lunch?" a voice hailed her from the open doorway, what seemed a few minutes later. She looked up to see Bethy's smiling face. She realized Larissa was already gone to get her own. Some vague memory surfaced of her giving her a wave of her hand, bidding her go on without her.

"I thought I'd wait until the crowd had settled a bit," she replied, smiling as she returned to the moment.

"That should've been about twenty minutes ago. Come on, get out of that chair! You're going to end up as flabby as I am," she chided her friend with a teasing laugh. Ryes shook her head in surprise, as she smiled.

"Oh, heaven forbid!" she responded with a laugh, storing her program, and getting up. She had been sitting for far too long today! She stretched, before going one step further, with Bethany now laughing merrily at her display. Then they left together, walking close to each other.

"Not going out on that hunt, are you?" she questioned, as they were heading down the corridor, her eyes serious as she sought the truth.

"I can't," Ryes replied with a heavy sigh. "I can't face things dying right now," she admitted, "not after Hallys."

"Not after we almost lost you," Maren scolded as he and Dotti joined them, coming up from behind as they paused to talk.

"It's not my own death I fear," she told him, then saw the shocked look in his eyes and knew it was the wrong thing to say to him. "We haven't saved good ol' Dirt, yet," she teased, trying to get him to let it go for now.

"First, you'd better look out for your own life," she heard Garth's voice firmly admonish, as he and Sabin joined them, as they all stood in the corridor. Ryes and Garth had quietly argued her viewpoint early this morning, but he finally made up his mind and decided this was the time to lay it to rest. She'd never openly oppose him, before the others. "If you can't take care of yourself, you can't help anyone else when they're lives are endangered too."

"Secondly, you're going on the hunt to help coordinate things from the base camp. That way, in case there's an emergency, you'll be close enough to lend a hand. We're going to have enough inexperienced starmen and humans along to make it a necessity. I learned a few things on our trip to Matlowe and the fact that you were there to stop a fatal, catastrophic event, opened my eyes. And finally, until you can come up with a solid plan for saving this aunt of yours, you're not allowed to go Time Walking in Hailys again. I can't see you risking Rhin on such a venture, either. You must have a plan to keep the both of you safe," he ordered. She saw the hard look in his eyes and knew this was the way it'd be, no matter what she felt. Maren saw the pain in her eyes and knew she hated to have things spelled out exactly, but also knew she very rarely crossed Garth when he did it this way, where they could all bear witness to his decree.

"Alright, I'll go," she gave in with an unhappy sigh. Bethany looked uncomfortable, as did Dotti, but they both knew this would be best for her all around. She only hoped Ryes meant it.

"We'll figure out something," Sabin assured her, smiling encouragement. "Just remember, you have plenty of time on this end of things to plan," he reminded her. She seemed to relax at this, giving him a wane smile and nod of her head.

"That's true," she agreed, feeling as if she lost her appetite now. "I guess I'd better figure out what I'm going to need for the hunt, after all," she surrendered. "Who's all going?"

"Almost everyone," Bethany told her with a laugh. "Not only do the former villagers feel it's long overdue, but most of the humans are interested in coming along. Since we live here, we feel we should be familiar with being able to provide something for the dinner table, other than just vegetables and the machinery to cook them with."

"You're not going, are you?" Ryes demanded, shocked. She knew Bethy's son was due the end of the spring!

"Bethy and I are going to help you with the base camp," Dotti stated with a laugh. They turned to the dining hall as Ryes thought on this. There seemed some tension between the two old friends, wondering what it was? She smiled for them, turning to face the others as they stepped over to get their trays, resisting tapping in lightly with Mind Voice to delve further, feeling that would be too intrusive and abusive of her friends.

"Then I'll make sure the both of you are very safe," she assured them. Maren gave her a nod of his head, feeling better if she were there to watch over Dotti, while he hunted.

"Let's get something to eat! I'm starving!" Bethy suggested, heading straight for the serving room. Ryes laughed as she and the others trailed after her.

"They got her out of that office, at least," Ardis commented to Neil and Brenda as they were finishing their lunch. Neil chuckled and gave her a nod.

"It's a good first step, to pull her out of her hidey hole," he agreed with a smile. Brenda smiled merrily.

"It's a start. Hopefully, she'll find herself soon and come back to us," she added, then her brows furrowed thoughtfully. "What did she see in Hailys? Really?"

"Sabin won't talk much about it, but I think it had to be something horrific. Until she lets that go, we might not actually get her back any time soon," Ardis pointed out with an unhappy look in her eyes.

"Then, let's get her to show us what she saw back then," Neil suggested, seeing a simple answer. "Among all of us, we should be able to come up with an answer to help her let go." Ardis nodded her head in agreement.

"That's what we need to do," she replied, finally smiling. "I'll talk with Raya to see if we can get her to help out."

"Exactly what we need," Brenda agreed with Neil nodding his head.

Ryes finished showing Raby how cute her hair looked with a couple of braids to pull it back on the sides while leaving the back long and free. Raby was laughing as Sayer finished tying on a sparkly bow to dress it up. This small space of time for them to share was helping her reconnect with her family again, while Garth was spending some time with his siblings and Sabin, so they could all practice their Talents together.

"Oh Mom, these are great!" she declared as she turned her head this way and that, as she looked in the mirror. She put it down and threw her arms around Ryes, giving her a kiss. "Thank you!" Ryes laughed as she let her go, then grabbed Sayer to give her a kiss, too. "Thanks for insisting, Sis," she added. Sayer laughed too, her eyes merry.

"I tried to tell you," she teased, after Raby let her go. Then there was scratching at their door. Ryes gave the girls a nod of her head and turned for the door.

"Come in," she invited, then smiled as she saw Ardis pushing her stroller with her sons inside, Katas following in her wake. The boys were sound asleep, as were Ryes' younger cubs. Right behind them were Neil and Brenda with little Samantha, which surprised

Ryes. And behind them were Maren, Dotti, and Tars with Karis and Rowis trailing them. Kovin and Raya entered with their two cubs, also sleeping in their stroller. She laughed lightly, as Kovin let their door drape drop behind him.

"We got this Mom," Raby assured her, as she Katas and Sayer took over the strollers, figuring things out on the instant, and went off to their room to chat with Tars, as her siblings joined them, at Maren's urging.

"So?" Ryes started with her hands open in invitation as her friends filled her chairs and couch, letting them answer her question.

"We brought some sweets and cheese cubes," Maren offered, grinning mischievously. He sat the large basket he'd brought down on the coffee table to tempt her. She shook her head as she smiled.

"So, where is Air Empath going tonight?" she asked as she pulled her remaining chair over close to the couch and the other chairs, internally preparing herself for this friendly visit. The time she'd spent with the girls had finally relaxed her inner fears somewhat, letting her simply connect with her friends again. She knew she had to, or Garth and her grandparents would be upset. She'd have to face Darman and Rinna very soon; it was almost time for the Great Spring Gather.

"We're not looking for a sight-seeing trip like that, tonight," Ardis came straight out, as she met her eyes. Her face reflected her inner search for the right words.

"We need to understand what's going on with you, now. You've never worried about something so much, as you've been since you went to see your aunt in Hailys," Neil pressed, concern coloring his blue eyes. She gave him a nod, a little embarrassed they noticed.

"You all deserve to see it, but," she stalled, now uncertain as her smile melted, "it's heartbreaking," she warned with a concerned frown and pain in her green eyes.

"Help us break our hearts, to help mend yours and ours," Brenda pressed, with an understanding look in her eyes. Ryes closed her eyes, suddenly finding it hard to face her friends. Then she felt her hands being taken. She gave them a nod as tears started at the corners of her eyes.

Raya formed up the meld, and once she had everyone settled down in the commune, she turned her attention fully to Ryes.

"Come, show us all what've you've seen in Hailys past," she urged, as she felt her reluctance to open up. She'd never been so resisting, before. She felt her inner conflicts; she wanted to protect them.

"Ryes," Maren pressed, "please?" His heart was in his sending, and she knew she couldn't refuse them, after all.

She finally began, but instead of first opening with what she discovered on this last trip back to Hailys, she first showed them her whole experience of her first trip into the far past. They marveled at the huge city and its futuristic look, pausing often so they could fully see all the details, many of them she hadn't noted at the time, being overwhelmed and excited by the experience, itself. At the time, she truly knew nothing about technology, nor how the machines operated. It was all magic to her. Even the humans found it an amazing city and Kovin was deeply inspired, seeing Hailys in her time and glory, a real super city. Hadu genuinely startled everyone, as he had Ryes, herself, the first time she met him. Aunt Adina also caught everyone's interest and she felt they wanted to know her more. When that memory finally ran its course, Raya pulled from Ryes' Booster and had everyone ready for what she wanted to share next.

She gave them her second visit, so that they could understand more of her dedication to saving her Great Aunt; as she was more than just a connection to her mother's family, but was connected to her personally, now. And this one, with Sabin accompanying her, gave Ardis an appreciation of what he experienced as he travelled with her into the past. She enjoyed seeing his reactions. And now they all had questions they each wanted to ask Adina, to understand the world and time in which she lived, but this was only a memory. There was so much to still understand!

Then finally, she opened this last visit and the actual attack upon Hailys. The starport was amazing and the group marveled at the operations and look of the busy starport. The humans compared it to their own starport operations on other worlds and seemed to appreciate it and understand. But then the attack began. It horrified everyone in the inner commune. The destruction, the buildings being destroyed before their eyes, the fires, the way people were crushed, or died in the wild flames; it tore at them, and in this moment, Ryes opened her heart, full of love, to them all. She showed them what she'd done to stop the wall of fire from engulfing her aunt and Hadu, as they tried to flee with a small crowd of other people. She felt the amazement and pride from her dear friends and family at her courage to act – even if it was far in the past. Then, slowly she gently brought them all out and back to the present.

"We have to save her and the others!" Maren insisted, now understanding it fully from her memories.

"But how?" Dotti pressed; her mind awhirl with all she'd experienced through Ryes' recollections. It was far more a city than she could ever imagine Hailys to be, before now. And the attack had been a horrid nightmare. Now she understood her reluctance to be around anything dying.

"That's what I've been trying to work through," Ryes admitted. She suddenly realized this deep sharing finally allowed her to let go of her deep, inner pain. "I have to save all those I can save."

"With our help, too," Raya assured her, along with Kovin's hearty agreement.

"We'll help you find a way," he added. "But why does your son need to be a part of this?" he asked, puzzled.

"He's a Booster," she assured him, humor in her mental tones.

"He's more than just a Booster. He helps us focus our Talents and even if his Talents haven't opened up yet, I believe he has another new one," Maren insisted. "He'll be key in this venture, in helping your Talents focus to save them."

"I know you're right about him, but it still makes it hard to have to use him is such a way," she admitted, tears threatening to form again.

"So, your mother was a Talent of One," Ardis commented to distract her before her sorrowful emotions blocked their open sharing. "Have you ever tallied up how many Talents you actually have, Ryes? I bet you have at least fourteen, yourself." She felt her surprise at this as she considered it for a moment.

"I've never really thought to count them, before. And I know my Molecular Manipulator is something never seen in the memories from the past, from those in Doran's valley."

"Also, your Empath seems very different from what stories have told the way that Talent usually works," Raya asserted. "I bet you may have far more than just fourteen Talents. Didn't you say, you felt the way Nalin's Water Shaper pulled at something within you?"

"It did, but I've no idea how to use it," she admitted. Then her humor sparked, and joy filled the link. "I don't know when I'll get the time. I must go out on the hunt tomorrow. No time for evil?" she asked, not quite sure of the quote. She felt humor from the humans in the link.

"No time for the wicked," Brenda teased, her own happiness was clearly felt. "It's to keep someone who's prone to getting into trouble so busy he, or she, has no time to think up more mischief," she explained.

"Ah, now I understand," Ryes returned, seeing the truth. "That's why Garth insisted I go out on this hunt!"

"Frankly, I feel safer knowing you're going to be there," Dotti supplied, "especially after Matlowe and that exploding door!" The others caught the wisps of her memories of the event, itself. The way the fire froze upon Ryes' command, then she released and directed the huge door. which hurtled upwards high into the air, then came crashing down, only to be stopped in mid-air for a few moments, to allow people to run and avoid being crushed, astounded them.

"Wait! Exactly what happened? I never saw the whole vid," Brenda demanded, needing to know. "Ellen's over there doing important studies. I thought it was only a hidden library. Is she going to be in danger?"

"No danger for her, now. I made sure of the site, myself," Ryes assured her. "I even reshaped the power core to be safer."

"And Sonta swore to keep her and Setta protected," Maren supplied, sure on that score. He realized he fully trusted his oldest cousin, now. Before their last couple of visits, he would never have believed him!

"And the limiter collar on Korman will help with that, too," Dotti added in.

So, Ryes and the others then shared their Matlowe Village experience for those who hadn't gone, for a few minutes. They finally decided it was time to dissolve the commune and just chat for a while and enjoy each other's company. And savor the tasty treats. The knotty problem of saving people in the far past was set aside for the present.

Small Treasures

Chapter 3

"What's wrong, Tennan dear?" Rebin asked, seeing her disgust as they were setting up the shelter which would house the showers; the same as they used at the gather.

"I don't want to be here," she protested, just short of whining. She was pouting as she worked and appeared close to tears.

Dotti sighed at this, saying nothing, as she turned back to making sure all the camp lights were set up, operational and ready. By the time the hunters would be back this evening, they'd be needed and already lit. She finished the last one in this spot and quickly headed for her next area, leaving the others to their own tasks.

Their outdoor shelters were already up and settled. Bethy was helping Ted set up the outdoor emergency treatment area, while Ryun, Raby and Katas were helping to watch the cubs. Chuck and Raya had the outdoor kitchen up and going. And Ryes, Wynne, Brenda, and Katie were monitoring the ten teams, which were spread throughout Hailys, to make sure everyone knew where each other was, and in case of any emergencies. Everyone who could, was out on a hunting team. Even Ardis was on Sabin's team, having a great time. The humans were bold adventurers having the time of their lives; the rich green and life in the forest enchanting them all. Rowan was out with a new lightweight crossbow and a spring in his step, which the younger men couldn't match. The only surprising exception was Dr. Cruthers, who opted to stay in Winterhaven to help manage things at home. Metta and a handful of others stayed behind too, keeping Winterhaven safe and running as normal.

"Listen child, if I could heal others as you, I'd understand why it's so important to be here. You'd never know if something might happen and only you could save a life. You missed a lot of fun when we went to the Caravaner's Spring Gather. I'm truly looking forward to the next gather, which is supposed to be far larger. Are you going to that one, dear?" she asked to help distract her.

She knew that Tanns had her days when it was best to be elsewhere and now wondered if her daughter, Tennan, also suffered from such drastic ups and downs? At least Tanns had left her younger cubs in Maren and Dotti's care for the time being, while she spent all her time with Brenda and Wynne, teaching them about the native plants of the region and her concoctions; making plenty from the stores of plants they had already collected, taking over from Ryes. It was the one and only thing she delighted in doing anymore.

"No. I may go in the fall, but not for the spring one. Teris and I will be mating soon, and I'd rather be comfortable at home, than out on the road somewhere," she admitted. "Did Maren tell you if you caught, or not, yet?"

"Yes. Missa and I are expecting a daughter! I can't believe how young I feel again! And Ryun's pregnant with her first cub. You can't imagine how overjoyed she feels!" Tennan finally smiled at this, glad her brother could grant miracles for both women. It was what truly made it worth being a Healer, in her heart. "And Aril had come back with Ryun, to help take care of her and their son, so she wouldn't be alone when he's born, as Missa came to help me."

"Are you going back to Matlowe?" she asked, wondering. Rebin paused a few moments, thinking on her question, pondering it herself.

"Only if I had a very compelling reason to return," she finally ventured aloud, "I now think of Winterhaven as my home! And it'd have to be one extraordinarily strong reason to ever set foot in Matlowe again," she asserted, smiling. "I'll have to go back to fetch the things I'm not ready to part with, yet. Most of my old things can go to what's left of my grown family. At least they don't have their old mother to worry about anymore! After Maren's healing, I feel as good as I did when I was a teener. And the things Riss is learning in school are amazing! I know our future lies with Winterhaven, not back in Matlowe Village, it's behind us both, forever." Tennan nodded at this, fully agreeing with her in her own heart.

"Last year at this time, I would've never imagined being here in Hailys, nor having a Talent all my own. I know sometimes it feels like things are going so fast, but somehow, it's not fast enough. Now that I'm in Winterhaven, I want more and know it's where I belong, too. Matlowe Village is a past I'm happy to be well rid of," Tennan admitted, smiling now. Rebin laughed merrily.

"I hated being considered an elder and basically waiting out the rest of my days. I was miserable, but now, even doing simple things like this, is fun."

"What about Metta? Is he going to stay in Winterhaven, too?" Tennan pressed, curios now. Rebin laughed lightly at this, shaking her head no.

"He's planning on returning in a few months. He wants Sonta, his oldest son, to get some experience being the head elder for a while, before going home. Metta will oversee setting up the underground library for others to use. And I'm certain to make sure Matlowe profits from that fancy Inn, Kovin and Phil have planned out for him. I heard they're planning on running power to the Matlowe Village homes. Didn't I hear them saying that they're going to be building a new house for Karr and her family, back in Matlowe? Is she going back, too?"

"Yes. She says she feels too exposed, being so far from the forest, out in Winterhaven, from what I heard her say to Gann. And she hates living underground. I can't say that I'll miss her screaming at everyone," Tennan replied.

Tennan breathed out a sigh of relief, feeling guilty, knowing her mother was still good friends with Karr. She was glad she'd be leaving and thought she heard Sabin and Garth remarking how they set the construction of Karr's house ahead of most of their other projects - even in Winterhaven. She wore out her welcome long ago! They're going start Karr's house after the Great Spring Gather. She saw they were planning to build a smaller version of their apartment homes there, too. She thought Maren was telling Justin that they were for Winterhaven's research teams and resident scholars to live in, while working in Matlowe Village. She didn't care. She never intended to return to Matlowe. And she'd come to hate her father, especially after Teris told her what he did to him, before and after, the last time they mated. She never wanted to see him again!

"I won't miss her screaming, either," Rebin chuckled merrily. They heard laughter of agreement as Raya came to join them.

"You have to be talking about Karr," she added, grinning merrily. Both women nodded with guilty smiles upon their faces. "I saw Ted and Maren try their best to find a 'cure' for her, but nothing has worked. I won't miss her screaming when she leaves," she admitted, "and I hope it's soon. Are you both about done? We've got some fresh iced tea and cookies, if you want to take a break," she offered.

"Just finishing up," Rebin assured her, hooking up the hoses for the pumps. "Let's go get a snack, then we'll run our final checks, after we take a break." Tennan smiled and nodded her agreement. It wasn't that the showers were difficult to install, just that it was a tedious job, of the type she was rarely called to perform, but Tennan knew she didn't want to help Ted today; she'd be spending plenty of time the medical tent soon enough.

"That sounds great," she agreed, helping with the final connections, making sure they were correct - not wanting to redo them all, later. Raya gave them a nod, then walked toward the communications post.

"Where's Kovin?" Raya asked, hoping he was all right. "He's not used to being out in a forest anymore," she added, worried. "He's more focused on the beauty of structures and compositions of the materials he'd need to build them strong, now." For the first time, she wondered what their children would grow up to be like? Ryes smiled for her, pointing to a golden point upon their 3D holo display of the hunt.

"His team just pulled down a large bounder someone wounded earlier, so the groups are still a little scattered. We're getting them to tighten up again. We don't need anyone getting lost already," Brenda explained, as Raya closely examined the image, seeing how far they were from the camp, and wishing he were closer.

"We have some cookies and a fresh pot of iced tea all ready, if you ladies want to take a break," she informed them straightening up, giving Brenda a nod and smile in thanks.

"That sounds like a good idea," Wynne stated, "mind if I take ten?" she asked Ryes, turning to meet her friend's eyes.

"Go ahead. You and Brenda may as well go while we've got the chance. Katie and I can keep an eye on things for a short while," Ryes agreed.

"How's it going, so far?" Raya asked Ryes, sitting down in the chair Wynne vacated, seeing Katie was focused in on something she heard over her headset.

"Overall, pretty well. For the most part, the teams have been acting like a bunch of overgrown cubs, out for a day of play in the woods," she replied, shaking her head as she smiled merrily. "Even with the obstacles of shattered buildings and open pits, they've had a great time. The humans say it's like one of their virtual games come to life. If I could get a better handle upon this death-sense I have, I'd show them how to properly hunt." Raya laughed, recalling the times Ryes fussed at the others about some of the things they'd do, when they first settled into Winterhaven. She remembered her telling them they were supposed to catch it off guard, not drive the prey off.

"Do you think you'll EVER be able to get around that?" Raya questioned. Katie looked up to Ryes speculatively, as she heard the question.

"I don't know," she sighed out, letting her shoulders drop as she realized it was the truth. She might never get over it!

"Why would you?" Katie suddenly pressed, "I think you'd have to cut out your own heart to get away from it, and we rather like you the way you are." Ryes smiled as she thought she was correct on the matter. "We don't need you to hunt to keep food on the table. So, it's not as important for you to lead the hunts, anymore. And I can't see you disconnecting yourself that much from life, when you have so many sweet little ones who need you and your big, warm heart." They exchanged understanding smiles.

"She's right," Raya agreed, standing up, "I've got to help get stuff ready for dinner. The fresh meat will be great, at least." The women gave her a nod in response, then turned back to their monitoring.

"Ryes, you'd better take this. Monty got separated and is lost," Katie suddenly prompted, hearing his call for directions. She switched over her channel, hearing him, then activated her mic.

"Hang on, Monty. Give me a few seconds to lock in on you," Ryes told him, trying to reassure him. His voice sounded panicky to her ears. He was supposed to be with Garth's team, but they had fanned out to try to drive some tuskers toward Sabin's team; thinking between the two teams they could handle the dangerous prey. She got the fix from the computer's directional, then thought to try to double check on him her way, using Empath. She closed her eyes, centered herself and extended out toward him. She felt the stirring of life around them, reaching outward from their camp, veering away from the touches of death she found, and finally finding him. He was truly separated, seeing it from his own viewpoint. She sighed as she let him go, surprised and yet not so, at how clear the contact had been. When she tested the humans for Talents, she discovered Monty's was Mind Voice, but he hadn't taken time yet to train with Raya.

"What do you think?" Katie asked, as Dotti stepped over to them with questions in her eyes, seeing their concern about something.

"He's all right but has been cut off. We're closer to him than the rest of Garth's team. I'll go find him and bring him back," she told her. "Dotti, would you mind taking over here for me, for a little while?"

"Sure. What do I need to do?" she asked.

"Just make sure they don't all end up trying to track and take each other out," Katie teased, smiling. "You can see where each of the team leaders is, on our display and the other team members can be pinged and added to the display, if needed." She indicated the colorful markers, which seemed to float and move in slow, random directions. She noted small names next to each marker.

"I think I can handle it and keep an eye on Maren, at the same time," she agreed, smiling. Ryes gave her a nod of her head, surrendering her headset to her friend as she stood. She knew she was almost as skilled with computers as Neil, so hoped she wouldn't be bored. Dotti took it, donned it, and sat in her place. Ryes stepped over to her things and put on her light trail pack, decided against her bow stave, then hefted her old spear, smiling.

"Be right back," she promised, trotting off into the nearby forest.

"Where's she going?" Bethy questioned, joining the women at the com station, knowing Ryes wasn't hunting today.

"To find Monty. He got separated and is lost," Dotti explained.

"Oh," she replied, then knelt next to Dotti, seeing she had her full attention. "I want to apologize about yesterday," Bethy breathed out, to her friend in a low voice. "I got a little carried away by the whole idea. Guess I'm not used to pushing my personal convictions in such a way. It was an eye-opening experience, after all. But I wanted to tell you, you've got the right, and I should've never blown up at you like that. Your daughter's a wonderful treasure! I'm so ashamed." Dotti met her eyes, seeing she meant it, then smiled graciously.

"I was a little too huffy, myself," she replied, blushing. "We can talk about it later," she suggested, shifting her eyes to the side, to indicate Katie behind her. Bethy nodded and smiled, catching on.

"We will," she agreed, glad their old friendship was still holding, after all the shouting. "Need a hand?" she offered, standing up.

"Sure, grab a chair, a headset and tune in," Katie offered with a gesture, wondering what they were talking about, sure she'd hear it later, but was curious.

Monty stood in the bottom of the deep, narrow cut he'd fallen into, trying to figure a way back up. There was just a sliver of sunlight above him. Standing in the cold, tiny rill didn't make him feel entirely cozy, either. He'd awoken wet and shaken after his unexpected fall and immediately called in to see if anyone was near enough to assist him. He'd felt Ryes' awareness touch him briefly, amazing him with the clarity of the contact! He finally took out his beltknife, which Ryes had given him during the gather, telling him he was naked without one. Since then, he found it was an amazingly handy tool and agreed with her. He hated being this helpless with his boss lady on her way to rescue him, so he began to dig into the soft soil on the side of the cut, trying to form his own hand and foot holds to climb out. If nothing else, he was determined to be ready to go as soon as she arrived.

After almost twenty minutes of struggling, he finally gained the upper ground. He lay on his back panting for a few moments, with an intense headache and queasiness in his stomach, then realized he was covered with muck and leaves. He got up, ignoring his stomach, cleaned off his knife and put it away, then sat down on a nearby rock as he brushed off his clothes, glad for the leather overtunic Garth insisted everyone wear. It protected him during the fall. He took a quick inventory, realizing he still had everything, including his pistol, but saw his bow stave was gone. Monty started casting about, looking for it in the leaf litter and brush nearby. Unable to find it, he looked down into the cut, seeing it lay on the bottom, half-immersed in the tiny rill below and appeared broken. He realized there was no way he was going down after it now. He felt woozy still from the original fall, and his head was still pounding, so returned to his rock.

"Monty?" he heard Ryes calling out, still sounding far off.

"Here!" he yelled in response, smiling to himself. He immediately felt better just hearing her voice. He was her protector at times, but realized he felt safer with her nearby. "I'm here!" He stood back up, looking for her.

"I'm almost there, hang on!" she returned, relieved to hear from him. "Are you all right?"

"Yeah, I'm fine. Just a little scraped up." She finally found him, locating him by his voice this time. She didn't want Empath called up with the hunting going on nearby.

"And it looks like you could use a good scrubbing, too," she commented. "Let me get a look at you," she offered, stepping closer with a smile. He gave her a nod of his head, knowing she wouldn't be happy until she made sure he was fully all right. She closed her eyes, laying her hands lightly upon his shoulder. He felt a strange, wonderful warmth inside whenever she did this. She opened her eyes after a few moments and smiled.

"Okay?" he asked. She gave him a nod and picked her spear back up.

"Now you are. Took a tumble? Let's get you back to the base camp, so you can get cleaned up, too," she stated, then after he gave her a nod and looked ready, she led him off through the forest, taking the quickest route through the trees and broken stone. After a few seconds, she stopped and searched the woods around them, frowning.

"Shhhh," she cautioned, stepping back, and touching him with an outstretched hand, to make sure he was close behind her. "Don't move." He stood, hearing nothing but his own breathing for several long moments, then he heard the sound a soft scrape and a rock skittering against another. He glanced up and to his left to see two long-snouted animals considering them quietly, from atop some plant-covered rubble just a few feet away. Their fur was dappled gray, black and tan and their teeth appeared too many, and too sharp. He held very still.

"What are they?" he breathed in question.

"They're called trotters, kind of like Earth's wolves. Alone, or up to three, no problem, but we're surrounded by a pack of eleven. Our hunters have disturbed their haunts and now they're hunting us. Give me a moment," she said, closing her eyes while every instinct screamed at her to keep a watch on them. She reached down for her Talent, using Empath to reach out to the trotters. They were unhappy and hungry, but not sure enough to rush immediately to the attack. She pushed at their minds with the thought of darkness and fire tied in with their scents, trying to drive them away as she had the jungle marl before. They quickly fled the area, crying as they believed their tails were aflame. She sighed as she opened her eyes again.

"Wait, what's that?" he questioned, his pistol in hand as he saw a giant gold and white viper slithering through the forest floor, approaching them in a hurry.

"Don't shoot. It's sort of a friend," she ordered, keeping herself between Monty and the serpent. She recognized this viper, as he knew her. "I freed him from Doran's Valley of Death and turned his heart back to Tayna, once again. Before, he was one of Doran's servants, who she used to kill intruders into her valley; mostly men," Ryes explained. Monty gave her an unseen nod as he held himself still, once again. She reached out to the long, huge serpent with Empath, keeping her eyes open as she did so this time, not needing to establish a strange new contact with this creature.

"Sorry we disturbed your rest. We were trying to avoid the area where I last saw you, so to leave you in peace."

"A great hunt, all places awakened," he responded. "They are your hunters. He is yours?"

"Yes. He is mine. The hunters are mine. Please tell me where we must stay away, to leave your hunting area alone?" she requested, feeling Monty's presence as he was now "listening in" on their conversation.

"This is mine," he told her, filling her mind with his perception of his territory, as she used Empath to have him show her his true range, as he was comfortable with doing this before with others in the past. His tongue flicked out to "taste" both their boots, making sure he knew them well and all the scents of the others they carried.

"We will leave it be," she assured him, understanding the extent of the territory he considered as his own, now. She'd make sure it was marked on their maps and fed into their holo system.

"I live to serve," he offered her.

"I don't need your service right now," she assured him as he lay in large, loose, relaxed coils at her feet. "Maybe at another time?"

"You will find me," he replied, feeling better that she'd need him. She finally bent down and gently scratched his head and the ridges over his eyes for a few minutes. He closed his eyes in ecstasy.

"I will come for you here," she assured him. Then gently withdrew and signaling Monty to step back. When they were well clear of the area, Ryes let out a long sigh of relief, as Monty finally re-holstered his pistol.

"He wants to serve you?" he questioned, still shocked at the close contact she and the serpent had, and the way he communicated his thoughts so clearly!

"Yeah, but it's not exactly the kind of `pet' I could have slithering around Winterhaven. I'd be constantly counting the cubs to make sure they hadn't become his next snack!" she reminded him with a laugh. "I freed him from Doran's Valley of Death, and he's decided that he's supposed to be serving me now. For Doran, he used to kill men who trespassed in her valley. He's probably centuries old and I'm hoping that someday old age will catch up with him. It may be why he wants to stay with me now. So, I'll provide for him as he grows old. Being around Doran has made him far from a simple, stupid animal, but I don't know what else to do."

"It's a real problem. If I think of anything, I'll let you know," he promised, with a smile lighting up his face. "Leaving him here in Hailys may be the best idea for now."

"So far, it's all I can come up with," she agreed, wondering how much longer he would live?

"Ah, that smells good!" Maren declared as he and his team returned to the base camp. Dotti laughed as she ran up to him, wrapping her arms about him and giving him a big kiss in greeting.

"It's a special marinade Raya and Chuck invented to go with fresh bounder. The first steaks should be ready pretty soon. The smell's been driving the rest of us crazy," she told him, once they pulled back from each other. He smiled down into her bright, blue eyes.

"So, who got the first bounder today?" he asked. They had bets up for this one!

"I think Torr did, but his team's not in yet. This one Monty got, using Ryes' spear. So, was the bet for who killed the first one, or the first one to be brought back into camp?" she teased. His team, as well as Rowan's, had brought in plenty of game birds. They were putting them into the cold storage boxes on one of the largest rovers.

"I think it was for getting it back to camp," he replied with a sigh. Monty was unexpected and he'd have to ask Kovin about how it affected their bets. "All we found were pleip birds." She laughed, recalling the sounds the birds made all the time. Pleip about described it. "Didn't I hear that Ryes had to go out to find him?"

"Yes, she did," Dotti replied, daring her husband to pry her secrets from her eyes.

"Then how did he bring back the first bounder?"

"I showed him how to track and bring one down, on our way back. After we practically stumbled across him, how could we resist?" Ryes demanded of her cousin. "Since Monty lost his bow, I lent him my spear. He found it much easier than the bow, too." Maren laughed at this, seeing how it all fell together. After all, he knew she couldn't bring herself to kill anything, with that strong Empath of hers.

"Ryes!" They suddenly heard shouted out. She turned with a frown upon her face, then ran for the showers. Monty stood in one of the stalls with the curtain pulled aside, he was half-dressed, and his face was pale.

"Calm down," she ordered in a low voice, wondering what it was? "What's the problem?"

"There's something in my pocket. I don't know what it is," he breathed out, appearing shaken.

"Stay still and give me a few seconds," she urged, as she realized half of the camp now stood behind her. She closed her eyes, letting her tension go, reaching out to feel what actually lay in his shirt pocket. She found it was a serpent. A very young one and that she was aware, as her father was, of more than a normal viper would be of the world around her. She used Manipulator and gently lifted her out of Monty's pocket, trying to unravel how she came to be there, to begin with. Maren joined her as she gently sifted through this young one's mind to find her answers.

She saw she was trapped in the cold, water-filled place and had come to its walled end. Monty's sudden fall had at first frightened her, then she realized he tasted of the ones her father tried to tell her about. She realized with him lay safety, so quickly found the most warm, secure place she could find and cozied down for a nap. She liked his smell and the beating of his strong heart and wanted to stay with him. Ryes pulled back from her consciousness for a few moments to contemplate this scion of her enemy's servant.

"Let me have her for a few minutes," Maren urged, bringing up his Healing, as she gave into his wishes and floated the tiny snake over to his hand. She didn't feel threatened, so she hoped she wouldn't try to bite him. After a few moments, she saw what Maren intended. So, as he extracted her poison sacs, she held them aloft, knowing they contained enough toxin to kill all the people present in the camp!

"What do I do with this?" she asked. Then Ted stepped forward with a test tube in hand.

"I'll take that," he urged with a smile. "If we can analyze it, we might be able to develop an antitoxin, in case we ever need it in the future," he explained. She released the sacs, and all the poison Maren removed from the serpent, into the tube, feeling relieved. Ted was glad he'd grabbed a sampler kit as well as his treatment satchel, as he heard Monty call out.

"What're you going to do with that snake?" Monty asked, stepping close to get a good look at her.

"Actually, she's very fond of you," Ryes teased, "she likes your smell and heartbeat. We'll find someone to take care of her. I don't think she'll get as large as her father."

"You mean that big one we ran into?" he questioned, reaching out to stroke her tiny head. He saw her eyes close in pleasure and smiled.

"Yes, that one," Ryes assured him with a sigh.

"Can I keep her?" Monty suddenly asked, extending out his hand to Maren.

"But I thought she frightened you?" Ryes asked, feeling this was an unexpected turn of events.

"She startled me. I used to have a red racer when I was a kid. He died of old age long before I went into the academy," he explained, hoping.

"Only if you promise to take good care of her," Maren decided, meeting his eyes to see if he meant it.

"Of course, I will," he vowed smiling. Maren passed back the snake, but Ryes gently grasped his wrist, meeting his eyes.

"Let me show you," she explained to the questions in Monty's eyes. He gave her a nod, knowing he should try to get used to this telepathy stuff, since it seemed he had the Talent, after all. She smiled as she reached out to him and showed him the whole event from the tiny serpent's point of view. As she released him, he smiled down at his precious burden.

"If she wants me that badly, how can I refuse to care for her? She's a precious bit of unexpected treasure," he stated, sounding more himself. "I'd better get my shower finished. Chuck promised me the first steak off the grill."

"You'd better," Maren agreed. "He'll probably make all of us wait, until you're ready."

"You'd better get a shower, too," Dotti scolded, teasing as she poked her husband in the ribs with a finger. She was three years older than Maren, but when they were together, she felt it was the other way and realized how much more she enjoyed life with him.

"Ow," he protested, getting into the game. "I'd better, or you'll torture me," he agreed. There was laughter as the rest started to break up, going back to what they were doing before.

"I'll go get our things," she replied with a laugh. Ryes shook her head, turning back to check on her cubs.

"What's that about that little snake's father?" Ted asked her in a low voice, falling into step with Ryes.

"We should all discuss this over dinner. It's a problem that I don't think will be going away too fast," she told him with a heartfelt sigh. She spaced her fingers around, as if she were trying to wrap them around one of Garth's thighs with a large spacing between them, unable to make contact. "He's as big around as this and trained to kill others on the whim of a very dangerous woman." Ted let out a low whistle as they stopped to face each other.

"That sounds like a problem, all right," he agreed.

"Wait until everyone's gathered and fed, then we'll try to find a solution to this headache," she urged, smiling. "At least he takes my direction for now and we've got his territory mapped out as to be strictly avoided. But he's used to being a servant and since he's getting very old, I think he wants to be taken care of in his retirement."

"And he's bright enough to know what kind of benefits package to ask for?" he asked, wondering.

"Yes. He's way above the intelligence level of an animal. I think he's centuries old and has been listening in on Doran's ravings for most of that time, until I freed him. At the time, I was trying to save Garth's life, so this is my burden to bear," she explained.

"We're all in this together," Ted assured her, gripping her shoulder in comfort. "We'll find a way to solve this, together." She met his eyes, then gave him a nod of her head, understanding what he was saying. She smiled.

"I'm surely out of ideas, so brainstorming is the next, best option. Thanks, Ted," she replied. He smiled and nodded his head, then headed back to the treatment shelter. He wanted to get this sample safely stored. He wondered how bright Monty's infant snake would be when she was grown?

Matlowe's New Light

Chapter 4

"You're not going to sleep with her in your pocket?" Torr asked Monty, as they were sitting around the large campfire after stuffing themselves on his very tasty bounder. The cubs were all in bed now, as were at least half the people in the camp; tired after the day's vigorous hunt. He smiled as he shook his head, finally winding down, himself.

"Ted's set up a small incubator for her while we're out here, then I'll set up a more permanent tank for her to sleep in, when we get back home. My grandfather got me a red racer from Earth, when I was a kid, growing up on Trinity. He was just a little bigger than this, when I got Streak. I loved Streak and had him until he finally died, years past when he should have. I'll keep her with me during the day and see if I can remember how to watch out for her," he explained, smiling when he saw the disgust in Torr's eyes.

"Why would anyone keep a snake?" Raya asked, wondering with questions in her eyes. The little golden-colored one in Monty's hand looked like she was exploring her new environs, wanting to get to know them all, but even as she left him to check the rest, or catch bugs to eat, she continuously returned to Monty, as if she knew he was her safe-haven.

"To control varmints in and around your house," Neil explained, smiling, "I used to have a pair of cats, myself. I gave them to my sister when I enlisted." Ryes smiled at this, knowing the intense curiosity the starmen had for cats, seeing the way the humans liked to compare them to these mystery animals, all the time.

"Actually, there was a farga I used to play with when I was a cub. She used to follow me when I'd go out hunting," Ryes admitted, "so I'd sometimes share some of my kills with her." Rowan started laughing loudly, nodding his head, and gasping for breath.

"Tanns was so mad about it. She said some of the villagers started calling you the farga's cub," he told her. Maren chuckled, recalling the arguments his mother and grandfather had over Ryes' pet. He recalled wishing he could make friends with one, too.

"That's where that came from?" Sabin asked, laughing as Ardis nudged him hard in the side.

"What's a farga?" Becky asked, puzzled.

"It's a kind of pest. They're long, furry, lean, and curious about everything. They live in dens under old trees, or crumbling buildings and will steal anything not nailed down, if you're not keeping an eye out. You never want to corner one, accidently, or otherwise. They have a strong musk and nasty bite," Garth explained with a smile, putting an arm around his wife. "It sure explains a lot," he teased her.

"Garth!" Ryes protested amazed and amused, she blushed as laughter started up around them.

"We still have to figure out what to do with little Shimmer's father," Monty reminded them, once the laughter died down some.

"How about if we take him back to Doran's Valley?" Mitt supplied, "Maybe he won't find his way back out, again?"

"I truly need to go there to check on Doran, anyway. But now that he's out of her valley, I'll never take him back. You've no idea what you're asking in such a thing, Mitt. It's not only instarman, but I'm sure he'd figure out what we intend and would fight being returned. No living creature should ever have to tolerate her presence within its mind and heart. I tuned the serpent back into the pulse of Tayna, herself. I can't do it. I won't..." Ryes replied, seeing it all in her mind's eye, once more.

Raya's face went white as she recalled her relating the whole experience to her, Tennan, Maren and Bethany once before in a deep inner commune. Garth looked at Ryes, curious. He noted the look in Maren's eyes and saw Bethy and Raya's faces. Even Tennan's eyes looked dark and shadowed. How would they truly know about Doran, to react so strongly?

"Who's this Doran and why do you have to check up on her?" Chuck gruffly demanded, seeing Kovin trying to comfort Raya. "What is it about this person has everyone upset, so suddenly?" Ryes gave him a nod, but no smile graced her lips now.

"She was sentenced, long ago, back on Kahmarr itself, to be placed in an eternal, cold sleep for murdering a cruel prince, who was chosen to mate her. She wanted all women to kill all the men and take over the world. Because she was of noble blood, they couldn't execute her. And she was pregnant with his son, and tried to kill their son too, when he was born. So, after his birth, they dumped her here on this out-of-the-way, isolated, game preserve to be forgotten. They placed her in a small building in the middle of a wilderness area. Still, her followers found her and built a large marble temple around her imprisoning tomb, worshipping her as a goddess. She had strong Talents and was able to extend herself far beyond her body, enwrapping every living thing around her with her madness. She used a Stone of Power, as my Aunt Adina named it, to control everything living in the valley. It was stolen by her followers, and I intend to take it from her. She doesn't need it to maintain her life; the equipment for that is separate. I feel sorry for the women who're still in suspension cases, joined with her in her endless sleep, but since my own mother broke free of that place long ago, I feel if they truly wanted lives of their own back, I think they could've broken free of her by now," Ryes told them with cold conviction in her green eyes. Maren shuddered, as if an icy breeze from hell brushed by.

"Especially since you made sure she didn't have control over the valley, anymore," he finished for her. She gave him a nod of her head.

"How did you do that?" Dotti questioned sharply, seeing Maren's intense reactions to her short tale.

"I burned away her Talents," she explained, "The creatures, which were under her control, are now free, and the valley will now experience natural seasons once more. The Stone of Power amplifies Talent tremendously. It opened the rest of my sleeping Talents, as I used it to help me overpower Doran. Her handmaidens tap it, too, as a tool to toy with each other and the creatures in the valley, at their whims. It's not that we need the Stone in Winterhaven, but that I'd feel better if it were in our keeping."

"A Windrose Stone," Ted suddenly spoke out into the silence, which had fallen after Ryes' tale. There were curious looks cast his way. "It's a mythological gem which is supposed to amplify a telepathic ability," he explained, "there was supposed to be one found on Trinity, that was about the size of a man's fist," he finished, looking to see the affirmation in Monty's eyes.

"Yeah, that was the tale," he agreed, suddenly reluctant to voice it, wondering how much of it Ted actually knew? There was a bit of his own family history tied up in it, and he knew the one which was generally let out, and the one which was only passed down orally through his family. No wonder he has this Mind Voice Talent, as Ryes released from within! It only verified what his great-grandmother told him about the Windrose Stone; it shaped and sharpened the families who had it in their care and keeping.

"Well, what if we set up a kind of limiter on Shimmer's father, to keep him here in Hailys for the time being? Then go on over to this valley and free that stone from that evil witch and her crew?" he suggested, dodging the curiosity in Ted's eyes, feeling he had to know something now, with the intensity of his gaze. "We have time before the Gather."

"A limiter? Now that's an idea," Neil agreed with a smile and nod, wondering what Monty wanted kept secret about that stone? He seemed deeply bothered with its mention, and he was from Trinity.

"I'd rather we create a special enclosure somewhere near Winterhaven and offer it to him when he feels it's time to retire and be cared for, for the remainder of his life. Something like a private zoo with one resident," Ryes countered, feeling it was a better solution. Jim gave her a nod of agreement and smiled.

"Both sound like good ideas," Garth decided, relaxing at having this problem being addressed, at least. He now wanted to know what Ryes had gone through in Doran's Valley, while he'd been helpless and in that witch's clutches. Ardis appeared curious and he saw the same in Mitt's eyes, too. So, this was something she hadn't related to them, yet. And he intended to get it out of his wife tonight.

"We'll discuss getting something set up for Shimmer's father tomorrow morning. Hailys might be too big a territory for a limiter.

We've got a long day ahead of us tomorrow. We'll see how well we do with the hunt, before deciding how long we'll need to finish filling our stores," Garth told them. He got nods of agreement as many of today's hunters realized how sore they still were, after the day's unaccustomed activities.

"Sleep sounds like a good idea," Maren agreed, standing up. He pulled Dotti to her feet. "Goodnight, everyone," he said, as they headed for their shelter. They were wished goodnight in return by the others.

"Goodnight," Ryes called out after them, sighing as she realized she was tired, too. She then saw the look in Garth's eyes and realized that even if he was tired, he had something on his mind. It could end up being a long night after all.

"No, Uncle. I've already spoken with Aric, and he says that he cannot remove that collar without killing you outright," Sonta asserted, exasperated as he was trying to talk with one of the humans working on what they termed an excavation site, here in the middle of Matlowe Village. Korman's approach had encouraged Setta to return to their own encampment, which was set up behind the elder's platform, behind the lines of their protective measures, meant to keep Korman at a distance.

He noted he now wore his tunics closed all the way up his neck, to try to hide the glowing collar he sported. He'd participated in the markings made upon his uncle's body and hadn't made any move to stop the others. With his silent approval, his uncle had been covered from forehead to toes with all types of written slurs against his character. It'd been a brilliant stroke of genius and a good way for Ryes, and quite a few other villagers to extract a little vengeance, without actually physically harming him. His own wife had added in her statement, having suffered his claws when she was younger, herself. Ellen had assured him the markings would fade in time. And he'd saved the marking pen for any future, true needs; he loved the way it could shift colors readily and go from narrow to wide tip, with the proper manipulations, as she'd shown him.

"There has to be some way to get this humiliating collar removed!" Korman insisted, almost growling. He knew his brother would be hard at work looking for a solution, but Sonta didn't seem to care at all.

"The humans don't have the key to it. It's only in Garth's keeping, back in that village they're living in now. He was afraid that you might become unreasonably violent and wanted this as a measure to help protect his people from your temper. My father went along with this and is now taking a vacation at their new village. Perhaps when he returns, he can see about obtaining your release from Garth, if you commit yourself to controlling your temper," he offered in hope, knowing better from long experience.

"He and his slut wife and their pets!" he scoffed in return, disgusted. "It's hopeless!"

"You should be thankful the elders voted to allow you to continue to live in Matlowe, after your attack upon Tanns. Even if you stated that you knew Maren was now a Healer and wouldn't let her die, you still used her in a callous and heartless manner, to your own ends. You're extremely lucky Ryes only `stunned' you, as one of the humans, or even your own son, could've killed you outright."

"It's against all rights for a woman to use weapons against a man!" he shouted, angry now with his oldest nephew, who was older than himself, in truth.

"No, that's only custom, not the law," Sonta replied, pointing back to the tall silver pillar, which displayed the twelve laws decreed by a crown Prince of Kahmarr, to stand for all Tayna.

One of the flying machines from Winterhaven had brought back the copy to Matlowe two days ago and a party of humans and starmen erected it next to the elder's platform, as it had been in the holo, from so long ago. The Elder's Platform itself had been rebuilt, so it too was new once again. The pillar clearly stated that a person was allowed to bear arms and use force to defend himself, or herself, or those they held under their protection, from any life-threatening danger. He began to suspect that some ancestor of his objected to women being able to defend themselves from men they didn't want to mate and had damaged the old pillar. When they found it in Aric's workshop, this was the one and only law which was defaced. After having to sit and watch the actions of his uncle Korman through the years, he could well believe it'd been someone very much like him.

"Where did that come from? It's never been here before! How do you KNOW it's truly from Kahmarr? It could be something Garth and his pets created, telling you this story it was from Kahmarr," Korman protested. He knew tomorrow there was a celebration planned to honor the pillar being raised in the Village Center square. He had no intention of having anything to do with that frivolous activity! Sonta laughed heartily at this.

"I saw the holo myself, uncle, when it was found under our very feet. And the original column was retrieved from Aric's workshop. It's in Winterhaven being restored now, as it was beyond Aric's and his father's skills to fix. When the original is returned, we'll have things here, as it was at the time when Hailys was destroyed. Too bad you didn't watch the holo the Winterhaveners played for us all a few evenings ago, or you'd know the truth, too. Once we regain our starships, we'll have to prove to the other remaining colonies that we deserve to be counted as civilized. Restoring these ancient laws is a step in that direction. These laws are recognized and will be honored by all citizens of Matlowe, uncle. Including you," he replied, dropping his voice down low at the very end. Korman's eyes narrowed as he met his nephew's, seeing the threat they held. His nostrils flared as he turned on his heel and headed back home. Obviously, Sonta had no intention of helping him at all.

As Korman walked down the narrow alleys, he realized he deeply missed Tanns. He wondered if Maren had been able to heal his tiniest sibling, which Tanns still carried? He hadn't wanted to hurt her but needed to lure Ryes away from her protectors. Aric told him how she floated him in the air to apply the sap-like substance she used to glue him to the wall. He couldn't believe it! Ryes with Talent and able to use it, with tiny cubs to nurse! She had to be using one of the human's machines, which Aric didn't see. But he felt a deep need to hear Tanns' gentle voice, or her teasing him by playing with the tips of the hair at the base of his ears, sending chills of pure delight up his spine. He wondered what she and the cubs were doing? He realized he'd even welcome Tennan's scorn-filled looks.

But Maren… He'd never tolerate his son's presence again! He was one of Ryes' pets now. He remembered seeing him holding one of those human creatures, as if they were mated. It gave him the chills! How could he ever mate outside of his own people? He tried to show him how to choose a good woman to mount, but that shibler never appreciated the things he tried to teach him, when he was small. Karis was of Maren's mindset, wanting nothing to do with him either. But he missed little Rowis and the squeals of delight as she'd practically launch herself to his arms, whenever he walked in the door. And Tars and her quiet smiles, as she'd serve him dinner. She was too big to sit on his lap now but loved to sit beside him as they sat to eat their meals.

He went into his darkened hut, fighting back an upwelling of sorrow. He missed his family. He missed his girls. He wanted to hold Tanns in his arms, once more. Had she made it? He wanted to ask Sonta if there had been any news but ended up getting into some kind of argument every time he got near him. He tried to approach one of the humans to ask, but they retreated whenever he came near. Apparently, Garth didn't think they could stand up to him alone, so had warned them away. He had to find out. Where were his cubs and wife? Where had they taken them? He was sure they would have some of the Winterhaveners present at the ceremony tomorrow. Perhaps he could get some information? Some word to ease his mind and heart about Tanns. Garth couldn't deny him this, at least.

"Garth," Maren warned in a low voice, seeing his father approaching them from some nearby shops, as if waiting until he had to come out into the open to show himself. They'd just arrived and were watching the equipment they brought being set up, before the formal ceremonies. Garth turned, already guessing who it'd be from the tone of his voice. Korman slowly approached, stopping only a couple of paces away. The sight which greeted the Winterhaven men's eyes was astonishing. Korman had lost weight and his face looked haggard. His eyes were shadowed and there was sorrow there, which tugged at their hearts. Garth hadn't even been sure it was Korman, until he stopped close to them. Sabin crossed his arms, keeping the expression on his face neutral, as he gave him a nod of his head, to give him permission to speak.

"All I want to know is if Tanns and the cubs are all right," he finally asked in a croaking voice. Garth gave him a nod of his head, understanding now. He wondered how he'd appear if Ryes were ever torn from him suddenly, and he had no way of knowing how she and their cubs were doing? Would he even fare as well? Of course, he'd never use Ryes the way Korman had used Tanns!

"They're well. Tanns has recovered and will be delivering your new daughter in a few days' time. Your older cubs are in Maren and Dotti's care and are doing well," he answered. "We're setting up a contact station here for the villagers to use. If Tanns chooses to take the call, you may speak with her through it," he offered as a small gesture of comfort. The relief on his face was well understood, as he gave him a nod.

"Thank you, Garth. If you'll teach me how to use this machine of yours, I will try to speak with her later," he replied. The lines around his eyes seemed to ease at this news, as his heart was lightened.

"Everyone will be taught how to use it. We're also going to be setting up some formal schooling here in Matlowe, so everyone will be taught how to read, write, cipher, and some of our own history. Your brother is heading the committee, which is setting up plans for Matlowe's growth. I'm sure he could use your help," he suggested, not sure what Korman would think of such a concept. Maren told him they learned how to read, write and cipher from his mother, knowing his father never had the patience for the task. He wasn't even sure if Korman knew how.

"I will consider it," he returned. "When are you teaching the use of your talking machine?"

"We start the lessons later tonight," Sabin answered, "You can try talking with Tanns then." Korman nodded his head to this, then turned to leave. After taking a step, he turned back, and his eyes met Maren's.

"Take good care of your siblings, or you'll answer to me," he warned him with a low growl. His face was suddenly a mask with his hatred plain for all to see. His eyes practically glittered in bloodlust.

"I don't need your threats," Maren quipped back with his own ire igniting. "I love them and will make sure they have the best future they can have, in spite of all you've done to them." Korman stood with his and his son's eyes locked, the air practically shimmering with the built-up hatred between. He finally turned suddenly and walked off. Maren was taking a step to follow, when Garth grabbed his arm, stopping him.

"Let it go. He isn't a part of anything which truly matters to you, anyway," he warned his friend. Maren stood still for several long moments, then sighed, the tension leaving his shoulders at last.

"What is it about him that does this to me?" he suddenly demanded, as Garth released his arm once again.

"You're too much alike," Sabin teased him, then laughed as Maren looked at him with amazed shock in his eyes, and his mouth hanging open.

"It looks that way to me, too," Neil supplied, smiling. "Not that I'd ever think you'd do the things I've heard he's done, but that you both have the same stubborn attitude," he explained.

"It goes deeper than that, but they're right," Garth agreed, smiling. Maren closed his mouth and looked thoughtful, as he gave his friends a nod of his head and turned to go down into the underground site. He had to think about this and knew where some comfy reading chairs could be found below, a perfect cozy spot for a bit of private introspection.

"Maren?" Sonta asked, having found him heading down the stairs going to the library below, "there's need for a Healer with some of the new Easterners. A woman has a cough that's not stopped in days, and I'm concerned." His face displayed his inner distress. Maren gave him a nod of understanding. This was far more important.

"Where?" he asked as he turned, then paced Sonta back up, noticing his slight limp for the first time. Sonta gave him a nod and directed him toward some of the still-standing older huts. Maren knew he had yet to take the full measure of health for many of the Matlowe villagers! He led him to her, as she sat on an old stone bench nearby. Maren noted she appeared very weak and was shivering in the warm sunlight.

"May I please help you?" he asked as he knelt in front of her. The man next to her appeared nervous, but with Sonta standing with him, held his peace. She looked up at him with questions in her eyes, puzzled. Here was a young starman dressed in a manner she'd never seen before.

"You can help me?" she asked, not quite understanding, as if she couldn't focus her thoughts.

"I'm a Healer. Please let me help," he offered. She went into a spasm of coughing, cupping her hand before her mouth. It was a forceful chain of coughs that ran on for several moments. Maren decided to take the initiative and closed his eyes and grasped her other arm. He deployed his Talent and eased her body's cramping from the coughing first, then delved in deeper to take care of the infections raging within. He fixed some other issues she had and strengthened her body as well as the little cub she was now carrying. Finally, he opened his eyes and smiled up to see the joy in her face.

"You're going to be having a very healthy son in a few months, so have plenty of time to pick a good name for him," he told her, smiling in return, "and I hope you're feeling much better now?"

"Thank you, Great Healer! I've never felt so good in my entire life!" she assured him, hugging him in joy. He laughed at this, giving her a nod when she finally let him go, once more.

"It was my honor," he told her, giving her a small bow, and standing back up. He made sure the air around her was clear of the contagion, too. The man next to her stood up, giving him a nod of his head.

"Thank you, Healer," he said, extending his hand palm up, "we have nothing to pay you for taking care of my oldest daughter," he admitted, appearing pained. Maren smiled and crossed his palm with his own and then shook his head.

"I never ask for anything for my Healings," he assured him, meeting his eyes squarely. "In Winterhaven we simply take care of each other."

"As we do here in Matlowe Village," Sonta assured the man, with a smile.

"I do want to check everyone in Matlowe that I can," Maren told them both, "Starting with the Chief Elder." Sonta appeared surprised, then chuckled, giving him a nod of his head in agreement.

"How about next to the Elder's platform, so you'll be out of the way with all the activity going on today?" he suggested. Maren gave him a nod, then went to grab a couple of nearby chairs, giving Garth a nod when he noticed him setting them up. Garth smiled and nodded in return. Maren's previous anger was now gone, as Sonta sat down next to him, and he opened both his Healing and Booster Talents. This could be a long afternoon, he thought, as he saw Setta run by with some tools in her hands, as she headed back down the nearby stairs below.

"Everything's in place and all ready," Neil advised Garth and the elders. Rowan, Metta, and Ethan had joined everyone this evening for the actual ceremony, having been flown in by Shadd an hour ago. She had the chopper locked up over in New Matlowe right now, needing the middle of the Village clear today.

Sonta had been trying to catch up to his father, but found himself astounded, more than anything else, of the changes in him. He was no longer an "elder," who had to struggle each and every day to just do simple tasks! He was an active ball of energy, who moved with purpose, and had the light blazing from his eyes as his mind considered new possibilities every moment. He knew it was more than just a good healing which he, himself, had earlier today from Maren. This spoke of his being exposed to new horizons and he not only had the courage to go after them, but to lead others onto new paths in life, which he now openly embraced. He was still his father, but never as he'd been before in his whole life. He found himself giddy, just being around him.

Shadd finally got her family to understand that she was never coming back to live in Matlowe Village, ever again. She was amused that her mother instantly understood about Torr and approved of Mason as a much better match. Still, she wasn't happy with her leaving Tobin for a stranger to raise.

"I promise to keep any new cubs to come with me," she assured her, smiling. Sivann sighed heavily as she gave her a nod.

"Please do, as you'll find for all the work you put into raising them, they're a rich reward in themselves when they get older," she advised her middle daughter, as best she could, then gave her a hug to help take the sting out of her words. Shadd laughed as she hugged her mother tightly.

"I love you, Mom," she whispered.

"I love you, too," she replied, as tears were now in her eyes. Once they broke apart, Setta approached the women and gestured for them to join the others gathering in the main square. Shadd laughed and nodded, as she smiled.

"Thanks! We're ready," she told Setta, as they followed her over to the Village Square. "Oh, the Elder's platform and the seating area look great," she commented in a low voice to her mother, who nodded her head, with a huge smile on her face. The sun was finished setting and the shadows were thick now.

"It's so exciting! Who knew what a little cleaning and paint would do?" she returned; the pride obvious in her voice. Shadd nodded, then grabbed her hand as they found a spot and sat down, all ready.

"I've noticed Old Matlowe now looks nothing like it did last year when we left!" she declared in a low voice, waiting for the elders to begin the ceremony.

"Your friends and humans have been our best blessing, as well as some of the folk from Riverward. There's a good family with a carpenter, who's teaching us all how to make our homes better. After this is done, I've got to show you our home. You'd never believe it," Sivann told her, teasing her with the laughter in her eyes.

"I can't wait!" Shadd replied, then noticed a group of elders with Garth and another starman she didn't know, were now grouped before the Elder's Platform, appearing to be ready. Others in the crowd around them quieted their conversations too, granting them their full attention. Neil stepped over and Garth gave him a nod of his head. He turned to face the gathering with a broad smile.

"As has been said before, 'Let there be light,'" Neil shouted and spread his arms wide. Suddenly lights came on in the Village Square all around them. All the major paths were now lit and every home around the middle of Matlowe was also brandishing lights within. A great cheer went up from everyone in the Village. This was a historic day for Matlowe! And the humans were laughing as they recognized Neil's joke, as he now stepped back behind the elders.

"In honoring our beginnings, we're giving back to Matlowe Village, so as Winterhaven grows, so does Matlowe," Garth spoke up loudly, so everyone could hear him once the cheering had quieted down. "This gift of power for all the original homes and new ones, so you can have a few of the comforts we have taken for granted in our new home. More expansion is coming soon, and you'll see Matlowe will become a center to be treasured upon Tayna!" He stepped back, then Metta stepped up to speak next.

"I want to first recognize all the people who contributed to this day's celebration. The Hidden Library and all the treasures it holds will be our contribution to all of Tayna. First off, I would like to honor Ellen, Minn, Poinsettia, and Taroom. Also, Kovin and Phil, who are not only designing Winterhaven, but now working on Matlowe Village and the future path it will hold. And with our homes having light, we can now see where we need to clean," he joked at the end, getting plenty of laughter and agreement. "We cannot thank them enough for this miracle of the past brought back to us all!" He stepped back next to Garth. Sonta now took his turn in front.

"I am so very proud of our new future! We can do this together, to recreate our Village to be so much more," he said with pride shining in his eyes. "Also, there will be lessons in how to use the distance communication station now set up behind me, near the Elders' Platform. We can use it to directly talk with our friends and family in Winterhaven. Lessons will begin in a few moments. We have tables loaded with food to help celebrate this event tonight and I've been told some dancing to be enjoyed. Please everyone, let's celebrate!" As the villagers got to their feet, cheering happily at the end, the music started up.

"That sounds familiar, but not so," Garth commented to Neil, who had supplied the music and device to play it. He chuckled and gave him a nod.

"I recorded the caravan musicians at the gather, so some are new tunes you might not have heard before," he explained. Sabin laughed and thumped his shoulder in joy.

"Great idea!" he replied, then stepped over to see his oldest sister, as she signaled to him to join her. "Later," he said in parting.

"Let's all go eat," Garth suggested, giving Neil a nod and smile. He gave him one in response and followed Garth and a mirthful Ethan to the tables. Power in Matlowe Village was a historic event for everyone to celebrate tonight. He wished Ryes were here to see it, knowing she'd be scanning the drones' coverage, as soon as she could tonight.

Battle for the Stone

Chapter 5

"He actually said that?" Ryes demanded merrily, trying not to laugh. She saw the look in her cousin's eyes and sat back in her chair, thoughtful. "They have it wrong. I think it's because you're both such total opposites. I don't mean about just attitude, but the things you believe in. Your father wants to maintain his crumbling tyranny, while you want change and a future which means something more than just a mean existence," she started. He suddenly looked up, meeting her eyes, seeing what he should've realized for himself yesterday. He'd been pointlessly torturing himself, turning their words around within his mind and heart, trying to see if they'd spoken truly. He didn't want to end up being anything like his father! Now he saw the truth. Ryes was right!

"I should've come to you about this last night. I don't think neither Dotti, nor myself, got any sleep over it," he sighed out, relieved at last.

"Take the rest of the day off. I want you fresh when we land in Doran's Valley tomorrow morning. I got everything ready for this venture, while you were over in Matlowe yesterday. And when we were hunting in Hailys, Garth had me show him exactly what happened when we were last in that valley, and I'm sure has passed it onto Sabin by now. This isn't going to be a fun outing you know, and I feel like I'm taking everyone into dire danger."

"We'll be fine. That fight against the southern Talents, along with your memories, have given me an idea of what we can face. What if those frozen followers of hers object to us taking that Windrose Stone? You'd better brief Mitt, and probably the rest of the team, too," he reminded her, feeling they should have all the bases covered. She sighed, nodding her head, knowing she should've addressed this earlier. Being aware of the possible dangers gave the teams the best chances of succeeding.

"I will, later this morning. I think you may have a point, but I think our greatest danger will still be from Doran, herself, still trying to direct the others' Talents," she pointed out.

"At least she has no idea what your Talents truly are, since you didn't know yourself, until long afterwards," he reminded her. "And since you're giving me the day off, I'm going to see what time classes let out today, so Dotti and I can catch a quick nap before my siblings get out of school."

"Sure, the two of you are going to take a nap," she teased as he laughed and got up out of the chair.

"I'll get some rest, at any rate," he promised as he gave her a wink. "Catch you at dinner tonight," he promised. She gave him a nod of agreement, then he left. Ryes sat thinking for a while. Then she turned to her terminal and entered a message for Mitt. It was time she knew it all, anyway.

"We'd best get a good aerial survey of the entire valley, first," Dr. Cruthers suggested, as Garth hovered for a few moments over the edge of what they usually called "The Valley of Death." It looked peaceful and green with no signs of violence of any type. Still, there was something here which set the nerves on edge, he had to admit to himself.

"That's what we're doing right now," he agreed as he activated the sensor array. He nudged the chopper into a low, slow sweep of the valley below them, making a circuit of it for the scans, creeping cautiously towards the temple in its center. It was a deceptive place, as he could still feel the power and evil emanating from it, even up here in his air vehicle. How could he have missed it before?

"This place gives me the creeps!" Mitt declared over his headset, on the open channel. She was piloting the second chopper, following her brother's lead on this one. "And you brought Ryes here as a place to camp?"

"I wasn't as sensitive to it then, as I am now," he admitted with a smile and chuckle, the first one this entire morning. This valley truly made him feel uncomfortable.

"It looks quiet," Tennan observed, looking out a window.

"Too quiet," Sabin countered with a sigh, as he sat in a co-pilot's seat. They were now seeing the temple more clearly, but Garth was making his sweep of all the outlying areas first, before heading toward the building in the center.

"That structure looks marvelous, even from here," Phil commented in a low voice, having forgotten his mic was open, wanting to see it closer now.

"Not really, considering what it holds and what atrocities were committed within," Ryes chided him, smiling tightly, as she sat in the seat in front of his. Doran knew she was here and was already trying to lure her closer, using the Talents of others to channel her desires. They just didn't have the reach she alone had before, but this is what she'd feared the most, that she'd find ways to still control the Stone and her handmaidens, even without her Talents.

"I'm glad I can shut that calling out, now," Raya told her, turning to see the set look upon Ryes' face. She gave her a nod of her head.

"Look at that," Torr's voice could be heard over their headsets. Everyone was starting to cast about to see what he spotted. Then down below, some of the tall trees' lower branches parted and a massive, misshapen head peered up towards them. The teeth displayed, as the animal opened its mouth to issue its challenge to them, looked as long as Ryes' hand from heel to longest fingertip.

"What is it? It's huge!" Dotti returned, holding tightly onto Maren, now.

"I've no idea," Garth assured her with a sigh, "Let's hope they still avoid the main temple grounds, otherwise we might have to delay this outing until we have heavy enough armament to defend ourselves."

"I can keep it away," Ryes assured him, "I'm telling it to go back to sleep now." As they hovered overhead watching, she reached out to the monster and urged it back to its den; that she didn't need its services today. It suddenly disappeared beneath the foliage, vanishing from sight. "It's another one of her servants, but no one from the Temple is actively urging it to attack. They're still unaware."

"Just leave this one here in the valley. We don't need any more pets seeking you out," Maren teased, seeing her blush at this, as laughter sounded over their headsets.

"What we brought in from our hunt in Hailys would only feed that thing for a few days. I wonder what it eats here?" Gann asked, looking around to see if there were any herd animals nearby. He didn't see any, but then there wasn't much of this valley visible from the air.

"I don't care, as long as it isn't us," Sabin told him.

"It moved quickly, for something so large," Torr added, still amazed at Ryes' control over it. Suddenly some huge hunting birds flew upwards, flapping in front of the choppers, screeching out loudly, disturbed by their presence. They were each almost as big as the smallest chopper back in Winterhaven! Again, Ryes reached out to them and ordered them to return to their nests, that she didn't need their services. They heard her and quickly plummeted downward again.

"Busy day, already," Mitt commented with a smile. "Glad you can manage those things, Sis."

"Me too, at least I'm not having to wrest control of them from someone else," she returned, as Garth glanced back to smile at her. She smiled in return for him, but Doran was starting to give her a headache. She was trying to block her lures and attacks, as much as possible, for herself and the rest of the people with her.

"Alright, let's set down next to the main attraction," he said as he returned his full attention to his aircraft. He maneuvered his chopper to land on the grassy verge in front of the main structure, leaving plenty of room for Mitt to land hers. "As soon as we cut the engines, I want four teams to comb the area for any immediate dangers. Stay on the alert and keep only in the grassy area near the temple. Do not, under any circumstances, enter any of the buildings," he ordered. Affirmatives were voiced as he cut back his engine. Sabin unstrapped and went to open the rear door, then he, Gann, Maren, and Monty jumped out; each carried rifles as well as their pistols. The door was sealed behind them, as Garth began his shutdown procedure.

"Are you all right, Ryes?" Raya asked, seeing she had her eyes closed and a look of concentration upon her face.

"Yes. I blocked her out, but I'm trying to check the area with Empath to see if there're any dangerous animals nearby. Doran may not control them, but they've lived exceptionally long lives with only the purpose of protecting the temple from men, foremost in their minds. At least they obey me when I order them to leave the area," she explained.

"Good," Garth started, glad she was making a sweep of her own. "We'll have only the strong Talents going in first. The rest can wait outside, until we declare this area secure. If you don't feel safe out here, feel free to wait inside the choppers. If something comes close while we're inside, and it's too big to handle, take off in the chopper and we'll handle the situation, as soon as we get the inside secure." There were affirmatives voiced once more, as Ryes opened her eyes and gave him a nod of her head.

"All clear, but I'll wait until the guys are sure of it, too," she told him, smiling.

"Why do we bother?" Maren questioned over the headset with a hearty laugh.

"Because I only checked on the creatures nearby, not on the physical traps. I didn't want you to feel unneeded, after all," she quipped back, smiling impishly. They heard his laughter in response.

"Thanks, Ryes, we'll remember that," Torr returned, still laughing.

"Scanners report it's clear," Sabin finally reported after several long minutes of boredom for those waiting. Ryes kept a light check on any wanderers into the area, keeping them away.

"Let's go," Garth suggested, seeing his wife looked like she was concentrating upon something, but did have her eyes open. She met his eyes, then smiled brightly, giving him a nod of agreement. Ready or not, it was time to face off Doran again and settle things once and for all time. They quickly exited the choppers, closing the doors behind them. They mount the stairs as a tight group, with Phil taking scans of the graceful building with his drones, as he walked. He already had two headed out to catch the back and sides of the main building with everything being relayed via the chopper's com back to Winterhaven. He wanted a solid record of this visit for his structure studies - and just in case anything happens.

"I can't believe this place," he breathed, reverently touching the carved marble column near the main entrance. "This looks all hand-carved."

"You won't believe the inside," Ryes told him, smiling, "but these women weren't right in their minds," she reminded the whole crowd gathered nearby. "And Doran's madness only pulled them further down a path I'm not sure they ever anticipated. Don't be surprised by some of the reliefs," she warned, getting nods from the other women in agreement, while the men appeared neutral.

"We understand m'dear," Ethan assured her, seeing she was suddenly nervous. He didn't think it was the upcoming confrontation, but maybe what these abused women may have depicted in their artwork. She didn't want to be associated with them, even if she was because she was a woman. Rowan nodded his agreement, stepping forward to hug Ryes.

"Be careful, granddaughter," he warned. She smiled for him and gave him a quick kiss, which he returned. "And you too, grandson," he ordered Maren. He laughed, giving the old man a kiss and hug, too.

"We'll be fine," he assured him. He saw the curiosity in Metta's eyes as he examined the beautiful entrance before them. It looked innocent, like the gardens around it, hiding the evil which lay coldly coiled in its heart. Maren recalled Ryes' memory of her visit here when she and Garth had been separated from the rest of them.

"What about us?" Torr asked. He, Gann, Monty, Leon, Sadie and Minn were their weak Talents and were to be held in reserve.

"You're going no further than the entrance to the main gallery. If we need your help, we'll call for you," Garth ordered, keeping the layout of the place clear in his mind, from his wife's memories. Ryes gave him a nod of agreement, thinking it was still too far into the danger's path for them. He got nods of agreement from the others, then turned and led his teams down the corridor, with Ryes at his side. The crystal lights still burned brightly, illuminating the few mounted weapons left upon the walls around them. Monty started to reach for one, but Sabin blocked his move, shaking his head.

"We don't need to get Doran any more agitated, just yet," he warned in a low voice, as what he felt had to be her voice screeching within his mind. He was trying to figure out how to block her out, remembering she didn't hold the power she originally held, and was glad Ryes removed what she could, earlier. Leon nodded his agreement. Monty understood and quietly relented. He was starting to get a headache from the awful noise in his head, that wasn't a sound heard by ears!

Ryes and Garth reached the main door of the cavernous room, while the corridor continued onward to other rooms on this level. As Garth and the rest were surveying the room before them, Ryes strode forward to the ghostly image Doran projected further into the room, to have her focus upon herself, freeing their teams. Maren recognized her from his nightmares and as she cackled with her mad glee, the hair on the back of his neck stood on end.

"Come a calling, daughter?" she maliciously taunted Ryes, "Missed your rightful home?"

"I've come to make sure you can't harm any others," she replied, anger suddenly flashing in her emerald eyes.

"And I see you've brought along plenty of men to sacrifice upon our altar. We haven't had a good sacrifice festival in some years. This could be a fun time."

"You can't touch us," she snapped back, trying to cool her anger, so she could deal with any stunts Doran might pull. Her handmaidens still had control of a few of the energy streams from the Stone, which was why she could project her image again. Doran's eyes suddenly took on a deadly focus, as if recognizing Ryes for the first time, out of the clouds of her hazy memories.

"Oh yes I can," she assured her, "and I will return every kindness you have bestowed upon me, tenfold. You've brought men into my sacred dwelling and for that you shall pay with your very life!" The vehemence in her voice dripped with the acid poison of her cold, bitter hatred. Her face was a mask as she drifted almost nose to nose with Ryes. "You will pay for what you did to me, and pay for it dearly, child."

"Everyone who's with the first team, form up a circle over there," Garth directed, suddenly feeling they'd better establish their inner linking fast. This witch was even more unnerving in person, and he didn't like the way she was threatening his wife! The others moved to comply, as if awakening from a trance; the shock of seeing the initial confrontation between Ryes and Doran having rooted them for a moment. Ryes stood facing off Doran, still not ready to break off, until the rest were ready. Torr and his team stepped back into the hallway, but close to the open doors. Torr wished they could put something between them and that scary woman, as a protection of some kind. Sadie hissed out, feeling the evil around them.

"How dare you!" Doran suddenly screeched, streaking over to confront Garth. "I know you! And I will still have your soul to feast upon again!" Even if a small part of his heart trembled at her nearness, he faced her off as Ryes did.

"You're not feasting upon anyone," he told her evenly. Ryes stepped over to his side, glaring at her.

"You're not touching my husband, nor my friends - ever," she stated, then put herself between them. "Get the circle formed," she suggested to Garth in English, seeing he wasn't doing as he directed everyone else. Doran tried to shove her aside, but Ryes countered it easily and stood her ground. This got her focus again.

"You have learned some new tricks, daughter," she stated with an evil-dripping growl, "but it is not going to do you any good in the end." She pulled back and quickly drifted over to their support team near the door. "So shy, little ones? I'll have your little alien girl help lay you out upon our altar, one at a time." Ryes trotted toward them, but Sadie shifted in front of Torr and spat at the ghostly image.

"I only do what I want to do, and I don't follow you," she stated, sneering. Doran reached out to Sadie but found herself blocked. These were Talents and even if not strong ones, they could still fight back. She smiled wickedly as she threw back her head to laugh madly.

"Little children playing with firesticks," she declared, "you will soon get burned!"

"Ryes!" Garth called out, seeing she was running toward the other team, and away from them. They were as ready as they could be, having formed up the inner link. Ryes stopped, knowing she couldn't be in two places at the same time. So, she extended her will and pulled Doran away from her friends, knowing it was more an effort with the way her heart was split in this moment.

"Just a few new tricks," Doran laughed, then suddenly streaked back to envelope Ryes within her astral form. Garth stared in horror as Ryes suddenly was surrounded by Doran's spectral image. She started pulling at her throat as if she were choking and struggling for air, as she was being lifted into the air. Doran's mad laughter echoed throughout the gallery, as Ryes was fighting for her very life.

"Ryes!" Maren started to go to his cousin, if no one else was going to help. Garth and Mitt grabbed him, pulling him back to them.

"She'll be all right. She can handle that witch, if she remembers that she can," Mitt scolded him, seeing the anger in his eyes. He saw the worry in her own, and relented, but he remained ready, in case.

Ryes suddenly felt as if invisible hands were squeezing her throat, trying to choke the life out of her. She struggled, fighting for air, hearing Doran's mad laughter and furious with herself to be so caught, off-guard. She realized her struggles were ineffective and the only way to break Doran's hold was to call up all her Talents fully. She closed her eyes, retreating inward with her every instinct screaming at her to fight against the hold upon her throat. She fought her own instincts and centered herself. Then she shoved Doran away forcefully, throwing her presence across the chamber, over the alter. She opened her eyes as she landed lightly on her feet and saw the surprise and absolute fury upon Doran's face and knew she should've had all her Talents called up before walking in here to challenge her. She turned to her family and friends, seeing their relief at her victory.

"Let's get this done," she said, stepping over to them as they reformed their circle. She massaged her throat, then extended her Healing to take care of it.

"You're all right?" Maren pressed, worried.

"Yeah. Just kicking myself for being so stupid, to be caught like that," she admitted with a smile, stepping between Sabin and Garth, taking both of their offered hands. She closed her eyes, reaching out for their link, melding into it with the others. She wasn't going to be the linchpin for the commune, leaving it to Raya. She knew she was still Doran's number one target and needed to concentrate upon other things, ready now to begin.

Ryes stretched out, taking control of the energy streams from the Windrose Stone, letting them flow through her being. She felt the others pressing for a chance to try this too, as they stirred within the linkage. She never realized how intoxicating it might seem to someone who'd never touched them before. She wasn't sure of the wisdom of this. Slowly, carefully, she released one for Raya to try to call to herself, thinking she could use it to help support the link. Mitt beat her to the punch, calling it to herself, before Raya could quite figure out how. Mitt felt as if she were being seared by a pure burning fire, deeply within. She struggled against it, fighting the pain, trying to cut its power off from herself. Ryes quickly called it back, leaving Mitt reeling from the experience.

"Mitt! Are you all right?" she demanded, fearing for her very life.

"Just took me by surprise," she returned, after what seemed an eternity. Garth was going to reprimand her, but Ryes cut him off.

"This isn't a game. I'm not sure how I do this. I'll let you try to call the energy, but please only one at a time, in case I need to pull it back from you. It may be too much," she warned them, deeply concerned. This was distracting her from keeping a sharp eye on Doran! She opened her eyes to see Doran pacing one of their drones around the chamber, as if curious where the little device came from and what it was doing in her temple. She hoped Phil could keep her busy for a few moments, blessing him in her heart.

"Let me try," Sabin insisted. He felt her reluctant agreement and saw how Mitt called the earlier one, so extended himself and called the energy to him. It was pure fire, lighting up his very soul!

"Let it flow freely through you. You direct the energy as it passes through," Ryes encouraged him, seeing he was handling it better than Mitt. After a few seconds, he realized he could control and direct the energy, himself. He realized he was barely managing the one, wondering how Ryes was taking almost all the streams and directing them as she willed?

Maren called one to himself, recalling his cousin's shared memory of her earlier experience. He didn't have the emotional goad, nor desperation to spur him on, but he found it wasn't impossible to accomplish. He felt the fire coursing through him and felt he could reach out and do anything he could imagine doing with his Talents! Such power almost scared him, he realized, not envying Ryes and her inner pool for the first time.

Garth and Mitt reached for streams at the same time. This time Mitt let it flow through, barely wondering how her sister-in-law managed so many? It still burned, but she pulled her Talent up and looked at the rest of the temple around them. She could SEE it clearly. She KNEW where the traps lay and how to permanently disarm them. She reached deeper into the link, tapping Ryes' Manipulator Talent and set to work, making this place safe for all of them to tread. The others noted how she worked, Ryes letting her tap into her Talent as needed.

"It burns," Garth told Ryes as he held onto his sanity and let the bright fire flow through his being. He felt a tremendous rush, as if he now held immense power to use as he willed.

"If it's too much," she started, but he held her back. If she could direct all of these intense streams of energy, he could direct one. He saw his younger sister calling another one to herself subconsciously as she worked, taking a deeper draw from both her own and Ryes' Talents. Raya pulled one to her, knowing the pain the others were in, but determined to learn how to do this too. It burned, but she held herself through the pain, bringing her Talent to the fore and doing as Mitt was, focusing upon using it, augmented by the wild, coursing energy. Tennan called one, fearful, but determined that if her brother could do it, she could too. She stubbornly hung on as she let the energy flow through, conquering it and her fears in the process.

Maren turned his attention to the Sleepers in the chambers, hidden in the alcoves. He suddenly tapped Raya's Talent, in order to clearly communicate with these women, wanting no misunderstandings. It surprised Raya, but she realized his purpose in this move and allowed it. She wasn't ready to face Doran. Ryes was facing her off, keeping her at bay from the other team and their men, as she had opened her eyes again to watch what Doran was doing.

"Who among you would like to be free of this place?" Maren directly questioned the women, whose presences were gathered nearby, to support and watch their raging leader.

"You're a MAN. We have nothing to do with men!" one scoffed, then tried to attack him with her Talent, insulted that he dared to address her, here. Ryes easily blocked it, letting the energy of her attack dissipate.

"What would we do away from here? The world as it is now, is not an easy place to live," another pressed, reaching out to Maren. Ryes recognized her as the one who'd befriended her mother, when she'd been captive here, as she listened in on their exchange.

"No, it's not, but at least you can live out your life. We're taking the Windrose Stone with us when we leave. You'll only have what power your own Talents grant you," Raya explained, focusing in with Maren, while maintaining the main meld. "Do you want a life of nothing and darkness? Your machinery will maintain your chambers for some time, but what kind of existence is it? To eventually die, cold and forgotten?"

"What is a Windrose Stone?" a third questioned.

"What you call a Power Stone. Our humans call it a Windrose Stone and we like that name better. A windrose lays out the directions on a map and this stone helps us direct our Talents far better and functions something like a windrose," Maren returned with humor coloring his mental tones. "We're very fond of our humans and if you choose to come out of here with us, you'd have to at least treat them in a civil manner. Both the men and the women."

"You are the one Ryes showed us, before," the second suddenly broke in, happiness in her mental voice as she realized it. "You are Maren?" she pressed.

"Yes, I am," he assured her, feeling amusement, as the others, who were watching what he and Raya were doing, hearing their exchange. He wondered what Ryes told them?

"What did Ryes tell you of my brother?" Tennan questioned her directly, wondering too.

"Only this," she returned, offering her memory of the earlier contact and the warmth and protectiveness Ryes felt toward Maren, even when she barely knew him, as she did at that time. He was embarrassed while Tennan and Raya were amused, adding in their own feelings of love for him, too. This outpouring surprised the other women, taking them aback. They'd forgotten what it was like to care for another being, much less a man, and to be so loved in return. What these three women felt for this one man, who felt he was seeking to save them from an endless pointless existence, daunted the Sleepers, greatly disturbing them all. Maren opened up his inner feelings for the people he lived with in Winterhaven. Dotti, Ryes, Tennan, Raya, Mitt, and the others, both human and starmen were in this sending, showing them that while they cared for him, he loved and cherished them in return.

"But all men only seek to use women to their own ends!" the first one protested, feeling confused by these strangers' charged emotions. The Winterhaven women were amused by her viewpoint.

"Women use men in the same way, at times," Tennan asserted with humor.

"I will try, if it is truly all as you have shown us," the second one voiced, trying to feel courageous. Tennan and Raya opened themselves up to the sleepers too, showing them it wasn't a lie, that their lives were enriched by the closeness they all shared.

"You're more than welcome to stay with us, or venture anywhere upon Tayna your heart takes you," Maren assured her and the others, "As soon as Mitt finishes with what she's doing, we'll have her figure out how to safely remove you from your chambers." Ryes saw Maren and the others triumph, where she failed with the Sleepers before, then noted Doran was planning something, with a gleam of wickedness in her eyes. She worried what it could mean? She thought she had everything covered.

"You only think you have won, daughter," Doran directly addressed her, once more. "I'll be the victor in the end."

"There's no prize here to gain. You'll only win your own solitary confinement, if you choose to continue walking this path. However, you can let go of your past and seek a new future, we'll release even you, Doran, to make a new life in this world," Ryes offered. Garth closely attended to what she was doing, trying to figure out what the dark witch was up to, himself. He did recall some of the tortures she put him through now, as she toyed with him, slowly consuming his very soul. She was dangerous and he knew it.

"This is what I think of your pitiful world!" Doran shouted, launching her attack. It was vicious and far more skilled than any which had been thrown at her before. Ryes tried to divert the energy of the killing, mental blast, but saw on the instant that it wasn't the way to deal with this one. She floundered, losing control of most of the energy streams and almost dropping out of the link, as Garth and Sabin came to her defense. Garth absorbed what remained of the attack's energy, diverting it back at the witch, while Sabin pulled Ryes back to the link, more strongly. Doran laughed gleefully as she reabsorbed her spent energy, so happy these inexperienced cubs had no idea what they were truly dealing with. Ryes found her center again and exerted her control over the streams, once more. She finally found what she was looking for - the ones still feeding Doran through her followers - and called them, too.

"NO!" Doran wailed as she realized what Ryes was doing. "You cannot take the power from me!"

"Oh, yes I can," she volleyed in return, then got an inspiration. Garth and Sabin saw what she envisioned, giving her their full approval and support.

"Let me, I want to pay her back a little," Garth offered, seeing her concentration was taxed enough, as it was. She allowed him, hoping it'd work. Garth was determined. He pulled up his Talents fully, then tapped into Ryes' Talents. He reached out to Doran. She shied away, as if she knew he had purpose in this contact, and she wanted nothing of him now. He extended himself and pinned her down, as Ryes held onto her beam control. She was tiring. He realized he barely knew how to control his own Talents, much less attempt to use one of hers, but wasn't going to let this witch hurt anyone else again. He delved into Doran's very being, seeking the inner link she was using to control the Talents of the others. She fought him here, viciously, as Sabin and Tennan joined him, trying to divert her attacks upon him, freeing Garth to do as he thought he needed. Her attacks, for all her years of experience and the darkness in her heart, were nowhere as dire as Gurri's had been, which surprised Sabin.

Still, she resisted them, using her followers' Mind Voice and Manipulator Talents to the fullest. She started hurling everything she could break free and grasp with one of the handmaiden's Manipulator. Small statues and stone carved benches from the main chamber, even the remaining weapons from the entry corridor flew toward Ryes and the group, as they stood in her hall, all at the same time.

"Look out! Hit the deck!" Monty shouted, as he dropped to the marble floor, as a sword whizzed by his head. Sadie was struck on the face by an axe, a glancing blow, as Torr pulled her down with him. Minn dropped, barely avoiding being skewed by a pike, but was still deeply scored along one leg. Leon narrowly dodged a hammer as he dropped to the floor and rolled, also getting a glancing blow that left him disoriented for a few moments.

"She's not aiming at us, we just happen to be in the way," Torr told the others, realizing they were safe on the floor. He extended his weak Healing Talent to help Sadie's face and stop the bleeding. He felt her trying to add in her own Talent to his efforts and smiled as he felt they were both fumbling along. "It's a good thing the stronger Talents know a little more about what they're doing for things like this!"

"She's a nightmare," Gann breathed, glad they were out of the main battle. He'd barely missed being cut in half by a very heavy sword, but his arm was bleeding where the blade barely scored him. "Still, I think we're safer with the rest of them."

"You're probably right," Minn agreed as he ignored the pain, unhappy to see Mitt in the middle of the maelstrom.

Ryes was deflecting the physical attacks, diverting some of the energy and Talent Mitt was borrowing from her, to do so. Mitt suddenly noticed what was happening and turned her attention to the battles within and without, helping in their efforts and deflecting the hurtling objects from striking any of them, leaving Ryes her full capability to exercise her Talents for inner defense.

Debris rained down around their circle. The benches broke in the fall, with the shards being a hazard for everyone. Mitt managed to deflect them away from everyone in their circle, feeling regret she'd been unable to divert the thrown weapons before their second team was harmed. They now lay upon the floor about them, too, as she drew the energy that kept them aloft away, using Ryes' Molecular Manipulator. She suddenly craved to open up her Inner Sight and Ryes' Molecular and regular Manipulator Talents to reshape things here, as she saw they should have been done, before. But the fight was not over, yet. She kept alert to any more physical attacks.

Finally, Garth reached through to the goal he sought. He recognized the link she had with her handmaidens with his Empath. He found his focus slipping as Doran redoubled her efforts, desperate as she realized what he was attempting. Her ghostly visage showed the fury and desperation on its face. Ryes saw it and turned her attention within to Doran, leaving Mitt to protect their physical bodies, taking up where Garth was faltering, as if they were tag-teaming now, still leaving Sabin and Tennan to deflect Doran's attacks.

Ryes grasped that strong link Doran established through the longs centuries they'd all spent here, adding in the pure power of the energy she was channeling through her being and severed it completely, extinguishing it fully. Immediately, all Doran's attacks stopped, and Ryes pulled back, concentrating upon the energy streams. The projected image of Doran had vanished as well. All remained quite as Sabin and Garth double-checked, to make sure she was truly without access to any Talent. The sudden silence around them was even more deafening, than the racket raised as Doran was hurling things at them a few moments ago.

Recoup

Chapter 6

"It's finished," Garth assured Ryes, speaking to her within their link. She slowly released most of the energy streams, keeping only a bare few to use, as they might still need. She saw the hall before them was a mess, as she focused back on what lay around them, again. There were statues shattered, weapons askance everywhere and stone benches lying in strange places. Some were broken, some not. The alcoves were mostly intact, as far as she could see. Mitt resumed her work, taking full control of Ryes' Talents, glad the real contest was over.

"Is it safe yet?" she heard a voice call out. She found it was a struggle to find her own vocal cords for a moment.

"Not quite, Torr. Hold on until Mitt has all the traps disabled," she warned, unable to see him from her angle of view. "But Doran's been eliminated as an active threat."

"You didn't kill her, did you?" Dr. Cruthers demand. She smiled to herself. They weren't supposed to be inside the building, yet! But with the main battle over and the sudden silence, she could guess he'd investigate – to be sure. A drone whizzed by her, as it was headed deeper into the room – taking scans.

"No. Just removed her connection with her followers, so she can't hurt anyone through them, anymore," she assured him. "She has no Talent and now no support from her handmaidens."

"Ah, geeze Ryes, this place looks like a real battle happened here," Sadie teasingly scolded, as she, Minn, Leon and Gann surveyed the main chamber. Torr was quietly talking with Dr. Cruthers and Phil out in the hallway. Sadie saw the small group stood with their backs still to each other, hands tightly clasped, and their eyes closed. Ryes was the only one with her eyes open and a smile upon her face.

"Well, you know what it's like when new management moves in," she teased in return. "Stay back. Mitt's not done, yet." Ryes closed her eyes, sinking back within, feeling at the limits of her strength with controlling the few streams she still held. Garth and Sabin were now helping Mitt, having discovered Ryes had a weaker version of Mitt's Inner Sense available too.

"You do realize Ryes, that you're just like your mother," Sabin told her, as he worked.

"What do you mean?" she asked, not understanding what he implied.

"That you're a Talent of One," he assured her. "Have you ever tried to figure out how many Talents you actually have? I'm sure if you took the time, you'd realize you have at least all fourteen of them. You could always check yourself with your Catalyst Talent when you get a chance." Ryes was still for a few moments, too numb after her battle with Doran to grasp what he was telling her.

"But my mother never had any power. That's what Rowan always said," she returned, defensively. "How can I be a Talent of One?" She suddenly felt humor from the others in the link, realizing they were all listening in on them.

"Well, you do have the power; it probably came from your father. So, you're one up on your mother," Maren teased, knowing her lifelong battle for recognition of her own merits, living in the shadow of all her mother could do and had been. "I wonder what with a little real training, how powerful some of these `weaker' Talents you possess, could really turn out to be?" he speculated, thinking Sabin had to be right about it. It felt like the answer...

"There's no one to train me, so it's a moot point," she returned.

"There's your Aunt Adina. She's locked in the past, but I wonder... if you could cast back your spirit and use your Talents back then from our present, why couldn't you bring her and Hadu forward into our time?" Maren pressed, suddenly getting an idea.

"No!" Garth quickly interjected, a trace of fear in his sending. He wasn't going to risk her in such an impossible attempt!

"But we have the Windrose Stone. Why can't she do it with the power of this stone?" Sabin unexpectedly spoke up in full agreement, seeing his chance at last.

"She has more than the Stone. She has all of us to back her, too!" Mitt declared, finally finished with the traps, hidden panels, and floorplates. Now she was gathering all the broken stone in the main chamber and piling it in a heap, in one corner, then pulling the good benches from wherever they landed, stacking them nearby. The weapons she gathered and left lying atop a raised platform where the altar stood, only next to it. She was enjoying using Ryes' Talents with the Windrose Stone to enhance everything.

"No!" Garth repeated, starting to get upset with his sister over this. Sabin's support was unbelievable, as far as he was concerned. "What even makes you think Ryes can do such a thing?" he suddenly demanded of his blood-brother, wrestling to understand it clearly.

"Remember the wreath of flowers? She was wearing it when we went Time Walking. Well, when we returned from the past, it was gone. I saw it fall off her head, as she stopped a wall of flame from descending upon her aunt and the others, who were trapped. After you carried her off to the chopper, I checked the ground around us. It was gone. I checked the path behind you. It wasn't there, nor was it in the chopper, nor in the blanket. She left it in the past!" Sabin insisted, opening up the full memory of what he saw and experienced, as they were Time Walking, and his subsequent search sparked by his curiosity. For the first time the rest, who had not seen it when Ryes shared it earlier, saw how truly dire the destruction was, and how desperate the people were, who were left in the far past of Hailys. Even Garth was appalled.

"You're right. It just disappeared, but I was so caught up in trying to save Ryes, that it slipped my memory," Maren stated, "We can't leave those people to die, trapped between two walls of flame, in the collapsing ruins of the building, itself!"

"Wait. I can control these energy streams to some extent, but how can I hold my focus upon opening up a pathway from the past to the present, while trying to juggle the energy we'll need to get the job done?" Ryes suddenly questioned, too tired to make sense of it all right now. "I'm reaching my limit here. I'm going to have to release the Stone's power. Are you ready?" she asked the rest. She got a sense of all clear from everyone, then released the rest of the energy streams to flow as they would naturally.

"We'll think of a way," Sabin assured Ryes, feeling her distress over being reminded of her great aunt's peril.

Raya dissolved the link, feeling it was time. Sabin clutched tightly to the memory of the Vision he had this morning; of them using the Windrose Stone to this end, but she still needed Rhin to help maintain her focus. He knew Garth didn't want them using their son in such a way, so felt once he realized it was the only way they could accomplish it, himself, then it would happen.

They opened their eyes to see their backup team standing next to them, looking relieved. With their weak Talents, they were still better than no-Talents, when it came to internal battles.

"We'll discuss this later," Garth ordered them aloud. He knew Sabin had to be right, but the only way to verify it was to go back in time and see if the flower wreath was truly in the past now, or not. He realized he'd have to go into the past with her, to make sure of it.

"Discuss what?" Torr asked, wondering what they'd been discussing.

"Using the Windrose Stone to rescue Ryes' aunt out of the past," Mitt explained, smiling. "Where's Phil? He's not going to believe this place!" she declared with a mischievous smile, as she deftly changed the subject. She noted Maren was busy healing the people injured during the attack, then he finished and looked to her.

"Mitt, we have some Sleepers ready to try living with us in Winterhaven, but you're going to have to have a look at those freezing chambers they're stored in," Maren spoke up, wanting to get her to check on their chambers, now that they talked almost half the remaining women into it. Raya smiled, giving him a nod of her head in support.

"Okay, which ones?" she asked as they lead her off toward the alcoves. Dr. Cruthers came across the room to stand before the statue of Doran, herself.

"Sadie, your face," Ryes realized it looked badly scratched up, with smears of fresh blood on it, too.

"I'll be all right," she assured her, blushing, but Ryes stepped forward and extended her Healing Talent, anyway.

"There, now you will be," she replied, smiling at her friend. She'd done the repair correctly and removed the blood from her skin.

"Thanks," she returned, grateful. She tried to follow what Ryes did, and realized she needed more practice with this Talent of hers. Ryes gave her a nod of her head in answer, as she smiled, then turned to see if any of the others who still needed healing, noting Maren had taken care of them, already. Garth still looked unhappy.

"Beautiful woman," Ethan commented, "but, so sad an ending." Ryes stepped over to him, not ready to take on Garth at the moment, still feeling his anger over Maren and Sabin's suggestions. Her grandfather and Metta stepped over to look at the statue, too.

"This large black monolith houses her suspension chamber. Should we release her after all this, or not?" she asked, wanting his opinion, if he had one formulated yet. Ethan looked at her, a contemplative look in his eyes. Raya had previously shown both he and Rowan Ryes' earlier confrontation in this temple to help prepare them both for this venture.

"I think she'd only feel the need to tear you apart, for what you've done to and taken from her. Would releasing her truly be wise?" he volleyed in return. Ryes sighed, realizing she should've expected such a response from him. Rowan looked at her with questions in his eyes, too.

"I don't think she'd have anything to contribute to our little establishment in Winterhaven. Karr's more than enough for us to put up with, all in herself," Garth suggested, smiling finally, as he stepped over and put an arm around Ryes' shoulders. The others chuckled in agreement, with a few nods. "Ethan, did you happen to see what happened to the flower wreath Ryes was wearing on her head, when she was Time Walking into Hailys' past?" he suddenly added, wanting to see if he'd made some kind of observation about it, too. Ethan turned to meet Rowan's eyes, as a smile passed between them.

"It disappeared, shortly before she and Sabin returned to us," he assured him, turning back to meet Garth's eyes. "I described the happenstance to Rowan, and we've been speculating as to where it disappeared off to," he offered with a jovial smile. Garth sighed at this, shaking his head.

"Let's get what we came for here secured, before I'll even begin to entertain any thoughts of Hailys," he decided aloud. Ryes tried not to smile too broad a smile, as Rowan winked at her, and Ethan was grinning merrily.

"My gosh, these things still work," Phil delightfully declared as he and Mitt had three of the thirty operational chambers cycling to revive their occupants. There were another fifty-three with the remains of their occupants lying desiccated within and would need burial later. They left them sealed until then. And finally, seventeen chambers were open and empty; one was surely Tyra's former prison.
"We succeeded with some, at least," Maren commented as he was standing by in case the equipment failed after all. Garth smiled at his enthusiasm, as Ryes chuckled.
"How many will be returning with us?" she asked Maren, seeing the look of worry upon his face, even so.
"We could only talk eleven ladies into taking the venture. But I did promise to return at the end of the summer to see if anyone's changed her mind by then," he replied.
"They're so afraid of everything," Raya told her. "I remember when I was living out on the plains and it was how I used to feel," she explained. Ryes smiled at this, nodding her head.
"Then you fell in with our little wild bunch," she reminded her. "I recall you being timid, but then, so was I at one time."

"You used to be so shy, no one hardly ever saw you. It was like tracking the wind," Garth agreed, remembering Ryes used to be so elusive. "It'd take days before I'd catch a glimpse of you, when they were living back in Matlowe."

"Yeah, we ruined you, too," Maren piped in, smiling at last. "I guess we'll just have to work our charms upon these fine ladies, also."

"You sure have a thing for women in freezers," Dotti teased, pausing as she was taking scans for Dr. Cruthers now, tracking her drones and using other recording devices. Maren wrapped his arms around his wife, pulling her in close.

"But you were already a part of my life, long before we met, m'dear," he reminded her, kissing her. She giggled as she pulled away.

"And you were in my dreams, long before you were even born," she agreed, smiling happily. "I'd better get this done first. I'll be right back," she warned him with a saucy wink, heading upstairs to the other wing of the building, at Phil's earlier urging. He laughed, giving her a nod of his head.

"She dreamed about you, before you were born?" Garth questioned, wondering if it was true.

"Yes, she did," Ryes answered for him, then leaned up and gave Garth a quick kiss. "It's too bad we put off for years, what we could've had much sooner, ourselves," she teased.

"I kept hoping to catch you alone, and the one and only chance I got, I could barely put two words together in my head," he admitted, recalling when she led him to the moss-eater's carcass in the forest. She sighed then chuckled, recalling that day and how he never spoke a word, just stared at her in amazement.

"Some things only happen in their own time," Ethan reminded them, stepping over to join the youngsters.

"Yes," Rowan agreed, having heard them too, "Otherwise, Korman might've tried to kill Garth, long before he was able to challenge him and win."

"I hadn't thought of it that way," Garth admitted, as Mitt nodded her head in agreement.

"He would've, and you know it," she scolded him.

"How was Dotti a part of your life, before you met?" Ethan asked Maren, curious. He blushed but gave him a nod of his head.

"When we were on our way to Hailys, I started having very intense dreams, as my Talents were beginning to awaken. There was Doran, whom I called ol' green creeps, who was trying to kill me, then Ryes' mother, who usually saved me from Doran. Then there was Dotti, and her I worshiped," he admitted. "I always figured if I ever met her in truth, I'd probably be too embarrassed to actually talk to her."

"Talk? We could barely get you to set her down upon one of the chairs," Mitt teased, laughing.

"So, you dreamed about each other," he commented, turning it around in his mind. "So much like Shelley and I. When we first met, it was as if we'd known each other all our lives. As if we'd fallen in love long ago, even if we were far too young at the time for it ever to have happened."

"That's what it felt like," Maren agreed, smiling.

"Oh, Garth, Phil, you've got to see this!" Gann urged his brother and friend, then noticed it looked as if they were all discussing something. Garth laughed at his interruption.

"And back to the here and now," he added. "How much longer will it be before these chambers finish reviving the ladies?"

"Another hour for the first three. We didn't want to tax the systems. They may still function, but if we try to cycle all eleven of the chambers at once, it could overload and take them all out. They're not running on the same equipment as Doran's crypt. You can clearly tell it's been added on," Mitt explained, as Phil nodded. She wondered what was up, now?

"I'll watch them. You go on," Ryes promised, waving at Mitt and Phil to go ahead with Gann. Garth gave her a nod of agreement, then the four of them left, heading for some secret stairs they found between the Windrose Stone's ring and the steps up to the altar.

"I recall you showing me the memory of your earlier confrontation here, but seeing this place for myself has been interesting," Maren told his cousin with a sigh. He pointed to some very intricate carving, into the stone slab on the back wall of this alcove. The scene depicted four beautiful women smiling in happiness, with the bodies of six men lying in a pool of blood, at their feet. "How could they set something like this to stone? The women happy, alone, would've been plenty."

"Perhaps Doran had this carved to represent particular men, who treated these women badly?" Rowan conjectured with a sigh. But he thought his grandson was correct in his observation.

"I wouldn't want to have to see Toron's face ever again, even if it were carved as if I triumphed over him like this," Raya admitted, "By doing this, they've immortalized their enemies, too."

"I agree," Ryes stated, crinkling up her nose at the thought. "I couldn't see putting Korman's face up on a wall. It doesn't make any sense."

"Sorrow and revenge rarely make sense to others not involved," Ethan told them. "If you need me, I'll be below, investigating what they've found in the chambers down there." Ryes gave him a nod of her head as she smiled. Metta then caught up with him and Rowan. He'd been giving the entire place a very thorough sweep, outraged at some of the depictions carved upon the walls. "Metta? Would you like to stay here with the young ones or go below to see what else they found?" he asked, turning to see him.

"I'll go see what's below," he replied, deciding it sounded the better option. The three elders left. Ryes sat down upon the cold, stone floor, feeling tired.

"Did that sound like another trip to Hailys, or what?" Maren asked, sitting down beside her. Raya sat too. The floor was better than those benches with all the carvings they had upon them.

"Garth was truly upset with Sabin," she admitted with a sigh. "I never noticed the flower wreath falling off, but it was pretty clear from Sabin's point of view."

"You looked like you were a bit busy at the time," Maren scolded. "I did see it disappear, like it fell off your head, but you tried to return shortly thereafter and was having a hard time reconnecting to yourself. I was too worried about you, to worry about a silly circle of flowers disappearing into thin air," he admitted, now mildly upset with the event again.

"For the flowers to now be in the past, then for the barest instant, you had to actually be in the past, too," Raya spoke up, still recalling the memory Sabin shared with them. "To bring your aunt and those other people here to their future, you'd have to find a way to connect them here, like those flowers were to there."

"Sabin's holding something back and Garth was too mad at him to see it. I wonder what it is?" Ryes conjectured. "And how would I create a bridge from the past to our present?"

"By bringing your Talents into full use, in both times," Sabin said, stepping around to see the trio sitting on the floor. He'd been nearby, listening in. "But instead of letting go, you'd have to hold them focused, until everyone is clear of the danger."

"But in order to do that, Ryes has to be back there, herself," Maren pointed out, feeling unsettled by his suggestion, "It means she could die in Hailys' destruction, too!"

"You've had a Vision!" Ryes declared, seeing his confidence in such a risky plan. This brought Maren up short, seeing she was right.

"Will Ryes make it?" Raya asked, needing to know now.

"I don't know," he admitted as he sat down opposite them. "I do know we make the attempt and that it will work. I don't know of any complications which could happen, after the small window into the future, the Vision left me with."

"Could you show me?" Maren requested, getting an idea. If Dotti were there, he could gauge by her pregnancy's advancement. Sabin met his eyes, then gave him a nod in understanding.

"But not Ryes. She'll have to figure out how to do this, all on her own. So, you'll have to promise to keep it from her and Garth for now," he stated. Maren gave him another nod in answer. "I'll show Garth, when I know it's the right time." Maren crawled over to Sabin's side, then closed his eyes. The two of them were quiet for several, long moments, as if they were discussing something internally. Ryes sighed, smiling to herself.

"Are you all right with this?" Raya asked her friend, putting a hand upon her shoulder.

"Yes, I think I'll be fine. I've had to do everything in my life `the hard way', as the humans say it, so this doesn't truly daunt me.

I only feel sorry for Garth for having to constantly keep an eye on me, trying to keep me safe."

"You're not going to peek?" she teased, smiling.

"No. Why spoil the surprise?" she quipped back, with a small laugh. Maren and Sabin opened their eyes looking at her strangely.

"What surprise?" Maren asked, wondering.

"Whatever you two are discussing," she returned with a smile.

"Do you feel it? Those women are restless and afraid," Raya said, casting her head upward, looking toward the chambers.

"They've been totally cut off from Doran for the first time in a long time. I saw some were checking to see if she still exists, but none have tried to reestablish a link with her. Give them time to realize and enjoy their first true freedom," Ryes replied, still smiling.

"Maybe more will now decide it's time to let this place go," Maren added, looking hopeful. Raya nodded her head and smiled as she met his eyes. They could hope.

After a long day's work, they finally secured the Windrose Stone, four shield barrier devices, and several other interesting devices, which they thought might prove useful. Due to the late hour, and needing to prepare for it, they decided to put off the burial of the ones who'd died in their chambers until after the Gather. That way it could be done with all due decorum.

Dr. Cruthers and Sabin decided to install an investigative team here, as soon as the main efforts in Matlowe were completed. There were other machines, which might prove of future use, as well as a study of the ancient power systems, both the one maintaining Doran's chamber, and the other one powering the rest of the buildings and sleep chambers. The study of the cult was also of some interest, but Ethan kept this idea low key for now, seeing Metta and some of the others' intense disgust with these women.

As for the Sleepers who decided to come out into the world once more, Raya and Mitt took charge of them. They loaded up the helicopters with the equipment returning with them, then their rescued survivors. The Winterhaven residents had to crowd in, and with some passenger exchanges back and forth, they barely managed to fit everyone in within weight tolerances for the machines to carry. Ryes was relieved, as she envisioned having to spend the night out in the fields, on the other side of the creek, as before. Of course, sometimes that was called a vacation nowadays.

"Here you are," Gann said, as he helped his second lady down from the chopper, after they finally arrived back in Winterhaven. She

smiled very briefly but he felt her revulsion over him having to help
her down, since they were unloading out of the back, still he smiled
broadly for her and gave her a nod of his head, gesturing for her to
join Raya nearby. He turned for the next woman.

"Thank you, kind sir," this lady told him, as he set her upon
her feet. Gann smiled more genuinely as their eyes met. He thought
his heart was going to stop. She had the most amazing lavender-
colored eyes! These had to be something contrived, like the way
Sadie liked to dye her hair red, he thought. She was looking up into
his eyes, as if she found it hard to pull away, too.

"It was no effort," he offered in return, removing his hands
from her waist quickly. "If there's anything you need, I'm at your
service. My name's Gann." She laughed lightly at this, nodding her
head.

"My name's Saree of House Delancee," she introduced herself,
feeling strange to be speaking with a man, after such a long time.
She knew she should've left with Tyra, long ago. He gave her a nod
of his head as he smiled. She liked his smile.

"Raya and Mitt are briefing everyone over there. They'll get
you settled into your room, shortly," he advised her, still smiling.

"Thank you, again," she replied, and turned to join the
women, but hesitated and turned back. Gann was now helping Dunn
of House Ebs out of their flying machine. She stepped aside to wait,
as Dunn thanked him also. She noted he didn't linger to look into
Dunn's eyes, as he had hers. This pleased her for some reason she
couldn't name. She noted his muscular arms and clean braided hair.
He looked like a Forester, with his easy manner. After he helped the
rest of the remaining women down, he turned and noted she was still
standing near him. He appeared puzzled, but his eyes held delight.

"Is there something you need, Lady Saree?" he asked.

"I felt you hold a Talent, and yet you labor as a commoner,"
she stated.

"A Talent's only another tool. It alone doesn't make me any
more special than anyone else, only able to help others in special
ways, when needed. I still have plenty of other work to do," he
replied, thinking it sounded like a silly question.

"What kind of work do you do?" she pressed, wondering, and
feeling the need to know.

"Right now, I'm an electrician, installing the wiring and
breaker boxes in the new buildings we're raising here in Winterhaven.

As soon as we finish the school, we'll be heading over to Matlowe Village to work on Karr's house, some new apartments, an inn, and a school we're planning on erecting in the village."

"Then, I will not see you, when you are working in this village?" she questioned. For some reason she felt disappointed by this notion. He laughed lightly at this.

"Phil and Kovin will have us on a four-four work week. We'll be in Matlowe for four days, then have four days off back home, here in Winterhaven. But I know my brother and he usually has plenty of things for me to help him with here. So, my days off are usually pretty busy, like today. He wanted me to help with this jaunt out to Doran's Valley."

"Then, I may still see you around, sometime?"

"Yes. I'll be available if you need me. Just type in a message into the computer system to me at any time, and I'll receive it. That way we can arrange our schedules," he assured her, smiling. "Raya will show you how we use our equipment here shortly, and acquaint you with English, the human's language." Saree stared up into his dark, brown-colored eyes and smiled as she felt stirrings within her breast, she hadn't felt in such a long time. She suddenly blushed as she thought this was far too soon for such strong emotions to be moving within her.

"Then, I will see you later, Gann. Have a good night," she offered.

"You, too. Sweet dreams, Saree," he wished her, then walked beside her, escorting her over to Raya's knowing eyes.

"You're not supposed to sweep them off their feet, so soon," she teased Gann, speaking directly to his mind. He blushed as he gave her a bow and nod of his head.

"That wasn't my intention," he fumbled in return with his own Mind Voice Talent. "Goodnight," he bid her aloud, then turned and retreated for the ramp down to the main entrance to Winterhaven, his heart pounding. So, Saree felt the same attraction for him, as he felt for her. Why? He kept asking himself. He went to the dining hall to get a late snack, seeing the place filled with most of the day's party, eating too.

The Dust Settles

Chapter 7

"Gann, get your tray and join us," Garth urged, just getting his mug of tea. "Karr's already gone to bed. I think she's finally given up on thinking she can order you around every minute of the day. Chuck held dinner for us, tonight, too." Gann laughed at this, nodding his head.

"I've got to talk with you, later," he told him in a low voice, stepping closer.

"Let's eat first, let me check on the cubs, then we'll take the whole night, if you need. I have things weighing upon my mind, too," he warned with a smile. Gann was relieved. He knew he wasn't going to get any sleep with Saree playing on his own mind, anyway.

"You've got a deal," he assured him. He got his tray, then returned to brother's table. He was starting to sit more with them, glad to be able to distance himself some from Karr, now. Glyn still loved her and stuck by her side and while he merely thought him a little crazy for doing so, it was Glyn's choice.

As they were discussing some missing flowers and where Sabin thought they disappeared, Raya and Mitt entered with the eleven former Sleepers from the valley. They were showing them the facilities and explaining how things were done here. They then encouraged the women to take trays, picking what foods they wanted to eat, and what they wanted to drink, then took them to some empty tables and let them get settled down for a few minutes. Saree saw him sitting with the others and instead walked straight for their table and sat down next to Gann. He blushed as she smiled at him, his stomach suddenly filled with flutter-wings.

"Is it all right for me to eat with you?" she asked.

"Not a problem," Ryes replied for him, smiling. Garth chuckled as Sayer came into the room holding Shaysa. "Ooops, guess I'm needed," she commented.

"Mom, I think she's got a slight fever," Sayer told her as she passed the cub to Ryes. Her eyes took on a more serious look as she stood and took one of her white-haired daughters into her arms and closed her eyes, cuddling her up to her chest.

"She does. Maren? What do you think?" she asked, opening them and meeting her cousin's eyes. He stood and took her and closed his eyes for a few moments.

"She's just cutting her first tooth," he assured her, smiling as he passed the infant back. Ryes sighed in relief. "Here, see for yourself," he instructed her, reaching out to her with his Talent and directing her own, so she knew how to recognize it now.

"Ah," she replied, relieved, "Guess I need more practice. Maybe I should spell Tennan, when she comes into season?" she suggested, turning to her husband with a question in her eyes. He laughed with a nod of his head, as she sat down.

"How're you going to fit that into your schedule?" he demanded.

"I think it's a great idea," Tennan voiced out, as Teris chuckled. "How do you expect her to strengthen her Healing Talent, if she never practices it?" she added. Maren nodded his head as he sat down next to Dotti.

"We're going to have to work our weaker Talents, in order to bring them to their strongest points. I just have no idea how to work this Booster Talent of mine," he admitted.

"I am a Booster," Saree offered, blushing as the others turned their eyes to her. She saw no animosity here, nor any derision, nor greed, and Gann had finally relaxed. She felt more at home in this primitive-looking place, than she ever did in her parent's plush home! "I could try to show you how I was trained," she finished, smiling.

"I'd appreciate it," Maren told her, meaning it. "My strongest Talent is my Healing Talent, which is why I've somehow ended up running the medical facility here in Winterhaven," he explained, "Ryes is a Booster, too, as well as her son, Rhin. We've never had anyone to actually train us." Sayer got a mug of tea and sat down next to Garth, wanting to hear what the adults were talking about.

"Are you really going to go Time Walking in Hailys, again, Mom?" she asked, having heard Sabin talking with Torr about it in the corridor outside, as she was bringing Shaysa in.

"Yes, I have to," she replied, settling Shaysa into her tabletop carrier. The cub was sleepy, and she wanted to finish her dinner quickly, while she still could. She looked up and saw how this upset her, so smiled for her. "I'll be all right. I won't try to do anything dangerous, like stopping a wall of fire this time."

"I'll be with her to make sure," Garth assured her, ruffling her short, reddish-gold hair as he smiled.

"Listen, your mother will be fine. We had a Vision which won't happen for a few months, yet. And she was in it," Maren told her as Dotti nudged him in the side.

"Ryes, you're going to have to show it to me, too," she insisted, appearing frustrated, "He didn't get much sleep for several nights afterwards."

"No," Maren ordered, meeting Ryes' eyes. She could understand why, but knew Dotti had the right to know about it too.

"I'll think about it," she offered. It was the best compromise she could come up with. "And you're not allowed to pry either, young lady," she told Sayer, feeling her attempting to find the answers for herself directly. "I thought we taught you better Talent etiquette than that?" Sayer blushed, nodding her head.

"Your daughter has Talent?" Saree questioned, surprised. Ryes looked too young to have a daughter so old!

"Actually, all our children, except Raby, have Talent," Ryes told her with a sigh. "When our younger cubs get older, I'm going to have my hands full. Sayer and Raby are our adopted daughters."

"Your mother told me she was a Talent of One," Saree started, unsure if she should voice something like that here. "She ran away from a marriage because of his family's ambitions, and he was reputed to be an abusing man. I would think you would be very strongly Talented, too."

"My father was a Booster and a strong Healer, as is my cousin, Maren," she told her. "And yes, I do have strong Talents too," she replied, not ready to voice that she was a Talent of One. Garth seemed to approve of her wording.

"What's a Talent of One?" Sayer asked the newcomer. She was sitting next to her uncle Gann and looked happy. He kept looking at her, as if he couldn't believe it, and was smiling. Maybe she was planning to mate him?

"It is a person who actually has all fourteen Talents. It means all Talents born into one person. It is exceedingly rare."

"Ryes has quite a few Talents, but I don't think she has all fourteen," Gann told her with assurance, while Ryes blushed.

"No, she doesn't," Garth agreed, glad Gann hadn't heard about Sabin's idea of Ryes being a Talent of One. He sipped his tea as his eyes met his wife's, smiling. She smiled in return, nodding her head.

"May we sit here, too?" Dunn asked, her tray in hand as she stood near Saree.

"You're more than welcome," Garth invited her, seeing they wanted to hear what was being discussed. Sabin and Torr had trays now and joined them, sitting on the other side of Maren and Dotti. Two of the other women drifted over and sat down, too.

"I just talked Kovin into mounting that Windrose Stone above the Phoenix's fountain, in the center court of our new apartments. What do you think?" Sabin asked Garth.

"No one will be able to casually touch it up there and it'll be protected from the weather. It'll do for now," he agreed. "And will match your and Dastin's Vision." This brought out a surprised smile from Sabin at the reminder, giving him a nod of agreement.

"If we need to tap it for any reason, it'll be close by," Ryes added, relieved, recalling that changed battlefield too, once their shared Vision opened up. Dastin had affected that change and she blessed him in her heart, as she felt it gave them all the boost to win.

"When do we get to see it?" Sayer asked.

"At our Founder's Day Celebration," she replied. "Not too much longer now. When do you think we should all start packing up our things?" she asked Sabin.

"Are you kidding? Ardis already has all of our small stuff packed," Sabin replied with a laugh.

"Where are you moving to?" one of the new women asked, wondering.

"We built some new apartment homes up topside. That way our families will have more living space, with plenty of room for the children to play. We could either house you ladies down here in our original facility, or in some of the ones set aside for the caravaners, until we get ones for you built too. It's your choice," Garth offered.

"Phil, I hope you realize we're going to need eleven new residences," Ryes called out to him as he appeared in the doorway. He closed his eyes a moment as if he were in pain, then he laughed as he nodded his head. He got a tray and came over to join them for dinner, after a few moments of making his own choices.

"I should've seen this one coming," he agreed as laughter sounded from the others around him. "I was just checking. It seems Ryun and Aril are planning upon returning to Matlowe to expand her cheese making business, but Rebin says Winterhaven's her home now and doesn't intend to return. And unbeknown to you, our fair Chief Executive Officer, Kovin and I were planning ahead, and already have built twenty more apartments than we thought we'd need, so everyone will have their own place already. We only have figure out who wishes to live in which one," he informed them. Ryes clapped her hands, laughing in surprise. The rest joined her, equally delighted.

"Excellent!" she declared. "Once we get those new apartments built in Matlowe, I don't think we'll have too many of the other villagers wanting to move here. After all, they'll see what they can create themselves, if they want to."

"Already tired of immigrants?" Maren teased, smiling.

"No. Just people like Karr," she admitted.

"Yes. I heard you're sending her back to us," Metta teasingly scolded as the three elders joined them. Ethan had insisted upon personally seeing to the security of the Windrose Stone first. Rowan and Metta simply decided to stay with him.

"Look, I can't handle my sister anymore," Garth admitted, chagrinned, "Nothing makes her happy."

"That's the truth," Gann agreed, "But I'm staying here. If Glyn wants to stay with her, that's his choice."

"She could drive a saint to drink," Monty spoke up in agreement, having to help distract her, when Garth was busy before. It was a chore he absolutely hated!

"I see that in a few short months, even you humans have gotten the full measure of her temper," Metta commented as he chuckled. He sat down next to Rowan, who sat across from Ryes. Ethan sat down on Rowan's other side.

"If she could find something other than her own interests to focus in upon, she'd be a far more enjoyable person to be in the company of," Ethan observed with a long sigh. "Your mother doesn't share her temperament and I've seen how she's tried to encourage your sister to change."

"She's the only one she'll halfway listen to, anymore," Garth agreed. "If Karr only knew what she truly wanted," he started, still unable to reach her himself, "I'd gladly help her achieve it."

"Stop trying, Garth. Karr will have to find her own way through life, and I think that's really the way she prefers it," Mitt scolded. "I'm only glad she's finally given up on running my life, too. I know I'd never treat our little sister, nor my cubs like that!" She'd stepped over with the other Sleepers who came to the main dining table, ready to assist them if needed.

"So, when's your season due, Mitt?" Rowan asked, knowing it had to be soon.

"Oh, that's right," Ryes suddenly voiced, looking to the Sleepers.

"What?" Mitt asked, curious.

"Got to make sure our newcomers understand one of our base tenets," she told Mitt, then stood up, "Attention, Dear Ladies, I want to make it perfectly clear that here in Winterhaven we women choose whom we mate with, as long as the man's willing, of course. We don't allow any challenges," she informed the women, noting most of them still looked a little dazed. She sat down as they now appeared shocked.

"Is this true?" Saree questioned Gann, startled by her announcement.

"Yes, it is," he assured her. "The women here are pretty tough, and we know better than to cross them," he teased, winking at his sister. "Mitt may be my younger sister, but she could still beat me, if she had a mind to." Mitt blushed at this, as the others laughed, nodding their heads.

"What was it I heard about Mason at the gather?" Tennan asked, after the laughter died down.

"He tried to make a play for me. He knows Minn and I are happy and I've no idea why he'd want me, when he has Shadd to toy with? If he tries that again, I'll knock him silly, so help me," she stated, meaning it. Minn was laughing and nodding his agreement.

"I'll talk with him," Sabin told her, as Ryes nodded her head.

"No, I will," Maren declared. "He's my half-brother after all, and there're a few things he's never known about our father. I can't see him trying to go Korman's way, especially here! Do you mind if I borrow your services, Raya?" he requested, seeing she'd joined them now too. The rest of the Sleepers followed her over.

"No problem. Just let me know when and I'll make sure the contact's clear," she assured him. He gave her a nod of agreement, then stood up, yawning.

"He's never listened to me," Minn added, "please do what you can?" he asked Maren, who nodded his head, understanding.

"It's late and been a long day. Goodnight, everyone," Maren said as Dotti gave him a nod of her head in agreement. They gathered their trays and put them into the cleaning machine on their way out, amid the goodnights the others wished them.

"I've decided we're all taking tomorrow off," Garth told Ryes and the rest at the table. "I'll send Dotti and Maren a message later. I think we should practice our teamwork and joined Talents more, so it won't truly be a day to play. But we're not meeting until after lunch, outside near the windracer pen." He got nods and voiced responses of agreement from the rest, then gave Ryes a quick kiss. "I've got a few things to see to before bed. You and Sayer go on without me," he told her.

"Do I get to practice too, Dad?" Sayer suddenly spoke up. A frown crossed his brow for a fleeting moment, then he gave her a nod of his head and smile in agreement.

"Yes. It's time we did start training you more formally in using your Talent," he agreed. She gave a shout in joy and leapt up, wrapping her arms around his neck, giving him a hug and kiss. Garth laughed as he kissed her back, then grabbed her into his arms and started tickling her, like he used to do to Mitt when she was younger, making Sayer squeal and laugh. The rest were laughing with them merrily.

"Now get to bed and get some rest," he ordered her, as he released her.

"Yup," she agreed, happily wiping the tears from her eyes, then grabbed Ryes' tray as Ryes stood, picking up Shaysa.

"Don't stay up all night," she warned him. He gave her a nod of his head, but she suspected he had no intention of obeying her directive. Sabin stood, too.

"I'd better git, too. I'm sure Ardis is up waiting for me," he announced. The three of them left together, Sabin talking to Ryes in a low voice, on the way out the door. Gann watched them, wondering what was afoot?

"Still got the time, brother?" Garth asked him, seeing his eyes upon his wife and friend. Gann turned back to him, smiling as he gave him a nod of his head.

"If it's all right with Mitt and Raya, I'd first like to escort the Lady Saree to her room. That'll give you time to make sure your cubs are all tucked in for the night," he replied.

"We wanted to keep you guys at a distance for a few days, before letting the ladies get used to having you underfoot all the time," Mitt teased, smiling.

"But I would not mind if Gann escorts me to my chamber," Saree spoke up quickly, hoping it'd be allowed.

"Saree!" Rhodi scolded, in a disapproving voice.

"I am a free woman, Rhodi. I can do as I choose here, as long as I am not endangering anyone else," she quipped back, a frown upon her brow. She swept aside a strand of her white hair, which had fallen in front of her eyes, and noted the look of amusement upon Mitt's face. She didn't dare turn to see what emotions Gann held in his eyes. The family resemblance between them was very obvious and they seemed close, too.

"That's the truth," Raya agreed, smiling. "But we didn't want this all to be too much of a culture shock for you, right at the start," she explained. She had Garth's permission to "peek" if needed, but somehow felt more intrusive with these women in doing so.

"Do we let her?" Mitt queried Raya directly, mind-to-mind.

"Let's, just this once, and see how they handle it. He doesn't seem to be trying to be other than a gentleman so far," she returned, in a like way, meeting her eyes.

"All right. If you feel that strongly about it Saree, Gann may escort you to your room. Gann, could you please first show her the bathroom and bathing facilities, so she'll know where they are and how to operate the machinery?" Mitt requested.

"Not a problem," he responded, giving his sister a nod of his head. The look in her eyes promised a talk later, too. He smiled as Saree turned to him with joy upon her face.

"Thank you, Sir Gann, for your kindness," she told him.

"I'm at your service, dear lady," he replied, not used to having to be so properly polite all the time, but for some reason it wasn't a true strain addressing her like this. "Whenever you're ready," he offered. Ethan chuckled merrily at their exchange, wondering at the way these two seemed to connect, so instantly. Could it be something like both he and Maren experienced, when discovering their first loves?

"I am not used to eating. So, even if this food is very interesting and tasty, I am full. Could we go now if you are finished?" Saree admitted. Sleeping would be another obstacle to face. She was used to ignoring her body, having existed upon a mental plane for so long, and now had to reacquaint herself with its needs.

"It's a common problem for anyone who's been in suspension for a long period of time, my dear," Dr. Cruthers advised. "Even with Maren making sure our bodies were back in their proper rhythms and balances, it was an adjustment to relearn to attend to things such as eating, elimination and sleep cycles. We were only in our tubes for seventy-five Taynan years, I can't imagine what you face, with your far longer containment."

"It is true," Dunn replied. "This will take us a little time to relearn how to listen to our bodies' needs."

"So, even for a non-Talent, there is a freedom of the mind and will?" Rhodi of House Klark asked, curious.

"Yes, apparently so," Dr. Cruthers replied, chuckling.

"We best go. Goodnight," Gann stated, not wanting to get pulled into an intense discussion at this hour of the evening. Not with he and his littermate were planning a session of deep discussions of their own. Saree nodded, saying her goodnights too. Gann stood and gathered both their trays, heading for the cleaning belt and the exit, Saree beside him.

"So, I'm going to have to go into the past with her, to verify it for myself. Sabin wouldn't lie, but it just seems too incredible! How could those flowers be in the past?" Garth related to Gann as they sat in his office. They had opened a large bottle of mead and after two hours, had almost drained it between them. It was one of the better bottlings from the caravaners, from which he'd set a few aside for special occasions.

"Sabin wouldn't support something so risky unless he's already had a Vision about it. Did you ask him if he had?" Gann pressed, thinking he might have a good answer. Garth's face looked surprised for a moment, as he was mentally kicking himself.

"That has to be it! I can't believe I didn't see it before! Still, even if he's had some kind of Vision, I still feel I need to check whether or not that stupid wreath of flowers is now in Hailys of the past," Garth sighed, determined to see this through, Visions, or no.

"I wonder what he was telling Ryes when they left together tonight? Does she know about his Vision?" Gann asked, draining his glass. "I'm glad you finally got what you wanted with Ryes, but I don't think I could've ever handled the headaches you've gained from having her as your own."

"Ah, but she's still worth it!" Garth sighed as he smiled. "Just go slow with Saree. She probably still doesn't know what she wants. She's spent who knows how many centuries living as a being of pure thought, and now has to deal with her inconvenient body again. Just don't get too hopeful, if she just uses you for a while," he warned his brother, worried for him now.

Gann, like him, never had much interest in the women in Matlowe. There was Kaytas for a few months, but she had decided to go solo for a while, again, unwilling to move to Winterhaven. And he was having to constantly cater to their older sister's whims all the time. Since he had the time to choose, he'd been caught up in the new construction projects and hadn't taken much time for himself, yet. Now this tall, willowy exotic-looking woman was purposefully seeking him out, and he had no idea what to do about it.

"I'll be all right. I can't believe the color of her eyes! It has to be contrived, somehow. They can't be that color naturally," he commented. And the glimpse into the gentle soul on the other side of them tempted him, as no one had ever before, in his whole life. Not even Kaytas had held him so deeply. Garth laughed, nodding his head.

"They're a pretty bunch of flowers, but we're going to have a time getting them settled. I only hope Maren can find a way to reach Mason. We don't need him starting up any trouble, either. I'm going to have to make sure we know exactly what Talents they have and what kind of training they've had for them. They might be the resource we need, after all."

"No. Ryes is still going to have to go back and rescue her aunt, and you know it," Gann scolded his brother, seeing what he was trying to do, to get the mission set up with others to take it on. Garth sighed and nodded his head, seeing it too.

"Well, time for bed. I've got everything set up for tomorrow, so I can sleep in. Ryes can always run interference for me."

"You're right. I'm going to catch a quick shower, first, then get some sleep. I think the practice session's a good idea. You should set them up weekly, at least for a couple of hours," Gann suggested as he stood up and set his glass down. Garth drained his, then gave him a nod of agreement.

"That's a good idea. I could use a shower, too. Come on. We've got lots to get finished before next week's Founder's Day." He got up and corked the bottle, setting it up on a shelf. They left his office, turning off the lights and headed down the corridor.

"Gann?" he heard a voice call out to him from outside his door drape. He'd just returned and was getting into bed. He pulled on his sweatpants and went to see who it was. Saree stood outside his drape, looking scared.

"Saree? Is there something wrong?" he asked, wondering what could've upset her so, here?

"Could I sleep with you tonight? I had a bad dream and cannot sleep now," she admitted. She hoped his presence would drive away her nightmare demons from her long past, which had risen to haunt her for the first time in centuries.

"Are you sure this will help?" he pressed, uncomfortable with the thought of taking a strange woman he didn't know, into his own bed.

"I think so. My father used to beat me terribly and I do not want to sleep alone. Please?" she requested, with tears in her eyes. Gann sighed and nodded his head. He held the drape aside to let her into his room. He recalled the times when Mitt would come crying to the furs he and Garth shared, when there were fierce thunderstorms raging outside. She used to look like this, so they'd sleep with her between them, to let her know she was safe. There was just no way he could refuse Saree, now.

"Sorry, my room's a bit of a mess," he apologized, as he started picking up the clothes he'd discarded, up from the floor and depositing them into the proper receptacle for the dirty laundry. She giggled at this and sighed.

"I did not come here to inspect your room," she teased, smiling. "May I?" she asked, indicating his bed. He nodded his head and let her crawl under the sheet and covers, then got in, leaving his sweatpants on, damping down the lights from the controls over the bed. He got settled down, then she snuggled in against his back. He quickly dropped off into a deep sleep, realizing in the process that her presence didn't feel strange to him, after all. It was as if this was the way it should be for them both and felt so very right...

Happy At Last

Chapter 8

"Who's this?" a loud voice intruded into his dreams. Gann's eyes snapped open, and he saw Karr standing beside his bed; her eyes were practically aflame with fury. His mind fumbled for a few seconds, as he had to wrestle with her anger and recalling Saree's tearful request, late last night.

"She's a friend of mine and none of your business, Karr. Go away, I went to bed late and it's too early to deal with your needs," he told her in an even voice, knowing it was the only way to talk to her when she was this way. For the first time, in a long time, he didn't immediately jump to her demands! Maybe it was having someone else, who needed his protection, but he suddenly understood the stand Garth took against her back when they were in Matlowe, and he told her he was going to move out beside the river, no matter what she thought of the matter. He felt Saree shift, as if to leave, but he put a hand out to stop her. Karr's eyes bored into his own at this, her ire stifling.

"How dare you!" she screeched, her voice scaling up as she screamed.

"I have a life of my own, sister," he reminded her in a low voice. "I'm not a cub, and am not going back to Matlowe with you, when you leave. Garth and I will make sure you're comfortable and will never starve, but we're grown men and don't need you to tell us how to live."

"We'll see about that!" she yelled, then turned and stomped out the door, malice in every line of her body. Gann got out of the bed and stood there for a moment – to be sure she was gone.

"Who was that?" Saree breathed out, now wide awake and shocked by that woman's intrusion. The way Gann calmly faced her off had been astounding!

"My older sister, Karr. I'm sure she's now on the way to yell at Garth for the way I told her to leave. He was going to sleep in today, too, so I'm sure it'll fall to Ryes to deal with her. Let me close the outer door, lock it, then get a quick message out to our mother. She's the only one who can handle Karr," he said.

"Is she always like that? I do not mean to cause you any problems," she started, feeling uncomfortable now.

"Yes, she's always like that, and you're not causing me any problems at all, Lady Saree," he assured her, turning to smile at her. She looked so young with sleep still clouding her lavender eyes and her snow-white hair disheveled. Gann quickly turned and closed his door, locking it, then sent a quick message to his mother, asking her to help Ryes and a basic sketch of the situation Karr found them in, which set her off this morning. He smiled at the response he immediately got, relieved that things would be settled soon.

"Should I go?" she asked as he came back to bed.

"Only if you want to," he offered, "I'm going back to sleep. I was up way too late, to be ready to face the day, yet." She smiled, then scooted back to allow him room again, and lay down upon the long pillow, once more.

"It is too early," she agreed. Gann chuckled as he got back into bed and settled himself again. Saree suddenly lay her head upon his shoulder and cuddled up to his side. He knew Mitt would be furious about this, but he realized he didn't care, as he drifted back off to sleep.

"I want to see Garth!" Karr loudly demanded, with wild fury in her eyes.

"He was up late last night and won't be up for some time, yet," Ryes told her, doing her best to hold her own temper in check. Karr screeched out in frustrated anger at this, causing two of Ryes' cubs to start crying. "You're going to have to leave. I have enough work to get done this morning, without you upsetting my cubs too."

"I want to see my brother! Do you know Gann has a strange woman in his bed with him this morning?" she demanded, hoping this would move her. She hated this outcast and the hold she had over her brother.

"Gann's old enough to sleep with whomever he wants," Ryes assured her in a tightly-controlled voice, doing everything she could to hide her surprise, guessing who the woman might be. "Now get out of my rooms and go help out in the gardens, like you're scheduled for this morning," she ordered. Raby had Rhin in her arms, trying to comfort him. Sayer looked upset as she was picking up Jann. The others were now starting to fuss with Karr's shouting.

"GARTH! GARTH!" Karr called out, stepping over to open the metal door Ryes had closed for him this morning. It was locked, so she started pounding on it with a fist, then Ryes pulled her back from it, putting herself between Karr and their bedroom door.

"Leave him alone. He needs his sleep," she told her, pulling her toward the door outside. Suddenly, Karr turned on her and threw herself at her, her claws fully extended, wanting to tear at her, for her insolence.

The unexpected attack shocked Ryes as she felt Karr's claws bite deeply into her face and shoulder. She made a grab for her wrists as they went down in a tangle, hoping to keep her away, but she only managed to get one for a moment. Her claws raked her face deeply, as she pulled the one hand away from her. Luckily, she missed her eye! It'd been too long since she was in any fight, and she realized she was losing this one badly, as she felt Karr's claws now sink into her arm. She heard Sayer shout something, as Raby was crying. Then Karr's weight was lifted off of her, and she lay panting as she tried to see what was happening now, but there was blood blinding her. She swiped at it, annoyed, ignoring the intense pain from her face, neck and arm.

"You are never allowed in my quarters, ever again," Garth told his sister, absolutely furious, as he put her back on her feet, away from Ryes. He saw his mother and father arrive, as well as Maren and Dotti. The shock in their eyes said it all. He released Karr, shoving her back, and bent to pick up Ryes from the floor. "Are you all right?" He saw she was bleeding from several deep gashes.

"Give me a few moments," she replied, realizing who held her now, "and I will be. The girls are really upset. I was trying not to let anyone awaken you. I'm sorry," she apologized.

"Let me help," Maren offered, rushing across the room, as he saw she was covered in blood, with plenty still flowing.

"You've nothing to be sorry for," Garth chided her with a sigh. "I should apologize for my sister's violent behavior. Thanks, Maren," he said, surrendering her to his care. Dotti came in and had her arms around Raby, trying to comfort her, while Sayer was now crowding Maren, trying to see how badly hurt Ryes was.

"I just got a message from Gann," Marla told her other son. "We got here as soon as we could. Sorry, son."

"It's not your fault, Mother. Karr is an adult and should be responsible for her own actions," he assured her, then turned back to Karr, having come to a decision, which could split his own family. "You're now formally banished from Winterhaven. Pack up your things; you're going to be flown back to Matlowe, as soon as Axel has a helicopter ready for departure. Your violence and behavior are inexcusable and will not be tolerated. If you ever even raise your voice to my wife again, there'll be dire consequences," he promised, sure on this point now.

"How dare you threaten me!" Karr's voice dripped venom, as she faced her younger brother. "I don't want anything to do with you, or that slut of a wife of yours, ever!" She turned upon her heel to stomp out of the room, grabbing the heavy fabric of their door drape to tear it down on her way out, when Maren quickly stepped over, reached out and brushed her arm. She fell to the floor unconscious, laying half in the hallway and half in the room.

"Jim, take her," Garth urged, seeing he was at their door now, looking in. He gave him a nod of his head and bent to pick her up, glad she was out cold. Maren finished with Ryes and then put her back on her feet.

"Better?" Maren asked Ryes, now he had blood on his clothes too, but that didn't bother him. She gave him a nod and a smile filled with gratitude. Sayer grabbed Ryes and just hung onto her for several long moments. She hugged her back, understanding her inner panic, which she projected through, with her budding Talent.

"Let's get Karr settled back in Matlowe with as few disruptions possible," Maren explained, seeing he had Garth's and Jim's full approval. "Let's head over and tell Glyn and make sure he knows he does have a choice." He and Jim left with Karr. Dotti understood and stayed, and continued to offer comfort to the younger ones too, now helping Raby. Sayer finally let Ryes go and gave her father a hug, too. He chuckled, breaking his own anger now, and returned it.

"We were just coming to see if you wanted to go to breakfast with us," Dotti told Garth, as he stepped over to make sure the cubs were safe, as they were all crying now. He smiled at her, giving her a nod of his head.

"Sorry about all this," he apologized with a sigh.

"I'll talk to her," Marla offered, stepping closer, again.

"Talking isn't doing it," he returned. "The banishment stands. I won't have her hurting Ryes, again."

"But why didn't she try to knock her out with her Talent?" Garvin questioned, puzzled, as he smiled and picked up one of his grandsons.

"Because I've told Ryes countless times to never hurt others with her Talents," he explained. "I'm going to have to rescind that order now. Karr intended to kill her. I felt it clearly, when I pulled her off her," he admitted. Karr's emotions had been so strong, he couldn't miss it, whether or not he had his Empath called up. He wondered if she had a background operating Talent, too? She'd skipped the testing session Ryes' held before.

"I'm fine. I just need a quick shower," Ryes assured him, stepping over to join them. "You can go back to bed." Garth shook his head at this.

"Until she's well gone from here, I'm not letting you leave my side," he told her. "Get our things, we'll both take that shower together." Ryes saw he meant it, so nodded her head and quickly ducked back into their bedroom. She wanted to first comfort her cubs, both their two oldest daughters and the little ones, but saw Marla, Garvin and Dotti were helping them already. They were the better parts of her family!

"Glyn, this is the first time you're truly being given a choice," Maren said, as he helped him pack up Karr's things into some containers he'd picked up on the way. He was slightly amused to note she now had two dozen pairs of shoes. Karr lay upon their bed appearing peaceful to all unknowing eyes. He knew the tempest still ranged deep in her heart and mind, and she was truly never sated. On the way to her quarters, he'd adjusted her body to change her claws to now resemble human fingernails, so she'd be unable to harm others as badly, again. And lengthen her season cycle out to the fullest, so it would be a long time before she'd have cubs again.

"I have a choice?" he pressed, still uncertain and fearful.

"You're an excellent jewelry maker, and a fine metalsmith, as well as a wonderful father. Do you really want to drag your girls back to Matlowe, when they're doing so well here?" Jim asked, as he helped with the packing, too. The faster they got Karr out of Winterhaven, the better for everyone! Glyn paused a few moments, to think of what was being offered.

"She'll be so mad," he breathed out, as his hand started shaking. "But I'd love to stay in Winterhaven, and I know Jons is learning so much in school here – far more than we ever thought to teach our cubs in Matlowe! And Kala and Tian love to play with each other all the time. Marla and Garvin get to lavish a lot of love on the cubs here. We have time to simply live our lives, instead of always barely scraping by and working hard for each meal." Maren nodded, understanding him too well.

"You might not be able to go there to see her for a long time," Maren warned. "Eventually, she might see how she was the one to drive everyone away from her."

"Maybe when she's truly old, she might realize it," Glyn offered, as he calmed himself, having come to a decision and took in a deep breath, letting it out slowly. "The cubs and I are staying in Winterhaven. We'll miss her, but I can't live with the constant anger anymore." Jim clasped his shoulder in comfort and encouragement. Glyn gave him a nod in appreciation of his support.

"It might be a long road, but I know you'll feel better about it, given time," Maren assured him, knowing it was the best for him and his cubs.

"At least they have a new home in Matlowe for her," Jim added, stooping down to pick up a box. "I should get a cart for her things. I'm not sure if they had time to finish, or furnish the house, yet."

"Let's ask Axel to use one of the bigger choppers and we'll haul out some new furnishings with her," Maren suggested. "Let me get the request in to him," he suggested, turning for the computer terminal, now very well practiced with the machine. Glyn grinned, happy for their company and help, as he started pulling out her clothes from the drawers and folding them, placing her things into a box, neatly with steady hands. He realized he was starting a new path to a new future and there was no fear in his heart anymore.

As Ryes and Garth returned to their room after their shower, Jim met them inside, appearing worried.

"Is something wrong?" Garth asked, seeing he was unsettled about something, which was so unlike him.

"Karr's house in Matlowe isn't anywhere near being done. Kovin just told me," he explained. "We were hoping to get her settled there with no reason to come back." Ryes smiled at this, giving him a nod.

"I'll take care of it," she assured him with confidence. Both men seemed puzzled, but Kovin soon appeared at their doorway; having been called over by Ryes.

"You need me?" he asked, knowing she wanted him immediately; she'd summoned him with Mind Voice, letting him know it was an urgent matter. She gave him a nod.

"Remember the bridge on the road to the gather?" she countered. A light seemed to come into his eyes as he smiled and gave her a nod. "We're going to take care of Karr's house right now, in the same manner." Garth instantly understood, giving them a nod as he went to put their shower things away.

"I'm leaving this in your hands," he assured her with a chuckle. Raby trailed him into his bedroom, wanting to talk with him. Ryes signed for Kovin and Jim to take seats, with a smile.

"Me, too?" Jim asked, wanting to be sure. Her smile widened as she gave him a nod.

"I'm letting you supervise her placement there, so yes, I'd like your input, Jim," she assured him. Kovin chuckled as he sat down, looking forward to this small foray.

"And soon I need you to help with that bridge over the Yuri," he teasingly threatened. Ryes laughed and nodded her head.

"Let's get some of our team's housing done, as well as some of the apartments we were planning for Matlowe, while we're at it?" Ryes decided on the spot. This got some shock and delight from both men and a look of surprise from Dotti, from across the room.

"It would be very appreciated," Kovin replied, trying to appear sober when his heart was flying, and he was practically giddy. "What a surprise for the villagers!"

"That's one I'm counting on," she promised cheerfully. She sat down next to them, and they got down to work, with Sayer appearing to want to join in, so very much. Still, she finally got Shaysa down for a nap and needed to help Dotti with Jann, who was still unsettled.

"Ah, you slept through all the fun," Mitt scolded Gann, as he and Saree finally appeared for lunch. He looked puzzled as they sat down at the table together.

"What fun?" he asked.

"No. It wasn't fun at all," Garth countered, just sitting down with his lunch tray, too. Gann realized he looked tired. Ryes was just settling the cubs into their carriers and giving them biscuits, not even having her tray, yet.

"You didn't get enough sleep," Ryes scolded her husband. "We can put off this training session until tomorrow," she suggested. He met her eyes with an eyebrow raised. She blushed as she gave him a nod of her head, then went to go get her lunch tray.

"What happened?" Gann questioned. Raby and Sayer sat down on Garth's other side, and both of them looked upset.

"Karr's been formally banished from Winterhaven," he replied. "She tried to kill Ryes this morning. You haven't read your messages yet, have you?" Gann shook his head, shocked.

"She looks all right," Saree said. "Is she all right?" she asked. Mitt smiled and gave her a nod of her head.

"She's pretty tough inside, and Maren got to her fast enough to take care of the outside," she assured her.

"I am sorry. I may have been the cause," Saree offered, realizing who they were talking about. Ryes returned, hearing this as she put her tray down.

"No, Saree. This has been building for a long time. She's tried to get me before, and I should've known better than to have let my guard down around her," she assured her as she sat down. "Did you sleep well?"

"I had trouble at first... so many old, bad dreams kept waking me up. I was exhausted and did not know what to do. Then, I went to Gann, and he let me stay with him. I have never slept so well, in my whole life," she admitted, blushing as she recalled waking up before him and curiously examining and admiring Gann's body. He'd slept only in a light pair of house pants. Mitt caught the barest wisp of this from her mind.

"Had you ever slept with a man, before?" she suddenly asked, wondering. And found herself wondering if she had been a virgin if she was still one?

"No. I ran away from home when I was young, hiding among my cousins to avoid my father's wrath. He was a very cruel man. I finally found Doran's valley and was put immediately in the sleep chamber, for my own protection. Doran did not want him able to hurt me anymore," she admitted. "Of course, through time, I came to know how deeply Doran could hurt me. Tyra of House Li was my friend and helped shield me from some of her cruelty. I wanted to leave with you Ryes the first time you were there but had no idea of how to escape the sleep chamber."

"I'll have to take you to see where we buried Tyra, near Hailys," Ryes told her, smiling. "Through you, I got to know her better than I ever had before. She was killed when I was an infant, so I never had the chance."

"So sad," Saree agreed trying to wrap her mind around that life, "Yes, I would like to visit her grave. Doran used your memories of the story of Tyra's murder to torture me, for wanting to go out into a world, which would allow a vicious murderer to live free, and continue hurting others. I was still determined to go, for she never saw your courage and good heart. You reminded me of the things which could still be, like love, and good family, and the freedom to seek a better life. My cousin Sams was a lot like you, and I still miss her." Ryes was taken aback. She never thought she was the reason any of the Sleepers broke free of Doran, at the last. She didn't know what to say.

"I'm sorry you had to suffer because of me," she finally told her. "But I'm glad you found a way to break free of her madness." Saree smiled grandly at this, her happiness clear in her beautiful eyes.

"But I have found joy here in your world and could not even begin to repay you for the way Gann has blessed my life!" She threw her arms around Gann as she laughed, then boldly kissed him. He chuckled as he returned her kiss, still not sure how he got caught up in all this. He never thought of himself as a blessing before.

"Gann! You didn't, did you?" Mitt demanded, needing to know.

"No, I didn't," he asserted, blushing now.

"Mitt," Garth started, not sure what to say exactly. "There should be more between two people, before they take that step."

"That is very true. Your brother treated me more like I was his little sister, and for the honor he has paid me, I cannot thank him enough. It is not that I do not know about sexual intercourse. I learned more than I cared to know from Doran and the other women, but that I am not ready to take that step yet. It would be another matter if my first season were to befall me, but until that event occurs, I only seek to get to know both myself and your brother better. Nothing more," Saree explained. Raya and the other women had approached the tables with their trays and heard the whole exchange.

"I'm sorry," she apologized, blushing, "I guess I was a bit wild and went through almost every man who caught my interest, last year. Since last winter, Minn and I have finally come to understand each other and with our adopting Sernn, I know he's the one I want to be with for my first time, too. Garth was gone at the time and poor Maren was trying to keep an eye on me, in his stead. I really caused him some headaches," she admitted with a small laugh.

"You sure did," Ryes agreed, shaking her head as she tried not to laugh, "Course, I gave him plenty of headaches, too."

"You were after the other men, too?" Dunn questioned her, sitting down nearby. She saw five little cubs set out on a table next to her and wondered. Ryes laughed at her question, as did Mitt and Garth.

"No. I exchanged true-mate vows with Garth when we mated. Maren had his hands full making sure I stayed out of trouble, then delivered my cubs when they decided to come early."

"And what a chore that was," Bethy piped in, stepping over to the table. Since her and Jim's usual seats were taken, she sat across from where Sabin and Ardis would be sitting soon.

"I'm glad you were with me, Bethy. It gave me someone else to focus in on, instead of wishing for Garth to be home," she admitted. Her friend laughed at this, nodding her head.

"All these cubs are yours?" Denas questioned, amazed.

"I gave birth to four of them and Garth brought home our fifth. He sent home Raby and Sayer with Darman, before he could return, so we adopted them too," she explained.

"True-mate vows?" Saree breathed, shocked, "You have actually done this?"

"Yes," Garth affirmed, knowing it was frequently asked, now.

"No wonder you had to save him from Doran," Rhodi commented, smiling mischievously.

"That was before we spoke our vows. Even then, I knew my life would be lacking without Garth. My mother spoke true-mate vows with Ronn, my father, and even in her spirit form, all she wanted was to rest with him. If you ask my grandfather, Rowan, he'll tell you the full tale of Tyra's life, after she left Doran," she informed her, seeing a haughty look Rhodi's eyes; curious about it. She feared within, that Rhodi was still chained to Doran in some ways.

"Oh, I almost forgot. Denas is of House Clenons as your other grandfather, Tair. I think you are cousins, but I am not sure to what degree your relationship goes," Saree pointed out, smiling at Denas as she told Ryes.

"Your grandfather was Tair? Then you are my third cousin!" she declared, standing up. "Why did you not tell me sooner, Saree?" she playfully scolded.

"Tyra asked me not to reveal it to you, as she was afraid Doran would use it against the both of you. Now that we are free, I can inform you."

"She was right," she sighed out, her face suddenly downcast as she thought of all they lost in that endless, cold tomb. Then she looked back up to Ryes and smiled as she stepped over to her. Ryes stood, not knowing what she wanted; this being the first she'd heard of her family line. "Cousin!" she called her and threw her arms about her, hugging her tightly. Ryes returned the hug, a surprised smile upon her face.

"This is a delightful surprise," Ethan declared, as he and Rowan stepped over to the group. "It's a small galaxy."

"I hear you've called a group practice session for all our Talents," Rowan said, speaking to Garth. "Are you going to need someone to help with the cubs? They're a bit much for Raby alone," he offered.

"Ryes was thinking of putting them outside upon their blanket near us. But if you want to come help, you're more than welcome, Rowan," he replied. Denas released Ryes to look at all her children. One of her white-haired girls latched onto to her finger as she offered it, cooing and smiling as she looked up to her. Denas found herself smiling, in spite of herself. Suddenly, she realized she wanted a child of her own. Mating wasn't the horrible specter she'd come to view it, if it bore such wonderful results! She saw Ryes' smile of pride as she surveyed her children too.

"So many," she sighed happily, "Are they not a lot to manage?"

"Yes, they are, which is why it's always nice to have lots of help around. Thanks, grandfather, I appreciate your helping Raby to keep an eye on them today." Denas returned to her seat, her eyes still glued to the cubs.

"Could you tell us about Tyra Li, while you watch them?" Saree asked Rowan, smiling. "She was a friend of mine."

"I'd be delighted," he replied, realizing these women knew Tyra probably better than he did, in truth.

"I believe I'll join you. I've yet to hear the full tale, myself. We were interrupted the last time," Ethan said, glad the opportunity had come again. This time he intended to record it!

"What tale?" Maren asked as he and Dotti squeezed in next to Bethy and Jim. Sabin, Katas and Ardis were right behind them. Ardis put her sons into their carriers as Sabin set down both their trays.

"The one about Tyra," Rowan told him. "I'm telling it again, while you're practicing your Talents."

"I've wanted to hear it," Dotti said, smiling. "May I?" she requested. Rowan gave her a nod of his head, delighted he'd have a large audience again.

"At least you'll better understand why Ryes glued Korman to that wall," Maren teased her, grinning.

"Do you still have a copy of that vid, Maren?" Raya asked, "I didn't get to see it and Kovin only saw him right before you left Matlowe. He was in stitches for days over it."

"Yeah, I still have it. But if you ask Sadie, she'll make you a copy," he told her.

"Kovin was in stitches for days, I'm still laughing about it," Sabin declared, seeing Ryes blushing. "If nothing else, it lets everyone know there're consequences to getting on your bad side, Ryes."

"She let him off too easy, considering what he did to my mother," Maren commented, then sipped his tea. There was still a gleam of ice in his eyes. Ryes saw it and knew she had to find a way to get him to shake free of his pent-up hatred of Korman.

"You saved her. Let it go," she urged him in a low voice, "You only hurt yourself by holding tightly to your hatred. By doing this, you still give him power over you. I'd rather see you free, cousin."

"Who is this Korman and what did he do?" Dunn questioned.

"He's my father and he terrorized Matlowe for far too many years," he replied, then saw Metta approaching and decided to subside. He and Metta had had their differences of opinion, the last few weeks.

"Garth? Am I supposed to be in on this `practice' you've got scheduled for today?" Sana questioned, as she and Justin came over to the tables. She saw their seats were already taken, but that didn't bother her.

"Yes, you're included," he assured her. "I'm giving everyone another half hour to finish their lunch, then we'll assemble outside."

"Slave driver," Ryes muttered, teasing her husband with an impish smile. He grinned as he put an arm around her, hugging her to his side.

"You know me too well," he returned with a laugh.

Karr opened her eyes, noting dawn's light was showing through a nearby, curtained window. She sat up. She was still dressed in what she was wearing earlier, but she had no memory of what happened and how she got to this strange room. She lived underground for some time now. How could she be seeing sunlight through a window? The bed she sat upon was larger and even more comfortable than the one they actually had. There were no sounds around her. No one was stirring on the other side of the nearby door.

"Glyn? Where are we?" she called out. She waited, but no one responded. Then, as she moved her hand, she realized she brushed a piece of paper. Frowning, she picked it up to see a neat, bold print upon it.

It read: "Welcome back to Matlowe Village, Karr. Glyn and the cubs will be staying in Winterhaven for the time being. There is a new communications station near the Elder's Platform which you can use to communicate with them, or anyone in Winterhaven. This is your new home. We have stocked it with the things you might need and have made sure all your things are here for you to unpack. We hope you will take the time to find your better heart and mind. You are still loved!" It was signed by Garth.

Tears sprang up and rolled down her face as she read it through a second and third time; trying to grasp all that was being said on this one piece of paper. Finally, she cast it from her and got out of bed. She wiped at her face, feeling grimy now. Then she noticed her hands. Her claws were gone, and she had human-looking fingernails instead! And they each had been painted and sparkled! She paused revolted and flattered, both at the same time. No sure what to do about it, she got off the bed and admired the light blanket that had covered her. It, too, was sparkly and yet was soft. The colors drew her, so she carefully folded it and left it on top of the bed, admiring her sparkly fingers each time her hands moved. How did the human girls manage to get anything done with their fingers painted all pretty?

She went to explore her new surroundings. She found a spacious closet behind one door and several boxes were stacked inside, ready to be unpacked as promised. There were shelves, drawers and long poles with hangers inside the closet. It was at least half the size of her bedroom. The box on top was opened and she saw her shoes were in it, as she lifted the lid all the way. She signed in relief as she stroked the pair on top, gratefully. They were her most comfortable and prettiest.

Another door revealed a Winterhaven-style bathroom with both a large bathtub and shower. She turned the handles and was delighted that the water flowed freely. She smiled now, as she looked in the mirror – finally able to do so, then was studying her face solemnly, unsure what to feel now. She used the waste chair, and decided to shower in a little while, as she realized she was starving! She found two smaller bedrooms with a shared bathroom and a room which could be set up as a craft room with tables and shelves. There was a large great room and a big dining room with well-equipped kitchen on the other side of it. And a washing machine with dryer in a small room off the kitchen. There was a tiny waste chair room next to the laundry room! Something she could let guests use, or herself if she was busy cooking. She realized she should be furiously angry with being dumped back in the Village with no say in the matter, as they'd done, but all in all, she was truly happy for the first time in her life. She wrapped her arms about her body and hugged herself in happiness. Even her odd-looking fingers were delightful. She was special!

She had a home that was beyond her original dreams, when living in Matlowe Village before, and she had all she could want, seeing the panty closet was well-stocked. She didn't have anyone in her way, nor needing to be scolded. She swung around in a circle with her arms open in joy. After a moment, she started up the small music machine, washed her hands and pulled out things to make herself a good breakfast. After her shower, she intended to see what was happening out in Matlowe and catch up on the local gossip! And show off her new shoes, new fingers, and clothes, as she knew no one else here could match them! And she now knew she was of a royal house! Karr of House Ladearis, and even if this wasn't a palace from stories of old, it was hers and she was deeply, truly, happy at last!

Practice

"Alright, this is too important for all of us. We're not used to battles using only our Talents, nor working in a large, melded group. We've had to face both these situations now, and I don't want anyone caught unawares, if an emergency happens. First off, I want the more experienced Talents to teach our newer people how to center themselves within, and consciously call up their Talents. Then, when we have that accomplished, we'll form a greater inner link. Raya will be the one to form the larger meld," Garth told the large, gathered group of starmen and humans.

They separated and formed up teams, quickly. Wren went to group with Maren, Leon joined Mitt's group and Max walked over to be part of Garth's. Of their new residents, whom they now commonly called the Sleepers, only Saree was present for this practice. She stuck to Gann's side, as much as possible. Somehow, he'd become her protector. They joined Sabin's team.

"I know you've seen me do this before, but I've never actually shown you how or what I do," Ryes said, turning to Sayer. Sayer smiled, uncertain, but eager.

"What do I need to do, Mom?" she asked, trying to appear grown up.

"Close your eyes and relax," she instructed, smiling, "Like we did at the river." She nodded, understanding.

"Can you show me, too?" Sadie asked, stepping closer to her and Sayer. Ryes saw her, with Scott and Monty right behind, then gave them a welcoming smile and nod of her head.

"Might as well go ahead and do your first, little mind linkage while we're at it," she told them, motioning the others closer, deciding it on the spot. Sayer laughed as she realized she was practically quivering with this chance to be an active part in the commune. She wondered what the human minds would be like? "Everyone join hands, then close your eyes and relax," Ryes urged. They complied, stepping closer to them. She centered herself, then reached out to them, pulling them into the linkage she formed. She showed each one how to go about centering her, or himself, then how to allow thoughts and experiences to flow through to each other within the commune, while keeping other thoughts more personal. This brought relief to all the others – knowing everyone else didn't need to know every thought that flowed in their minds.

"I tried to help Torr heal my face, but I didn't know what I was doing, any more than he did," Sadie told her, opening her memory of the experience. "I then tried to follow what you did for me, but you work so fast." Ryes smiled mentally at this, agreeing with her friend.

"You should see Maren at work when he heals!" she lightly teased, "Let's do a check on your little one and I'll show you how to basically direct your Healing Talent. The rest of you can watch and see how you need to focus your Talent to use it more effectively."

She felt Sadie's nervousness, especially with the others present, but she gave her consent, as she really wanted to learn how to do this herself. Ryes brought up her Healing Talent, mentally urging Sadie to bring hers up for use. After a little fumbling, and some light-hearted encouragement from the others, she managed to accomplish this small task. Ryes delved into Sadie's being, first taking a quick measure of her body's health, seeing she needed some nutrients she was lacking. Sadie noted this with her own Talent now, surprised.

"No damage yet, but you'd best see Ted about it for some dietary advice, or supplements," she advised.

"I will, as soon as we're done here," she agreed, promising from the heart. Then Ryes delved down further, seeing the new life she now bore. She found him, barely perceptible as separate from Sadie's own body, but her health sense showed her that he was well and growing at his proper rate. Sadie was excited at being able to perceive her own son, as the others reveled in her joy, and being able to touch a new life for the first time, through their Talents, too.

"Then your Healing Talent tells you when something's wrong?" Scott questioned. He was glad this last attempt to impregnate Sadie had worked so well. He was proud and immensely moved by being part of the team helping to create this small life. It was amazing!

"Yes, on that level it's instinctive, but for actual healing, or more definitive work, you have to do a deeper draw upon the Talent. Practice makes it more immediate and easily focused."

"Have you picked out a name for him?" Sayer asked Sadie, still amazed at seeing her son this way.

"We haven't decided upon his name, yet. Gleds wants to name him Karl, after his true father, but I think it should be something new, since Karl won't be the one here to raise him," she told her, with humor tinging her mental voice. "We still have plenty of time to find one that suits both of us."

"By tradition, we usually use older family names, from either side, or something based upon an older name to honor that person, for our firstborns. Gareth, I named in honor of his father, since Garth insisted none of our children will carry his name," Ryes explained.

"I want to change my name," Sayer complained. "My mother was named Sayer, but she died fishing four winters ago when the ice broke away from beneath her. Since you're now my mother, I'd like to change it to something from your family," she begged. Ryes was taken aback. She hadn't thought to ask either of her older girls if they wanted to change their names.

"Then we'll have to come up with something pretty for you, or do you already have one in mind?" she asked.

"Not truly yet, but I was thinking of Mada, in honor of your grandmother, whom Rowan described for me, but thought I'd ask Dad about it first," Sayer replied, happy she was giving her the choice.

"Most definitely," Ryes agreed. "Let's see what he thinks first. Now I'm going to open my eyes, so we can see what else everyone's doing. It truly takes practice to be able to call up your Talent, yet still hold onto what's happening out in the world around you. It's important, and I want each of you to practice this skill when there's nothing critical going on. We've been practicing this for some time now. Sabin used it during our battle with the southern Talents and it bought us all back to ourselves, so we expect everyone to learn how to do it," she warned, then opened her eyes, letting her physical perceptions flow inward, so they could see the others around them. There were still small knots of people in groups of three's and four's scattered nearby. Everyone else still had their eyes closed, except Maren and Mitt. Ryes smiled at them, giving them a nod of her head. She got smiles in return.

"This is freaky," Scott said, seeing himself standing with his eyes closed, through Ryes' eyes. "Can more than one of us open our eyes?"

"You could try, but I'm going to help filter the views, so we don't have too much chaos, as we try to figure out which view belongs to whom," she offered. Sayer opened her eyes slowly, seeing she was standing between Ryes and Monty.

"This is interesting," Monty commented, smiling. He saw his face smiling in response, through Sayer's eyes. It amused him even more, as his smile widened.

"Could you show us what happened when you were fighting Doran?" Sadie suddenly asked. She projected her memory of seeing Ryes enveloped by Doran's ghostly image and her acting as if she were being choked. This greatly disturbed both Scott and Sayer, as they actually saw a piece of the battle for the first time. Ryes knew she couldn't sugarcoat it. The confrontation with Doran was why they were now having to practice their Talents together like this. She urged them all to close their eyes.

"I'll show you it from my point of view, and some of what was happening within the linkage, but you've got to understand this was a necessary operation for ours and others' future safety." She felt them all acknowledge what she said, not truly understanding why. So, Ryes opened the full memory, from the moment she stepped into the great hall, until Mitt was busying herself with the clean-up, after Doran had been neutralized. She felt it was a bit much for Sayer, but thought it better prepare her for whatever she may come to face later in life.

"Amazing! Then we can tap into each other's Talents at will when we're joined together like this?" Monty questioned, feeling he just beat Scott to the punch.

"Yes. Try tapping into my Healing Talent and take a `health reading' of yourself," she invited. She felt his fumbling attempt, then helped direct him in this venture. As they were doing this, Sadie tapped her Manipulator Talent, opening her eyes to watch as she made several small rocks near them float up into the air. She sent them on a crazy lazy dance, delighted with the skill. Sayer also tapped it, as Sadie wasn't taking a deep draw upon the Talent and she snagged her water bottle from nearby, adding it into Sadie's rock dance.

"How many Talents do you have?" Scott questioned, wondering. Ryes mentally sighed.

"As far as I know, I have Catalyst, Healing, Booster, Time Walking, Manipulator, Empath, Mind Voice and Inner Sight, which only works on machines and non-living things. Of those, my Healing and Inner Sight are considered my weakest ones," she responded.

"And what kinds of Talents does Dad have?" Sayer asked, dropping her water bottle as she turned her attention inward. Scott lifted it up, delighting in being able to focus his mind this way, while Sadie smiled and listened, as she watched things with her eyes open.

"He has Fire Shaper, which is a very old, rare one, and Empath."

"But isn't Empath sort of like Mind Voice?" Monty questioned, recalling the snake.

"Not in the least. With Mind Voice, as you, Scott and Sayer have, you can communicate directly with another individual's mind, whether, or not, that person has Talent. With Empath you have an awareness of the life around you and can use it to communicate with creatures, which barely have organized thoughts. You can direct their actions, or just get a scope of what's in the vicinity."

"Could you show us? I loved it the last time," Sayer pressed, wanting to know how a windracer thought.

"Not yet" Garth interrupted them, having stepped over and joined in their inner meld, tapping Ryes' Mind Voice. "Let's get the whole group linked up now, then you can show them Tayna, as you've shown her to me. I still haven't been able to achieve that deep a contact."

"All right," Ryes replied, embarrassed to have forgotten how long they'd been playing around with their abilities. Scott and Sadie were reluctant to let go of her Manipulator but knew this was part of what they came out here to do today. She dissolved their inner link, then smiled as they noted the others were gathered into a larger circle now, sitting on the grass, waiting.

"Just like a bunch of kids, out for a day of fun," Garth teased her. She nodded her head to this.

"Of course," she replied with an impish light in her green eyes, "It's the best way to learn them." They walked over to join the rest, sitting down. Maren took her hand as they rejoined their hands and closed their eyes, centering themselves, and falling into the new much-larger link. There was a jumble of scattered thoughts as Raya fought to get everyone organized. Ryes lent Raya her strength and Talents, so they got settled quickly, thereafter.

"You were letting them play with your Talents, already," Mitt accused her, humor in her mental tone.

"How else does one learn to control a Talent? You have to learn to play with it, first," she returned merrily. "You only wanted to use my Manipulator again."

"First off, I want Ryes to open her Empath. Rein, Gann, Teris and I all have this Talent too, but not to the degree Ryes does. I want all of you to see Tayna, herself, as Ryes can see it," he said, knowing this was the only way to get everyone to understand how precious their world truly was.

"I have seen the others use Empath before. They like to use it to toy with the beasts in the valley," Saree stated as she joined them, not sure if she wanted to participate in this after all, even if she was here to be with Gann.

"This is so much more," Maren assured her, with humor.

"It's far more than that," Garth assured her, too, then gave Ryes the go ahead to take control of the link.

"Hang on tight," she teased, as she took control and unleashed Empath fully. She first floated upwards, taking in the life within and around Winterhaven itself, showing everyone the myriad sparks of life around them. Pausing here and there to further delve into the presence of a creature's mind, but not exerting control over any of them, surprising Saree. Then Ryes took them further afield to soar upon the wings of a hunting bird, dipping and turning in the icy winds, far above, as she looked for prey. As the bird dove, Ryes let go and wandered further once more, latching onto some wild windracers, running for the pure joy of racing across the open grasslands. Next, she dove into the ground to see what it was like for a small, furred animal to live below the windracer's feet, in his cozy den.

After a few moments, Ryes moved onward again, but delved down deep into their world, and tuned to the life pulse of Tayna, herself. Giving everyone a chance to know their world had her own life pulse. Feeling their astonishment, and knowing the humility they each felt, well. Through Tayna, she exploded upwards, high above the clouds, looking down and seeing the long stretch of the great Yuri spreading out below them. She could feel the sense and order of life, itself, below them, clearly making out cities and villages.

The continents drifted beneath the group, as they danced among the clouds. The fury of a fierce thunderstorm practically left them all breathless. But they saw even the storm had a purpose and place and was a part of the world balance. Ryes turned her attention outwards, taking in the dance of their own solar system, with great Monrush at its center. The other stars beckoned them further outwards, but she refused. This was as far as she would go for now. She stretched out and touched a part of their star's heart, which was a heady experience. Finally, feeling it was time, she drifted back to Tayna, herself, slowly returning them all to their original place, as tiny beings near their small, but growing, city.

"We were actually there? A part of Monrush?" Torr questioned Ryes, not believing what she just showed them.

"Yes, and that's as far as I'll go for now. Tayna's our main concern after all," she returned merrily. She realized they were still reeling from the experience, except for Garth, Sabin, Mitt, and Maren.

"And I could do this, if I can learn to open up my Talent the same way?" Teris questioned, shocked. This was what his Talent was all about? Tennan was proud of him.

"You might need the help of a Booster to get out so far, but yes, you should be able to do this, too," she replied.

"Forget Manipulator, this one's much better!" Sayer spoke up, still excited from their shared journey. "Can we go again, Mom?" she pressed.

"Later. We have other things to do right now," she reminded her.

"Right," Garth spoke up, recalling he wanted them to practice working together. He'd thought this was the best way to get their Talents in concert and saw he was right. "First, let's share what we recently went through in Doran's temple. I'd never usually choose to press a fight, but in this case, it was to ensure our future safety. It's important, as we've no idea if we'll ever be placed in a position like this again and should know how to defend ourselves and still remain flexible enough to use and lend out our Talents to each other at need," he pressed. He got concurrence from the Talents who'd participated, then got them to open up with a shared, joint memory of their experience in Doran's temple for the others to understand what he was trying to tell them.

Saree just absorbed their experiences and understood so much more, getting to see their blended memories of their experiences there. It gave her a better view of these people she was now living with, and she found, seeing their hearts and minds, she could trust them and find her own place among them now. It was where she felt she belonged! Finally, their shared memories came to a close and they each sat in contemplation of the whole event.

"Ryes was letting us practice using her other Talents, but I don't know how to lend out my own," Scott said, once they were finished and everyone was quiet. It'd been more in-depth and interwoven than just the one Ryes shared.

"That's what we're all going to learn to do. I'm scheduling our practice sessions for a few hours, once a week. Prince Callas said the only way we'll be able to defeat the Snagospin Talents is to use our own Talents against them. We know we're stronger when we work together, and with the humans sending out a task force to eventually reach us, we need to be able to defend ourselves if they're followed. We're not going to let Tayna be bombed again, if we can possibly help it, and someday we'll take the fight out to the stars. With Ryes' Empath abilities, I hope we can see them, long before they reach us. With using her Catalyst Talent in reverse, I hope we'll be able to burn out their Talents. But we don't know the kind of Talents they have, nor how strong their Talents might be. It could end up being a true battle in the end," he warned, letting them all know his intensions. This was serious business, and he wanted his people as prepared, as possible.

"That's a lot to take on," Gann stated, seeing now how determined his brother was about it. He realized he didn't doubt his ability to get them through all this. "But I'm with you."

"You know you can count me in," Ryes assured him.

"Me, too," Sabin, Torr and Maren all pressed at once.

"I'll help too, Dad," Sayer stated, determined she'd be a part of it.

"This world has been my sanctuary for a very long time. I will fight to protect it," Saree spoke up, realizing she meant every word, to the core of her being.

The rest offered their allegiances to his cause then. They knew this was their only home and they had to be able to defend it, if it came down to it. It gave Garth a feeling of warmth, to know he had their willing support, even the face of impossible odds.

"What about the caravaner Talents?" Maren put in. "They were originally part of the forces to protect this world and her peoples. Do you think Darman will throw in with us?"

"He already has," Garth assured him, "It's a part of our new treaty. It's what Dara and Kyma are also considering. If this comes to be as we envision, we'll be training the rest of the Talents from across this continent within the next few years. After that, we'll see if we can reacquaint all of Tayna with what we were meant to be - a world united once more."

"This is getting tiring, even tapping into Ryes' abilities," Raya reminded him.

"Alright, Raya. Practice, but be careful not to hurt others," Garth advised, giving Raya permission to dissolve the link. She gently released them, and they opened their eyes, most seeing the world very differently.

"How many Talents do you have?" Saree asked Ryes, having felt the pure strength of the one she openly displays in taking them on that journey. She'd never known an Empath to be so strong!

"Several," Ryes replied, smiling. Saree saw her reluctance. Was it because she was once one of Doran's followers, or for some other reason? Or did she even know it herself, she wondered?

"And the day after tomorrow, we're going back to Hailys, so we can check on the whereabouts of a certain flower wreath you were wearing the last time," Garth reminded her.

"You value flowers so much?" Saree teased, smiling.

"Only if she accidently left them off in the starport, while she was Time Walking over three hundred years ago," Maren replied, grinning.

"But that is impossible!" she stated in shocked surprise, trying to wrap her mind around such a concept.

"We thought so, too," Gann assured her.

"Saree, I'd like to do a thorough check upon each of you ladies, to make sure you're not experiencing any health problems. If you and the others have the time," Maren requested. Saree smiled, her cheeks dimpling.

"I believe our schedules are open. Am I correct, Raya?" she asked, seeing she was standing nearby.

"Yes, and that's a great idea, Maren. I forgot all about it," Raya told him, but he gave her a nod of his head at this.

"Good, then let's go gather the rest, if Rowan's finished with his storytelling," he offered, gesturing for Raya and Saree to come along with him.

"I will see you later, Gann," Saree said in a low voice, blushing. They'd shared a little of themselves with each other, before being called into the greater meld and she found her attraction for him growing. He had an equal attraction for her but wanted them to take things at a more cautious pace. She wasn't sure if she had the patience anymore. She wanted to know what a physical joining would be like. He'd shown her three other women he'd known intimately, when he lived in Matlowe before, but had never formed lasting attachments with them. He'd never formally mated anyone and was actually considering her, if she wanted him in return. She realized, like Mitt, she wanted to explore a little first, but was sure her path would probably lead her back to Gann.

"Yes, my lady," he replied, smiling. "See you at dinner," he promised. She smiled for him and nodded, then turned and followed in Maren and Raya's footsteps, seeing them collecting the others nearby.

"She surely has her eyes on you," Ryes commented, smiling. It was worth the scratches to see him happy, she thought.

"And I can't keep my eyes off her," he agreed with a happy sigh, thinking the jeans and T-shirt looked good on Saree, even if the filmy robe she wore in the temple revealed more. "Well, I'd better go catch up on my messages and see what else I was supposed to have done today on this day off," he said, giving his sister-in-law a knowing wink. She laughed merrily at this, giving him a nod of her head. Most of the others were drifting back toward the main doors, some talking in small groups as they went.

"Now that we have the important stuff seen to, let's gather our children and I'm going to take a nap with the cubs," Garth told her, putting his arm around her shoulders. She laughed at this, nodding her head.

"They may take a longer one, if you're with them," she agreed. "I'll keep an eye on things," she promised.

"I'll help," Sayer put in, hoping. She wanted some time to talk with her mother alone.

"I'm always glad for the company," she assured her, smiling. They walked back to where they left the little ones, seeing they were being well looked after. "They're going to spoil them, holding them all the time." Garth laughed in agreement.

"Saree, I cannot believe your behavior with that man!" Poli declared, glad they finally had a few minutes alone. They'd each been examined by Maren, who removed their neural nets, but they managed to finally gather in one of the empty conference rooms.

"Leave her alone, Poli. She is going to mate with him soon and even looks happy with her choice," Rhodi broke in, diverting her anger. It did them no good to get mad when they were in an inner commune, it only clouded their contact with each other. This brought Poli up short, puzzled.

"You have had a Vision?" she questioned, seeing it as the answer. "I thought you stopped having Visions long ago?"

"Yes, my Visions have returned!" Rhodi was absolutely joyous, the first time in a very long time and they all felt it clearly in their link.

"I will mate with Gann?" Saree asked, almost afraid to believe.

"Yes. I have seen you pregnant, dancing around a Winterfest tree with him. It makes me envious. I hope that if I can ever find the courage to give myself to a man once more, that he will be as the one you have chosen," she told her, then showed them all the brief glimpse she was granted.

"You do look happy, Saree," Denas agreed, getting excited. "It looks like a fun party; everyone is so happy."

"Dancing. I have not danced in an eternity," Lissel stated, wistfully and wanting to dance now.

"And the music seems lively," Ruan added, with longing in her heart. "It does not appear as the formal ceremonies I recall from what is now, far in the past."

"What are we going to do about the new homes they are offering us? It seems so much for them to grant us our own homes. We are all still strangers. What do they expect from us in return?" Almas questioned, not settled about it at all.

"Raya has been very truthful with us. I have read little deception in her mind. She knows when I am looking, as if she has been with us all along, but has been polite in not looking at our minds, without permission. She saw nothing wrong in the offer of our new homes and considered it our right, since we are now living here in Winterhaven. The only thing I was able to get was the sense that we will have to contribute to the community through our skills, or labors, as we will, and as is needed, as they expect of everyone who comes to live here," Dunn explained, letting them see what she'd found.

"Our skills?" Lissel asked, "in what way?"

"As teachers and defenders," Saree told them, "I was included in their `practice' today."

"Show us," Poli ordered, needing all the clues she could find to unravel this mystery. Saree paused a moment, then did as she was bid and showed them most of the session, as the larger group melded in unity. When Ryes opened her Empath Talent fully, taking the entire link on her journey, the rest were awestruck at the ease with which she wielded such power. She left out the sharing of the battle in the temple. She felt they didn't need to know it now. And Saree realized she was still working her way through it, herself. Seeing it from both sides had been amazing!

"And she has more than one Talent?" Poli pressed, after Saree showed them her experience. They'd all been dazzled by it.

"Yes, she herself has admitted to it. Garth is planning on her taking a Time Walk foray into Hailys' past. Maren said Ryes lost a wreath of flowers, over three hundred years ago in Hailys. They are going to verify it was truly lost then. I think Gann said something about she needed to rescue her great aunt, Adina of House Li. I am not sure of what she plans, but there was talk of Sabin having a Vision about the rescue attempt," she informed them of all she knew.

"Her cousin, Maren, is the strongest Healer I have ever felt in my entire life. And Ryes is Empath, Manipulator, Catalyst, Time Walker and has Inner Sight. Are you sure of these Talents?" Minya asked, almost afraid of such a person.

"Her mother, Tyra of House Li, was a Talent of One. What do you think? All the cubs born to a Talent of One have strong Talents, themselves," Saree stated, sure on this matter; it was part of the histories her grandmother taught her when young.

"Tyra was a Talent of One? No wonder she was able to escape Doran when she felt ready for it!" Renes said, understanding many things now about both Tyra and her daughter, Ryes.

"I wish I had known Tyra was my cousin when she was with us, but I was barely talking to anyone then," Denas commented, feeling as if she lost something precious, when she'd turned inward away from them all, for a very long time.

"It is all right. You still have blood ties to Ryes. We might have to make use of these ties someday. And Gann is the brother to Garth, the leader. It is good that you will be mating him after all, Saree," Poli stated. "We must keep our options open. We are stuck in this tiny colony of theirs for now. We will cooperate and help them, as we can. We do benefit in that we will have our own dwellings and will not starve. And if problems arise at any time in the future, we will have resources we can tap. Having them at the top of their command chain is to our benefit. Having the Stone available too, will only play to our favor. So, put on smiles ladies and do try to fit in for now."

"Remember, they fought Doran and won. They are Talents to be reckoned with, if we cross them. We tried for years to break free of that mad woman and could not. It only took a mere handful of these untrained people to succeed, where we failed, even over a hundred strong," Renes warned them.

"For all their lack of experience, they fought as a team. It is something we never learned, as Doran kept us divided from each other with petty squabbles occupying our minds. We must learn to meld as they do, if we ever have to stand against them," Ossa reminded them.

"We will," Poli promised, "But for now, we have new things to learn here. And at least we are free to choose if we want to have anything to do with men, or not, with no one making us do things we truly abhor. That makes it wonderful to live here."

"That is the greatest blessing about living here in Winterhaven," Dunn agreed, heartily. She had lived for too many years with these women in the evil dark of Doran's ravings, but knew if it came down to it, she would side with Ryes over Poli, always.

Flowers

Chapter 10

"He's parking the chopper closer this time," Ryes told Maren in a low voice, grinning mischievously as they were landing.

"That's not funny. You truly gave us a scare, last time," he quipped back, keeping his voice low too. "No pranks today," he warned her.

"I can't. Garth's going with me this time. Course, I didn't expect that I could do what I did the last time, either," she returned with a sigh. Saree and Denas were with them to help. Garth decided to form a link this time, in case of any problems. "I'm not sure about telling our newcomers all that I can do. What do you think?"

"They were in a fair amount of shock over my Healing Talent the other day. They're still strangers to us in many ways. If you're not comfortable about telling them, then don't," he advised. Then Mitt cut the engine and he saw Sabin tugging at his headset as a signal that they should have theirs on. He smiled than nodded to Ryes, as he put his own back on and activated it once again. She saw the look in Sabin's eyes and knew she must've missed something, so quickly copied Maren with a light laugh.

"Now that we have everyone back online," Garth commented, smiling. "We'll have Ryes sweep the area first, then I want Sadie, Jim and Ardis to double check her. Once the area's declared all clear, then we'll go out and set up our team."

"I'm going to do another sweep for that missing wreath," Sabin told Garth. He smiled as he gave him a nod of his head, knowing he wanted to be out there with his wife, too.

"Ryes?" he prompted. She nodded her head and closed her eyes. She centered herself and called up her Empath ability. Since they were utilizing Saree and Maren this time as Boosters, they thought she could do a more thorough job of a sweep with her Talent, than just the security team on foot. She swept the area around the chopper first, then continued outwards, urging any animal which could cause them harm away. She was surprised at the amount of life these grasslands held! After a few moments, she opened her eyes and gave Garth a nod of her head. She kept a light touch with their surroundings in case anything significant wandered into the area.

"Alright, security team, do your job," he ordered them. Sadie opened the door and the four of them jumped out, Sabin closing it behind them. Mitt continued with her shut down procedure. After what seemed far too long, Sabin gave them the all clear. Maren opened the door and helped the women out. Garth and Mitt jumped out of their own doors.

"No fresh wreaths," he teased his wife. She grinned and nodded as they walked to where they'd been before. Sabin already had the groundsheet and blanket set up, just like then. Ryes snagged one of her favorite pink flowers and put it into her hair anyway. Maren shook his head with a laugh, recognizing her stubbornness. As they sat down upon the blanket, Ryes did one more sweep, then let go, hoping nothing new would nose them out. The jungle marls still stuck in her mind.

"Let's form our link. I think this should work," Sabin told them, then closed his eyes ready to provide the support for this venture. At least he was almost as familiar with Ryes' Time Walking Talent, as she was now. The others fell into the link, leaving Ardis, Sadie and Jim to keep an eye on things around them. And even if Sadie has Talent, they needed her sharp eyes to keep them safe today. Garth and Ryes were physically separate from the others, only linked in through her Mind Voice. Denas and Sabin controlled the main link with their Mind Voice, drawing upon Maren and Saree's Booster Talents. They felt this was the safest approach.

"Ryes, go back to when and where you last left your aunt," Garth urged. "All I want to do is verify what Sabin saw."

He felt her compliance, then that tremendous wash of wild energies as she released her Time Walking Talent. He held onto her tightly as she cast herself back into the far past, zeroing in on her Aunt Adina and Hadu. The intense wrenching sensation almost had him doubled over in agony. He'd only taken the shorter "local" trips back with her to when the humans were the lone occupants of Winterhaven, never these longer, deeper trips. He felt as if he were awash in a golden light, which blocked his senses. Then suddenly it cleared, and he and Ryes sat near what had to be her aunt. She willed them unseen, as they stood up.

Adina was displaying something she held in her hand for a tall slender man to see. It was Ryes' wreath of flowers. The shock on both their faces was clearly seen. She raised a wall of dirt to block the doors and keep the flames at their backs away for a little while. The people turned desperate eyes toward Adina, expecting her to save them. There was still fire freely burning in the stairway ahead of them and the entire building was shaking, as if it were being torn to pieces around them. Some were having a harder time keeping their feet under them, as the lights of the building around them flickered madly. Smoke drifted in the air around everyone, causing many to cough. They were in terror! Adina put the flowers upon her head and gave a nod to Hadu, then turned around and put out her hands before her, as if she were pushing an invisible wall. The actual wall seemed to flow apart, and it looked as if she were using her Talent to create a tunnel for them to freedom; a new one with no flames to block their escape.

"No, remain unseen. Don't distract her," Garth urged, sensing Ryes wanted to help. He watched Adina's efforts for a few minutes more, than saw she didn't have enough energy to fully win their freedom. The other peoples moved over and started digging in desperation, knowing this might be their only way out and the only way to save their lives. "Return us to our own time. I've seen enough," he finally surrendered. Ryes reached back for herself, feeling that wrenching sensation as always. With the presence of the others anchoring them on their end, it was far easier for her to connect with herself, pulling Garth back, making sure he was safe first.

"Was I right?" Sabin demanded, letting their link dissolve as he saw both his friends were all right.

"Yes, you were," Garth admitted, chagrinned, "It fairly shocked Adina too, when she realized what happened. Was that tall strange one, Hadu?" he asked.

"Yes, he is. She was trying to tunnel up through to the surface. Is she an Earth Shaper?" Ryes asked, looking to Denas and Saree.

"Yes, it sounds like one. I can shape water to some degree, but it is weak. My Booster Talent is much stronger," Saree explained.

"Where is the starport? You said it was here," Denas said, looking around at the grassland around them.

"Over here," Ryes said, standing up and offering her a hand. She led her cousin to the edge of the pit, with Saree following them. "There," she told them, her arm sweeping to encompass the great, depression below them.

"You said Hailys was destroyed and several who had the Talent saw its destruction in their Visions and Dreams at the Temple, but this... Are you sure?" Denas demanded. Ryes turned back to her, seeing sadness and desperation in her eyes.

"Did you have family in Hailys?" she asked, wondering and uncertain now.

"My mother, grandmother and other family members lived there," she admitted, with a nod of understanding. "It was why I came here first."

"Let me show you what I've seen from my previous Time Walking journeys here, and what we just saw a few minutes ago," she offered. Maren had stepped over and was looking down into the pit too. Denas met her eyes, not certain if she truly wanted to know it so surely. Then decided she couldn't go on without knowing, so gave her a nod of her head. Ryes didn't seem cruel and had been truthful so far.

"Yes, please show me," she begged, a strange light in her eyes.

"Do you mind if I see it, too?" Maren prompted.

"Yes, you can, you sensation junkie," Ryes teased him, smiling. Denas chuckled too, understanding him only too well, after Saree's sharing of her Empath journey before.

"Me too," Saree declared, not wanting to be left out. Ryes gave them a nod of her head, then closed her eyes. She opened her memories for them, as they clasped hands and created an inner commune. Mitt and Sadie had joined them, determined to know what was going on. After showing them all her trips back to Hailys and most especially both her last journeys, she realized there was a deep upwelling of sorrow coming from Denas. She comforted her, knowing with a pain like this, only time would truly heal it. The others with them sought to ease her sorrow too. Denas found herself awash in an outpouring of love and support. It eased her heart a little, but she still deeply missed her family, now feeling totally cut off from them through both the disaster, and time.

"I need to see Hailys!" she suddenly demanded, "right now!"

"You truly don't want to," both Ryes and Maren urged her, but she stubbornly clung to her demand.

"I'll fly us by the city, and you can see it for yourself. I'm sure they never felt anything, as the attack came in fast and furious, leaving few survivors," Mitt told her. They dissolved the link, but Ryes held a tenuous contact as she half-carried her sobbing cousin back to the chopper. She wasn't going to let her go through this alone! Maren brushed against her, keeping a check upon them both - just in case. He opened the door and the three of them climbed in and settled down, waiting for the rest. Saree joined them shortly, climbing up all by herself.

"You could've waited for one of the others to help you," Maren teased her, grinning. She smiled in return, beaming proudly.

"I have seen, as long as they are able, the women look after themselves. I can too. I am not a child," she told him with a light laugh.

"That's the truth. You're definitely not a child," Maren agreed.

"Why do you mate a human, Maren?" she finally asked, her curiosity burning to know. There were several mixed couples and they seemed happy with their chosen mates.

"Dotti and I are true-mates, and we believe that we must've been true-mates from a previous life. We dreamed and fell in love with each other, long before we met. It's hard to explain it all fully, but she's my life," he told her. She saw the passion in his eyes and felt he spoke the truth. It was an amazing concept. A human and starman as true-mates? She realized she wanted to ask Gann about it, for his insight on the matter, since he'd known them longer.

The others joined them shortly. Ryes had headsets already upon herself and Saree. She decided Denas didn't need to listen to the aimless chatter they sometimes fell into on the longer flights. Maren had his own already on, too. Mitt powered up the aircraft, once everyone was settled, then flew them east toward the main ruins of Hailys. The trip took a very short time, and, as they hovered over the ruins of a once great city, Denas cried out in agony, collapsing into a tight ball. Mitt angled the chopper to avoid the great crater and took them on a heading back home. Maren reached out with his Talent and put Denas deeply to sleep; the pain in both his and Ryes' eyes almost tore Saree's heart out. They cared and suffered too, having unintentionally given Denas great pain.

"I'll take her to medical," Maren offered, but Ryes shook her head.

"I'll put her in the spare bed we have in Sayer and Raby's room. She's my cousin and I'm partly to blame for this. I don't want her to awaken cold and alone in one of your recovery rooms. The girls can help me keep an eye upon her. We'll find a way to bring her back to us," she told him. He nodded his head, seeing it might be the best way after all.

"We'll do that," Garth agreed, thinking Ryes had the right approach. "I don't know how we're going to keep the cubs quiet, but we'll work it out, somehow."

"But she loves your cubs," Saree told them, smiling to see the surprise in Ryes' eyes. "She was telling me yesterday that she could now look forward to her next mating, if she could have beautiful cubs like yours."

"Then your pack of noisy little crawlers ought to be the best medicine for her, after all," Maren told her, smiling in relief. Ryes sighed as she sat back in her seat, her arms still around her mysterious cousin.

"I'll just pray for a miracle," she replied, smiling a little at the thought of her small horde being the best chance for Denas' recovery.

"Maren, can you tell when my season will be coming? Rhodi said she saw me pregnant and dancing with Gann around a Winterfest tree," Saree suddenly requested. There was surprise in Ardis' eyes as she and Sadie exchanged looks.

"Rhodi's a Visionary?" Sabin asked, wondering. They still didn't know what Talents their Sleepers possessed. It could be extremely important to all of them! Garth met his eyes appearing to think the same.

"Yes, she is, and has Mind Voice. She used to be an exceptionally good Visionary, but for a long time she saw nothing. She was so happy when she saw the one about me; she thought her Talent had died within her long ago," she explained.

"We'll have to know what Talents you ladies do have," Garth told her, thinking on it. "In case of any future problems or needs."

"I am a Booster and have a weak version of Water Shaper," she told him, straight out, trusting these people wholly in her heart. "Denas is a Catalyst, but I believe her Mind Voice is her stronger Talent."

"Do you want me to check you right now?" Maren asked, thinking it might be best while they had the time. She smiled and nodded her head.

"Please?" she requested. Maren smiled and closed his eyes, then put a hand lightly upon her abdomen. After a few moments he opened them and met her eyes.

"Your first season will be starting in just a couple of weeks. So, you should be able to go with us to the Great Spring Gather, if you wish. I know this doesn't leave you much time to choose a mate. I can delay it if you want," he offered. She smiled warmly, seeing the great gift he was offering in letting her choose whether, or not, to be a slave to her body, by delaying her season. Even Ruan and Minya couldn't do that for all their Healing Talents! A woman's body has a very delicate balance.

"I want to talk with Gann first and see how he feels about it, then we'll give you our answer," she replied, thinking it would be the best course to follow. She had a friendship beginning with Gann and wanted to continue with it. This was the best way to let him know where she placed her trust. But she knew she had to pass this information onto her friends. Maren was giving them a choice they'd never been granted before in their whole lives! Sabin huffed a laugh at hearing her response, as Garth chuckled.

"Fair enough," Maren replied, giving her a nod and smile.

"Gann truly has his eyes upon you, Saree," Garth assured her, seeing Mitt smiling and nodding her head, too. "He only wanted the two of you to take things slow, so that you'd know it was the right choice for the both of you."

"I'm sure you'll be able to make the best choice together," Ryes assured her, seeing her blushing.

"Maybe we could find Denas an acceptable man and she could have cubs of her own, too?" Saree suggested, suddenly seeing a way to help heal Denas' heart.

"That would have to be her choice," Maren warned, "I don't tinker with others' bodies, without their full knowledge and consent."

"But it is an option you could offer her," she countered, understanding why such a strong Healer would need strong convictions.

"Yes, it's a consideration," Ryes agreed, nodding her head. "First, we'll see how Denas feels about things, before we even think of presenting her such an option. But time may be the only way to heal this wound."

"What do you mean, we've been challenged?" Garth asked Torr, as they were settling Denas into the girls' room. Torr laughed at the puzzled look on his cousin's face.

"See for yourself," he offered, handing over an old-fashioned parchment. Garth took it with a frown, unrolling it. After several minutes, he threw back his head and laughed with abandon. Sabin looked curious, as did the others in the room.

"What?" Maren demanded, now needing to know.

"We've been challenged to a Field Ball match by the Matlowe villagers," Garth told them. "The game's scheduled for right after the Great Spring Gather and they want to hold the match on the field over here. It says that at least we have more level ground to play on," he finished, still chuckling as he passed it to Sabin.

"Field Ball? When are we going to get time to play Field Ball?" Maren demanded, grinning as he considered the idea of a match. He mentally tallied who might be playing on the Matlowe team.

"I think it's a great idea," Mitt assured them. "You guys are all out of shape. We're going to be hard pressed to come up with a workable team."

"That's the truth," Ardis agreed with a merry laugh.

"What do you mean?" Sabin demanded of his wife. She merely laughed again at the look on his face.

"When was the last time you lot worked out consistently in the gym? I work out more than all of you men," Mitt scolded. Ryes smiled, nodding her head in agreement, as she headed back to the larger bedroom again, to be with her cousin. She'd hear the details later.

"Is the team supposed to be all men, women, or both?" Torr suddenly asked, reaching for the parchment. Sabin held it out of his reach, but Maren managed to snag it. He looked at it as Mitt read it from beside his elbow.

"It doesn't say. We'll have to issue a response anyway and request a meeting to clarify rules and team structure," he told them, lowering the paper to look at the others.

"Mitt, Minn, Ryes, Jim, Kovin, Phil, Justin, Scott, Maren, Sadie, Ted, Leon, Dotti and I, all use the gym fairly regularly. There's a little time to try to get you guys in shape for the match, if you want to represent Winterhaven, but not much," Ardis told them, laughing. She saw she'd scored by the look in the eyes of the men around her. It served them right, she felt.

"We'll have a meeting to discuss this and the final preparations for our Founder's Day celebration tomorrow morning," Garth told them. It stung that what the women said had some truth to it. They were all too busy to get the exercise they knew they now needed!

"Excuse me," Poli said, pulling aside the door drape to see the room was fairly crowded, and they looked to be laughing about something.

"Come in," Garth invited, having snagged back the message, wanting to examine it again. He looked up to see it was one of their Sleepers. "I'm sorry. We just returned from Hailys and were discussing a message we received from Matlowe. Ryes is with Denas, through there," he informed her, indicating the drape over the door to the girls' room.

"Thank you," she replied as she and Ruan stepped into the room, heading toward the indicated doorway. She pulled the drape aside to see Ryes sitting beside Denas, a look of deep concern in her eyes. She looked up to see them, gesturing them to join her. The room was large and neat with two twin beds set headboard to headboard on the opposite wall from the bed Denas lay upon. Beyond them were five cribs, set so you could easily walk between them to check on the young cubs. There were dressers and a door that lead to a large closet, partly open. And the room smelled fresh, as if there was a flow of outside air vented into the room.

"Isn't this a lot of noise for someone who needs quiet, to find her healing?" Ruan questioned Ryes sharply; a look of disapproval upon her face, as she stepped closer.

"Actually, I think Saree may be right; that Denas needs the sounds of friends and family life around her, to help her find a way to say good-bye in her heart to those she loved deeply," Ryes countered, calmly facing these women, who were older and more experienced in the world. But she knew her own truth in her heart and would not back down on this decision.

"May I examine her?" Ruan asked, feeling put off by her answer. Still, it did hold some merit. She might be young, but she displayed no fear of them, as she recalled she faced off Doran all alone, before. And won her freedom!

"Maren put her into a deep sleep to help her rest. He said she should awaken late tomorrow morning. He's putting himself on call, in case she needs him," she informed her, but stood up and let Ruan have her seat. She gave her a nod of her head, took the offered seat, then closed her eyes to check upon Denas herself. After several long moments, she opened her eyes and sighed.

"It is as you say. Her spirit is badly injured. The sleep will do her good. Will you keep a watch upon her?" she asked. Ryes nodded her head in response.

"It's more than just a familial obligation to me. I feel responsible for not seeing she wasn't ready to see Hailys as it is now. I didn't know her mother, grandmother and other family members lived there at the time of its destruction," she admitted.

"Was it truly destroyed?" Poli questioned, needing to know it for herself.

"Come with me," she suddenly offered, stepping over to the door drape and holding it open for them. "I'll show you." They looked puzzled but did as she bid them. She worried about them as she recalled Garth calling them a bunch of pretty flowers. They did seem fragile, she thought, but recalled Saree's strong, determined spirit. It gave her hope.

Ryes stepped over to their computer access and keyed in a quick command. The screen blanked as she stepped out of the way, allowing them to see it clearly. The computer slowly displayed a slideshow of images taken by the original team of humans to explore the city, then ones taken by their own teams, as they took various forays into the ruins. Poli sought out a nearby chair, her face ashen.

"To see that great city, which was once filled with so much life," she said, looking to see the understanding upon Ryes' face and the concern from the others in the room. "I can only imagine that in person it is an even a more gruesome sight."

"Did you have family there, too?" Ardis asked, wondering if she could handle such a time shift, losing all her family, friends, and everything she'd ever known growing up? It was the one thing she worried about with their humans; that all that they'd known was forever changed or gone.

"No, but I did love to immerse myself in it, using my Empath Talent. From these pictures, I would imagine it is much changed now."

"This will be hard for Minya," Ruan said, looking sad too, "She grew up in Hailys."

"We'll break it to her, after we pull Denas through this," Garth advised, stepping closer. "Maybe the pictures are better? They're not as personal, as seeing it with your own eyes."

"That is true. We will see what we can do to help her through this tragedy. And I would like a few moments to speak with you, Maren, if you have the time to spare?" Poli requested, glad Saree had come straight to her, as soon as she returned. He was offering them a priceless salvation!

"Not a problem," he assured her, stepping closer. Ryes returned to the computer display and exited the program. She then pulled up her message box, seeing she was falling behind. But there was no way she'd desert Denas now! Raby appeared pushing the stroller with one hand and a cub over her shoulder. The other four were in their seats, trying to squirm out of them, even if they were strapped in. Katas was right behind her with Ardis' two cubs in her stroller. Spann had made the strollers for the new mothers two months ago and they still couldn't thank him enough.

"They're plotting an escape," Raby told Ryes, "and I've got the ringleader right here," she said, handing over Gareth.

"Oh, you'd never know he was your son, Garth," she teased as she took him. "It's almost lunch time. Go ahead and get yours. Is Sayer still in class?"

"Yup. She should be out soon," she told her. Raby went into her room then came immediately back out, questions in her eyes, as she was trying to frame what she needed to ask.

"Our cousin Denas will be staying with us for a little while. Don't worry, you don't have to be quiet, nor keep the horde quiet. In fact, the cubs might be the best medicine for her," Ryes explained. "I know it's crowded enough, as is," she teased, smiling. Raby laughed, nodding her head.

"Another roommate," she mockingly complained with a big grin, then went back in to change. Being covered with baby drool didn't do much to attract the young men, whose interest she craved! She'd be sixteen years old in three months and wanted to make sure she had her future mate pinned down, long before she hit her eighteenth birthday!

"I'll go get our lunches," Garth told Ryes, as Raby emerged in fresh clothes. Ryes was playing with the cubs and getting ready to feed them. The crowd in the room had dissipated down to them, Poli, Ruan and Maren.

"Thank you," she replied, glad he was still taking the time to eat his lunches with them. "You don't have to eat with us, Raby. I'm sure Katas would miss you if you did." She saw a look of pure relief in her eyes.

"Thanks, Mom," she told her, giving her a quick hug, then dashed out the door. Garth chuckled at this, leaning down to give Ryes a kiss.

"I'll be right back," he promised as Dotti appeared in the doorway.

"Maren, lunch time," she reminded him. He gave her a wave in acknowledgment, almost ready to join her. Garth slipped out past Dotti, giving her a nod inside, as he did. She got the idea and came on into the room. "The kids are a handful," she commented, sitting down next to Ryes.

"Yes, they are. I like the human's idea of school lasting most of the day. Sure, it's for a better education for the children, but the mothers and fathers must love it even more," she told her, chuckling.

"It does give the parents a break," Dotti agreed, laughing with her. "Wait until yours are old enough."

"Ah, by then I'll have grandkids to watch for Sayer and Raby, and heaven knows when my next season will come," she reminded her with a shake of her head. "I'm doomed!" Dotti laughed merrily at this, nodding her head in agreement.

"Probably so," she told her.

"You don't have to agree with me! How many are you and Maren planning?" she suddenly thought to ask, wondering.

"Let's see how our first goes, before we make plans for any more," she replied in a low voice, blushing. "It surely makes sense to me that your season only happens once every few years. We're vulnerable every month! Did you know about Brenda? Already?"

"Yes, and unplanned. Maren told me. I can't believe it! We're just going to have to come up with a better birth control for you humans to use, so you can get a breather between kids."

"Do you think we'll ever have any grandchildren?" she suddenly asked in a low voice, meeting Ryes' eyes. It was a question that had plagued her off and on the last few weeks. She wondered...

"She feels `right' to both of us. I'll bet she'll be able to marry anyone she wants and have as many kids as she feels like bearing," Ryes assured her, also in a low voice, seeing it did haunt her friend's thoughts.

"Who?" Maren demanded, surprising them as he walked up behind them, wondering who they were talking about now?

"Maren!" Ryes complained, as she saw smiles upon the other women's faces at his craft, as they stood back from him. The humor in their eyes was good to see, she realized. Ryes smiled giving them a nod.

"Thank you so much, Maren," Poli told him, then she and Ruan left as quickly as possible.

"What was that all about?" Dotti asked him.

"Laying down a few rules for Ruan, seeing she's a Healer. I asked for her and Minya to start working and training in the medical center. I also let them know I can delay their seasons, if it's a pressing matter, since they're very new here and need time to find men they find acceptable. But I also let them know I'm not eliminating them entirely. It'd be unnatural and might do them more harm, than good," he explained, smiling. "So, who were you talking about?"

"Your daughter," Ryes explained, shaking her head. "I was just telling Dotti that I didn't think grandchildren would be a problem."

"Grandchildren? Oh, you're making me feel so old, already," he complained, a hand to his heart. The women laughed at his merry display, then he met his wife's eyes. "She'll be fine and will have as many kids as she feels like having," he assured her. She suddenly grabbed his neck, pulled him close and kissed him soundly.

"Alright, you two. Go get your lunch and leave this soon to be grandmother alone!" Ryes urged them with a laugh.

"Since when are you going to be a grandmother?" Garth asked, as he stepped back into the room.

"Give Raby a couple more years, dear sir, and you'll see," she reminded him, smiling at the shocked look on his face now. "She'll be in her own home with her own new family - starting out."

"You're right! I forgot! I'm going to have to make sure the young men know they have to have my approval, before they'll be allowed to date my daughters," he agreed.

"Oh, Dad!" Sayer complained, stepping in behind him, her face scrunched up in protest. "I'll never find the right guy that way!"

"That's the way it's going to be imp," he teased, "I kept your Aunt Mitt chase for years, just ask her."

"I will," she threatened, grinning, as she plotted it in her mind. "Going to eat my lunch with Raby today," she told them, then dashed into her room. She came instantly back out with a puzzled expression on her face, as questions danced in her eyes. "Who?"

"Your fourth cousin, Denas. She's not well and needs us to look after her. Don't worry, you can make as much noise as usual and the same goes for the horde. Your cousin Maren put her under, so she'll sleep through until tomorrow," Ryes told her. She gave her a nod in relief, then dashed back into her room. After a few minutes, she emerged, wearing one of her new blouses with big holes sewn into the top of the shoulders.

"Later," she said, running out the door amid the laughter.

"I think you're already losing the game, Garth," Maren warned, with a laugh. "We'll see you later," he promised as they left.

"Ah, just the seven of us now," he said, setting down their trays upon the low table and sitting on the floor beside her.

"Just so romantic," she agreed with a laugh.

Founder's Day

Chapter 11

She realized she heard crying, and laughterm and voices which held a lot of affection, all sounding at once, coming from nearby. She didn't recognize the room she was in as she opened her eyes, nor the human man, who sat near her, reading a real book. He suddenly looked at her in surprise, as he realized she was awake. She looked into his lively blue eyes, mesmerized for a moment.

"Sorry, Lady Denas. I'll get Ryes right away," he apologized. She put up a hand to halt his immediate escape, seeing he looked as if he were in a half-panic.

"Just call me Denas, please. What is your name, sir?" she asked, wanting an introduction at least.

"His name's Montigue of House Elbridge," Ryes answered from the doorway, a smile upon her face.

"You can just call me Monty, ma'am," he assured her, relaxing a little and granting her a small smile.

"Thank you, Monty, for watching over me as I slept," she told him, meaning it for the first time in too many years.

"It was no trouble, ma'am," he replied, getting up and stepping over to Ryes.

"Thanks, Monty. I appreciate it, too," she said. He blushed and gave her a nod of his head, then ducked out the colorful drape behind her, book in hand.

"He is not badly put together. I have seen a few mixed couples here. Are they compatible?" she asked, not sure if she would follow what she meant, with her phrasing.

"Oh yes, both male and female," Ryes assured her, realizing this might've been her first chance to see a human man up close. "How do you feel?" she asked, stepping over to take Monty's chair, so she wouldn't be looming over her.

"This is odd," Denas sighed out, relaxing back into the bed. "My body feels rested, yet within I feel utterly exhausted. I can guess from the commotion outside, that I am not in my own quarters."

"You're our guest. I'm sorry to say, but the girls and cubs all sleep in here, too. In a few days we'll be celebrating our finding Winterhaven. We have a very spacious apartment home ready for us, with lots of bedrooms. The girls have most everything unnecessary already packed and ready for the move. Garth decided, to be fair, no one's allowed to move any of their personal items in, until after the dedication ceremony. And his injunction applies most especially to us, since he's our leader. So, until then, we'll have to make do with the cramped quarters," she explained. She saw the amusement in her eyes as she related the circumstances they had to live in for the moment.

"Then, I am staying with you and your family, cousin?" she asked, wanting to be sure.

"Until Ruan, Maren and I can all agree that you're ready to venture out on your own again, yes, you're living with us," she informed her, smiling, "I'm so sorry, I didn't wholly understand what actually seeing Hailys would do to you!"

"No, do not be sorry. I spent a long time under Doran's captivity, where I retreated from everyone. I do not know if I was seeking to run away, or a death she was denying me. I was an outcast in a close-knit society for too many years," she explained, realizing it was her truth.

"Then we have much in common," Ryes told her, smiling again. "I spent most of my life as an outcast in Matlowe Village and spent my days running in the woods. Then Garth and his friends approached me, asking me if I'd teach them how to hunt, my way. My life hasn't been the same since, and if it hadn't been for Garth, I might've died last year; either by my own hand, or beneath Korman's claws. When you have no one to truly care, nor anywhere to go, what choices does an outcast have?" Denas met her eyes, seeing her truth. She might not have lived as long a life, but hers hadn't been an easy one, either.

"Would you happen to have a robe I could borrow? I believe I could use a trip to the bathroom, and a shower," she told her. Ryes smiled at this, nodding her head.

"Got one right here," she replied, having placed some clothes for Denas in Sayer and Raby's wardrobe, having anticipated her needs. "I believe some concerned friends wanted to drop by after lunch, if you feel up to a little company later," she offered, helping her get up, subtly using Healing to help steady her balance.

"Ah, lunch does sound good," she agreed smiling, realizing she was hungry, but not sure of any company.

"Well, lunch around here can sometimes be a circus with wiggly cubs to feed, while you're juggling your food and mug of tea. But what's life without adventure? Right?" Ryes teased merrily.

"Too true," Denas agreed, smiling now, hoping she could find a way to enjoy all this attention. She blessed her cousin in her heart, seeing what truly lay at the base of her inclusion into her small, active family. It'd been too long since she had family around her.

"In recognition of that momentous day one year ago, I hereby dedicate these new homes to our original, intrepid explorers. Without their courage and spirit of exploration, the rest of us wouldn't be here today," Dr. Ethan Cruthers declared smiling grandly, then gave the signal for Garth and Sabin to cut the cord with the ridiculously large pair of gold scissors, displaying the symbol of the Phoenix, which Phil had made for this occasion. A loud clapping and cheer went up, as the light cording dropped to the pavement. Garth handed the scissors back to Phil with a big grin upon his face.

"Thanks," he told him with a laugh, as Phil gave him a nod and smile in return. Sabin had his arms in the air, cheering with everyone else. Ryes, Ardis, Shadd, Mitt, Kovin, Maren, Raya and Torr, who were out in front of the rest of the residents were also cheering and clapping; happy with being recognized by the rest of the Winterhaven residents.

"Now, everyone may start moving into your new homes, but don't take too long as the festivities begin soon," Ethan urged with a chuckle. He ran his hand through his now-thick blonde hair as he smiled merrily and cut off the mic, seeing most people already had boxes and bags at their feet, ready for this moment. There was a mad scramble, accompanied by jokes and laughter, as the new residents rushed to find their names upon their doors, eager to see them for the first time.

Several of the apartment homes had two levels, for the larger families, while some had an upstairs apartment and a downstairs one, which were reserved for the bachelors, or couples with only a child. They were arranged as eight or sixteen units to a building and the buildings had been arranged to give ample play areas for the cubs and small gathering spots with tables under pavilions and outdoor grills near them, so if the residents wanted to enjoy some time outside when the weather was nice, they could do so. Each building had trash and recycling collection areas, too. And none of the homes had anything more than a small kitchenette, as the community dining hall was where the leaders of Winterhaven felt everyone should take their meals.

"Here's our place!" Sayer declared as Ryes was laughing at the silly antics around them. She knew where her home sat, but the other residents all made it a game, even the Sleepers got into the fun. "The door's beautiful! It looks like Honey's carved into it!" Sayer fingered the artwork, following the graceful curves carved into the sturdy, stained wood and grinning with pride. The paint accents were perfect!

"Well, open the door," she urged, pushing the stroller with the cubs. She had her backpack on and was carrying her old spear in one hand, thinking it was perfectly suited for this occasion, since if she hadn't decided to go ahead and teach a bunch of clumsy villagers how to hunt, they wouldn't be here on this day!

"Oh!" both Sayer and Raby declared as they stood in the open doorway staring at the room beyond. Denas laughed, getting excited about it too. Moving days were usually times of stress, but here it was filled with fun and joy!

"There's new furniture in here!" Sayer added, as she looked back to Ryes and Denas.

"Go on in. Your bedrooms are upstairs and are supposed to be marked," Ryes laughed out, seeing their surprise. She'd been in here over a week ago, to make sure everything was working and tweaking the arrangement of the layout, not wanting any surprises, so already knew what it looked like.

"Oh, it's so spacious," Denas declared as she stepped in behind Ryes. Garth appeared in the doorway behind her, his arms loaded with three boxes.

"Excuse me, coming through," he told the women, wanting to set them down inside. Ryes and Denas stepped aside, letting him pass. "I'm putting all our things over here, then we'll sort it out tomorrow morning." He told his wife, after setting down his burden against the far wall of the main gathering room.

"Good idea," she agreed, then stepped over and stood her spear up in the corner behind the boxes, not wanting anyone to get hurt playing with it. She was going to mount it upon a wall, unless she needed to go out hunting again.

"Why tomorrow?" Denas asked, as Garth disappeared out the open door.

"In another hour, the party with food and games starts up next to the Phoenix fountain, and then the drinking and dancing later in the evening. I don't think anyone's going to be in shape to get anything done until tomorrow," she explained, smiling. "Come, let me show you to your room," she urged. She employed Manipulator Talent to lift the stroller upstairs ahead of them, bringing out laughter from the others. There was a small sitting area at the top of the stairs with a hallway off from it. They passed Raby and Sayer's rooms as she showed her down the hall, pointing out what would've been one of their spare bedrooms for her use, with her name already upon the door. She then pushed the stroller into the bedroom across from hers, the one set aside for the cubs. "The Horde" was proudly displayed upon their door. They were squirming and wanting out now, appearing excited too.

Denas smiled as she opened the door, then stood there with her carry sac upon her shoulder, looking at her room. There was a window, which looked out to a courtyard outside, a large, comfortable-looking bed, which already had a colorful bedspread, and there was a wooden dresser near the door. An over-stuffed chair was by the window with a small table and reading lamp. A mirrored door which was partly open, revealed a large closet, then another door beyond, which she wasn't sure where it led. She stepped in, throwing her bag upon the bed, opening one of the dresser drawers, noting the scent of fresh wood. Someone had put time and effort into making it, for it looked elegant yet was sturdy.

"Oh Mom!" she heard Sayer shout, finding Ryes in the cubs' room, "Thanks!"

"It's beautiful!" Raby declared, tears of joy sounding in her voice. Denas sighed to herself. This is what she missed most. Home. She then recalled they had a party and dancing ahead of them still, so quickly unpacked her carry sac, thinking she could put her things away, first. Exploring, she stepped through the second door and was delightfully surprised to discover she had her own private toilet, sink and shower. She stood there looking at herself in the mirror as tears of happiness ran down her cheeks unchecked.

"Oh, you're wearing me out," Garth protested, sitting down. "Go torture someone else!" Ryes laughed at this, shaking her head as she sat down beside him. She grabbed her glass of water and almost drained it in one long pull. She hadn't had this much fun dancing, since the winter before last, when the caravaners were wintering with them in Matlowe.

"Nope. The only one I ever intend to torture is you," she declared, smiling mischievously. "And that's what you deserve." He grabbed her and kissed her, chuckling as he did so, before letting her go.

"May I have this next dance, ma'am?" Monty asked, stepping over to their table. Garth met Ryes' eyes and he knew she couldn't refuse him.

"I'd be happy to dance with you," she agreed with a big smile. She'd already danced with almost everyone else this evening, yet still had energy to burn. She jumped to her feet and Monty took her out onto the dance area, near the fountain at the base of the huge, towering Phoenix, in the middle of their new complex. Below their feet was the thick, sturdy glass-like ceiling for the underground swimming pool. The lights reflecting up from off the water below gave a wonderful, magical feeling as the dancers twirled around the dance floor.

"I'm out of shape!" Gann declared as he and Saree sat down next to Garth. They both looked so happy.

"Want to play on our Field Ball team?" he asked, smiling. "Matlowe challenged us to a match." Gann looked surprised at this, then threw back his head and belly chuckled as he shook his head.

"Oh, no. You're not dragging me into that one! I'll be over there working for a while, starting next week," he reminded him. "The foundations have already been laid and the first walls go up, at the end of this week for the rest of our projects. It'll be bad enough being around Karr again."

"Do you think you'll be able to break free for the Great Spring Gather?" he asked.

"I don't know. I'll have to check the construction schedule," he told him, not truly wanting to attend. He and Saree were talking about her upcoming season, and he was still undecided about her putting it off a while. He realized he wanted her badly now, but didn't want his time with her divided, as he had to work over in Matlowe. He wanted her to be the full focus of his time and energy, with no interferences - even from his own littermate!

"All right. Just let me know," he replied, seeing something in his brother's behavior which implied his interest in Saree. Perhaps he had other, more pressing matters to attend to, such as her season? He smiled to himself, understanding him too well.

"How are you feeling, Denas?" Saree asked, seeing her watching the dancers with happiness in her eyes. Denas was sipping her drink, which appeared to be stronger than water, with a big smile upon her face.

"Much better now," she replied, sounding merry. Her eyes were dancing with a light coming from within, and Saree was relieved to see they truly had her back with them again. She'd worried and while she'd had Ryes' assurances that she was getting better, it now appeared a miracle. Still, instead of sitting with the other "Sleepers," as they've become known, she stayed with her new family and friends.

"Have you had a chance to dance?" she asked, wondering. Most of their number had been enjoying the party with both starmen and human men asking them out onto the dance floor, all so very polite and respectful towards them.

"The music is strange, if lively," she replied. "Garth and Maren have both taken me out now. But I enjoy sitting and watching everyone, truly." Ryes and Monty returned to the table at the end of the song, with Ryes now out of breath.

"May I ask you out for the next dance, Denas?" he asked, seeing she hadn't danced much with anyone else. She hesitated for a moment, then laughed lightly.

"I would be delighted," she replied with a smile lighting up her eyes, standing up. He smiled as he bowed to her, then offered her his arm, taking her off to dance floor.

"She still seems so sad within, somehow," Saree commented.

"But she's getting better," Ryes assured her, smiling as she leaned against Garth's shoulder. "You know it's almost time for the announcements," she reminded her husband.

"Oh, yeah... I almost forgot," he said, with a sigh.

"What announcements?" Gann asked, not having heard of anything special being spoken about lately.

"It's a Big surprise," Ryes assured him, smiling. She stood up and pivoted on her heel to face them. "Do you want me to make it? After all, I had a hand in it."

"No, but you can stand beside me, Sweet One," he told her, standing too. "The break's right after this dance finishes, so let's make sure everyone has a fresh drink in hand." They left, leaving the others at their table with puzzled looks upon their faces.

"What could it be?" Garvin asked his wife. They were taking a break, having danced most of the evening, already. She shrugged, not knowing.

"The shuttles are due for their first test flights this week," Ardis commented, trying to divert their curiosity for a few moments more. Dotti was starting to show a little and Sana was having a time trying to hide her pregnancy now. It was definitely time. Sabin chuckled, nodding his head as he lifted his glass.

"`bout as ready as we'll ever be," he commented in a low voice.

"Ah, that has to be it," Saree agreed. "Have you ever been in space before, Sabin?" She wondered at their boldness. They didn't leave the dangerous first missions to subordinates but went themselves. Maybe since they'd been the people to establish this colony, they felt responsible for the dangers?

"No. This'll be our first experience. Other than needing motion sickness medication, no one's said much of what to expect," he told her. She laughed lightly at this, nodding her head.

"It is not like any other kind of flight! You will love it, once you get used to the gyro turns," she assured him.

"So much to look forward to," he replied with a shake of his head. Ardis laughed as she hugged him.

"I wish you'd let me go," she complained, smiling.

"You'll get your turn," he promised, meaning it. He'd had a Vision about journeying with her aboard a larger ship. The same one which he and Garth are supposed to pilot someday! "Looks like they're ready."

There were servers going to all the tables, offering fresh drinks and light snacks to everyone. The dance was winding down, everyone looked ready to take a break. As the dancers finally drifted back to their tables, Garth and Ryes took the platform, at the end of the dance floor. Monty led Denas back over to her seat at the table and took a seat next to her as she gave him a nod and smile. She stayed next to him and seemed happy to have him with her.

"We have a couple of announcements we'd like to make, while the musicians rest for a few minutes," Garth said, speaking into the mic. There was laughter and shouts of agreement from the crowd.

"Is everyone having a good time?" Ryes asked first, smiling as she surveyed the scattered tables around the edge of the courtyard.

There were shouts and hoots and comments - all expressing their happiness. She laughed at hearing them, hoping they were ready. "We wanted to make this day special for us all! We're so proud to have our very own Founder's Day!" She got more cheers and laughter of agreement from the gathering. It took a few moments for the energy to die down, but when it did, Garth took control of the microphone again.

"First off, I'd like to announce that our two shuttles are now ready for their maiden voyages. I'd now like to dedicate The Defender and The Avenger as the first starships in Winterhaven's fleet. They may be small, but they're the first two in what we hope will be a true fleet, someday," Garth said. A cheer went up from the crowd. "Could the crews of our ships please stand up and take a bow?" he requested. Ethan, Rowan, Axel, Mitt and Sabin all stood to clapping and cheers. There were big, proud smiles on each of their faces.

"Our first mission, as a part of testing the craft, will be to place satellites near Tayna to extend our weather watch, and communication's abilities, then to go out into the Dark to place a few warning satellites, to help keep track of any activity in our solar system. So, we should know if anyone, other than our ships, is approaching Tayna." This got applause, but the seriousness of the mission was noted on the faces of the people around them. The crews took their seats again, as the clapping died down.

"Secondly, I'd like to announce that our population has grown, again. We have eleven newcomers, as many of you already know, who've been learning to adjust to our small community here and have enriched our community with their graces." There was laughter and cheers, so the ladies stood, as the group encouraged them, smiling for everyone, amazed at being so presented. They stood and waved, and all appeared embarrassed, but pleased. After a few moments, the Sleepers took their seats once more, too.

"And finally, I'd like to say that while most of our women here are either pregnant, or have small children to care for, we have two very special pregnancies to announce tonight. There was a lot of soul searching, love, and effort put into bringing them into fruition, so you'll know that it wasn't a casual matter," Garth said into the mic, seeing he had everyone's attention once again. "Maren and Dotti are now expecting their own daughter, as Justin and Sana are expecting their two sons. We'd like to congratulate these two couples and look forward to the birth of their children. These children will bring both our peoples together as never before!" The pride in his voice was clear to everyone gathered. There was at first a scattered clapping, as this last piece of news was still sinking in, then there were shouts and cheers and loud clapping in support of the two couples from both the starmen and humans. Ryes laughed at this, relieved. She still knew the next few days would be the worse for all of them, as the questions would start pouring in.

"Way to go, Justin!" Scott shouted, surprised to hear the news. His friend gave him a nod of his head, blushing at all the attention. Sana was laughing as she held onto him, almost quaking in reaction.

"Now I understand why Senna and Tanns were taken ill with headaches, after dinner tonight," Marla remarked. Rebin turned toward her, then realized the reason, too. She laughed, nodding her head.

"Those are my little nephews you're talking about," Sabin teased, as he winked at Ardis. She gave him a nod then turned and saw Torr was laughing as he hugged Maren, as Bethy was hugging Dotti, both women crying in joy. She'd get her turn, so waited a few minutes.

"How can that be? Are we so closely related to your people?" Denas asked a shocked, yet happy, Monty. He was still clapping.

"I guess it must be closer than we thought. Even for all his Talent, I don't think Maren could've done it, otherwise," he told her. "Excuse me a moment," he offered. She gave him a nod of her head, so he jumped up and went straight to the knot of people surrounding Maren.

"You're not surprised, Rowan," Gann pointed out, seeing his beaming face.

"I'm going to be the great-grandfather," he stated, "Of course I already knew." Ethan chuckled as Metta laughed, at the look of pride in his eyes. "She'll probably be as pretty as her mother and as stubborn as her father," he assured them, soliciting more laughter from the others at the long table.

"I'm going to be a great-uncle!" Metta added, smiling with pride, "and she's going to be simply beautiful!" He got up to go congratulate the happy couple.

After hours of partying, the celebrants finally started drifting off to their new homes. It'd been an event-filled evening! While Saree and Denas had been openly supportive of the two mixed couples and very happy with their pregnancies, Ryes noted the rest of the Sleepers were still trying to process this news, as they were

unsure if it were something to be happy about, or not. It'd definitely
been a surprise to them, as the other Winterhaveners.

Monty slowly walked Denas to her door, as Ryes and Garth
had gone in ahead of them, wanting to make sure the cubs were all
settled for the night, in their new home. Raby and Sayer with Tars
and Katas had taken all the younger cubs to their home to watch
during the dancing, giving them some fun dress-up time, and giving
the parents a break. Ardis and Sabin went in and claimed their cubs,
both the older and younger ones, then headed quickly off to bed, so
Senna couldn't harangue Sabin before they reached the safety of their
home. Maren had collected Tars and his younger siblings quickly too,
wanting to get home before Tanns caught him outside.

By the time they reached her door, Denas had completely
forgotten how late the hour, and was happy to just talk with Monty
about his life before being locked into his suspension capsule on the
Star Quest. They sat upon a bench in front of the house, by the door.
His simple life intrigued her. He'd never known of the lives of royals,
nor had been involved heavily in politics. Like the starmen, he'd had
a direct brain connection into their "net," but it had been completely
severed with both distance and Maren having removed it when
restoring his body. And like her, he realized he didn't miss the
constant uninvited barrage of others into his life. Her talking about it
gave him a moment of perspective to realize while he'd lost something
which was useful, it'd had been controlling his time each minute of his
day. She too, no longer missed hers and was glad Maren had
removed it, too. He tried to explain how simple life was on a colony
world and for the first time missed Trinity, if only a little.

Denas tried to explain how she loved to be away from the
pressures of being part of an extensive family, who loved to control
everyone's lives constantly. And with the pressures added by being
related to the royal family, everything she did was criticized
constantly, as if they were honing her to be the most perfect doll, to
be put up on a shelf and forgotten, unless they needed something of
her. She didn't miss it, except for the family life she'd had at home
when growing up. They'd both grown to love this small
establishment, which was more of a blend of the two peoples into a
new whole.

"Is she still there?" Denas asked in a low voice, amusement
coloring her tone. He gave her a nod and smiled too.

"It's getting late, and while I know Garth declared tomorrow a
day off, I know I'll still have duties to take care of," Monty said,
reluctantly. She put a hand atop his and gave him a warm smile.

"Then, I will look forward to seeing you tomorrow," she
replied, meeting his eyes, and finding only warmth and happiness

there. It truly warmed her own heart. He stood and offered her a hand to help her to her feet. They were both laughing again. She finally gave into her heart and wrapped her arms about him in a hug, her head resting against his strong chest. Monty willingly returned the hug and was reluctant to let her go now. They stood together for several long moments, just holding onto each other. As they parted, her lips sought his and he willingly joined her in a long, heart-felt kiss.

"I…" she started to apologize for the kiss, but he shook his head no and smiled. She could not get enough of his deep blue eyes!

"Let's sleep on it, and see where we go with this tomorrow," he promised, then reluctantly released her. She smiled and nodded, then sighed and walked slowly to the door.

"Sweet dreams, dear Denas," he wished her, not having moved. She turned and smiled.

"Sweet dreams, dearest Monty," she wished him in return, then turned and went inside. She realized leaving him was the hardest thing she'd ever done, as she closed the door behind her.

Monty turned for his own home, his heart was dancing. He wanted Denas so very much, but there was no way he was going to ever rush her. Somehow, she'd become precious to him in just a few days. He passed their stalker and gave her a nod, knowing she'd thought herself well-concealed, as she'd watched them tonight. One of the Sleepers was keeping an eye upon Denas and himself all evening long. Light laugher was heard in his wake as he continued home.

Space

Chapter 12

"I need a few minutes to escape, where no one will bother me," Maren said, as he plunked down into the chair next to Ryes' desk. She nodded her head in understanding. It'd been a few days since the announcement, and she knew the reactions would start up.

"So, who's more outraged? The starmen, or the humans?" she asked, knowing he'd have the knowledge firsthand by now.

"The starmen, for sure," he informed her, closing his eyes and leaning back in the chair. "Funny though, I thought I'd get the loudest screams out of Metta, but he's been one of our best supporters. Just when you think you know someone," he sighed out. She was shaking her head.

"Metta sees some kind of advantages here. After all, he's your uncle. Is Dotti all right?" she asked, shutting down her terminal and giving him her full attention.

"Oh yeah. I think everyone knows that to bother her is like issuing you, or Ethan a challenge, and Sana falls under Sabin's protection, so the women have been mostly left alone. Justin and I, on the other hand, are the scum men who insisted upon doing this to our wives. And I have the added attention, since several have figured out who had to have done the nefarious deed."

"You knew the job was dangerous when you took it," she teased, "but all you were thinking it was only when you helped change your baby's dirty diapers." He opened his eyes, saw her small smile and laughed at her humor. "Actually, I'll let it be known that I was the linchpin in the procedures and for them to get off your back. You've got far more important concerns to worry about."

"I don't know if that'll help, and I don't want people focusing on you and your Talents," he said, sitting up straighter. "We'll weather this, and things should be fairly calm by the time the cubs are born. Actually, you look pretty calm today," he commented.

"Calm? Me?" she retorted, with raised eyebrows. "I'm going to go have lunch alone for the first time in weeks, and you think I look calm?" The smiled had melted from her face on the instant, as a frown creased her brow.

"They'll be fine. What's the big deal with placing a few satellites?" he asked, "And, I'll have lunch with you." Ryes sighed at this, smiling for him, knowing he was trying to be supportive.

"I don't do too well when he's gone like this. I keep thinking of the last time and how they only went out for a few days, to draw up a peace treaty," she replied, recalling how the days had turned to weeks, then to months.

"A few days is it. Unless they feel like wrestling a chunk of ice out in space for air and water; they don't have any other source of fresh oxygen they can breathe. That does put a limit on the trip," he reminded her, smiling. She gave him a nod of her head.

"Don't remind me of any other, possible problems, which can occur," she quipped back, trying not to get gloomy about it.

"He'll be back before you know it. Mitt and Axel won't let them tarry about, too long. And you can always check up on them, your own way, since your Talents aren't dimmed by a pending birth," he encouraged her. She smiled, remembering that she could. She'd give it a try right after dinner, when things should be quieter.

"I bet Mitt's having the time of her life! She and Axel make a good team." Maren laughed at this, nodding his head.

"What about Dr. Cruthers? He's like a cub being let out for his first night away from home!" Maren said, still laughing. He was accompanying Garth and Sabin, while Rowan was with Mitt and Axel. "And I never thought Rowan would take on such a thing, either. How come he outranks us? I wanted to go," he pressed. Ryes shook her head in response, as she sighed. Somehow, she was struggling to find the humor in her heart, today. Seeing them off this morning had been so hard to do – even surrounded by family and friends!

"Hey, are you two going to lunch, or not?" Dotti demanded, looking into Ryes' office. "I'm starving!"

"We're ready," Ryes assured her, standing up.

"I'm only glad there're no ice storms raging outside," Maren teased her. Ryes laughed at last, shaking her head. Somehow this was the release she needed. Dotti's eyes looked startled for a moment, as she recalled that day, then she smiled and gave him a nod of agreement.

"Me, too," she supplied, as the three of them left for lunch, laughing now. Larisa smiled, relieved they'd finally gotten Ryes to release her worry. Then realized she was hungry too, so quickly rushed to join them, closing the office door behind her.

"Approaching Trinity, Sir," Ensign Tiller reported from his station, looking relieved to see it at last. The first leg of their dangerous venture was over, with a hopefully safe harbor to set to. He looked up to see the thoughtful expression upon Commander Kaminski's face.

"Any response to our hails, yet?" he asked the communications officer. She looked up from her board to meet his eyes, since he had turned to her.

"No Sir," she replied, appearing concerned, "I read they're receiving us, but aren't responding. I'm monitoring short range communications and there's some chatter about us, Sir," Ensign Ortin warned in a low voice, hoping it didn't carry far.

"Pipe it to my station," he ordered, noting her concern. She was too attentive to her duties for him to ignore it.

"Aye, Sir," she replied with a hint of a smile, and small sigh of relief.

"Anything to report Mister?" Captain Walker asked as he entered the bridge and approached Kaminski's board. His second in command swiveled around to face him, still partly listening in on what the colonists below were saying.

"From all scans, it appears Guardian Starport is dead. We'll be within visual range in another forty-five minutes, Sir. And as far as Trinity's concerned, they refuse to respond to our hails. From the local station gossip, there's fear running through them like wildfire; that we'll bring the Darkens back down upon them with our presence," he reported. Walker's face was grim. It wasn't unexpected, but they sorely needed repairs. If the starport was usable, then they'd utilize it, otherwise they'd have to deal with the colonists face-to-face.

"First, we'll see what's left of Guardian, then deal with Trinity, if we have to take that step. We can call them upon their allegiance to United Terran Fleet and the Terran Republic of Worlds. We'll remind them Earth hasn't fallen yet, and they still owe her several obligations. How many ships are still with us?" he finally asked, worried about the stragglers.

"Six. The Carpenter still hasn't reported back, Sir." There was a sigh of regret in Kaminski's voice at this. He hated handing out suicide missions. The Carpenter had dropped back to divert the three

pursuing, Darken ships. They still had The Gungnir unaccounted for
as yet, too.

This dropped down their original twelve ships to seven. They
only lost three, breaking through the Darken's lines. The Aries'
Wrath, herself, had sustained heavy damage, as had The Orit's Tablet.
If Trinity's colonists were unwilling to help them effect repairs, it'd be
a long time before either ship would be ready to return to Earth - if
ever. The Aurora and Freedom were damaged, but if they could
salvage equipment off Guardian, they'd soon be fit once more. This
left The Dagger, Malta and Mjölnir to carry on their original mission.
He had them lagging behind, in case the Carpenter failed, until they
were sure of their welcome, or a solid opportunity to be repaired.

"We'll make it," Walker assured him, clasping his shoulder to
encourage him. "They can't all be ostriches." He saw doubts in his
First's eyes, but neither one said anything further in front of the
bridge crew.

"I'm more concerned about them firing upon us, right now.
They sound crazy down there, Sir," he netted him, offering him a
com-bud, so the Captain could hear some of it for himself. He
frowned as he took it and put it on. He fingered up and down through
the channels, himself, as his frown deepened in concern.

"I see what you mean. Stay on the alert. Until they can get
someone with some guts to stand up and respond to our hails, we'll
officially maintain ignorance. Keep a sharp eye to Trinity, and let me
know when the starport's in view, and if at all possible, keep Guardian
between us and them," he ordered, making his decision. He wanted
to get on the wire and tell those ignorant, backwoods colonists exactly
what he thought of their situation. As far as he was concerned, let
the Darkens have them as soon as they were gone! He wondered
how things fared out among the other surviving colonies? And what
of this station on Monrush IV? Would they have the supplies and
know-how to help them with any real repairs?

"That does it with this one," Axel reported as he and Garth
drifted in space, far above the elliptic of Monrush's solar system,
having just released their first warning satellite into space. They had
released the communications-weather satellites shortly after take-off
from Tayna, early in the morning four days ago. Those had been easy
comparted to this one, but they'd already sent Mitt and Sabin back
inside, doing the final adjustments. Garth smiled at this, admiring
space. It was so like the view Ryes had shown him before, through

her Empath. He hoped someday to be able to see Tayna and space like she did, with his own Empath Talent.

"Well, next month we can always start building our first starport," Sabin teased with a chuckle. This brought laughter out of the rest of them in response.

"I'll review your designs next week," Garth replied with a laugh. He signaled to Axel that his scans were indicating the satellite had acquired a stable orbit. "Mission complete. We'll check on her again on our return," he ordered.

"Heading back in," Axel agreed, smiling. A starport, indeed! Their resources had been taxed just building these few satellites! If only more real machine and electronic techs had survived. He and Mitt were hard pressed enough as it was, with trying to train others, and maintain what they still had. The salvaging of the two shuttles had been a blessing and a curse. They took him away from his other projects, including his wife Kerry, far too much. At least they were operational and proving to be useful.

"About time. I think Ryes is going to drive me nuts with wanting a report every five minutes," Mitt told them, hinting to her brother to talk with his wife.

"This is what I get for only leaving for a couple of weeks last fall," Garth assured her. He activated his thrusters and propelled himself back, along the length of his tether toward the Avenger. "Suggest to her to run the tests designated for the satellites, then place a call to Gracie and see how she's doing to test out the ones we set up before? That should keep her busy for a few minutes."

"Now there's an idea," Mitt agreed, watching Axel approach the Defender, relieved he was all right. She still worried about any micrometeorite swarms nearby. She switched her channel and transmitted Garth's suggestion as an order. It might buy them a little time. It wasn't that she didn't understand what Ryes was going through, but that if she'd leave them alone, they'd be able to complete their work more quickly.

"Coming in," Axel reported, as he reached the airlock. He set up the sequence for going back into the ship, getting green lights across his tell-tales, and notching down his stress level. He hated space walks!

"Affirmative," Rowan answered with a smile. "Mitt's talking with Ryes right now," he explained. There was laughter heard over the radio in response.

"Coming in, Sabin," Garth told him, smiling. His sister wasted no time, for sure. "Mitt? Tell Ryes that I'll talk with her in a few minutes," he requested.

"Affirmative," she replied, grinning. "She's initiating the test sequences on all four satellites now, with Neil monitoring her," she reported.

"Good," Sabin said, knowing Neil would keep her busy, and out of their hair for a little while, at least. As soon as the pressure equalized, he entered the main cabin, and Ethan helped Garth take off his suit.

"She does have cause," Ethan reminded him, in a low voice. "If it hadn't been for Maren last winter, we would've lost her and the children. None of us would've ever suspected she'd go out into an ice storm, in her efforts to try to reach the two of you. She was so heart-broken and desperate."

"I know," Garth replied with a heavy sigh. He'd meant for Maren to show him that memory through Raya, having heard the telling. He recalled feeling her attempts on Winterfest Day, but hadn't thought she'd go out to sit in the middle of an ice storm to do it! "I owe her cousin a heavy debt, I'll never be able to repay."

"What's a debt if it's all from the heart? There's no need for obligation, when it's close friends and family; only a sharing of the love you already give each other," he gently scolded, smiling merrily. "Debts only apply to strangers, whom you don't fully trust."

"That's true," Sabin agreed smiling, having floated to their lower aft cabin to see what was taking them so long. "Should we head out for our next target?" he asked. The sooner they placed the satellites, the faster they'd get back home.

"Let's get out of this area slowly and keep an eye to this one's stability. Then we'll head azimuth to place our last one. How many hours did Axel project until we'll be in the right place?" Garth asked. They had planned one high azimuth to the plane of the planets and one low azimuth, to help cover as many variables as possible.

"Somewhere around sixty-five hours," he replied, as Ethan nodded his head in agreement, placing the helmet and gloves upon their shelf, then sealed the compartment. As soon as Garth finished removing the suit, they could secure the locker and let the cleaning/decontamination cycle start up. The suit would be clean and refreshed and ready in under an hour.

"So, the sooner we get going, the more quickly we can get back home and ease Ryes' mind, somewhat," he ordered, smiling.

"I'll go relay your orders," Sabin replied with a knowing grin, turning back for the cockpit. The weightlessness wasn't anywhere as bad as he imagined. It was like a slow-motion dance, which he enjoyed. He could imagine what it'd be like to have Ardis up here with him. Even with just a few days between them, he found he missed her so very much.

"Sir, Trinity's Guardian Starport coming into view," Ensign Tiller stated. The Captain sat in his chair, seeing what remained of the huge starport for himself. Silence reined upon the bridge. They'd seen the signs from the scanner reports and the bits of debris scattered near its orbit, as they approached. As the Aries' Wrath stood out from the wreckage, Walker's heart sank to the bottom of his boots.

"Anything new from the scanners?" he requested, keeping his voice steady and business-like. He was The Captain, and calm and always in control.

"There're traces of life still aboard, Sir. They're not plant life and are too large to be small animals, but no one's responding to our hails from Guardian, either," Kaminski reported, "There're a few areas which seem to have power, and oxygen-filled compartments. Including a docking bay section."

"All stop. Maintain our distance, keep her between us and Trinity, and alert the rest of the ships to stand back behind us," Captain Walker ordered, coming to a decision. It was Command's orders to try for Trinity first. "I want a team sent over to determine if we can salvage supplies for our own and The Tablet's repairs. If there are any survivors who wish to accompany us, they may be brought onboard on the strict understanding they will follow all directives we hand down to them. Relay orders to the remaining ships and inform the captains that I'll hold a conference in two hours on the situation in our briefing room," he ordered.

"Aye, Sir," Kaminski responded.

"And let the rest of our ships know to be wary of the colonists," he added.

"Yes, Sir," he replied, seeing why with the increasing panic in the voices over the frequencies they were tapping. It was disturbing to think these were once civilized people. Captain Walker left the bridge, heading for his office. In a way he couldn't blame them. It appeared they'd been heavily bombed by the Darkens before, still they had to know they weren't here to attack them.

Kaminski set to work setting up the survey team to send to Guardian. It was an easy task and quickly done. The people under him understood the importance of even this seemly small mission. The fact that there were survivors gave everyone some small anchor of hope. He realized he felt better being able to rescue others, even if they, too, needed some kind of rescue.

"Sir?" Ensign Ortin requested Kaminski's attention, when he was finished. He turned to look at her, seeing the indecision in her eyes.

"Yes, Ensign?" he prompted, giving her permission to speak.

"I had a message from Fleet about one of The Star Quest's survivors, who'd come from Trinity. Should I still relay the packet?" she asked, hoping. Kaminski thought on it. Walker hadn't said they weren't to talk with the colonists, and it was from Fleet.

"Go ahead and send it. If any of his, or her, family's left, they might appreciate hearing it. I'll take full responsibility," he replied, smiling. He hoped it'd make some of them twist in agony a little. They were here to protect them, whether, or not, they'd ever appreciate their efforts. At least they'd made It this far. It was only because their telepaths had given them enough warning to keep them clear of most of the trouble spots. He hoped for the crews of The Carpenter and Gungnir. Commander Stefanovik was his cousin and was now serving as the captain of The Carpenter.

"Aye Sir, thank you, Sir," she replied. He gave her a nod of his head, then she turned back to her board with a smile upon her lips. He understood her! It'd only take a few seconds to relay, but she wanted to hear their responses. It might give them something to think on, other than their own misery. After all, if they brought news of a missing son, who was found, and still alive, it might give them pause to realize they weren't the only ones out here struggling to survive. She bet herself that as soon as they were operational, they'd be underway, straight toward the Monrush system. She didn't think the Wrath could stand much more punishment.

"Who's there?" a voice demanded out of the darkness, near the twisted wreckage of a ship's gantry. The trooper paused and stood his ground, on what was once one of the ship's docking areas in the starport.

"Sergeant Carrillo of the Aries' Wrath. We're here from Earth," he replied. The five other men with him shifted uncomfortably but held their lights steady, as he directed. They had their night vision scans up and could clearly see the dozen raggedy-looking survivors, who hid with indecision clearly upon their faces. "We're here to evacuate any survivors from Guardian."

"We can leave?" a woman questioned, her haggard face showing a surprised hope dawning.

"About time," another voice spoke up, as a thin young man stepped from out of a nearby doorway, a large case in his hand. He strode directly up to the waiting men, smiling, as if he expected to be openly welcomed among friends, who'd only gone out for a day's outing.

"Lieutenant Alec Scott reporting for duty," he said, extending his identification to the sergeant. Carrillo took it and scanned it as his corporal looked at the case he was carrying.

"We don't take pets," Corporal Hines declared, seeing a black and white furred animal within.

"Storme's a hemicat," Lt. Scott informed him, the slightest edge of ice in his voice. "She's not a pet." The hemicat stuck out her paw through the bars for him to scan. Surprised, he did so and saw she was registered in his system, too.

"Can we come too?" a man requested, having come forward, with the rest of the ragtag group following more cautiously.

"Come on out, we're leaving," Alec responded loudly, with a smile.

"If Alec thinks it's safe, it is," another added with surety in his voice, as he stepped up behind their leader.

"A psi," one of the troopers whispered to another with relief in his voice.

"How many are left?" Carrillo demanded, having already messaged back to command about the situation. An added telepath was a blessing right now. With the addition of his hemicat to boost his abilities, he was a good asset to have on hand.

"One hundred eighty-two total remaining. We have forty techs from different fields, twelve administrators, sixteen children, twenty-five firefighters, five paramedics, eleven security, sixteen dockworkers, two secretaries, three barkeeps, twenty-two ship crewmen, six housewives, twenty-three general laborers and me," Alec reported, smiling with assurance.

"All right, let's get everyone assembled down by the shuttles for evacuation," Carrillo ordered, motioning for his men to start gathering them in. As they activated their helmet lights, more of the timid survivors started stepping out of hiding. Carrillo could now see the tattered remains of a Fleet shipsuit upon the telepath. It was badly torn up and filthy, but he still wore it with pride.

"Commander Briggs requests you report directly to him upon The Aurora, Lieutenant Scott," he informed him, saluting him more formally. Lt. Scott returned the salute, then gave him a smile in return.

"It's been a while since I've seen Ash," he commented as he headed the group, walking toward the shuttles. Tears of relief, which threatened to blind him, were all he outwardly displayed at their rescue. Two years and they were finally free!

"One hundred eighty-two out of what might have been forty-thousand?" Walker asked, double-checking what he thought the landing party had reported over the com.

"Yes," James responded, not letting himself take it in right now, even after seeing the debrief vids. "Yun's already claimed the psi, since he's served with his crew in the past."

"That's fine," Linden replied, knowing the Aurora didn't have any psi's on her now, after that last skirmish. "Was there anyone else we could use? Any medical personnel?" he pressed, hoping.

"The firefighters, paramedics, some of the techs, but I'm not sure about the ship crewmen who survived. Security might be useful, too," he reported, looking at his comp display. "We only found a few scraps of humanity out of the destruction. From their stories, it was pretty horrific, and surviving the aftermath had been mostly a matter of luck. They tried to evacuate the station to Trinity last minute, but most of those ships were blown to bits." James didn't appear happy to deliver this report.

"Use all we can," Lindell said, knowing his First would have the matter well in hand, and might even interview the crewmen himself. "And the kids?" James' eyebrow raised at this as he shook his head, knowing children on working starships was not a good situation.

"Three mothers have decided to take their sons with them down to Trinity, when we can get a shuttle planetside for them. The remaining eight are being taken care of by one of the barkeeps, who is an uncle of two of them, and one of the administrators who was a friend of the mother of the eight-year-old. They're familiar faces for the children. They're going onward to our end-point destination in Monrush. They want to be as far away from here, as possible. They don't feel safe on Trinity," he informed him, waiting for his response. He didn't know how he'd react to children aboard.

"No promises, but if they want to come along, they can. Still, I won't have children running wild on the ship," he ordered in an even voice. James nodded his head in agreement.

"We'll keep them under control. They're still recovering from the trauma of the attack and the long isolation on the destroyed station. The doctors feel they're being too quiet, so probably by the time we reach Tayna, they should just be starting to behave more normally. They will not be an issue," he promised. "I've come up with a list of eighty-five people in total who're serious about relocating to Trinity, if we can convince them to let a shuttle land."

"Do what you can," Lindell ordered, nodding his agreement. "All I want is the area safe and clear, so we can get patched up."

"Aye, Sir," James agreed, "I'll make it happen." Lindell gave him a nod then stood up and left the room. James sighed, then called up his comp's com to get a few things started.

A View of the Stars

"This reeks to high heaven, Lin," Captain Wing Yun declared as his face betrayed his anxiety over their desperate situation. "Are the rest of the colonies like this," he wondered? The Aurora was his first ship, and he didn't intend to lose her!

"I know it stinks," Walker assured him. He was the task force commander, and the morale was quickly bottoming out, as the colonists sounded more aggressive over their continued presence. "But even if there are enough serviceable docks on Guardian, we don't dare use them. Trinity may decide to launch against us at any moment and we'd be sitting ducks. We could have the Tablet and Wrath pull in to load up with what we can and get some of the more difficult repairs done, but we'd need the rest of you standing out to keep an eye on Trinity while we do so. Command never took this situation into account."

"Perhaps out among the other colonies some sanity may still exist?" Captain Christa Kaplan suggested. "We need supplies, medicines, repairs and some good surgeons to help care for our wounded." Distress colored her voice, while she retained a poker face.

"I hope we'll find it, Christa," Walker replied, "but, for our money, The Wrath and Tablet are making a beeline to Monrush IV, after we scavenged what we can from Guardian, since the best we'll be able to do is limp along. We'll take the survivors with us. The rest of you carry out our main mission and get an assessment of any remaining colonial forces. Rendezvous with us at Monrush IV and we'll decide our course of action from there. We should have an idea of what that old Amitell station is capable of, by then."

"Shouldn't one of us go along to provide you with some cover?" Yun asked. "Who knows what Darken forces are still roaming freely in the starlanes, and wasn't it a system near Monrush where they were first discovered?"

"Yes, it was," Walker agreed, nodding his head grimly. "We might need the fire power and assist. Which is more capable right now of bringing a fight? The Freedom, or the Aurora?" he asked.

"The Freedom," Kaplan replied quickly, a puzzled frown upon her face.

"Then, we'll borrow The Aurora," Walker decided.

"Sir? There's a report," an ensign said, stepping into the briefing room after knocking. Walker gave him a nod of his head, activating his terminal. After a few seconds he smiled his relief. He waved the man out of the room.

"The Carpenter will be rejoining us soon. Mission accomplished, the Darken ships were successfully led off on a tangent. Commander Stefanovik reports all's secure with minimal damage to his ship and the loss of only two additional crewmen. I think the Fates are favoring us for the moment, ladies and gentlemen," he informed them, looking up with a smile upon his face. "Now, let's review our strategies in the light of Trinity's warm welcome," he suggested, calling up the star charts in the holo tank, in the center of the table. The remaining six ships' captains gathered closer.

"I never knew how beautiful it truly was out here," Rowan sighed as he tried to fall asleep in freefall aboard their small ship. It was strange with the push of the drive pulling against them in a direction other than the "down" he knew all his life. He was looking out the front port, as he was strapped in closest to it. Axel smiled at this, recalling his first time in space.

"I never tire of it," he replied with a sigh, "I was only five years old the first time I saw space up close like this. We were only on a vacation to Shangri-La on Deimos, but I've never forgotten it."

"Where's Deimos?" Mitt asked, not having heard him mention it before.

"It's one of the moons of Mars, the fourth planet of the Sol system. We lived on Mars. My dad worked at the University and my mom worked for an aerospace company. We had a big family, so as soon as I was old enough, I shipped out to go see what lay beyond our small solar system. Amitell seemed the best way, aside from joining the military. Even with all that's happened, I still don't regret being here. Mars was getting pretty crowded when I left," he told her.

"Oh, to be able to choose which world you want to live upon," she sighed in return.

"Even if we had real starships, I'd still live on Tayna. She's pretty comfortable," he replied, chuckling. "I'd like my kids to have a choice, but I think I've found my home. After all that red rock and sand, green trees and grass are refreshing."

"I'd still like to see what lies out here," Rowan ventured. "I've lived most of my life in one small village. It'd be nice to be able to tread on a new world, just once." Mitt laughed lightly at hearing the yearning in his voice.

"I'd like to go exploring, but I think Tayna's where I belong, too. Let my cubs decide things for themselves, but I know where I belong," she told them, smiling into the darkness. She and Minn had spoken true-mate vows and Tayna felt so "right" to her.

"Goodnight, Mitt, Rowan," Axel wished her as he yawned.

"Goodnight," she returned. "Goodnight to you too, Rowan," she wished.

"Goodnight to you both," he replied, still unable to tear his eyes away from the view.

"Well, time to pack it in," Brenda ordered Neil, as they were playing an intense game of Space Battles on their handheld minicomps. "Figure out who won and shut it down." Dotti smiled up at her as she and Maren were playing one of the teams.

"Just a minute, we have to finish up this round," Torr protested. Ryes, Brenda, and Ardis all exchanged glances. They'd heard this one before! Dodi just smiled as she watched them play, a sleeping Tobin in her arms. She looked like she'd found her true place and happiness, as they all welcomed her into their circle. Shadd merely chose to not come over if Torr and Dodi were around. Ryes and Ardis had adjusted to make sure to include her in other activities, when they could. Still, Dodi was welcomed in their homes.

"All the cubs have crashed and it's going to be a long day tomorrow," Ryes pointed out. She didn't want to say that since no one had left her alone for a minute, she hadn't had a chance to check up on the shuttle crews her own way, yet. She wanted to see for herself that Garth and the rest were all right! She was fidgeting and a bit restless now but was trying not to shove everyone out the door. Ardis caught her eye, seeing she was impatient about something, and that set off alarms in her head.

"What've you got planned, Ryes?" she pressed loudly, needing the others able to see it too. After last Winterfest, they decided to keep a close eye upon her, whenever Garth was away. She appeared startled by the question; her eye wide, as if caught in a plot.

"I want to check up on them - my way," she finally told her with a sigh and a dark gold blush, seeing the rest were now looking at them, too. There were questions in their eyes, then a dawning realization in some of them.

"Oh, to hell with this," Maren declared, deactivating his minicomp, before his turn was finished. "That's much more fun."

"You're including me," Ardis insisted, smiling, "It's been a while since I've gotten to venture out to see Tayna with you. I want to see it again."

"Alright, everyone who wants to see Tayna and how our two shuttle crews are faring, gather `round," she invited, finally giving in, knowing they wouldn't leave her alone until she included them all. Her friends moved to sit near her on the floor, joining hands with smiles upon their faces.

"You too, my dear lady," Torr ordered Dodi with a smile. She blushed as she lay Tobin down upon his blanket, in his stroller. "And the both of you, too," he said, nodding to Monty and Denas as they also delayed. They were talking in low voices, sitting removed from the rest. They moved to join their circle reluctantly.

"But I've seen Tayna from Ryes' point of view before," Monty assured him. Then saw the determination in Torr's eyes and gave in.

"Won't this be too much?" Denas asked, unsure.

"No," Ryes assured her. "I've been getting a lot of practice at this lately. I'm learning how to handle numbers," she told her. "I don't know if by stretching out with my abilities, I actually increase their power, or if by trying new things, I learn how to focus and handle things better. All I know is the more I push at what Dr. Cruthers calls `the envelope,' the better I become at utilizing my Talents."

"If you need to draw upon my Booster Talent, feel free," Maren reminded her, smiling.

"I think I have plenty of energy, but I'll keep it in mind," she replied. "Now everyone join hands and relax while we form our inner link," she instructed. She saw them complying, nodding her head to her cousin as he joined them.

Once the link was formed and everyone settled down, she opened Empath Talent, drawing freely upon her own Booster, then drew them out to experience the night life near Winterhaven. She reached outwards to encounter the sleeping thoughts of the inhabitants of Winterhaven, itself. Stretching out further she encountered their windracers, as they dozed in their paddocks, then she lightly brushed the minds of some skin-wings as she drew the others upwards. The skin-wings were feasting as they caught the insects in midair, which were drawn to the lights around their complex. The deaths of the insects drove her onwards. She moved higher, finding a hunting night bird as he scanned the soaring land beneath him, seeking for the warmth given off by his prey. As he dove for a scatter-chase, she pulled them upwards once more. They finally drifted high above the clouds, looking down upon Tayna herself, as they passed quickly through the atmosphere, catching up to the daylight side of their world.

"Watching a colorful world turning below is what I never tire of," Brenda sent out into their inner commune. There was amusement from the other humans and Denas, but amazement from the rest, as many were seeing all this for the first time. They had never imagined what their world would look like from up above.

"It's absolutely beautiful!" Ardis declared. Her heart was pounding with excitement at this journey. Each time seemed so different and amazing!

"I don't think I'd ever tire of it, either," Ryes agreed, smiling to herself. She hoped to never become so jaded as to take such a breathtaking view for granted. "Let's go find them, now," she warned, turning her attention outwards, away from Tayna. The pulse of life and dance of the cosmos spread out before them, amazing everyone anew. There was life among the stars too. It wasn't something they were used to, as they could clearly feel its rhythm.

"Some have said we're merely the children of the stars. Now I can see why," Neil dared, astounded to be so drawn to the stars themselves.

"That's what it feels like!" Maren agreed, joyfully.

"That's why I usually stop right here," Ryes told them. "I don't want to lose myself out there. Once I'm sure I can safely return to myself, then someday I may journey beyond Monrush, but for now, the only star I've brushed is Monrush."

"A cautious explorer," Brenda teased.

"At times, not cautious enough," Maren countered with a mental laugh. Ryes laughed in agreement, then stretched out, knowing their crews were heading azimuth to the solar system plane and found both shuttles, very quickly.

"It seems they've hardly gone anywhere, yet," Minn protested.

"They're not going very far in the first place," Maren replied as Ryes homed in upon the occupants.

"Not everyone can travel upon the wings of a thought like Ryes can," Torr pointed out, mentally chuckling. "If we could keep her awake and looking out here all the time, we wouldn't need satellites."

"Could you check to see if anyone's near us, first?" Neil questioned, wondering how far she could perceive things, which didn't belong.

"There're patterns to life. I can tell if it exists, and if it has a higher order, as we hold in our villages and towns," she replied. "There was a pattern of such likeness upon one of the moons of Monrush III, Tyssen, the one time I was out here exploring before, but haven't had the time then to investigate further."

"Could you show us?" Dotti pressed, needing to see if there were other survivors from the Star Quest, too. The others caught her concern.

"They could be another people, entirely," Torr warned her, not wanting her to get her hopes up too quickly.

"They could be more starmen," Brenda cautioned, seeing what Torr meant.

"Would the humans still have survived this long?" Dodi ventured, speaking out for the first time, surprising herself, having not meant to be so loud.

"Yes, they could have, but most likely it'd be the children of any survivors," Monty assured her. "A human's average life-span is now about a hundred and forty years. And there've been a few people who have lived up to a hundred and eighty years, or so."

"That's with good food and medical care," Dotti added. "Let's go check out that moon, Ryes," she urged.

"Yes. You started this and now we all need to know," Ardis agreed, feeling her reluctance.

"It still lies within the bounds of the Monrush system," Maren pointed out. "And we can always tell our intrepid astronauts what we discover, on our way back."

"All right," she finally gave in. Ryes reached out toward Tyssen, then hovered over the area on its moon which held order. It was unmistakable to all of them that here existed life, a strongly ordered life. She gently reached downwards. There was a thin atmosphere, much more so than Tayna. It gave her misgivings, but she plunged on downward, seeking them out. She found a great bubble resting upon the side of a deep canyon. It mostly protected the main living area, which appeared to be crude huts, overall. Also, it looked as if they utilized the natural caves here as dwellings too. There were two wells providing water, after a fashion. They had small, terraced gardens, which seemed to sparsely support the peoples, as well as some animal pens. All-in-all, it reminded Ryes too much of Matlowe Village.

"That's an environment shelter," Neil assured her, recognizing it. It appeared of human manufacture.

"Look, there are people in odd clothing," Denas pointed out, seeing them first. There was a small line of people walking with a small, covered wagon, heading towards the shelter. Ryes brought them closer. It turned out that here was another mix of starmen and humans. But instead of being an equality, it looked like the humans were enslaved, having to pull the cart under the crack of a whip. This brought out Ryes' anger suddenly, as a bright hot spark. She was outraged by what she was witnessing!

"How can they do this? We are almost the same people?" Denas demanded, puzzled, and deeply disturbed.

"Maybe we shouldn't contact them after all?" Maren suggested, feeling Ryes' anger welling up from deep within.

"No. We should save the humans from this, at least," Ryes decided.

"Look, we've been noticed," Dotti pointed out, indicating a starwoman, who was looking up to them, puzzled. She stopped, looked around the area about her, then closed her eyes.

"Who are you?" she demanded. She was using Mind Voice – being clearly understood.

"I'm Ryes from Tayna. And my friends are with me. How can you think of yourselves as civilized, if you enslave humans in such a manner?" she demanded right up front, needing answers.

"Who are you to judge us and tell us what to do?" she returned, not believing she could be talking with someone from another world! The rest of her hunting party stopped as they saw she was standing still, using her Talent, and wondering what the problem was.

"I'm the Chief Executive Officer of Winterhaven. These humans fall under my jurisdiction, and I will have them safely back!" she challenged her - directly.

"You can't do ANYTHING to us, if you're on Tayna," she retorted, smiling to herself, sure of this truth.

This was the last straw! Ryes suddenly reached out and flipped her head over heels, suspending her in midair with Manipulator. The woman screamed as she hung out of the reach of her friends. She would've lost her link with them, but Ryes held that firm too, at the same time. Denas opened her Talent to help Ryes, strengthening her connection to the meld and the pool of power. She immediately felt her gratitude for the assist.

"Don't tempt me," Ryes warned, then lowered her slowly to the ground once more. "The gravity's lighter there," she told the others gathered with her, so only they heard this observation. A ripple of amusement ran through their thoughts at this daring of hers, which this stranger clearly heard.

"I'm called Nesa. If you can save your humans, will you please return us to Tayna, too? Our great-great-greats came from Tayna and were shipwrecked here on Booda, as were the parents of our humans. We promise to change, if you would return us to our homeworld, too," she pleaded, all arrogance cast aside. This could be their one and only chance of finding a new life back on the world her ancestors originated. It was only legend to them all now.

"I will advise our Base Commander, my husband, Garth," she told her, still not trusting her. "The decision will rest with him. I'll return tomorrow to let you know what he says." With this she pulled back, feeling the first touches of her limitations. Maren added in his own Booster Talent, granting her his support. She showered him with her love and appreciation. It wasn't as if this outing diminished her pool of power, but that his was more focused than hers. She thought his training with Saree had helped and she'd have to study a way to improve her own Talent use, now.

"I never knew you could do something like that!" Denas commented, astounded. "Actually, extending your Manipulator and using it on another world! I am amazed and have never heard of anyone doing that in the before!"

"I didn't know I could do that before either. But, if I could stop a wall of flame from engulfing people far in Tayna's past, I thought why not try it at least?" They all saw a short wisp of her memory of that event, startling some of her friends. "Here're our shuttles, again," she told them, having drawn back that far, very quickly. She'd felt Denas' surprise at the way she used her Empath Talent, too. It must be a different kind than she'd known before.

"It seems they're just settling down for the night," Brenda observed. Ryes' anger over the way the humans were being treated amazed her. She cared deeply for them all and would protect these strange humans to the full extent of her amazing abilities.

"Then let's wish them a goodnight," Dotti urged. There was agreement from the rest, so Ryes lightly brushed their adventurers' minds, allowing everyone to say their goodnight wishes. Then she drew back from them to solely encompass Garth and Sabin's minds. She showed them their encounter with the inhabitants of Booda and asked what should be done about it. They clearly saw her heart and her need to rescue the humans trapped in such a hopeless life.

"We'll check out the situation, ourselves," Garth told her, seeing the way she could still reach out with her Manipulator Talent to reach another world. "I'll RADIO you about what we decide, after we place this last satellite."

"Why should we have bothered coming out here? She could've just as easily have placed it for us," Sabin suggested, humor in his mental voice. This sparked laughter all around, as both he and Garth had made their comments "loud" enough for the rest to hear them.

"If any problems develop with the satellites, we can always have Ryes check them out," Neil supplied, agreeing with him.

"And effect the repairs, if needed," Ethan asserted, happy with this idea.

"I'd better go," Ryes told them, feeling it was time. "I'll check on all of you tomorrow," she warned. She and Ardis gave their husbands their love, as well as the rest of the shuttle crews, along with the rest of their friends giving them their love, then Ryes released the shuttle crews. She returned her friends back to Tayna, and to themselves, once more, making sure everyone was safe. They opened their eyes, back in her living room.

"We touched another world!" Dodi declared, still amazed with all she experienced.

"And they definitely don't think like us," Maren pointed out with a sigh. "At least our own people are safe," he added, smiling as he looked at his cousin.

"I think this was what I was trying to do last winter, but the cubs were almost due, and my Talents were no longer mine to command," she told him, smiling. "And now they're much further away."

"Thank goodness there's no ice storms either," Torr returned, chuckling as he stood and extended his hand to his new wife. Dodi smiled as she took it and got to her feet.

"Maybe some floor pillows for next time," Dotti suggested, grinning as Maren helped her up. Then he turned to help his cousin, who was already on her feet, smiling impishly at him.

"That's a good idea," she agreed. "We might as well have some comforts."

"Goodnight, Ryes," Neil wished her, as first he, and Brenda gave her kisses and hugs, then to the others in the room. They gathered their daughter and things, then headed for the door. "Goodnight," they both wished before leaving.

"Goodnight," Torr and Dodi wished them. "Goodnight, Ryes, thanks," he told her, giving her a hug, too. The others quickly followed suit until only she, Denas and Monty remained.

"Goodnight, cousin," Denas wished her, wrapping an arm around Monty's waist. This shocked Ryes, while bringing out a chuckle of happiness from Denas. "Monty invited me over tonight if I wanted to go. If you don't mind..." she informed her.

"Not at all," she assured them, smiling. She stepped over and hugged them both, wishing them a whispered goodnight. "I'll see you both tomorrow, then."

"Yes, ma'am," Monty agreed, smiling in delight, finally relaxing. His stomach was slowly unknotting, having expected some kind of scolding, which he realized would've been out of character for her. "Goodnight." He picked up Denas' overnight bag.

"Goodnight," she wished them, seeing them out the door, then closed it thoughtfully. She realized she didn't want to see either of them hurt, but it was their choice. And after what Maren put her through last year, she was done with meddling with others' lives! Ryes turned off the lights and went to bed, sure in the knowledge Garth was truly still safe and sound.

Decisions

Chapter 14

"We're pulling into Guardian," Captain Walker ordered his First when he arrived back on the bridge. Kaminski looked surprised but turned to relay his order. "Have the other ships stand out and maintain a sharp watch for now," he added.

Ever since they transmitted the packet from Fleet about a missing ensign from Trinity, the colonists had quieted down. They had to be discussing things, at least he hoped. Since the virtual silence had reined for over four hours, he decided they should act, while they could and take advantage of the distraction.

The last of the survivors had been evacuated and spread out to the various ships, so no one vessel was loaded down with them. It also split them up; in case they decided they wanted to help the colonists below by making trouble up here. The station had been quartered and thoroughly searched, to be sure it was as safe as it could be, and there were no hidden traps, or other surprises.

"Orders have been relayed to the rest of the force," Kaminski informed him, as Walker took his chair. "Pulling into Guardian," he stated, as the ship banked and maneuvered toward one of the still usable docks, which was large enough to accommodate the Wrath.

"Easy as she goes," Walker ordered, seeing his helmswoman steering her with a sure hand.

"Aye Sir," she replied, not taking her eyes off her screens. It was an easy dock, but with the threat of the colonists below, it had her a little wary.

"Mr. Kaminski, have the repair detail scrambled, as soon as we have dock and seal, then have a salvage detail out to procure what other supplies we and the other ships need. Let's get what we can finished smartly," he ordered.

"Aye Sir," Kaminski replied, turning to his terminal, as he kept an eye to the screen displaying the view of the starport. "Detail crews report their readiness," he reported, after a few moments. He'd had the crews already scrambled and ready for his orders, so they were now ready to disembark as soon as they had dock and seal.

"Very well," he replied, smiling to himself. Kaminski was the best in Fleet, after all. He'd realized it himself, as they fought their way through the Darken's lines. He had no qualms with him serving at his side. The ship eased into the dock, touching the port seals with the most skilled, delicate touch he could imagine. Considering what they had to work with, it was inspired piloting with having to dodge debris. There was a flash of lights indicating they had docked, then another to tell them they were secure.

"Docked and sealed," Kaminski reported, "Sir, detail crews dispatched."

"It's only a matter of time, now," Walker sighed out, deciding to watch it from the bridge. If all went well, they'd stay a few days to affect their repairs, then back out and let the Tablet, Freedom and Aurora have their turns. If that went all right, then they'd give the remaining ships a chance at the docks. It all depended upon the colonists, now. He wanted them as ready as can be for any confrontations they might find, as they ventured further out into the Darken's older territory.

They finally wrestled the larger satellite out of the cargo area and into the dark void around them. It took all four of the younger crewmembers to handle it, leaving the two elders to manage the shuttles, themselves.

"Weightlessness doesn't mean things get any easier," Mitt commented as she realized she'd broken a sweat in this operation and was frustrated by not being able to wipe off her brow. She hit the switch to ensure the suit removed the extra moisture and smiled as it relieved her quickly. Axel laughed at this, giving her a thumbs up.

"That's the truth! In fact, I think it makes things harder," he told her, as she grinned and gave him a nod inside her helmet.

"Do you think the satellite will be safe out here?" Sabin questioned as they aimed the dish toward Tayna, checking the alignment using the signal input they had from Winterhaven's computer.

"No, but it's about as safe as it can be anywhere, except its own hangar," Axel replied with a laugh.

"So, are we going to go out to this Booda, or not?" Mitt asked as Axel checked the computer alignment. Garth and she stood ready, in case they needed to adjust the alignment by hand. Sabin was helping Axel with his computer screens.

"Yes, we are. I want to evaluate exactly what's there, myself. I ran up the computations earlier with Neil's help and we do have the fuel and resources for an investigation," he told her and the others, as they worked.

"What if they decide to try to take our spacecraft, to go back to Tayna by themselves?" Rowan questioned, concerned with such a journey with only the six of them to manage things.

"We have the safety interlocks set already, so only those who're authorized from Winterhaven can pilot these shuttles. We also have Ryes' backing. I'll have her assemble the Talents to keep an eye on things, as we stop to make a call upon our neighbors. With that pool of Talents, I don't think they'll get away with anything," he replied, sure on this score.

"Are we going to bring back any of the inhabitants?" Ethan questioned, just as concerned as Rowan. It seemed a risky venture with such a small crew, especially if the starmen were of a violent nature, to begin with.

"We're limited by our air, water and resources. We'll see," Garth told him, leaving it as a decision for later. It did no good to try to figure out what they could and couldn't do, until they got there and saw things for themselves. He realized, like Ryes, he couldn't tolerate to see anyone abused in such a base manner. He knew slavery would be outlawed upon Tayna, if he had anything to do with it. It was one of their own laws, after all. And he would see it upheld.

"You're right. It doesn't do any good to decide things, until we see what we have to work with for ourselves," Sabin voiced his support.

"Right now, let's get this finished, run our test sequences, have some dinner, then head out for this Boody place," Axel suggested, smiling mischievously.

"Boody, yeah, that's it," Mitt agreed, laughing.

"A wise man always lays a firm course of action," Rowan commented with a chuckle.

"I think so too, and do my best to be wise," Garth stated, smiling. "Is this a stable position?" he pressed.

"Yes. We don't need you two out here, anymore," Sabin responded, seeing Axel's thumbs up in agreement.

"Alright," he replied, "let's head in, Mitt," he urged his sister. He saw her smile and nod through the broad faceplate of the helmet, then turned to gather in his tether, as he activated his suit's small booster jets. They had a new course to lay into the computers and he wanted it done before they took their dinner break.

"Connor Elbridge of Grail City calling the Aries' Wrath, please come in Aries' Wrath," Connor spoke into the microphone set before him upon the console of the sole remaining computer center upon all of Trinity. They risked much in this venture, but he was determined to know all the available facts for himself!

"This is the Aries' Wrath, Mr. Elbridge, how may we help you?" Ensign Ortin replied, all smart sweetness in her voice. Bingo! Her instincts had been right! Here was one of Montague's relatives, probably wanting to know more. She signaled for Mr. Kaminski to monitor the frequency. It'd been a week, but planetary ground travel could be slow, she thought.

"Montague Daniel Elbridge was my great uncle, ma'am, and I need to know if you have any further information than what was included in the message you sent out to us," he replied, nervous as his father and several other elders stood around him as he spoke. It wasn't that he was speaking to a military ship, but that they were there to censure him if he mis-spoke, himself.

"Let me transfer you to Commander Kaminski. If there's anything further to be passed along, he'll have access to that material," she replied, then transferred the signal over to his queue, upon his signal.

"This is Commander James Kaminski," he stated, "Whom am I speaking with, and how may I help you?" he questioned with a smile upon his lips, as he stressed the last word in a leading manner, leaving it to the colonist to reintroduce himself and repeat his request.

"Sir, this is Connor Lee Elbridge of Grail City. Montague Elbridge was my great uncle. We thought he'd been lost long ago and here you pass on this official transcript, which states that he's still alive and living upon a world called Tayna. We've never heard of any world named Tayna, sir. Is there any more news about him you might have available?" he asked, hoping.

"Tayna is the name for the planet the indigenous population granted it. Since they were there long before us, it's now its designated name. It was formerly called Beda IV and the Amitell facility had no name previously. It's now called Winterhaven and is populated by both the indigenous people and what survivors they managed to retrieve from stasis chambers on The Star Quest. It lies near to the system where we first discovered the Darkens, but it appears safe for the time being. I have a few holos which were sent along with the report, if you'd like to see them," he offered. Ensign Ortin signaled that they had traced the signal's origin. He smiled as he gave her a nod of his head. At least they now knew where their main communications equipment lay, for future reference.

"Yes sir, we'd like to see them," was the excited reply. "I never met my uncle, but my dad says I look a lot like him."

"Fine. I'm transmitting the holos to you now," he replied. "Is there anything else we can do for you?" he questioned.

"Could you please tell us why you're here?"

"We're here to unite the remaining colonial forces. Sol system is still under siege, but we're confident we can raise enough ships to break back through and end it. Since Trinity has no standing fleet, we're taking our quest further out and will not bother you folks anymore," he assured him.

"The Darkens didn't follow you here, did they?" he asked anxiously. The computer had translated the data and It now displayed the holos. He smiled as he saw he did, indeed, resemble his uncle. Only Monty looked almost ten years younger than him. Those cat people around him looked odd, but they were all relaxed and laughing about something. One displayed a group of humans with some scattering of the cat people in with them. It looked like they were eating a meal and all talking and enjoying the company; unaware of the fact their pictures were being taken.

"We made sure that no one followed, and we'll be out of here as soon as we've procured supplies from Guardian. We've rescued one hundred eighty-one residents from the starport. We were unsure if any of them would be welcomed, if we tried to return them to Trinity," he replied. He wanted some assurances that they wouldn't be shot, if he sent down a shuttle with the ones who wanted to return to Trinity.

"Really? We thought everyone up there was dead," he replied, shocked. There was a low muttering from the others around him as he waited. "The elders say they'll personally welcome anyone who wants to return to Trinity and make sure they find new jobs and places to live," he finally added, noting the silence from the other end, while the elders debated this move. Was it some kind of trap, he wondered?

"We'll have a shuttle of the survivors ready for departure in about two hours' time. Let it be known that we'll offer to take anyone who wants to leave Trinity back with us, but it may be some time before we reach Earth once more. We're limiting the number of passengers to equal the number of survivors. Our resources are limited at this time," he offered. "We'll let you know exactly how many are heading down, as soon as we've surveyed them to find out."

"Sounds fair enough," Connor replied, smiling to himself again. He realized he'd never been up in space and wanted to go, as he had as a child. He wondered what it was really like? "We'll have this frequency monitored until then," he assured him, then cut off his transmission and turned to face the others in the room.

"They've been up there a whole darned week; does this mean they're leaving soon?" Elder Martin demanded, frowning.

"I'm betting they're patching their ships up. They're probably ready to go. Well, we'll know what they're really like in a couple of hours," Elder Elbridge replied, smiling down at his youngest son. "You did good," he assured him. Connor nodded his head, then stood up.

"Do you need me to monitor the station here?" he asked, wondering. He had some thinking to do and only two hours to get it done!

"No, I'll take care of it," his father told him, "You go on." He took the chair and looked at two of the holos displayed upon the grid beside the operator's chair. Connor grabbed a chip and slid it into the receptacle, taking another terminal and making a copy of the holos for himself, then threw in another one for his Aunt Pam. "Is that for Pammy?" his father asked.

"Yeah. I thought she'd appreciate it," he replied, done with the task. If Jim wanted his own copy, he could make it himself. "I'll be back before that shuttle arrives, in case you need any help," he assured him. Jim nodded in response, then gestured him out. The elders had important things to discuss now.

"Watch your step, ma'am," Connor said, as he helped the survivors, who'd decided to come down to Trinity, out of the shuttle. Only eighty-five had decided to join their colony. They all looked too thin and pale, and many had horrible wounds, in various stages of healing. The children were a grievous sight!

"The sun's so bright," she complained, putting a hand up to block it from her eyes. He chuckled at this, nodding his head.

"It's summer ma'am, and yes, it's bright," he agreed with a polite smile as he gestured her over to the small open-air tent they erected to receive and process their new colonists. "The shade's right over there, where we have a reception set up." She smiled at this and hurried over on unsteady feet. A junior quickly appeared to lend her his arm and assisted her across the tarmac and within.

Commander Ashton Briggs from the Aurora had come down with the shuttle to supervise the transfer and now he and his aide were speaking with the governor and elders under the tent. He seemed young but held the mantle of authority well. Once they traded handshakes, and were smiling, he turned and came back to the shuttle. Boxes of supplies were being quickly loaded through the cargo door now.

"That's everyone," a trooper corporal informed Connor, as he stood at the top of the stairs. Connor noted his crisp clean uniform and the smooth, precise way he moved. "Is there anyone coming aboard?" he asked, seeing the crowd gathered outside. There was a range of emotions upon their faces, although joy seemed to be the one most expressed. Still, it made him feel uneasy, but orders were orders. He kept his scans up.

"Just a few, really," Connor informed him, then turned to signal the departees to advance. Six men and five women stepped forward with relief in their eyes, as if they were returning to paradise. He could understand after a fashion, it was a promise of a better home.

"You're right. Just a few," he agreed, then signaled for them to come aboard. "As soon as we're loaded up, back away or you might get hurt in the wash," he advised as the anxious people stepped past him, carrying only their personal items in a small bag, as advised. Connor shook his head at this, grinning.

"I'm coming too. I want to meet my great uncle and see one of them cat people up close. They look like a friendly bunch," he told him, finally sure of his decision as he lifted up his own travel bag. His Aunt Pam had urged him to make up his own mind, and to stop living in his brothers' shadows. He found his heart was still turned to the stars, and knew this would be his last and only chance. He had no kids anymore; his wife and little ones having died two years ago in an unexpected flood, down in Heaven's Gate. His life had been empty, up to now. Adventure beckoned him onward, and Tayna was where he hoped to find it.

The corporal looked surprised, then smiled as he gestured him aboard, too. Connor waved good-bye to his family, surprising a few, then jumped up the stairs, eager to see what awaited him now. Another trooper motioned him to a seat, then secured him in. The Commander and his aide boarded and sat, strapping in too. After what seemed an eternity, they heard the cargo doors sealing. Their hatch sealed next, then the troopers strapped in. The small shuttle lifted gently upwards, away from Trinity's gravity at last.

"Alec, you wouldn't believe the strings I had to pull to keep you on the Aurora. It's only because we're accompanying The Wrath, that you get to stay," Ash told him as he sat down next to his friend in the officer's lounge, catching a brief break. He smiled as he looked up to him.

"I knew you could do it," he stated. Storme was curled up in his lap, sleeping. He looked much better, now that he'd had a week's rest and recovery. "I saw the holos from that world we're headed out to, and it looks intriguing."

"Yeah, all the cats you could want. Think all we'll need to keep them happy is an oversized ball of yarn," he returned with a chuckle.

"But these cats had star travel long before we ever did if that report's accurate. They must have colonies of their own out there, which might've survived!"

"As long as they're still on friendly terms with us, I don't care what they look like," Ash assured him. "I could wish for a few starships to lend us a hand, but it doesn't look promising. They were carrying spears when they first discovered the base. They laughingly named it Winterhaven, even if it snows there," he added.

"But they picked up our language and technology fast - even before they brought down the Star Quest," Alec retorted. "They're smart and learn things quick. What was this thing about Talents? Is it some kind of telepathy?"

"You would want to know about that, wouldn't you?" he replied with a chuckle. "Yes, they seem to have a few who have psi abilities, they call Talents. The most surprising one is a man named Maren, who can heal with a touch. He and Ryes were the ones who revived the humans from the stasis chambers, since the equipment was almost totally shot. It's a miracle any of them survived."

"That's the truth. I can't wait to meet all of them," Alec told him, still excited by the prospect.

"I want to get to know them, too," one of the colonists said, as he stepped closer to the two men. "My great uncle Monty's there living with them cat people, and he sure looked happy from the holos," he explained, smiling. Alec gestured for him to sit down, giving Ash a nod of his head that this one was all right.

"The Star Quest was a wreck, it was a miracle any of them survived," he told him. "It seems, from the holos, the cat people and humans now live all together, as if they'd been raised that way. I saw there was even one pairing off of a `starman,' as they call themselves, and a human woman. I only hope we're not bringing any problems out there with us."

"That starman is Maren," Ash informed him, giving him a nod of his head. "If she wants to cuddle up to him at night, that's her business. We're only out here to find a way to save the Sol system before our defensive lines fall."

"It's that bad?" Connor questioned, his intense blue eyes studying this officer's face, seeing it in his eyes that it was. "So, then we'll do our best to start recruiting others. There must be some ships left, which are able to fight," he told them. "My name's Connor Elbridge and up until my father's time, my family's always been tied to Earth Fleet. It's not that I'm enlisting right now, but you've got my help, if you need it," he assured him, giving them a sure smile.

"We may need it," Alec replied, noting Ash's silence. "I'm Lieutenant Alec Scott and this is Commander Ash Briggs. What do you think of my hemicat?" he pressed, sure of what he sensed earlier.

"She's beautiful," he replied. "May I pet her?" he requested, wanting to touch her, so very much.

"Yes, you may," Alec granted. Ash looked in utter shock. He never let anyone touch Storme! "You're a psi, aren't you?" he suddenly asked the colonist as he was stroking his animal. She dozed on lazily, but confirmed his suspicions for him, before dropping off into a deeper sleep once more.

"It runs in my family, but I didn't think I had any abilities," Connor admitted, nervous.

"Elbridge. Yes, now I remember. Your family had the Windrose Stone for a time, long ago. Now it's lost in the vastness of space, for eternity," Alec related, recalling hearing of his family before. All psi's kept track of what little true stories existed about each other.

"The Windrose Stone?" Ash questioned, astonished, "I thought that was only a legend!"

"It actually existed and was in our keeping, before. A pirate ship attacked the Quicksilver and destroyed her, taking the Windrose Stone with her into oblivion. We never found the ship, nor the Stone. It was said in their efforts to escape, they went well outside of any established starlanes, so she may never be found," Connor related, knowing this one well.

"What about the pirates?" Ash pressed, interested, in spite of himself.

"Their ship returned with its lone surviving crewman dying as he docked her in Starport Farone's dock. When the Quicksilver blew, she almost took the pirates with her. What was left of the ship was almost scrap, but they did find pieces of the Silver's hull embedded in the wreckage," he said, then pulled out a pendent from under his shirt. "I have a piece of the Silver, which my grandfather gave me when I was little." From the fine gold chain depended a rounded, flattened piece of silvery metal, which looked like a piece of free-formed art jewelry.

"May I?" Alec asked, reaching out to indicate he wanted to touch it. It was if he were drawn to it for some unknown reason.

"Sure," he replied, allowing it. As their fingers brushed each other and the piece of metal, the room before them no longer existed. What they saw was a bright, silvery starship, tumbling in the darkness of space, as her engines had burnt out. The pirate ship came into view, latching on to board her. Then a sudden blast almost blinded them, as the ship self-destructed, almost taking the other ship with her. The vision faded, leaving both men looking into each other's eyes.

"She'll be found," Alec told him, absolutely sure.

"I know," Connor replied, suddenly very sure on this score. "And she's in far better shape than we thought."

"Yes, she is, Captain," he agreed, teasing his new friend and partner. But he knew... someday... it would be the truth.

"You guys scare me," Ash told them, standing up to go get something to drink. "Be right back." He realized he had to get away from them, as he'd seen what he was sure they saw. A silvery ship tumbling through space... and the blast and knowing that silvery ship would be found soon. He knew he wasn't psi, but now had his first doubts. Maybe together they were so strong they projected it to him unconsciously? Or? He didn't know and wasn't sure he wanted to know, not now when he finally gotten a decent promotion, he knew he deserved! If it turned out he was psi, he'd be stripped of his current command and forced into the Psi military branch. He did not want that life! He'd seen the trials Alec had gone through; it'd been akin to legalized torture. Being childhood friends, he'd been there to support him, and help keep him sane. He didn't think he'd survive it, himself.

Changes

Chapter 15

Ryes hovered overhead, looking down upon the tiny colony on Booda. She realized if she were quiet, with no chattering going on, Nesa didn't detect her. She slowly did a head count, discovering there were sixty-two people scratching out a meager existence beneath that tiny dome and cave complex. She saw Nesa arguing with the starman elders that they had to let the human slaves go, or they'd never get off Booda. There was some serious debating going on afterwards, but it soon settled as the witnesses gave their own testimonies in Nesa's support. Finally, Ryes stood in the center of their square and made herself visible to them. A gasp went up from the assembly as they saw her, knowing she couldn't possibly be there with them, but some didn't seem so sure about it.

"It has been passed down, from the Laws of old, that no person may own another as property. Each man and woman is born free, to live their lives and make their own choices as they will, when they're adult. If you do not obey the Laws," she declared, pointing to a very familiar-looking, silvery tower with the laws etched into it, nearby. Brush had grown up around it, at its base, obstructing the view of most of the laws. "We will not help you. You're descendants from the ships, which had kept contact open between the colonies of the other starman worlds for Prince Callas, long ago!"

"Who are you?" an elder demanded as he stood, glaring at her interruption. She smiled, granting him a nod of her head.

"Ryes of House Li, Chief Executive Officer of Winterhaven, formerly known as Amitell Research station number ten-thirty-three. We've retrieved the Star Quest and revived those who still survived in their stasis chambers. We've repaired two of the remaining shuttles and my husband is not far from Booda, at this time." There was an instant buzz of low voices at this news from everyone gathered, both humans and starmen, as she'd spoken in both languages.

"If you continue to treat the humans as slaves, we'll not take you back to Tayna. We're practically the same people and equals, and won't tolerate them being so ill-treated," she stated. She saw the humans looked to her with hope in their eyes. It was almost painful to see.

"We will take your words under consideration," another elder stated, looking grim. Ryes gave him a nod, then turned and gestured, causing the plants and debris to fly back, exposing the full column for all of them to see. The laws were clearly etched and now in view.

"If Prince Callas were alive today, he'd take immediate action, especially considering you were the ones he entrusted to bring these laws to others, and see that they were enforced!" she pointed out, then allowed herself to be unseen.

There was a stirring from the starmen, as many of the men jumped from their seats to crowd closer to see it for themselves.

"What do we do, Huras?" one of the elders asked the glaring one.

"We'll discuss this in private, first," he returned, then stood to go see it for himself. He wondered when the plants had been set to grow in front of the column? Did his grandfather deliberately ignore what they'd been entrusted with so long ago, just for his own comfort? If so, they all had much to answer for. He wondered how much longer they had, before the husband of this woman, Ryes, showed up? She knew how to read and speak both languages fluently! That too was a surprise.

Ryes quickly withdrew, realizing it was time for breakfast and she'd be missed for sure. Too many people were watching her now!

"Garth sent in a message this morning saying he wanted us to be ready to form a link-up for when they land at Booda. He wants us to back them, as best we can," Torr informed them, as Ryes finally showed up for breakfast.

"Well, that's not unexpected," Maren replied, smiling at Dotti as she nodded her head in agreement. "So, what were you up to this morning, Ryes?" he pressed, thinking he already knew the answer.

"Nothing much. Just overslept a little today," she assured him, smiling sweetly, trying for a look of innocence.

"Sure, you did," he retorted, in a low voice. Their eyes met and he knew she'd talk about it with him later.

"What did you do to your ears?" Ardis scolded Katas loudly, as she and Raby came to the tables with trays in their hands. "And yours too, Raby?"

"We thought they looked pretty," Katas protested, instantly pouting. Ryes laughed lightly at this, giving her a nod of her head.

"Raby asked me if it was all right and I didn't see anything wrong with piercing her ears. The little gold rings Glyn made for them are kind of pretty," she told Ardis.

"Just because some people don't mind holes in their heads," she responded. "I didn't give you permission, Katas."

"Ahhhh, Mom," she returned with a frown, "everyone has them now!"

"Not Everyone!" she snapped back, tapping one of her ears and looking disgusted.

"If she changes her mind about them later, Maren or I could heal her ears back to normal," Ryes offered, surprised at how upset Ardis was over this small matter. Ardis looked to her, then back to Katas, as she and Raby still stood with their trays in hand, signing to the girls to sit down.

"We'll see what your father says," she warned her, then dropped the matter. Sayer emerged, joining them, her ears were pierced too. Ryes had healed the piercings for the girls, so they wouldn't be in pain, waiting for it naturally.

"Who started all this?" Torr asked, amazed. They didn't look too bad. He might get it done, himself.

"Who do you think?" Ardis returned, turning to take care of Adris, as he started fussing. He looked to see Dotti and Bethy with pierced ears, wearing dangling earrings. "Mitt, who else?" she finished, not seeing where he was looking.

"Did you see that she even shaved her legs?" Sayer put in, grinning from ear-to-ear. "I saw her swimming before they took off and it looked strange."

"I'd believe it," Ardis told her, turning back to the others.

"I thought it looked good," Ryes put in, barely keeping from laughing aloud. "I was thinking of doing it, myself."

"We're a bad influence around here," Bethy told Dotti, smiling as she did so.

"I never thought of myself as a fashion trend, before," she returned, chuckling at the thought.

"I like it," Minn told them, as he and Sernn joined them for breakfast. "Mitt's shaved legs are so sensual!" Ryes laughed in surprise at this, as did the other women.

"Never thought of it that way," Ardis admitted, frowning. Maren nudged Dotti, gently.

"So that's why you do it," he teased her. She blushed as she laughed, shaking her head.

"I'd feel like a gorilla, if I didn't shave," she replied, "but, I noticed you never objected, my dear."

"They are sensual," he admitted, smiling to himself at this. "I could try to discourage the hair growth on your legs, without disturbing the rest of the other functions those pores perform," he offered.

"That's a great idea!" Dotti agreed, delighted.

"That'd be wonderful!" Bethy agreed, enthused.

"Oh, could you?" Katas begged, hoping.

"Please, Cousin Maren?" Sayer asked, smiling as sweetly as she could possibly manage.

"I'd appreciate it, truly!" Raby added, excited.

Maren had to laugh heartily, as he suddenly had the attention of all the women and girls seated near him - both human and starmen. Their eager faces filled with delight, lightened his heart.

"Alright, I'll take care of everyone who wants it done," he surrendered, giving in, "except for you, Ryes; you're more than capable of doing it for yourself."

"I never thought about it, before," she admitted, her eyes dancing with mischief. "With self-morphing using Healing, I could even disguise myself to look like a human. I'll try it later. But for now, I've got a lot of work to get done this morning," she told him as she turned to Jann and Shyla, who were squealing with delight. Maren's eyes held shock, then he frowned as he thought on what she said. Bethy and Dotti exchanged glances, too. Monty and Denas stepped up to join them, sitting down across from Ryes.

"Good morning," Denas wished them, smiling happily.

"Good morning," Ryes returned, glad they both looked happy.

"Did you two sleep well?" Maren teased, as Dotti nudged him in the ribs for his impertinence.

"Very well," Denas returned, as Monty nodded his head, blushing. Two nights and they were still going strong! He wondered if it were too soon to move her in with him? "Have you seen Saree this morning? She and Gann are usually here by now." Ryes realized she was right, then frowned, wondering if it had come so soon.

"I'll have to go check my messages," she told her, smiling as their eyes met for a moment.

"Have you checked on the guys this morning?" Ardis questioned, hoping she was keeping tabs on them. The other night's adventure had utterly amazed her; it was far more than the exploration she took them on, when they first arrived at Winterhaven. She was going to ask her if she could take just her out tonight, when she went to check on them.

"They're just fine," she replied, smiling. "They should be to Booda tomorrow. I paid a quick visit to the colony. There's sixty-two people living there. I think they're descendants from one of the ships Prince Callas was using to keep in touch with the isolated colonies on other worlds. They even have a column of the Laws, which was obscured with plants. I showed it to them, to be sure they understood."

"Prince Callas?" Rhodi quickly questioned, stopping as she was on the way to the table she usually sat at, with some of the other temple women. Her face betrayed her great surprise.

"Yes, he identified himself on the last encoded part of the message he left for Garth," Ryes explained. "We finally got to see it shortly before we freed you. Maren looks and sounds almost exactly like him, only younger. We're descendants of his," she added.

"Yes, he does! Now I know why you seemed so familiar, Maren," she told him, smiling. "I used to spend time in court when I was younger. If I may, could I see this message he left behind?"

"You could see the unedited, un-encoded part, but the rest was only for Garth, so he'll have to give permission for that part," she granted. Rhodi frowned, wondering.

"How do you know it is for him, alone?" she questioned, her doubts plain on her face. Torr chuckled at this, nodding his head.

"He says his name correctly, straight out in the second part," he replied, breaking in, before Ryes could. "You'll see it soon," he assured her, as Ryes smiled and nodded her head.

"I'll have a copy made for you of the first part and sent over this morning," she offered, noting Poli and Ruan listening to them, too. "You may all view it. I should've set up a viewing for you, shortly after you arrived. It explains a lot of our whys."

"Thank you. I appreciate it," she replied, then continued on to her own table. Doubts and questions now alighted her bright eyes.

"It's a good thing you and Dotti spoke true-mate vows," Denas told Maren in a low voice, laughing lightly after Rhodi was out of earshot.

"Why?" Dotti asked, while Maren appeared puzzled.

"They were both younger when she was attending court, she was after Callas for a mating. She never caught, but I recall they were the only happy memories she had of any man," she related, smiling. Dotti chuckled as she looked at her husband. Maren was blushing.

"Thank goodness I found you, my love," he told her as he wrapped an arm around her waist. She sighed at this, nodding her head, then gave him a quick kiss.

"Next life around, we're not going to be playing such an odd game of tag," she warned, teasing him.

"You've got that right," he agreed. "So, how do you think we're supposed to retrieve sixty-two people from Booda?" he turned, asking his cousin. Ryes smiled, giving him a nod of her head in understanding.

"Actually, when I was taking a head count, I made sure to let them know that if they didn't abide by the laws they were originally supposed to enforce, we weren't going to help them. They had a column displaying the laws right there in their village square. Some plants had grown up to hide them, so I made sure they saw them all, and left them to chew it over. Hopefully, by the time Garth gets there, they'll be ready to listen to what he has to say. My best guess is that we'll have to make several trips over and back by shuttle," she told him, noting the others paying her words strict attention.

"Why not use your Talent to help them lift off from Booda with a heavier payload, then again when it comes to landing upon Tayna?" Bethany suggested. Jim nodded his head at this, wondering if Ryes had enough power to do it?

"Could you do such a thing?" Monty questioned. "We could help," he offered.

"I don't know if I care to risk so many lives that way. Not to mention they don't have enough oxygen, food, nor water, and it'd overtax the filters, having so many on the trip back," she pointed out, appearing concerned.

"Use your Talent to push them home more quickly," Torr suggested, smiling as they were trying to think of ways to get around her limitations.

"Hey, I can do some things, but I don't know if I can do all that," she protested, smiling. "Next thing you're going to want me to move some of the metal beams from Hailys to create a new spaceport near Winterhaven!"

"Now that's a great idea," Maren assured her, grinning broadly. "We could use one!" Ryes blushed at this, shaking her head. "You helped the Star Quest land, before you knew what you can do, I think you can help them get off of Booda, too!"

"I'm heading for my office, before you think of any more impossible things for me to do today," she finally said, standing up.

"I'll take care of the horde this morning, Mom," Raby offered. She figured it was the least she could do for her allowing them to get their ears pierced last night, especially in wake of Ardis' ire over them.

"Thanks," she replied, relieved, quickly grabbing her tray and headed for the receiving belt near the exit, needing this escape.

"How does she know she can't do it, until she tries?" Torr asked, frowning, puzzled by her behavior.

"She doesn't, but she promised Garth she'd behave. She'd have to get his permission first, before attempting anything so risky," Maren reminded him. "Give her time. She'll figure out a way to bring them all back safely to Tayna."

"Could she have meant it about the slavery thing, though," Bethy ventured, with concern in her eyes, "If they don't let go of it, she'll really leave them there to rot?"

"If you'd seen what we saw the evening before last, you'd understand why," Ardis told her. "None of us will tolerate what they were doing to their humans - ever." The fire in her eyes told Bethy the rest of the story. She gave her a nod in understanding.

"I was thinking of having Maren delay it, but with all that's been going on the last few days," Saree apologized to Gann, as they finally took a few minutes' break. He sighed happily as he traced the line of her jaw, smiling down into her eyes.

"Phil and Kovin aren't going to be too happy with this, but I know they'll understand. And I want to be able to be home, here with you, afterwards, but there're some projects they need me for in Matlowe. You could always take a few days to come out to Matlowe with me, when we're through," he offered. She smiled up at him, nodding her head to this.

"Yes. I want to be with you, especially now. This has been nothing like the other women were describing to me before. You are such a gentle man, Gann. I am so glad it was you," she started, then paused, not sure how to tell him of the joy in her heart. Gann realized this was something deep from her, so called up his meager Mind Voice Talent and reached out to her from within. She saw what he was doing and responded in kind, reaching for him with her Talent to Boost his.

"I'm glad you accepted me as your mate, too," he sent to her, opening his heart to her, so she could know what he felt for her. Saree was amazed, for he never before showed her the depth of his feelings. She opened herself up to him, showing him how much she'd truly come to love and cherish him.

"Is it so hard for you to express your heart?" she asked, her heart beating a strong rhythm.

"After years of having to help care for my older sister, yes, it's very hard to express what I feel deep down," he admitted to her. "Karr used my feelings against me and has been getting worse through time. I can't believe she attacked Ryes! I'm glad she didn't choose to go after you, too. I'd never let her near you, believe me."

"I do believe," she replied, realizing he'd been abused most of his life by his older sister – the polar reverse of Doran's followers. "Let us try something," she suddenly urged. She felt his hesitation.

"What?" he asked, wondering and unsure.

"Let us try mating while maintaining this inner commune," she suggested, excited by the inspiration.

"Do you think we can?" he ventured, wondering what it would feel like? Her excitement was starting to set him off, too.

"We can try," she replied. She was still feeling the hot, intense demands of her body, letting him feel it too. Instantly, he was feeling the demands of his body in response.

"Let's," he agreed as he knew he was ready to enter her, once again. "I hope at least one of our cubs has eyes as beautiful as yours," he teased. He felt her inner humor at this.

"It took generations to breed it into my family line," she
returned. "I don't know if our cubs will have them, or not."

"I hope so. I couldn't see them disappear with you. After all,
two of Ryes and Garth's cubs have her green eyes. We can hope."

"Then we will do that," she sent, then found herself being
pulled in by the physical sensations she was experiencing, barely
maintaining the contact between them. He opened himself up more
fully to her from within, uniting with her wholly. Saree opened herself
to Gann in whole, in kind, their shared joy carrying them onward for a
long stretch of time.

"Sana," Maren started, not sure how to tell her the news. She
looked up to him, hoping everything was all right with her sons.

"What's wrong?" she asked, suddenly worried. He sighed,
giving her a nod of his head.

"Let me call Justin in here for a moment, first," he told her,
wanting them both present for this news.

"Alright," she responded in a small voice, then he looked at
her face and smiled as he shook his head.

"It's not bad news, just unexpected," he assured her. She
appeared relieved as he stepped outside the room, letting the door
close behind him. A few minutes later, he returned with Justin.

"Okay, what is it you need to tell us?" he asked, having
stepped over to his wife's side, taking her hand in his, both appearing
worried now.

"You've fathered a sport," he told them. "Sana, you're
carrying two sons and a daughter, but she'll need adjustments to
make sure she'll be born as normally, as her brothers," he warned,
smiling and yet puzzled, still.

"You mean we've conceived a child naturally between us?" he
asked, not sure if he believed it, or not.

"Yes. It's why we usually cease having sexual intercourse for
two months following a mating, to prevent the occurrence of a sport.
The woman may occasionally still put out eggs, which can be fertilized
for a while after her season. A sport rarely lives more than a few days
after its birth and can sometimes kill its mother if it dies within the
womb, spreading toxins throughout her system," he explained.

192

"But you can make sure she'll be all right?" Sana pressed, hoping, and elated, all at the same time.

"I made sure Rhin was all right. I should be able to handle this little miss, too. So, it looks like you'll have to pick out another name, and I'm sure Scott will want a genetic sample, before I do any work upon her, for his research project. If you don't mind," he told them, smiling as he delivered the news. Their faces lit up with excited joy, as they clung to each other for a few moments in disbelief. Sana laughed and nodded her head.

"I'll go get him, right away!" Justin declared, then turned to Sana and wrapped his arms around her, kissing her as he realized he was practically crying in his happiness. She laughed as she returned his kiss and was crying. He released her and turned back to Maren. "I'll be right back!" He quickly rushed out the door. They could hear him shouting as he ran down the hallway outside.

"I thought starmen and humans couldn't..." Sana started, frowning, now unsure.

"So did I," Maren agreed. He knew he had to talk to Ryes about this, as soon as possible! And do another check on his own, dear wife! He realized it might be a good idea to check all the women of Winterhaven, who were of bearing age. Many had openly tried mating to those willing from one side, or the other. He wondered how many other natural crosses they had in the making now?

"Maren!" Mason called out as he was leaving the underground facility, heading topside and home. It'd been a long day, and it was far from over! He stopped and turned around, puzzled as to why he'd want to talk with him, but there was something in Mason's eyes, and he instantly knew he had a troubled heart. So, he stood waiting for him to catch up, noting he was carrying a duffle bag over his shoulder. He must've just returned from, or was heading out to, Matlowe Village.

"Is there something the matter?" he asked, as he approached.

"I need to talk with you, if you have the time," he pressed. Maren may be his half-brother, but they'd never bonded in all the years they both lived in Matlowe. Now, he found he needed his advice and was unsure of his welcome; he knew changes needed to happen.

"Let's go sit out near the Phoenix fountain," he suggested, smiling encouragement. Mason almost sighed in relief, making Maren feel guilty over being irritated about wasting the time. It must be something very important for him to feel a need to talk alone, this deeply. The two men walked in silence, until they found seats at one of the tables near the fountain.

"What's the problem?" Maren asked, after he settled, hoping it was something he could help him with, at least.

"After the time we spent with Minn in commune through Raya, I've been thinking about what you showed me of our father, as you knew him growing up," he began in a faltering voice, finding this whole thing as difficult, as it was troubling. "I know you and Minn were only trying to save me from something I had no idea of what."

"We saw signs of where we thought you might be headed and wanted to help you find other ways of approaching life," Maren told him, from his heart. "We didn't think the women here in Winterhaven would let you stay long, if you kept going the way it seemed." Mason met his eyes in surprise, realizing he was most probably right. With Ryes and the other strong Talents, there was no way someone like their father would ever be tolerated here.

"I've been working the last few days over in Matlowe, and had some time to actually talk with Korman in the evenings, after dinner. He's..." he started, not sure if he could still find the words to say what he knew he needed to say now. He looked up to meet Maren's dark brown eyes, "For years I was afraid to say more than a few words to him. There were so many stories. And when I came of an age to start exploring free mating, he showed up near whatever girl I was interested in, when we were together. It was unnerving. He never said anything, merely watched us, as if evaluating my performance."

"I saw he was haunting you, a few years ago, but didn't understand why. I knew better than to interfere, by then," Maren admitted. "I should've tried to talk with you, then," he apologized. If anyone knew Korman, other than his mother, it was him. He'd kept track of his father, except Garth, Sabin and Torr pulled him away, making sure he learned to laugh, and not caught up in things he could never control. They gave him an appreciation of the joys of life!

"No, it's all right. I got through it, and when I finally found the courage to approach him this week, he started talking to me. I can only guess he's been very lonely with Tanns and the cubs here. He's twisted... inside his mind... far worse than I ever imagined. You tried to hint at how deep his insanity went, but I didn't understand it fully, until last night. He means to kill you, Leand, Riss and Karis, Maren. Just because you're his sons. I was fairly concerned he meant me too, but for some reason he didn't say anything further. He told me Mellas turned up dead, for no known reason." The color drained from Maren's face. Mellas was another of Korman's sons, who was their age. That left only Leand, Riss, Karis and the two of them. At least Leand, Karis and Riss were here in Winterhaven now! He had to warn them tonight!

"He threatened as much, the last time I was in Matlowe. That's when Ryes glued him to a wall. He tried to get her, but she stunned him. I'll talk with Kovin. You shouldn't have to go out to Matlowe, if Korman's on some kind of death hunt. Even with the limiter, he's sneaky and will find a way to get you," he warned, gripping his shoulder as he looked into his eyes.

"I fully believe you. I'll talk with Kovin and Phil. We have too many projects still in the starting stages, here in Winterhaven. The above ground community hall goes up next," he told him, smiling finally. He recalled the ice in Korman's voice at the last, when he casually mentioned Mellas' demise, at the end of their conversation last night. It was like he was giving him a warning.

"Hey, there you are!" Shadd declared with a smile, as she stepped over to them. She saw they were talking about something and wanted to know what it was; she hated being left out of things.

"I was just telling Mason I'm going to have to check every woman in Winterhaven. It appears we now have two naturally occurring crosses between starmen and humans, which have appeared," Maren explained, winking at his half-brother, as he let him go. Mason's grin widened as he nodded his head. It did no good to worry Shadd about something like this. They'd both do their best to keep alert, whenever they were anywhere near Matlowe.

"And I was telling him that there's no need with you and I being as close as we are," he replied, teasing her. She came up to him and threw her arms around his neck, dropping down onto his lap.

"You betcha!" she told him, kissing him deeply for several, long seconds.

"I've been meaning to ask, exactly what did you do for my spunky lady here, when she came to have you dry up her milk?" he asked once their lips parted, now having both parties present, it seemed a good time for his question.

"I had Maren delay my next season a while. I wanted us to have plenty of time for each other, before having to worry about cubs to chase around," she told him, knowing Maren probably would, now that she was here with them, too.

"But I'd like for us to have cubs of our own, too," he protested, "How far did you push it back?" he asked Maren.

"I put it out at the five-year cycle. She would've otherwise had her next season next year, in the late summer," he informed him. Shadd smiled happily at this but wondered at the sudden sadness in Mason's eyes. Did he want cubs so badly, after all? Was that why he'd been after Mitt? It hadn't been that they'd once been lovers, after all! Everyone knew she was due for her first season soon.

"You can restore it to my normal rhythm?" she turned and asked, wanting to be sure. If it meant so much to him, how could she hold it back? It maddened her to see Torr so happy with Dodi. How could he? At least Mason was great in bed and seemed to truly love her. If it meant having a cub to keep him happy, she realized she'd go that far, but only for him. As long as he helped raise the child, she added, within her own mind.

"Yes, I can, anytime you want," he assured her. Maybe she was having second thoughts? It was obvious Mason wanted a chance at getting cubs of his own.

"We'll talk about it," Mason said, feeling this was something they needed to discuss. He didn't think it was him in particular, just that she wasn't ready to care for a child full-time, yet. They were both still young, after all. But that look in Korman's eyes... He hoped he'd be alive to father cubs when she was ready for them.

"Good. I'd best get home. Dotti's stuck with our siblings today, since it's their `off day' from classes, and they can be a real handful," he told him, grinning as he got to his feet.

"I keep forgetting that I have more siblings," Mason returned, astounded to realize Maren did consider him a brother, despite their living out of touch with each other back in Matlowe. He stood with Shadd still in his arms, putting her down upon the table, then hugged his brother heartily. "I'll talk with you later, brother!" he promised. Maren laughed, nodding his head.

"How about the both of you come over after dinner tonight, and we'll all play games together, or something," he offered. Shadd laughed out in surprise, as Mason nodded his head in agreement, a big smile plastered across his face.

"That sounds great. See you later," he promised, then hefted his duffle, and he and Shadd headed for their home, too. He had a lot of things on his mind and now wanted some time for a quiet discussion, with his lady. If it came down to it, he'd stay home and raise their cubs and she could go out and work! This was a change he openly wanted in his life, now.

Booda

Chapter 16

Early the next morning, Ryes finally came to a decision. As she watched the reports of the shuttles' approach to Booda, she put in a request for both Rhodi and Maren to meet in her office right away. When they arrived, both looking puzzled by the other's presence, she asked them to shut the door and take seats before they started. Maren politely closed the door, before taking a seat.

"I've been struggling with a decision," she admitted outright, after they settled into their chairs.

"What kind of a decision?" Rhodi questioned, before Maren could voice it.

"Usually, in our group melds, Raya forms, holds and controls the whole linkage of our inner commune. Frankly, I trust her to control things and keep a hold on matters, to allow us all to get to the work before us. With the complexity of this one task, and the dangers we might need to counter, I feel it needs to be layered to support what should be done. Raya will hold the outer team and I've been struggling to decide who'll hold my inner base team."

"So, you've narrowed it down to one of us?" Maren asked, smiling as he was proud of being actively considered.

"No," Ryes replied. "Maren, you I fully trust, but you don't have the experience I feel I need to back this one dangerous venture." The smile melted from his face as he gave his cousin a nod in support and understanding. He knew she was right, as he was still learning how to use his Talents.

"Then, you have chosen me?" Rhodi questioned, not wholly comfortable with such a responsibility. She barely knew these people!

"Not alone," she returned, now smiling. "I've decided upon the both of you. Do you think the two of you can hold a linkage intact and functioning, as a team?" She knew she was asking a lot of Rhodi, but felt she had little choice. They looked to each other, surprised, then back to Ryes.

"I don't have a problem with it," Maren finally said, smiling and confident.

"I am not sure," Rhodi admitted, blushing. "To work so closely, we must meld more completely than the others, in the larger link," she protested. "I do not know if I am ready to do such a thing with a m...mm..." She found she couldn't even say the word; it died upon her lips.

"A man?" Ryes finished for her, smiling as she tried not to mock her. "Or is it more that Maren's a descendent of, and looks like, the one man you once pursued?" she pressed. Maren gave Ryes a startled look at hearing the sharpness in her voice, as he recalled Rhodi's earlier focus. Rhodi's blush deepened.

"Maren's not your prince. Don't you think I'd understand how hard this is for you? I'd never ask it, but that I need the both of you, if I'm to do the work I must! I need your inner strength and control over others, and Maren's heart, strength, and power. He's more in tune with me than you are, and can anticipate my needs more readily," she explained, knowing she was being brutal with her truths. She felt she had to be with the time of their need approaching rapidly. Rhodi met her eyes steadily for several long seconds, then dropped her gaze as she considered her words, resisting the urge to look within her mind. Maren gave Ryes a nod of his head, seeing her reasoning clearly.

"I see. Can we truly be of any help to them, being so far away?" she demanded, needing to verify they'd have some effect upon the outcome of what Ryes looked to believe would be a confrontation.

"I can take care of things, as needed, but because of the distance, I need a solid foundation to be able to do what may be required," she admitted. "It's a potentially hostile situation, but unless I have assurances of your full support, it's for naught. I won't risk their lives so frivolously. If you cannot help us, tell me who else might have the abilities and experience?" Rhodi sat and gave the matter serious consideration for several long seconds, trying to determine if any of the others in their group could perform the task in her stead. In the end, she realized, she was the best choice after all.

"No one else here," she finally admitted, swallowing as she realized her throat had gone dry. If only Doran had been sane, willing, and able...

"I can handle it, Ryes," Maren volunteered, knowing Rhodi didn't want such close contact with him. He saw how this one decision tore at her very soul, and almost pitied her at how closely she clung to her ancient beliefs, still.

"Maren..." she began, knowing he'd do his absolute best to keep things in hand, as he could. She was afraid it wouldn't be

enough. Not only could he be harmed, but the rest of them were at
risk, too.

"I will do it," Rhodi interjected, feeling she was best suited for
this task. She knew life here would be trade-offs. For the things they
were freely granted, there'd be demands placed upon them in return.
The fact that this one cut so deeply, and so close to her own heart,
made it harder for her to face, but she was determined. Ryes saw the
look in her eyes, understanding were within her own in response. She
did comprehend what she was asking, but still did so because she had
little choice. Somehow this gave Rhodi comfort, as she accepted that
she had a role to play here, herself. She would leave her own mark
upon Winterhaven and make it a part of her being, after all. She'd
hoped to avoid such, being ready to leave quickly, if they found a
better place to live. Could Kahmarr truly be gone? Viewing the holo
last night had given her chills. It had been Callas, and he was so old!

"Thank you," Ryes replied, giving her a small bow.

"So, how much time do we have left to prepare?" Rhodi
questioned, putting her own interests aside for the moment.

"Another hour, at the most," Ryes responded with a sigh. She
turned her terminal screen about with the computer's report upon the
shuttles' location displayed, for them to see it for themselves.
"They're in preparations for entering Booda's atmosphere now."

"Where were you thinking of assembling the group?" Maren
queried, tallying in his head those in Winterhaven, who had Talent to
some degree. He knew Saree and Gann were still tied up in her first
mating and wasn't sure if they should disturb them.

"Which do you think sounds better? Beside the Phoenix,
topside, or in the dining hall?" she questioned him, smiling.

"The Phoenix! That way we won't be distracted by the
delicious aromas of dinner being prepared, so close by," he returned,
grinning as he gave her a wink. She started chuckling as she recalled
his endless interest in food, up until he found Dotti. Something about
having her to focus upon had curbed his restless hunger.

"It is a valid point," Rhodi agreed, smiling. She may not know
the why behind the look he gave her, but she knew it could be an
issue at times.

"Great. Then, I'll message everyone to gather in about forty-
five minutes."

"What about Saree and Gann?" he questioned, saying it aloud.

"I'll message them with the invitation, but I'm not counting on their attendance," Ryes replied, noting the odd look in Rhodi's eyes at being reminded of Saree's season and her choice of mates.

"Then, we'd best go and prepare," Maren told them, standing up with a smile upon his face. Ryes gave him a nod of her head.

"I'll be there shortly. I want to make sure the horde's being looked after first. I'm also bringing along Rhin," she informed him.

"Ah, your son, whom you believe is a Booster," Rhodi replied, seeing why she'd want to include him for this.

"It's not a belief. He is one, and very powerful," Ryes retorted with a tight smile, feeling her comment sharply.

"But I'm not allowing you to put Rhin into a nap state," Maren scolded her, looking serious. "It's unfair to him."

"I know," she returned, sighing as she considered it. "It just makes things far less difficult," she protested.

"He'll grow up resenting it, otherwise," he assured her, then turned for the door. "I'll get Rhin. You join us when you're ready." Maren opened the door, without looking at either of them, then left. This coming confrontation was playing upon his mind, and he wanted a few minutes to get clear and ready himself for both the melding and the task ahead.

"Maren is right about your son," Rhodi said, backing his opinion.

"I know, but even though Rhin's little, he's very rambunctious. I don't want him disrupting the concentration we'll need, to keep control of the situation upon Booda."

Rhodi smiled grandly at her, recalling other times when infants were used in melds. It was a mother's common concern, and valid. It was so very rare to find a young child with Talents powerful enough to be used, at such an early age. Males were even more rare.

"He will be fine, you will see. We will make sure he behaves," she assured her, as she stood up. Ryes smiled in response, giving her a nod of her head.

"I've got some quick messages to get out," she suddenly recalled, pulling her terminal back to check their progress.

"And I must prepare myself." Rhodi turned with a sigh, leaving Ryes to the work she still needed to accomplish, not envying her the tasks ahead. Larissa appeared somber, knowing the situation already, and casting her prayers for its success.

"Do you think it'll work?" Sabin asked Garth as they began their slow descent through Booda's atmosphere. Garth decided that even if they couldn't free the humans, this will be good practice for their landing back upon Tayna. None of them had ever attempted it before. Ryes had fussed at them for not getting in some real-time practice, before lighting out on their mission. Now he knew her wisdom. He should've practiced, as he found himself questioning his landing moves now! Was he doing it right?

"I fully believe in Ryes," Dr. Cruthers replied for him, seeing the hesitation in Garth's response.

"I worry that she'll try to overtax her abilities too much. We almost lost her the one time, and I don't like the thought of risking her like this."

"She'll do as she sees best. Grant her the grace to know when she's reached her limits, and the others the sense to pull her back, otherwise," Ethan told him, speaking in a low, gentle voice. "I fear for her, myself, but would never hold her back. I wouldn't want her to hesitate in a crucial moment where her own life, or sanity, would hang in the balance if she paused instead of taking action," he gently scolded. "You hold her will in too tight a grip." Garth turned, meeting his eyes. He wanted to tell him he had no right to speak out so about their relationship, but saw he had a valid point. He'd known Ryes all his life, but it was only in the last year that he'd truly come to know her - from within.

"Your words fall as shards, cutting deep," he admitted with a sigh, then smiled. "I'll do my best not to shackle her too severely."

"Good. She's bright, has an iron will, and will find a way around your restrictions, given time. I know from experience," Rowan's voice replied, coming over the radio. "You only save yourself heartache and headaches by looking at it this way."

"Should we try to meld with their link?" Mitt asked, wondering. They planned only on her, Sabin and Garth going out to meet these refugees for the first time - just in case.

"No," Sabin ordered. "Keep on your toes, as the humans say, and have your own Talent in use. Mind Voice is far handier, even if

it's your weaker one. I'm keeping mine up, too." There was light
laughter over the radio in response.

"I'll keep it in mind," she promised, as Axel gave her a nod in
agreement, smiling in his turn.

"They should be joining us soon," Garth reminded them, as
they fired their braking thrusters. He lowered the landing gear, as
Sabin scouted for a good landing spot near their objective.

"There, grid coordinates Charlie eleven, Yankee four-one-
twelve," Axel spoke up, seeing what looked like a promising spot. It
was a plain, flat area, free of large rocks and tall brush.

"Got it," Garth returned, punching it up into their computer,
relaxing a little at the controls now. He hoped Ryes and the others
were ready. He didn't intend to let anyone leave the shuttles, until
they joined them.

"All right, let's begin," Ryes ordered, feeling a little panicky
with time pressing upon them. She finally got Rhin to settle down in
her lap and was amazed as Rhodi caught him up into their meld with
great ease. He kicked his legs in happiness, his tiny eyes closed. She
breathed a sigh of relief, then surrendered herself more completely to
the inner commune. It took a far shorter time for everyone to settle
down this time. Maybe it was the fact they had real work before
them, with lives upon the line, or maybe it was Rhodi's years of
experience, but she was happy they were so quickly organized. Ryes
then unleashed her Empath Talent fully, giving control of her Booster
to Raya, Maren and Rhodi. Rhin's Focus Talent helped immensely.

For the first time, she didn't dawdle with investigating the life
upon Tayna, nor Tayna herself. She launched them straight upwards,
reaching out toward Booda, startling them all with her grace and
assurance. The Sleepers had never felt an Empath of this caliber, but
she didn't let their astonishment distract her. She searched for Garth
and the others, finding the shuttles just settling upon the large moon's
surface. She reached out to them, to let all of them know they were
present, too.

"About time," Mitt scolded her, playfully. There was a ripple
of amusement from the rest in the linkage.

"Behave," Minn cautioned his wife, so happy to know she was
still alive and all right.

"Who? Me?" she returned merrily, "You know me far better than that!" They watched as they all began to don the environment suits, knowing they weren't adapted to this moon, as the inhabitants who lived here were. These were far lighter, yet stronger than their space-venturing suits. Garth had everyone pocket stunners – in case. Even if the others were remaining behind, they still wanted to do an exterior check of the shuttles, and be prepared in case they were needed, having pulled out a pair of rifles from a locker and hand weapons were now strapped to their waists. All was ready.

As the party of three headed out, they were met halfway by a party from out of the dome. It was the middle of their night, but they'd been restless, anticipating the coming visit.

"You are Base Commander Garth?" a woman questioned, seeing there were two men before her. Garth smiled at this, giving her a nod of his head. He was finally getting used to being called so on occasion. He realized a smaller title was easier for him to bear than the larger one granted by Prince Callas.

"Yes, he is," Ethan replied, coming up behind the party, joining them. Sabin sighed, knowing they couldn't exclude him now.

"You speak Dolbith very well, for a human," Nesa commented, seeing he was an elder, at that. And no one reprimanded him for speaking to her.

"Yes. Ryes taught me Dolbith, long ago," he replied, smiling jovially at her odd compliment.

"We're here to see about organizing a return to Tayna for certain survivors," Garth told her. He noted there were no humans in their greeting party. Was it they didn't consider them important enough to include, or was there some other reason?

"Yes. Our council of elders is assembling at this time. I'm to bring you before them," Nesa replied, not liking being reminded of her duties. It was fascinating to see there were men and women, who were new and obviously not of Booda. The strange clothing they wore interested her. Did they truly need such here? She recalled old tales of when the humans first arrived. They were said to wear such suits.

"Then proceed," Garth ordered her, gesturing for her to lead them. She blushed, but turned, gesturing to the others. The four men fell into step around them, as she now walked next to Garth. Ethan stepped forward, walking beside him on his other side. This looked to disturb her, for some reason. Humans didn't seem to be equals in her mind.

"How long have your people been on Booda?" Ethan asked her, smiling at her discomfort. It appeared that Ryes was right about their view of humans. Nesa paused a long moment, wondering if she should respond to his question? Silence reined as they all awaited her reply.

"For more than two hundred and forty years, by Tayna's reckoning," she finally told him. "How is it you have such privilege?" she pressed, finally.

"What privilege?" he returned, enjoying baiting her, despite himself. Garth and the others chuckled, enjoying it, too.

"Dr. Ethan of House Cruthers is our head of Research in Winterhaven. In all truth, he outranks the rest of us and we're merely glad he allows us to be so at ease in his company," Garth informed her, as the rest of his small group laughed and nodded in agreement. Ethan looked merry, shaking his head in denial. She blushed darkly at this, almost insulted to believe a human outranked a starman. How could it be?

"You have strange customs," she replied. "We've been looking at the Laws, which had been passed down from long ago, but have yet to find a way in our hearts to grasp that humans are meant to be included. Could they truly mean all peoples?" she pressed.

"Yes, they did and still do!" Garth returned. "There're other peoples, other than humans, dwelling upon Tayna. Do you want to be slaves to them only because you're different? The Laws will apply equally to everyone, at all times!"

He felt his own ire rise within, knowing now how Ryes must've felt, the first time. How could such ignorance be allowed to live among them? At the very least, they should look into settling them into their own, separate enclave, if they returned with them to Tayna. He felt Ryes' agreement with his own thoughts, glad she was with them, now. The Boodans looked to him in shock, realizing his point was valid. Silence reined as they approached the dome itself, each buried in his, or her, own thoughts.

Garth and his team noted the worn condition of the plastic dome that protected this small, shallow valley. He stopped outside it to let the drones take a good scan and let them all observe its dulled and pitted surface. There were a few small rents at the bottom on one side of the entrance but appeared to still be stout and protective. Nesa and her hunters stopped with them and took it in, as if seeing it for the first time, themselves. He gave her a nod, then they all turned and entered their village. Nothing was said the whole time, but the drones seemed to puzzle the Boodans, as they watched them.

Nesa thought she felt the presence of his opinionated wife again but didn't want to stop to call up her Talent to be sure, at this time. She found she was a little afraid of this man, Garth. He was physically bigger and appeared stronger than any man here! She led them inside the shelter, then over to the stone seats set before the largest stone dwelling, where their great elder leaders dwelled. They were all gathered out on the steps, sitting, and awaiting their arrival. As they approached, Huras, the Chief Elder, stood up as she halted before them, giving them a bow, she rarely granted.

"Elder Huras, I present the leader of the starmen from Winterhaven upon Tayna, Base Commander Garth," she told him, after they entered the center circle. The others with him were glancing about, accessing the conditions of both where they lived and the inhabitants, themselves. The drones had flown off, covering the entire settlement.

Garth noted they were all starved and thin looking. It brought him no comfort to think of leaving any of these people here on this world, at all. Some wore remains of tattered clothing, while others sported what had to be woven plant fibers from the local flora. It didn't appear comfortable. An occasional scale-covered tunic was seen here and there too, which might be skins from some local animals. Everything was very primitive-looking and hand-crafted, from their simple tools, and clubs, to their baskets, ground mats and other strange possessions. While Matlowe Village had been a humble, poor village, this place made it appear a very rich community in comparison.

"Thank you, Nesa. You are dismissed," the head elder ordered, gesturing for her and the rest of her hunters to step away. There was a human elder, who stood next to this Garth, as if they were equals. It was curious, to his mind. "We welcome you, Garth, and those you bring with you. Your coming has been foretold," he informed him, wondering if he knew. Garth smiled at this, giving him a nod of his head in response.

"My wife, Ryes of House Li, always keeps me up to date," he assured him. Then it seemed Ryes appeared at his side, smiling up at him. His own grin widened, glad to have her image with him, even if she couldn't be so, herself. "We're here to see to the humans' release," he added. He pointed to the metal column, nearby. "You have the Laws, and they will be obeyed," he ordered with a snap in his voice. There burned a golden fire in his eyes, now.

"We knew not of the last four and have been wondering how to make amends to our humans. If you insist upon taking them back with you to Tayna, would you also consider removing us to your world? Our resources are severally taxed, with there being very poor hunting the last three years. Many have already died, due to our shortages," he told him, not wanting to beg, but feeling he had to for the sake of his own people.

"Yes, we can see you've not fared well," Ethan spoke up, a sharpness in his eyes. "We'll do what we can to evacuate everyone, but it'll take time and several trips. We only have the two shuttles working at the present time. The Star Quest was too severely damaged to be considered space-worthy, anymore." Huras blinked, not used to being so addressed by a human, but the others allowed it with absolutely no protest. There were even nods of agreement out of the starmen with him!

"We have a shuttle which might still work," one of the human elders said, standing to speak out. His Dolbith was broken, but understandable.

"Do you?" Mitt returned, using English smoothly, startling both the Booda humans and starmen. "Where is it? I want to look at it," she pressed.

"What did she say?" Huras asked, not understanding a word.

"She wants to examine the human's surviving shuttle," Garth explained. "She wants to see if it's still space-worthy or can be repaired. It'd be an asset, if so."

"Our own craft were destroyed in our landing and scavenged to create shelters. There were three human craft, which came down to Booda. But they're a far walk from here," he cautioned, narrowing his eyes but hoping, still.

"I'll go see," Ryes volunteered, but still a little afraid to leave them so vulnerable.

"I'm going with you," Mitt added. Ryes met her eyes, seeing she'd be the most qualified, but was afraid to leave them that much more defenseless, among these strangers.

"Don't worry, we'll be fine. You two go take care of it," Garth told her in English, seeing why she was hesitating.

"I won't let anything happen to her," Sabin added, also in English, as he stepped over to help support Mitt's body. She gave him a nod.

"And we'll help," the human elder insisted, stepping forward with the help of a young woman to support him. Several of the humans came with him. The savage marks and scars upon their bodies startled Sabin, but he gave them a nod of his head in agreement. These he trusted far more than the starmen around them! He felt their helping to guard them was a welcome sign and saw no threats in their surface thoughts.

"We won't be long," Ryes promised, then disappeared. She gently sifted through the man's memories, finding the location of the shuttles there, then welcomed Mitt's presence and the two of them took off to seek the site.

"Where do they go?" one of the starmen elders pressed, seeing Mitt's body slumping against the other man's, as if she'd truly left, and the ghostly image of the other woman vanished. Sabin wrapped his arm around Mitt to hold her up. This was a use of Talent he'd never seen in his whole life, and it left him feeling unsettled.

"To check on the human shuttles," Garth explained. "My sister has Inner Sight and will be able to see if any of them can be quickly repaired, in a very short time."

"Inner Sight?" Huras declared, astounded at the presence of such a Talent. "Mind Voice and Empath are all that we've seen here on Booda. My granddaughter, Nesa, is the strongest to appear in a long time."

"We have quite a few Talents in Winterhaven. Including six of our humans," Sabin told him, smiling. The thought of a human having Talent looked to shock them anew. He realized he might enjoy this, after all.

"My wife is the daughter of a powerful Talent, and you've seen how strong she is," Garth added, reminding them to not obstruct them, even in her apparent absence. Her wrath would be Fury itself, otherwise, he feared.

"You're Dr. Cruthers?" the elder questioned, in a low voice, needing to be very sure.

"Yes, I am," he affirmed, turning to get a better look at the man addressing him, wondering who he could possibly be?

"I'm Nicolas Reece, one of the maintenance techs, who helped build your special enclosures for your studies," he prompted him, seeing he didn't recognize him right off. It'd been years, so was no surprise.

"Young Nick?" he returned, seeing it really was him, after all. "You were barely old enough to be an Amitell employee. Weren't your parents there, working at the station?" he asked.

"Yes. My dad, Rob, thought it'd keep me out of trouble. I was only sixteen, at the time. I was heading toward my tube when the attack came. I had to see their ship for myself, so ended up being caught up in the evacuation. I couldn't believe how fast they took out the Star Quest! I'll never forget it," he related to him, his eyes casting back into the far past. "We crash landed here, after our shuttle took the edge of one of their beams and were quickly captured by the cat people. Our luck seemed to have gone from bad to worse," he finished. Ethan nodded his head at this, his eyes briefly meeting Garth's as he listened to the short tale, too.

"You're back among friends, Nicholas," Garth assured him, surprising him. "We all live together and work together to make Winterhaven our home."

"We found them, and it looks like two of them can be used, again. Mitt and I have already done all the quick repairs we can, but we're not sure about the one being able to make a landing upon Tayna. Axel should check it out, too," Ryes informed them, returning. She didn't project her image as before, feeling it was a waste of energy. Mitt opened her eyes, smiling and nodding her head as she stood under her own power again. She was leaving her Talent open and could clearly hear Ryes and the others with no trouble. Suddenly, a young human man ran up to the group of humans guarding them, panting in the effort of his haste.

"She's born, but I don't believe will live long," he told Nicolas and the other humans.

"Who?" Ryes questioned, seeing Huras had stepped over to them with curiosity in his eyes. He appeared to wish he'd learned more of the human tongue before. He wanted to know what was being discussed. The runner looked around, not seeing who'd spoken the question.

"We have a lady Talent among us," Nick assured George with a smile and nod of his head. "Show her," he ordered. George nodded his head, but as he turned to lead her to the mis-born child, he saw his younger sister, Abbra, coming toward them. He knew she shouldn't even be out of bed, having just given birth! He rushed to her, taking the bundle she held in her arms, as she was stumbling on uncertain feet. Suddenly, the bundle was lifted out of his arms, up into the air in front of them. Abbra, herself, had a strange look in her blue eyes, then she closed them, with an odd smile upon her face.

"It's all right," Mitt assured him, having stepped over and clasped him upon his shoulder. He flinched from her hand, as if she'd struck him. This greatly upset her. She'd never meant to bring him harm, nor fear. "Ryes and the others are healing them," she finished, meeting his eyes. George saw a sadness in her dark-brown colored eyes and wondered. She'd even spoken perfect English. He now saw she'd meant to be friendly and didn't know what to do to apologize.

"I... I'm sorry," he finally said, finding his voice, "You startled me."

"It's all right," she assured him, smiling again.

"When can we leave?" Huras demanded, still frustrated. Garth gave him a nod of his head, seeing his discomfort with being left out.

"As soon as we can get an assessment of how many the combined shuttles can hold. Are they truly ready, Mitt?" he asked.

"Axel can double check for me, but they look like it. I programmed their computers to have them home in on our own shuttles and land next to them. He should have his evaluation ready for us soon," she assured him. "There'll be plenty of room for everyone, as long as they don't bring along anything else but the clothes they're wearing. We can dump out the cargo we don't need, but it'll be tight with the water and oxygen."

"There's plenty of oxygen and water here on Booda to tap," Nicolas pressed, seeing this Mitt had responded to her leader in English. It appeared they all used it as naturally as their own language. He had to smile to see the look in Huras' eyes.

"Right! It'll take a few hours to run the compressors to liquefy the oxygen, then," Mitt added, smiling at this human elder.

"In a few more hours we can all leave. But you can't bring anything with you. We have weight limitations to keep in mind," Ethan informed the starman elder, smiling. He knew Garth and the others were deliberately ignoring him. They were here for the humans primarily. After seeing the scars all the humans bore, even the young children, he could well understand why. He wasn't sure he wanted to bring these starmen home, but he couldn't leave them here, either. Huras looked to him, giving him a nod of understanding, seeming to accept his instructions with no reservations about the source now. That was good, very good.

Realization

Chapter 17

"Look at this, Maren. She's a natural cross!" Ryes pointed out, what must be obvious to him, too. His humor rippled across the link, as he brought up his Healing Talent to care for the tiny child. Tennan, Minya and Ruan added in their Healing to help him and with her mother's care. Abbra was Talented with Mind Voice and readily joined their linkage with her own mind, relishing the warmth, love, and humor she found here.

"And what will you name your tiny daughter?" Monty asked as he turned his attention toward her. He wasn't as fumbling with his own Talent, as he'd been before. He and Denas had learned a lot from each other the last few days. "My name's Monty and this is my dear lady, Denas," he told her in introduction.

"I don't know. I hadn't expected her to survive! My name's Abbra Denzyl," she returned, still unsure of her welcome and skills. Denas' humor came through clearly, as did Abbra's life's story in return. They saw Abbra was only seventeen years old, and this was her first child; her brother had protected her from being raped for years. She had blue eyes and blonde hair and was a head-turner for a Boodan human. Nires found a chance when George was injured and took possession of her until she suddenly turned up pregnant. He then disowned her and the other starmen left her alone after that, as George grew stronger again, as he recovered.

"You will have plenty of time for naming her, on your way back to Tayna," Denas assured her. "She is so beautiful! I love her eyes! I am hoping they turn out as beautifully blue as yours."

"She's my first and I think you're right. She is beautiful!" Abbra realized she was starting to feel excited with the prospect of leaving Booda, now. She'd been afraid of leaving all she knew and understood behind, when first hearing of the approaching starmen and their shuttles. "Her father will deny her existence, but I don't care. She's mine."

"He will? Why?" Saree pressed, not understanding why a man would do such a thing to her and her helpless daughter.

"I was only for his pleasure and cleaning his home. He banished me from sight as soon as he learned of my pregnancy. His own, starman wife, Sciri, would be terribly upset if she knew he fathered her upon me," Abbra explained to them, embarrassed.

"Well, she'll never want for playmates here," Torr assured her merrily. "We've all had plenty of children born in Winterhaven the last few months, with more due soon. A few of them will be crosses, too." Tears of relief and happiness ran down from Abbra's eyes, as she felt his truth.

"Thank you for coming to take us away from all this," she replied, feeling they were finished with both her and her daughter. She opened them, as Ryes brought her infant down near her, for her to take back into her arms. She did, letting her contact with them slip away. She knew she'd be with them all, very soon!

"You're welcome," Mitt assured her in English, smiling, "You're riding with me in the Defender, Abbra. I don't want her father to get near either of you, while we're enroute home," she told her. George appeared astonished. He'd never told them his sister's name, nor of the circumstances of his niece's getting.

"You're right, Mitt. If there's danger of any retaliations enroute, we should separate the starmen from the humans. Only, who'll pilot both the other shuttles?" Garth questioned, wondering if any people with such skills still existed here on this world? They didn't have time for even the basic training needed! And he didn't trust the computers that much!

"I can pilot one of them," Sabin offered, chuckling that he'd have to remind his friend.

"On a second thought, I'd better take the other. Abbra can ride with Axel, though. I don't want her, or her little one to come to harm," Mitt said. Garth nodded his head, relieved that all the shuttle crews had taken the cross training.

"And Rowan's staying with Axel, in case he needs help," she added in Dolbith, seeing he might be about to tell them, otherwise. If it came down to keeping the Boodans entertained, Rowan was the one best suited for the job!

"Let's get to work, people! We have much to get accomplished, still," Garth ordered in a firm voice, first in Dolbith, then in English to be sure everyone understood. He saw the Boodans jump to his commands. It brought a smile to Sabin's face as he gave him a nod in understanding. Garth managed to keep a serious look on his face, but Sabin noted the mirth in his eyes.

"But what of the things we truly value?" Huras questioned, hoping they could take some things back with them.

"You may pack them up but leave them for later pickup. I'd rather see you saved first, than your things. We have plenty of resources in Winterhaven. And we can use this as an exercise for training the other shuttle crews," Garth decided, issuing the order. "Let's go look at what we've got to work with on those shuttles, and unload any unneeded cargo," he added, turning back to the rest of his crew. He saw the starmen on the steps and benches nearby looked hopeful, but wary. He realized if they truly wanted to stay, he wasn't going to stop them, but he refused to leave any humans, nor crosses, to live among them anymore.

"Yes, sir," Mitt responded, smiling. She motioned for Abbra and her brother to come with her, but George hung back.

"I'll go pack our things for later," he stated, but urged his sister to accompany them. He had sandy blonde hair, a hint of freckles across his nose and appeared the largest human here, even if he was gaunt-thin. Abbra smiled for him.

"Thanks," she voiced, then turned, ready to go where Mitt was leading them. Somehow, she felt no hesitation in associating with this starwoman. Having seen her mind and heart, she trusted her fully.

"I don't have anything worth keeping," Nick said as he fell in beside Ethan. A small group of the humans left with them, as did Nesa, which Garth noted. She walked near Sabin, a small carry sack in her hands. Her hunting party was trailing them, too, carrying bags.

"We need to help with the unloading," she explained to Garth's curiosity, smiling as she did so. She also wanted a look at her new niece, still so mad at her brother's folly, as Niles confessed it to her months ago. If she'd been made right, she'd do what she could to make friends with the human woman and make sure her niece would know she had two sides to her family. She lived and that was part Talent and miracle!

"Good," he finally responded, his doubts plain in his voice.

"And I intend to leave my things near to where you land, for later pickup," she added. He gave her a nod of his head at this, wondering if they could still pull this whole thing off so calmly? The presence of the hunters could spell problems, even with their simple weapons.

"See? That did not go badly," Rhodi stated, now that the meld was dissolved and they opened their eyes, seeing each other, once more. There was joy at the testing of their new skills in melding a greater team. She saw Ryes' earlier wisdom in doing it this way and now wholly agreed with her need to be able to respond to any potential violence. The whip scars and scratches on the skins of the humans had been horrific to see!

"Still, it was good practice anyway," Torr commented. He saw Denas, who was sitting beside Ryes, looking at her strangely. But Ryes was looking down at her son, smiling as she tickled him.

"You were so good!" she told Rhin, grinning, then picked him up, putting him to her shoulder. He was laughing and kicking at his mother's attention, then squealing in delight, waving a fist in the air at the fountain nearby. He looked to want closer to play with the cascading water.

"Ryes," Denas began, not sure of even saying such a thing aloud. While in the last of their contact, she'd felt it truly and now needed to voice it, while she had the courage.

"What's the matter?" she asked, granting her, her full attention. Denas closed her eyes, reaching out to take her hand. Ryes huffed out a breath in surprise, but responded in kind, wondering what could be so disturbing her cousin?

"I need to be sure," Denas sent, "May I use my Talent and examine you?"

"Yes, if you feel it's so important," she replied, puzzled but patient. After a few seconds, she realized it, too. Her own Catalyst Talent told her the truth, of what only Denas had seen for sure. She'd put it off for weeks now, partly not having the time and partly, not sure if she wanted it verified. Now she knew!

"You are, after all. I have never heard of it occurring from one generation to another and it may be why you have more than fourteen," she told her, seeing Ryes now saw it for herself.

"I'm a Talent of One plus," she stated, still trying to grasp the full significance of such a concept. "Can you tell me anything about it?" she pressed, knowing she'd been trained on old Kahmarr.

"All your children will be born with strong Talents, for one. You will need to train hard to bring out the full potential of each and every one of the Talents you possess. We have all had training to a degree, but not in some of the ones you have. I do not know who we could ask, since Kahmarr is supposed to be gone now," Denas said, feeling sad with such knowledge. After seeing the old holo and Hailys, she knew it too had to be gone.

"My Aunt Adina may have some ideas," she replied. "Please keep this between us for now, and I'll let Garth and Maren know. I'll have to find the time to get more practice in," she marveled in response, "Thanks, cousin!" She added an outpouring of warmth and love from within, appreciating her concern.

"You are welcome," she replied. "It was interesting to note they did have natural crosses there on Booda. Do you think the danger exists, with Monty and I becoming so close?" she suddenly asked, needing to know how she felt about their relationship. Ryes felt this clearly through their contact.

"You wanted a big family of your own, someday. It seems if you want to stay with Monty, you might still get your chance. I've already directed the lab staff into looking into developing some new birth control methods, for both humans and starmen to use, since we all seem so fertile here. It'll be up to the two of you, if you want to take the chance, or not. I'm only glad you both seem so happy together. Maybe you should discuss it with Monty?" she suggested.

"Could you check me, now?" Denas pressed, suddenly feeling it might be important. "I have never craved sex before in my whole life, and I was afraid with Saree coming into her season so soon, it might have tripped mine, too."

"As you wish," she replied, calling up Healing and doing so. It was true. She was having a mild season, but nothing like any others she'd sensed before. "You're right! You're going to have a child. Maybe you should have Maren make sure this little son of yours will be all right? I don't have the depth of ability he has," she admitted.

"Alright, but this is going to be very difficult for Monty and I to have to hold back for the next two months!" she returned.

"It was hard for me! But it seems you still have a few days left, so enjoy them while you can," Ryes urged her, humor in her thoughts. They both let go of their inner commune with smiles upon their faces.

"So, what was that all about?" Maren questioned. He now held Rhin, since Ryes was busy. He'd been about to wiggle free from her with the fountain firmly within his sight as a goal. He'd grabbed him before he fell and actually hurt himself, escaping from his mother's grasp.

"I'll tell you later," she promised, smiling as she stood and took him back. Denas nodded her head, seeing the curiosity in Monty's eyes, as he helped her up.

"Let us go home. I will tell you, too," she replied to his unspoken question, giving him a warm smile with her secrets dancing in her merry eyes. Monty smiled as he shook his head in response.

"I still have to stand watch in the computer room, before I can call it a day," he advised her.

"Nope, you're free for the rest of the day," Ryes assured him, smiling. "And that's an order," she added. Maren was thinking he could now guess.

"And I'll escort you back to your office. I have a few things we need to go over, before they return," he said in an even tone. This got her attention.

"I'm sure there're a few concerns," she agreed, then smiled as she stepped up to Rhodi. "Thank you," she told her, hugging her one-armed. Rhodi smiled as she gave her a one-armed hug in return, momentarily cupped the top of Rhin's head with her other hand; giving her a nod as she withdrew her hand and let go of their hug. The child still practically hummed with the seepage of his sleeping Talent. Amazing! The only more powerful Booster she'd ever felt in her life was his mother, and she wondered what his Talents would grow to become?   His Focus Talent was a new one and it amazed her!

"I finally feel as if I am a contributing member of this community. Somehow, teaching children of Kahmarr and of the Old Alliance's history is not as rewarding as I thought it would be. And my thanks to you, Maren, you are far more patient, and gentle a person, than I could ever have imagined." He gave her a smile and nod of his head. With this, she turned, heading for her own home, glad it was close by. Her heart was weighing her now. He wasn't her prince, and could never be him, but he would've been a wonderful replacement in her life, if he'd been free.

"So, what was that with your cousin?" Torr pressed, joining her and Maren, as they headed down into the main facility, outpacing the rest of the group. Ryes rarely walked at a sedate pace.

"She's a Catalyst, too. And as we were in such close contact, and sitting right next to each other, she discovered I'm a Talent of One, but unlike my mother, I have more than fourteen Talents. It shocked her more than I think it did me," she explained in a low voice, hoping no one else was close enough to hear her.

"I knew it!" Maren declared loudly, grinning merrily at this news. "You've got too many Talents to not be," he stated, in a much lower voice. "And what else?" he pressed. Ryes frowned at this, not wanting to voice her suspicions before Torr.

"The rest was personal stuff," she returned, "between the two of us, only." He felt there was more here, but glanced to Torr, instantly understanding her mood.

"Let me guess, nothing that would involve men?" Torr asked with a slight bitter edge in his voice, as Ryes shook her head at this.

"No. Only that her season is upon her. She wasn't sure about Monty fathering her cubs, but I think has decided he's far better than anyone else she knows. That's why I'm giving them both the next few days off, to take care of more important matters. If the Boodans have natural crosses," she started, smiling for him.

"And we already have two of our own," Maren added. Torr looked puzzled by this news.

"Who?" he demanded aloud. Dotti, he knew about, but who else now?

"Justin and Sana now will be having the two sons we helped create and a daughter they conceived naturally, who'll still need a few adjustments," he told them. "And Kaspin and Seth Fairfax are going to have a son. She was in season last month, but stuck it out with Seth, thinking they couldn't have any children. She came to me yesterday, wondering after the Founder's Day announcement. Seth's delighted with the news, but she wasn't sure what to believe. I don't think she expected to have any children with him as her partner. She's about your age and will have plenty more seasons, still. Either she'll have to get used to it or will have to pick her partners a little more carefully. It was obvious she's fine with Seth as a free mate, but not as an actual mate. They were discussing which home they were going to live in, since they now had a child due. I made sure to warn Seth about the two month's abstinence. That part seemed to disappoint them both."

"Isn't Kaspin from back east?" Torr questioned, wondering. They were now down in the main hallways, heading for the offices.

"Yes. She came out here from Riverward with her youngest sister. She's been working on the cleanup crew in the evenings," Ryes replied, "And, Seth usually pulls night watches, because he says he loves the quiet."

"And apparently, the action," Torr added with a chuckle, "At least they're both of an age."

"That's true," Maren agreed, chuckling with him as Ryes smiled and shook her head.

"I've got to get things wrapped up for the day. See you two, later," Torr said, stopping before his office door.

"Right... later," Ryes agreed, smiling. She and Maren continued down to her office.

"So, what else?" he finally pressed, needing to know.

"There's something not quite right about Denas' season. As if it'd been rushed or made to happen. She's a Catalyst and has Mind Voice, not Healing. Could someone have done this to her, or is it like she's thinking, caused by Saree's season coming on? They were close friends at one time. I know she's been so depressed over losing her whole family, but between my cubs and Monty, she's been back into the pulse of life again. With cubs of her own to hold, it might bring her back to us, fully. She and Monty already have one begun and heaven only knows what the next few days will do, but once her season's over, could you check her a little more thoroughly? I don't have the finer touch you have, cousin," Ryes admitted, needing his help for this one. They stopped outside her office, the corridors were clear for the moment.

"I'll take care of it," he assured her, feeling disturbed that someone would willingly tamper with another's body, without their active knowledge, nor consent. He'd never tolerate it! Rhin reached for one of his braids, making cooing noises. Maren smiled as he disengaged his tiny, grasping fingers, noting his little claws were just getting their first touch of hardness. It'd be another five years before they'd harden fully.

"Thanks, cousin," she breathed in response. "I'll see you soon, for dinner," she said, seeing his mind preoccupied with the problem. "There's nothing to do about it, until you can check her yourself, and it could be natural after the long time in stasis," she reminded him. He smiled, giving her a nod of his head.

"That's the truth," he agreed. "Let me know if you need us," he urged her, sure she'd check up on the others on Booda again, soon. Ryes smiled merrily at this, nodding her head.

"By the time we're ready for bed, they'll be blasting off Booda, bound for home. You bet I'll be keeping tabs on them!" she returned. "Oh, wait! If these people have been living in lower gravity conditions all their lives, will they be able to blast off so easily? Can they take the strain of the added g-forces? Those shuttles don't shield much against that," she asked. Maren looked thoughtful for a few moments, knowing it was a valid concern.

"I should've thought of that one," he agreed. "How about I'll go check on things in my office, then be right back, so we can do an evaluation of the Boodans, together?"

"I knew you'd find another excuse to go with me, again," she teased.

"Someone has to keep the trouble you get into to a minimum," he playfully scolded with a laugh, then gave her a kiss and headed for his own office. She sighed as she watched him go, so glad he was her cousin.

Huras looked disgusted at Lacon, as he was trying to quickly bundle what few possessions he had, in preparation of their departure. The elders had made sure their things were packaged up first, and only when that was done, did they allow the others to take care of their own things. They were using the ragged blankets and any other container they could find, or fashion, to keep their things together. They lined up the containers inside one of the biggest stone dwellings, along a back wall, keeping the human possessions separate from the starmen – just in case - as per the wishes of the elders.

As a gesture of the new conditions their lives were now taking, Huras cast his own whip into the trash pit and directed all the other starmen to do the same. There was surprise and reluctance, but they all complied. The humans were surprised and unsure if they should be happy with this voluntary change, or not. As if in expressing their relief, they might be punished for it. The starmen still had claws...

"I want everyone who's already packed up and not helping with packing the rest of everything else, to start heading towards these space-faring ships," Elder Pak ordered, first in his broken English and then in Dolbith. He was tired of the others milling about, scared, and unsure of what to expect next.

"The women and children, too," Huras added. The children were trying to add in favorite rocks, or leaves, or patches of old hides to the packing piles.

"Starmen, or humans?" Roya questioned, unsure. She practically jumped and quickly backed away from them, as both elders turned with anger in their eyes.

"Both!" Huras and Pak practically shouted at them. At this order, the rest gathered all the children and headed out, going in the direction they'd seen the strangers come in from, before.

George came in with another armload of meager possessions, dodging the rush of the people streaming out the door.

"This is the last from above and across," he told them, adding it into the starman side of things, sorting out the different bundles before standing and turning around.

"How much more?" Pak asked, giving him a nod for consideration.

"Only below, on the far side," he replied in his broken Dolbith. Chris came in with several bundles, putting them on the human side of the room. Lacon stepped over to their end of the room, finished with his sorting now, too.

"Let's go get the last of it, then double-check everywhere," he advised. The other two humans gave him a nod of his head in answer.

"How can we be sure you're getting everything?" Huras asked, frowning with doubts playing in his eyes. Chris huffed out a short laugh, throwing his arms open to encompass the whole room around them.

"This is for all of us! We're now one people – The Boodans. It's not starmen and humans, just Boodans. We do this for all of us," he explained. This surprised both elders with Pak giving him a nod and smile.

"It truly is! Thank you," he told them. This brought our real smiles, then they turned and headed out the door. "They're right," he assured Huras. "We're now The Boodans. It doesn't matter who our ancestors were, only what we make in our new lives. We have to lead them onward as one people." He finally gave him a nod of understanding.

"I hope they keep their word and return to bring our things back to us," Huras said as he turned to survey the treasure trove before him. The fingers of one of his hands twitched to explore things, but he resisted, as he realized these precious things were everyone's last memories of home. He turned and stepped away from the piles to finish his early breakfast, sure it was going to be a long day.

Launch for Home

Chapter 18

Sabin and Axel quickly had the unloading party organized, with everyone, except Mitt, Ethan and Nick lending a hand. Mitt was busy checking the systems, giving Axel reports directly, using her Mind Voice. He found he rather liked that she had this ability. Through her, he was able to provide a quick analysis of a given problem on the spot. It saved them both labor and efforts, time and again. The only drawback, as far as Axel saw it, was he didn't have the Talent himself, and had to rely upon Mitt contacting him first.

"There're eight suspension tubes, four of which are operational," Mitt informed him, from the lower level of the larger shuttle. She was now referring to it as Flutter-wing, due to its unstable flight characteristics on its short journey to their landing site. The other, smaller one she called Sand Burrower, due to her finding it half-buried in a sand dune. She had Ryes get it free with her Earth-Shaper and Manipulator.

"Chuck the dead ones and keep the live ones. You never know when you'll need to put a troublemaker on ice," he told her. She smiled to herself at this, understanding it only too well, and hoped she wouldn't have to use them, but she kept her stunner in her pocket at all times. "Anything else?" he asked, while she had their inner communications open for the moment.

"I've got the Defender's computer updating both the Flutter-wing and Sand Burrower's computers. There was some military tactics stuff, which I saved to storage and made sure I removed the cubes, so they won't get erased, or overwritten. I figured my brother might want to review it later. The compressors are going like champs and the water detail just arrived with some yellow-tinged liquid, they call water. I've got it being filtered out, before being added into the systems and them off for their next load," she informed him. She felt his humor at her efficiency.

"Not everyone has the privilege of growing up with fresh, clean well-water to drink," he chided her, smiling to himself. They were pulling out the weapon racks from the Burrower to make more room. He'd have to do new mass calculations, once they had all the modifications finished. "As soon as these racks are out, I'll need you over here to check out the suspension tubes on the Burrower. That's one piece of equipment I never want to see malfunction."

"Right, will be over there soon," she agreed, then let go as she had to direct the others in removal of the dead tubes. Every ounce could count! She didn't look forward to piloting this ship down through Tayna's atmosphere!

"Mitt!" she heard her named called out, then realized it sounded like Maren's voice. He had to be tapping Ryes!

"I'm busy," she sent in return, keeping her eyes open while using her Talent. She'd been doing it this way all day; not entirely trusting yet.

"We're going to have to check the Boodans to strengthen them for the g-forces of takeoff," Ryes insisted, knowing it was crucial. She stopped; surprise written in her eyes as she understood the implications.

"You'd better tell Garth and Sabin, right away," she suggested, realizing they were right!

"We will, but is there anything else we need to cover, that you can think of?" she pressed, wanting to cover all the bases, while they could.

"How about lessons in how to eat, drink and use the bathroom in a weightless condition? Not to mention, how many would be prone to motion sickness. We have a limited amount of the medication available and I'm not going to clean up after sixty some odd people!" she declared, not wanting to imagine that scene! There was humor from the other two as they did sympathize with her.

"We'll see what we can do," Maren promised, deciding to begin with the humans, who weren't involved in the re-tooling of the two Boodan shuttles. But Ryes pulled them over to Garth and Sabin first, who were just finishing with the removal of the weapon racks.

"Hate to bother you," Ryes sent to them both, "but we're going to have to check the Boodans to see if they can stand the g-forces of takeoff and landing." Garth was at first irritated by her contact, feeling she needed to get her own work done there in Winterhaven, but he realized she had a valid point.

"I never thought of it. They've been living all their lives under this lesser gravity, and we had our own time with it, when we lifted off Tayna," Sabin voiced aloud, seeing Garth's irritation, then understanding.

"That's a good idea, go ahead and do what you can," he encouraged, sure Maren was in on this, too.

"Thank you, O'Great One," she returned, teasing him. "And I don't check up on you every five minutes, as you seem to believe," she added in mild protest.

"Time's a wasting," he reminded her, resisting the urge to chuckle. "Get busy," he ordered. She withdrew, leaving them to their own work, noting the puzzled look in Axel's eyes.

"Alright, time for us to get things rolling," she asserted. Then, as they were centering in on Nick, Tennan, Ruan and Minya joined into their commune.

"We're here to help," Tennan told her brother and cousin.

"It's too much for just the two of you to handle," Ruan insisted.

"The more the merrier," Maren agreed, knowing they could use their help with sixty-three people to adjust, even with Ryes' pool of power. "Let's get this done," he pressed as he focused in upon Nick, once more. First, he contacted him, through Ryes' Talent and let him know what they were doing, then began their examination, seeing there was more needing to be accomplished than a simple adjustment to a heavier gravity. After what seemed a long time, they finished and backed off. Nick laughed aloud, smiling merrily as Dr. Cruthers looked puzzled.

"They healed me up. I've never felt this good!" he told him. Ethan gave him a curious look.

"They could've waited until our return to Tayna," he pointed out, wondering, knowing Ryes and Maren usually had good sense in this regard.

"It was initially to make sure I could survive the take-off. We've lived under this lower gravity for so many years, considering we don't have any special equipment to compensate for the g-forces. Maren and Ryes decided to try to adjust everyone, themselves," he explained.

"I forgot," Ethan admitted, glad Ryes was on top of things, once more. "They're such a blessing, always trying to anticipate our needs."

"And they were kind enough to make sure the rest of my body's in working order. One of the women was also making sure I remembered how to eat, drink, and use the null-g toilets. Guess they're trying to cover all the bases," he admitted. Ethan chuckled, nodding his head in agreement.

"We have a good, close team at home. You'll soon see," he assured him, relieved they were trying to think of everything ahead of time. He turned back to his computer entries, relieved. These systems truly were archaic, now. He wondered when he'd become so jaded, when their AI was older, yet ran far better after Ryes allowed that Prince's program to update it.

"I can't wait," Nick replied, wishing they were launching already! He went back to securing any loose items in the cockpit, as he'd already finished the cargo space area of this ship. Funny, as he seemed to remember this routine well, from so long ago!

"If we didn't have you filthy lot, there'd be room for more of my things," Mive shouted at a small knot of human and mixed children, who were awaiting their parents' direction, near the shuttles.

"They came here to take us back, first," Eris returned hotly, her eyes wide in panic. Would they let them leave now? Mive strode closer to stand over the gangly child, who was obviously a cross.

"Well, there'll be one less," she breathed out as she struck at her with her claws extended. Suddenly, she was tossed up into the air, as if a windborne leaf. She fell hard upon the ground; the wind knocked out of her lungs. It took her several long moments to regain her feet again. The ghostly image of that strange woman stood between her and the mouthy child.

"If you don't let go of your hate, you're not going to be allowed aboard, and you'll be left here alone to rot," Ryes scolded her. Maren was already seeing to the girl's healing, as well as the adjustments she'd need to survive. The other women with them were already taking care of the other children gathered.

"You animal lover!" Mive shouted at her, hate in her eyes. Toro ran over from where he'd been helping with the water; pulled her back, shaking her by her shoulders as he did so.

"Don't be stupid!" he ordered his wife. She focused in upon him, then hung her head in shame. She'd lost control again. It was happening to her far too frequently. "She means it."

"I'm sorry," she apologized to him.

"Not me, her," he told her, letting her go and turning her towards Ryes.

"I'm sorry. Sometimes I can't help my temper," she admitted, turning to face Ryes once more, sorrow was deep in her light brown eyes. Ryes didn't look convinced but felt Maren's need to speak with her.

"It could be a chemical imbalance in your body. May I check?" he asked, appearing beside Ryes. She looked to her mate, then seeing his expression of agreement, she stepped closer. Maren reached into her very being, delving for the wrongness he felt emanating from her a moment ago. He found it and set it to right, then did the adjustments needed for her and the two cubs she carried to survive the forces of their takeoff and landing. Also healing the cubs, but they were all pitifully thin and malnourished here, which tore at his heart. They had to save them all!

"I feel very strange," she told him, feeling he'd withdrawn.

"I found there was something wrong within your brain and took care of it, as well as made sure your body will be able to withstand the forces of takeoff and landing. We must make sure everyone has this last adjustment to survive the trip. I'll see about the other adjustments we'll need to do for your two cubs, so they'll be healthy, as soon as you reach Winterhaven," he promised. She placed a hand to the side of her bulging stomach, feeling them moving now.

"They've felt weak," she admitted, appearing worried about their survival.

"They'll be fine for the trip, and I'll make sure they'll be born healthy. I'm a Healer, after all," he assured her, smiling. "You're going to have to pick out some fine names for your two sons, soon. Now, let me see to your husband and the others," he urged.

There was a strange smile upon her lips as she stepped back. Mive found herself humbled and awed by the power and gentleness of this one man. She couldn't wait to leave. The air now seemed suddenly thin, making it a little harder to breathe. She wondered what Tayna was truly like?

"My thanks for the care of my wife and sons," Toro told this image of the foreign Healer.

"It was no effort. I'll be able to give each and every one of you a more thorough check, once you reach Winterhaven," he promised, "Now, do you mind if I adjust your body for the g-forces involved in takeoff and landing?"

"Do as you must. The humans need to undergo this, too?" he asked.

"Yes. Everyone from Booda must undergo this adjustment, or you'll die merely in the attempt of leaving this world. Tayna has a higher gravity, so it'll make it easier for you to live there, too," he explained. He saw this starman didn't understand what he was talking about and the others around him were looking puzzled. "If you take a sling and twirl it over your head, you're causing the rock within the sling to feel a greater force, than what you feel. Now put yourself in the place of the rock. The pressure is what you'd feel as the shuttle takes off. We want to make sure your body can withstand that pressure." The light finally dawned in his eyes, as he now grasped some of what he was telling them.

"Then, I'm ready to receive your touch, Healer," Toro stated, gesturing for him to approach. Maren smiled to himself, feeling relieved. He reached out to him and performed the required adjustments, then noted the others were gathered behind him, looking ready for theirs too, now they understood it more clearly.

"You'd better help out with the shuttles, now. There's still work to get done, and they could use your help," he urged once finished.

"We'll do so, immediately," he replied, then gathered Mive to his side, as they rushed off. The next Boodan starman stepped forward, ready. Ryes and the other women finished with the children, then turned their attention to the human adults, who'd come closer to see what they were doing. The children were now busy gathering some nearby fruits to bring as food for their trip, as Ryes suggested.

"It took a few hours, but we're finally ready to go," Axel reported to Garth, as the men were finally taking a break. The children and adult Boodans were sitting in a ring of mostly mixed starmen and humans. They were roasting some tubers they found, in a campfire, and it almost seemed homey now. Garth gave him a nod, as Mitt stepped out of Flutter-wing, wiping her hands on a rag. She smiled with a mixture of relief and uncertainty in her eyes.

They'd collected all the removed equipment from all four shuttles nearby in orderly stacks and rows, for later pick-up by salvage crews. Ethan and Rowan had gone and tagged the location of the Boodans' stored things and did a quick sweep of the area in their former village with the aid of drones – to make sure it was well deserted. They didn't want anyone tied up and forgotten on purpose. After spending hours working side-by-side, the attitude of both the humans and starmen had improved, but they still planned upon splitting them up to keep any conflicts minimized. The Boodans were getting excited about the coming journey and finally relaxing.

"As ready as can be," Mitt reported to her brother. He gave her a nod, stood up and dusted off his hands on his trouser legs, then turned to the Boodans. All eyes were turned his way, as this pitiful collection beings hoped now that they'd been shown there were other ways to live.

"We need to start loading everyone aboard. For your comfort and the flight capabilities of the shuttles, we'll be splitting everyone up," he informed them, getting nods of approval out of Rowan and Ethan for his wording.

"I'll take fifteen starmen with me," Sabin ordered, standing up next to Garth, with a no-nonsense look in his eye. Huras shuffled forward to stand before him.

"Where do you want us?" he asked. Sabin gave him a nod.

"Follow me," he replied, then gave Garth a smile and nod, and headed to the Sand Burrower. She might have a pitted hull, but he felt fully confident in her abilities to get them home. Huras turned to his people and gave them a quick survey.

"I'm taking my family and whoever else wants to join us," he told them. Nires stood, as did his wife, Sciri, but Nesa stayed seated next to Abbra and ignored him. He snorted and turned to follow in Sabin's wake. This was not the time to discipline the child, he realized. Once they had gone, Axel stepped up next to Garth.

"I'm taking the new mother, and any other humans who can come with me. I have room for sixteen people," he stated. Abbra appeared surprised, then a delighted smile blossomed across her face. She gave Nesa a nod and the two of them stood, with George and Nick joining them. They sorted themselves out and joined Axel, who smiled to see Nesa among the humans, as if this was her rightful place. He'd cleared her earlier with both Mitt and Sabin, to be sure. He gave her a nod, then turned to lead them over to the Defender. Rowan followed them over to the ship, as they previously agreed.

"All the families with young children will be with me," Garth asserted. There were a few humans, some crosses and a few starmen with children around him.

"And I'll take the rest of the starmen," Mitt announced. Nesa's hunters were the first to join her. She gave these men a nod and led off a group to the Flutter-wing, mentally praying to Aletagga that she'd lift-off safely. Ethan joined Garth as he and the families went to the Avenger.

"Cross your fingers," Axel suggested in English, now that the shuttles were finally ready for launch. They'd gotten everyone strapped in and as comfortable as possible, and as calmed down as possible.

"Hah! I don't think I can spare any," Mitt returned, grinning. She was nervous about this trip. The equipment she had to work with was marginal and she wished she had more time with Ryes' Talents to use for further improvements.

"Mitt, you could fly that thing in your sleep," Garth teased, knowing the way she could get easily keyed up over things. "Go ahead and launch," he ordered, feeling if her ship were the problem child, it was best to see if the Flutter-wing could lift, at all.

"Roger," she returned. She already had the engines up and online, with almost all the systems reading as ready. She took the controls into her hands and urged the ship to lift off. It balked, feeling far too heavy to leave even this weak gravity. Her heart sank, wondering what they were going to do? Then suddenly, she felt as if the ship was shoved from beneath and they were quickly rocketing upwards, leaving Booda behind them for good. She let out a sigh of relief, as she headed out on the pre-planned coordinates. The regular flight engines working like champs, at least.

"Thought you could use the help," Ryes told her, "But I barely managed that one. I don't know about landing her on Tayna, she's pretty heavy," she admitted, embarrassed that she was fully drained from this one small effort.

"You've been trying to do too much all day, again," Mitt sent, scolding her, smiling to herself. She knew the ship hadn't done it by herself!

"There's no way I could desert you, when you need my help!" she returned. "Life would get too dull around here without you!" Then she felt Ryes drop out of the link and was worried about her.

"Way to go, Mitt!" Axel told her, over the radio. "That old ship has some life in her, after all!"

"No. It was only because of Ryes that we made it. I'm having serious doubts about landing her on Tayna. We'll have to come up with a plan by the time we reach home," she warned. She saw the other three shuttles lifting and joining her upon her trajectory, by her instrumentation. At least they were all going home in good order, so far.

"We'll come up with something. Don't worry, Sis," Garth assured her, relieved Ryes had been able to help.

"Yeah, just kick back and enjoy the ride," Sabin suggested. If Ryes had been behind that launch, he wondered if she'd be able to help the ship land on Tayna? Or would Tayna be too much for even her? He'd have to radio in and talk with her about it, later. For now, he had a ship full of humans, who were all trying to ask questions at once. This was going to be a long voyage home...

"Ryes!" Maren cried out as she suddenly dropped out of the link. He was dumbfounded when she nonchalantly reached out and shoved the Flutter-wing up and out of Booda's atmosphere. He realized he should've suspected it'd been too much for her. When they were suddenly dropped out of contact with the shuttle crews, it shocked the others, gathered in the meld. Maren knew he couldn't just instantly drop the link with the rest still reeling from being cut off from Ryes' Empath Talent. Rhodi, Raya and Poli helped him restore some sense of calm and eased everyone back, letting the link dissolve naturally.

"What happened? Ryes fainted," Dotti told him, as she now held Ryes' still form in her lap. She was breathing, but otherwise looked unresponsive.

"Let me have her," he urged, taking her from his wife. He closed his eyes and concentrated. After several long minutes, he opened them with a look of relief upon his face.

"She will be all right?" Dunn questioned, astounded at the casual display of power she performed, just a few moments ago.

"Yes. She's resting for now. She's been doing too much today," he replied.

"Good. Then let us call it a night and let everyone get some rest, to help prepare for when it comes time for the landing," Rhodi suggested, standing up.

"That's a good idea," Maren concurred, "I'll go put her to bed." Dotti smiled, giving him a nod of her head in agreement.

        "If that is what she can do with her Manipulator Talent... I do not think I could ever do anything like that!" Almas despaired, in a low voice. Denas stepped over to comfort her friend.

        "No one expects you to be able to do something so grand," she assured her. Suddenly, Almas pulled away, meeting her eyes with a strange look in her own.

        "Maybe that is a part of it? We do not expect to be able to do impossible things, so we do not. Maybe if we believed we could, we would?" she suddenly voiced. "Ryes has no idea what she can, or cannot do, so goes with her heart."

        "You bring out a good point," Poli agreed, seeing it was true. "Could our formal training be working against us, allowing us to be shackled?" she wondered.

        "Why don't we talk about all this tomorrow?" Torr suggested, yawning. "When we can be more awake? Maybe we can do impossible things if we don't think of them as impossible?" he suggested. Monty laughed at this, nodding his head in agreement.

        "I never knew I had Talent before, in my whole life! So, this is the first impossible thing I've done," he stated. This got chuckles of agreement from the other, longtime Winterhaven dwellers.

        "That's the truth," Sadie said, "But I'm with Torr. It's too late to discuss Cinderella fantasies. I'm heading for bed." With this she left, heading toward her home and Gleds' warm arms.

        "Goodnight," Raya wished everyone, feeling Sadie had the right idea in mind. It was past time for bed!

        "Goodnight," Maren replied. He stood, holding Ryes in his arms, while Sayer looked at her with concern. The others were following Sadie and Raya's examples and were bidding each other goodnights and heading home.

        "Will she truly be all right?" Denas asked, in a low voice.

        "Yes, she will. She just overdid things, again. She keeps forgetting she does have limits," he replied, smiling assurance.

        "Good. Then we will wish you all a goodnight," she said, as Monty gave a nod of his head in agreement. They left, arm in arm.

        "Will Mom be all right?" Sayer whispered, as she walked back home with Maren and Dotti.

        "She'll be fine," Dotti assured her, playfully ruffling her hair, "Don't worry, kiddo."

"If you want, you could sleep with her tonight and scold, or tickle her, as soon as she wakes up in the morning," Maren offered, chuckling as he could imagine Ryes' surprise in the morning. Sayer grinned, liking the idea.

"I think I might," she agreed. Dotti and Maren laughed aloud at the look on her face, knowing Ryes was in good hands. As they entered their home, there was a red light flashing on the computer terminal, on the far side of the room.

"I'll go check it," Dotti offered, as she waved to Maren and Sayer to go ahead and take care of Ryes. She stepped over to the terminal and activated it. She was surprised to find Garth's anxious face filling the screen.

"Is she all right?" he demanded, seeing it was Dotti who was taking his call.

"She's resting. She overdid it today, is all. Maren says she'll be fine by morning," she replied. He looked relieved to hear this news.

"The computer told me she was under Maren's care, when I tried to have it put in a call for her," he explained. "I thought she was stretching herself too thin, with the situation on Booda. Could you post a note for her to call me as soon as she wakes up in the morning?" he requested. Dotti smiled, nodding her head to this simple request.

"It's not a problem, Garth," she assured him. "Have a goodnight," she wished. He grinned at this, nodding his head in turn.

"If we can get the kids to calm down and go to sleep. They just figured out how much fun a lack of gravity can be." She could hear the giggling and high-pitched laughter, knowing it sounded well familiar to her ears now.

"Good luck!" she added, rolling her eyes and smiling, "Try a bedtime story."

"Thanks!" he returned with a chuckle, then the screen blanked as he cut the com on his end.

"What was it?" Maren asked, coming back out to the living room alone.

"Garth was worried about Ryes," she explained with a sigh. "Let me leave her a quick note, then we can go home, too."

"Now that's what I live to hear," he told her, nuzzling her ear as she typed in the message. Dotti giggled, trying to concentrate enough, so to spell it correctly. Then she turned to her husband and threw her arms around his neck.

"You're mean," she accused, nibbling upon his ear in return. He scooped her up in his arms and gave her a teasing kiss.

"You know me too well," he admitted, as he headed to the door, barely able to reach the switch to open it. "Just wait `till we're home and I'll show you how mean I can be," he warned. Dotti chuckled as the door closed behind them, the computer locking it for them.

Snatch

Chapter 19

"That was a mean thing to do to me," Ryes scolded Maren as she finally came in for breakfast, the younger cubs in their stroller. He grinned, recalling what he suggested to Sayer last night.

"Just can't take a little tickling?" he returned. Dotti chuckled as she was settling Rowis and her tray in next to her. Karis was curiously listening, all ears. Ryes snorted at this, smiling. She pulled the stroller over and began putting her cubs up into their highchairs. Sayer trailed Raby into the dining room, heading over to get their trays right away. Sayer gave Maren a thumbs up with a huge smile, before she disappeared within. He laughed at this, nodding his head.

"I'm outnumbered as is and now you're teaching them to be ornery, to boot," she protested, having caught a glimpse of their exchange.

Tars emerged from the kitchen area, tray in hand. She'd gotten to where she loved to follow Sayer, Raby, and Katas about, trying to act as grown up, as she thought they were acting. It was comical to see at times. She sat down next to where she knew Sayer would be sitting.

"Good morning, Tars. Are you going to be learning anything interesting today in school?" Ryes asked. Her younger cousin smiled at being so addressed.

"Yes. We're learning about gravity and how it affects things like the way the shuttles fly," she boasted, grinning with pride. Surprise was written in Ryes' eyes as she gave her a warm smile.

"A very timely lesson," she returned in compliment, "Do the teachers always do such things, when we've got specific operations going on around here?"

"Yes, they do. That way the teachers can tap live data and vid files from the computers, to illustrate their lessons. They seem to pick things up more quickly that way," Dotti explained. She was now teaching part time and found she srather enjoyed what she originally considered a chore.

"So, the word is, don't mess up," Maren teased, seeing the surprise in his cousin's eyes. She chuckled in return, having finally settled all five of her little ones. Ardis came in with Katas and her two sons, heading over to their highchairs too, as Katas went on into the kitchen for her breakfast.

"Where are we going to settle all sixty-two Boodans?" Ryes suddenly questioned the others around her for ideas. The problem had been plaguing her all morning long! "I could see maybe letting some of the surviving families draw lots for the remaining apartments, but I refuse to let them occupy the ones we're building for the caravaners."

"Down here, would be my first, best bet," Jim replied as he and Bethy joined them, coming out with their trays. "Do you think they could become a security issue?" he questioned, seeing an unusual look of hesitation in her eyes.

"Yes. The humans were the starmen's slaves for almost all their lives to date, so I'm not sure about leaving them running around the underground facility - unsupervised," she told him with a heavy sigh. "I know Garth and Sabin haven't discussed it yet, but I want some suggestions available for when they start considering it."

"It could be a problem," Bethany agreed, frowning. "Was it really that bad?"

"Yes, it was Bethy. When they arrive, we've got a lot of work ahead of us," she informed her. "Maren, you'd better brief Ted and the rest of your team." He gave her a nod of his head, seeing there was still so much work to prepare, and they were still over four days out from Tayna.

"What about their landing?" Bethy asked, thinking she overheard Torr commenting about it to Ruan just a few minutes ago, but she didn't catch the details and was worried now.

"Mitt's shuttle, the Flutter-wing, won't make it. I don't know if I'll have the strength to help support her all the way down. We might as well find a stable orbit for her and ferry everyone down with the Defender or Avenger, seeing as the Sand Burrower still needs some time in the hangar to be up to our standards," she explained, as she gripped the edge of the table, looking to the others for help.

"Will Aunt Mitt be all right?" Sayer questioned, as she and Raby joined them, sitting down next to Tars.

"Do you think I'd ever allow anything to happen to her?" Ryes returned, with a bright smile. This brought out chuckles from everyone around them.

"But everything else is going all right?" Ardis pressed, needing to know.

"Yes, but they're having problems coming up with activities for the younger cubs. With the near weightlessness, they're a little wild, bouncing around the inside of the ships, and some of the adults aren't much better. Other than that, they're settling into things well. Our crew plans on going over the social do's and don'ts for Winterhaven with the Boodans, especially about our not allowing challenges," she assured her, smiling warmly, understanding her concern. "If you want to chat with Sabin, I've already entered my clearance for you. Use your com, anytime," she informed her, "I'm sorry I forgot to do that before." Ardis smiled, her eyes lighting up in happiness at hearing it.

"Thanks," she replied, relieved. She now intended to call Sabin, as soon as she had the cubs settled down for their nap, this being one of her days off.

"Let's go get our trays, since the girls can watch the horde plus, while we're doing it," she returned. The two women walked off companionably.

"Can't we use the fighters to help?" Sayer asked Jim. She was reaching for ideas to help out. He looked at her curiously, realizing she was Ryes' daughter after all, then shook his head.

"No. They only seat two each and you really need to know what you're doing, to pilot one solo," he explained. They'd managed to repair four of the salvaged craft from the Quest. Garth wanted crews selected and trained, but was going to hold them in reserve, against need. They weren't much more than gnats against the Snagospin ships, but they might buy them a few seconds of time as a distraction for an evacuation. He planned on taking the training, in spite of his wife's protests. It was his boyhood dream come to life!

"Where're we going to put everyone?" Katas asked, still wondering, having overheard it being discussed by others in the kitchen.

"Don't worry, honey, we'll manage it," Kovin assured her, smiling as he paused by their table. He had his cubs in his arms, heading for his own table. With Raya busy in the kitchen during mealtimes, he'd become quite good at handling them alone and felt closer to his children. "We'll have to delay our new community hall a few months, to start our first expansion to the apartment complex. I knew we should've built more from the start."

"That's the truth," Maren agreed, laughing, "we just didn't expect a large population expansion so soon."

"You're telling me?" Ryes returned, having appeared with two trays in her hands. She set them down on the table. "I'm sorry, Kovin," she began, but he shook his head at this, knowing how many things happened around Winterhaven unplanned, now.

"It's all right. Phil and I have come to conclude that we're doomed to have our projects interrupted, or modified by everyone else here, already. We'll manage it. But we're going to need help to scavenge some more building materials from Hailys. Perhaps we can form up a salvage crew once our new inhabitants arrive? After all, if they get to help build it themselves, they might appreciate more of what they're being given," he suggested.

"Now, that's an idea!" Ryes agreed, smiling.

"Wait a minute; we appreciate what you guys have built for us!" Maren protested, grinning. Kovin laughed, shaking his head in denial.

"Tell that to the repair crew, not everyone takes care of their homes," he suggested, then turned for his table, as his two cubs were squirming and fussing now. "Later," he said, over his shoulder. He knew now he'd gotten word to the one person who'd make sure word got out to care more about their new dwellings.

"Sounds like you need to post some reminders to everyone," Dotti suggested. Ryes nodded her head at this, her eyes far away for a few seconds.

"It's too bad. I thought we were all better civilized than that?"

"That's why peacekeepers exist, to remind us that we are a community and follow the rules and laws," Jim commented. Ryes nodded her head, then turned to take care of her fussing children, as ideas danced in her head.

"I'll take that one on," Torr volunteered. "It's what I do." She gave him a nod in understanding. He had a better understanding of what might be needed to establish a true peacekeeper force. Dodi smiled her agreement, as she finished feeding Tobin.

"Thanks, Torr, I'll leave it in your capable hands," she replied, happy to have one thing removed from her to-do list. "What truly has me worried is not this upcoming landing, but our attempt to rescue my Aunt Adina from out of the past," Ryes finally admitted to everyone. She realized if her one effort to push the Flutter-wing free of Booda had flattened her so thoroughly, what of the proposed trip back into Hailys' past, to pull people through time, into the future?

"What do you mean?" Dotti questioned, frowning as she wondered about it. Maren's eyes suddenly darkened, as he realized what she might've meant. Could they truly pull it off?

"Time Walking into the past is one thing, but actually trying to pull people out of another time, into our own... Can I truly do it?" she pressed, not really looking for answers from her friends on this one.

"If you can't, no one else can," Dotti assured her, smiling. "I'm sure you can do it."

"Why don't you try a practice here and now?" Bethy suddenly pressed, looking anxious. Ryes appeared puzzled by her suggestion, as she frowned and turned to offer Gareth a spoonful of cooked grains. He greedily devoured it as she smiled encouragement to him, then offered him another one, quickly, before giving a spoonful to Shyla, who ate hers quickly, too, burbling her delight.

"You mean pull forward one of the humans we know wasn't identified as dead?" Maren asked, seeing what she meant. Ryes turned back to them, shock registering in her eyes as she now grasped the proposal.

"Right!" Dotti agreed, smiling, "just sneak aboard the Star Quest, before she launches and pull a couple of people forward to our own time."

"But why the ship? Why not from the base?" Bethy asked, frowning. Jim was thoughtful, considering their choices.

"She's right. With the ship there's a greater chance of retrieving someone whom we haven't officially accounted for, and causing all kinds of problems with paradoxes," he said, speaking up. Maren nodded his head in agreement at this.

"But how do we choose whom to grab?" Ryes asked. "The entries in the Quest's computer were damaged and degraded from both the attack and through time. I don't want any paradoxes, which might bring disaster down upon us all," she cautioned.

"Actually, with the computer files being incomplete, it increases our chances of not creating a paradox," Bethy theorized.

"That sounds about right," Maren agreed. "There were plenty of people who were unaccounted for, from what Ted told me."

"But what if the ship takes off while we're doing this?" Ryes pressed, still unconvinced the ship, herself, would be their best choice.

"We know exactly when she lifted, from the AI here in Winterhaven," Dotti assured her, smiling. She could well understand her caution. "Just time it so we're finished long before she lifts." Ryes sighed, realizing they were right. It wouldn't be as far back a reach as Hailys, and it sounded very reasonable to stage a practice, before engaging in such a risky venture.

"And Garth only forbade me to go Time Walking in Hailys," she surrendered with a smile as she turned back to wipe off her Rhin's face. He was fussing, wanting more food, as were the rest now. "But who do we go after, then?" She was feeding her cubs, so didn't note the silence behind her right away. She turned her head to look to her friends, once she realized they were too quiet.

"That's the problem. We're so short staffed in too many fields and missing many friends," Bethy replied, a look of pain in her eyes. Dotti had gone pale as she realized the fate of others did, indeed, rest in their hands. She wondered about those who'd found new partners here among the other survivors, or the starmen, in the Winterhaven? She hadn't been involved with anyone else, but that didn't discount the rest. What would happen then? Maren put an arm about her shoulders, seeing how much this upset her.

"Let's leave it in Aletagga's hands," he suggested. "We'll go to a given point in the ship, which isn't being actively monitored, and see who he throws our way." Ryes smiled at this, nodding her head in agreement.

"He should be our patron god here in Winterhaven," she quipped, teasing him. He smiled in return. "When should we make the attempt? Should we wait until Garth and the others return?"

"No. There'll be enough confusion with trying to get the Boodans settled and leaving for the Great Spring Gather," Maren countered. "We roughly have a forty-hour window and still have plenty of time to prepare for their arrival. I'd say, gather everyone together right before lunch tomorrow for this. That way, we'll have time to rest up - if we're needed."

"That sounds good," Bethy agreed. Ryes gave them a nod of her head in concurrence and a happy smile of relief.

"I'd better get some messages out," Ryes stated, then turned back to her children. "Should we include everyone, or just a few?"

"All the stronger Talents, at least," Jim suggested, "and a few others, who should never be left out, like Torr."

"You better believe I'll be there," Torr chuckled, smiling at the idea of the attempt. "It'd be a good practice! But we should still keep this from Garth until we see if we succeed." Dodi appeared unsure but gave him a nod.

"Good idea and if I excluded you, I'd be in trouble with Garth," she returned, looking back to him with a smile. "Did you get a chance to check on Denas yet, Maren?" she added, wondering about it now.

"Yes. And you were right. I set things to right for her, but it looks like she and Monty will be having a son. She was pouting over the abstinence period, saying she had just found out why most everyone else enjoys sex so much," he related as everyone burst out in laughter.

"Talk about a sheltered life!" Bethy commented, grinning merrily as Jim tickled her. He put a hand to her swollen stomach, smiling proudly.

"She's definitely hanging around with the wrong crowd, if she wanted to remain pure and untouched!" Jim added, chuckling.

"It's the rest of the Sleepers I worry about. They still try to keep aloof from us," Maren returned with a sigh.

"Don't worry, we'll shake them free, eventually," Ryes assured him, finally finished with the cubs, so could now eat, too. She gave them each a teething biscuit. "Although, I'd never wish five on anyone!" This brought out more laughter in agreement.

It felt so strange for her to only have contact with the others in the link through her Mind Voice Talent, as she stood inside the half-circle. It was Rhodi's suggestion, since she needed to extend herself back into time to reach the people they hoped to bring forward. The rest didn't want to accidently get pulled back into the past, too. It still, somehow, made her feel as if she were alone upon this ambitious quest.

"We're ready," Maren sent her through Rhodi. Ryes took a deep breath and released it slowly, not sure if she was, then closed her eyes and unleashed her Time Walking Talent fully. She held nothing back, knowing she'd need the solid contact between the time she lived and what she sought out of the past. The protective golden veil enveloped her as a very familiar, wrenching sensation tore at her, instantly making her feel a few moments' nausea. She drifted back, getting a sense of when she wanted to go, quickly finding it, and opening her eyes to find herself standing in an open field, which would someday hold their apartments and the Phoenix fountain they were gathered near.

"Can you hear me?" she sent, then realized she did, indeed, hear the rest in the link, their humor, surprise, and other thoughts and emotions rippled through her mind and senses. It was as if they were merely conducting a regular practice session.

"Yes," Rhodi responded, sensing she was still unsettled about this bold attempt. Ryes smiled to herself, then saw where the Star Quest was sitting, just east of the main entrance of the research station. She saw a table set out near its base, with lights illuminating that small area. It looked way too familiar, so as she started trotting toward it, a smile graced her face. She slowed as she approached and saw Bethy and Dotti arguing with the two men manning the check point. Ryes willed herself to be unseen, smiling in amusement as she could now understand them.

"We don't need an armed escort. Dr. Cruthers has it clearly spelled out in these orders," Bethany informed the lieutenant. The ensign with him rolled his eyes at this. Dotti was also starting to get irritated with their attitude. She glared at the ensign for his impertinence but leaving the talking to her friend.

"They're not ship's crew, nor station personnel, so they will have an armed escort, or be taken aboard in an unconscious state," the lieutenant returned, sticking to procedures. Then Ryes noted Ethan striding toward them, with a look of fire in his eyes. It took her aback, for she'd never seen him angry before.

"What seems to be the hold up here?" he demanded, as he stepped into the lights.

"Sir, they won't let us board," Bethy informed him, before anyone else could speak.

"The native people will either be escorted by an armed squad, or be anaesthetized," the lieutenant informed him, standing a little more straightly in his presence, appearing to recognize him and his rank.

"My orders are very specific," he replied, seeing this young man was a bureaucrat to the core. "Bethany, Dorthea, are you armed?" he questioned. Both women produced stunners immediately. "So, it'd be a waste of manpower and time to enlist a squad."

"But Sir," he protested, uncomfortable. He hadn't thought to ask the women if they were armed.

"Get me the OOD, then," he urged, ready to play his game. Then motioned Alda over to him. He brought out his cutter and severed his bonds, freeing his hands. "That had to be uncomfortable," he commented, as Alda was rubbing his wrists. "I'm counting upon you to give us full cooperation and to look out for our three ladies, here." Alda met his eyes, then gave him a nod of his head in response. Dr. Cruthers smiled expansively as he gripped his shoulder in reassurance.

"I'll not betray your trust, Elder sir," he replied in Dolbith. He relaxed, waiting for the situation to be resolved. He was uncomfortable with boarding the monstrous machine, but if these people had no fear of it, he'd be brave, too.

"Sir, the OOD's on the line," the lieutenant said, gesturing for Ethan to take the portable com unit. He took it, listening for several long moments.

"Your procedures are only for potentially violent situations. These people are civilized and trust my staff and I," he informed the officer on the other end of the line. There were several more seconds of pause, as he listened.

"You will NOT! I'll not risk them so! These people will be going into suspension for the first time in their lives and we have no idea how they'll fare, as it is. I'll not allow them to be drugged, nor stunned. It'd potentially be issuing them a death sentence. And Petan is pregnant. I'll not see her child endangered by your policies either," he stated, icy tones dripping from his voice. It gave Ryes a chill to hear it! This was a new side to Ethan, to her eyes.

"Of course, they have their own names! Yes, of course," he replied, then handed back the com to the lieutenant without another word. The young officer took it, a small smile upon his lips as he put it to his ear, thinking he had triumphed.

"Yes Sir," he replied, after several long moments, then he cut the com and looked disgusted to Dr. Cruthers. "Your party is cleared to board," he informed him.

"About time," Bethy commented in a low voice, then turned to Ethan.

"I'll join you shortly in the lab storage area," he told her. She gave him a nod and a smile, then turned to the others she was responsible for and motioned for them to follow. The plains people and Dotti at the rear readily trailed behind her. Ethan watched them, smiling to himself. Then he thought he glimpsed a ghostly image of a petite, native woman standing nearby dressed in shorts and a T-shirt.

But she turned and was gone into the night. Most curious, he thought, as he turned back to finish overseeing the evacuation.

"I've never seen him that way," Maren commented. Ryes agreed.

"Let's get moving. We still have a mission of our own to finish," Torr prompted her. Ryes trotted toward the ship, going around her friends, grinning as she did so. She reached the base of the Star Quest very quickly, but instead of going up the regular boarding ramp, she headed aft to the cargo loading areas.

"How about a ready room, or break area?" she asked, bringing up her Inner Sight, so she could see the Star Quest as she'd been, before the Snagospin's attack. She was a thing of beauty and function, and Ryes found it suddenly hard to hold her concentration, as she searched for a likely area which wasn't being monitored. Now she could appreciate Mitt's fascination with machinery. With this Talent, it wasn't a dead lifeless thing, but was amazingly well ordered and alive! She found one at last, letting go of her Inner Sight reluctantly, realizing it was too addictive and kept her from being invisible from others. She was back to spirit form again, passing through the bulkheads, until she found the corridor she wanted.

"Hey, that's Kline," Monty stated, recognizing who was walking ahead of them.

"Was he accounted for?" Torr questioned.

"No," Sadie replied, "he's not accounted for.'"

"Great, then let's follow him," Maren urged. Ryes didn't need any more encouragement. Kline sauntered down the passageway, with a duffle thrown over his shoulder, until he reached a particular hatch, having passed others. He opened it and went inside, closing it behind him.

"The entertainment has arrived!" he announced to the others in the small room. Ryes noted, with relief, that it wasn't being monitored.

"Hey Kline!" a man shouted out with a huge smile and laugh. "You're still alive, after all these years!" Ryes observed the others were ship's personnel, dressed in shipsuits, making Kline stand out from them, even more, in his civilian attire.

"Oh, it's you," a woman commented, then turned back to her minicomp, unimpressed.

"Hello to you too, Parleer," he returned, then stepped over to clasp his friend's hand in mutual happiness.

"Good to see you, Kline," he said.

"Same here, Tuppins. So, what've you been up to, lately?" Kline asked. Ryes decided now was the time. She willed herself to be seen, as she stood in the middle of the room. A sudden silence fell upon the people in the room, as they immediately noted her presence.

"I need all of you to step forward, towards me," she told them. "Your lives are at stake."

"Am I seeing things?" Jake Tuppins questioned.

"The rest of us are seeing it right along with you!" another man in the room replied, standing up. "Isn't that one of your natives, Kline?" he asked.

"My name's Ryes of House Li, or by your method of naming, Ryes Li, and I'm here reaching into the past in an attempt to bring you into your future, or our present," she explained.

"Why?" the woman Kline named Parleer asked. Bitty Parleer stepped closer, trying to get a good look at her. This native was comfortably wearing a pair of jean shorts and T-shirt, which had a Phoenix on the front of it, as if she wore such clothing every day, but she looked a little see-through-ish, as if a holo projection that wasn't quite set up right. But there weren't any holo projectors in this break room!

"I can't give you the exact reasons, you'll just have to accept my belief that it'll be in your own best interests," she explained.

"Eloquent for a native. Thought they didn't understand English?" Jake Tuppins questioned his friend. He saw the shock in Kline's eyes.

"And do you gain anything out of this?" Bitty pressed. She was no illusion, that was for sure.

"Actually, I do gain something out of this," she admitted, grinning, with her eyes lighting up in mischief. "It's practice for a more dangerous attempt into the far past of Hailys, the nearby city of ruins, to rescue my Great Aunt Adina. If I don't try, she'll be killed as the Snagospin attack falls upon Tayna."

"These Snagaspin, who are they?" Kline asked, stepping forward to stand before her.

"Snagospin. You humans will come to call them the Darkens.
They're the people you're fighting right now, a few sectors away.
They attacked this world, named Tayna, hundreds of years ago,
destroying what there was of true civilization. Now your presence has
stirred them anew." Ryes explained, seeing they were gathering closer
to her to hear her tale.

"We don't have a lot of time, here," Maren warned her.

"Let me help," Monty offered, then opened his eyes and took
Denas' hand, which held his, giving it over to Sadie, who sat on his
other side. He used his own Mind Voice to retain his grip upon the
linkage, moving to Ryes' side, as she stood in the center of their
horseshoe-shaped grouping. He took her hand, feeling a horrid
wrenching sensation, but he focused upon Ryes and made it, as he'd
seen her do earlier, and willing himself to be seen, too. He appeared
out of thin air, taking the humans here by surprise.

"Monty!" she declared, turning to see he was with her. "This is
too dangerous for the both of us," she protested.

"We don't have time to waste, Ma'am. The Quest's going to
be taking off toot-sweet," he replied, grinning at his success. He
turned to Kline, a serious look in his eyes. "This is your one and only
chance at a future, Marc. Are you with us, or not? We can't hold this
connection open forever."

"This is for real?" one of the other women pressed, wanting to
be very sure, as she stepped closer – somehow believing them.

"You betcha," Monty assured her, giving her a nod. "If you
stay, you'll die. The future lies right here," he offered, extending his
other hand.

"I'll give it a try," Bitty Parleer answered, suddenly stepped
forward, offering them her hand. She looked excited and nervous, but
there was a look in her eyes which showed her belief in their truth.
Ryes reached out and took it, putting herself fully into the past. This
moment of real contact surprised Bitty.

"It's going to feel horrible and weird for a few moments, but
you'll be fine," she warned, then "passed" her back to the others, as if
they were standing behind them, ready to receive her. Parleer
disappeared from the room.

"Creepy," another woman stated, but stepped forward. "If
Bitty thinks it's on the up, I'm willing." She grabbed Ryes' hand,
grinning. "Ready." Ryes smiled, liking her spunkiness, then passed
her back, too. There was a ripple of amusement as the others in the

open circle found they had the two strange women suddenly among them.

"It's working!" Monty declared, grinning merrily.

"Ted says your time's running short," Maren prompted.

"Got to wrap it up. The ship's about to lift. Who wants out, now?" Ryes told them, realizing they were right. They could feel the vibrations of the engines through the floor plates, as her engines were kicking up in energy levels. Tuppins and another woman came forward.

"I like living dangerously, but at least it would be living, why not?" he stated as he grabbed Monty's hand. Monty handed him back, just as Ryes did the woman with him. There were three people left in the room. Another woman, a crewman and Kline.

"Come on, Kline. Because I recognized you and knew you weren't one of our `lost ones,' is the reason we followed you into this room, to begin with. What's the problem?" Monty pressed.

"I don't believe in magic," he replied, a cocky grin alighting his face, with his fears plain for all to see.

"It's not magic," Ryes assured him. "I'm using my Time Walking Talent, which I inherited from my mother. If your people had bred for your psi talents for tens of thousands of years, you'd be where we are, with distinct Talents, some of which are more powerful than others. This is it. Yes, or no?"

"Yes," he finally chose, slinging his duffle across his back, then took her hand, liking the feel of her warm skin against his. She smiled, gave him a nod of her head, then passed him back to the others. The remaining woman suddenly dashed up to them, throwing herself into Monty's arms. He laughed out in surprise, as he handed her back.

"I'm staying and taking my chances," the last man stated, hanging back.

"Then either get to an evacuation shuttle right after takeoff, or to a suspension tube," Ryes advised, then she urged Monty on back to the others.

"You're that sure?" he pressed. She nodded her head. He saw the human with her had disappeared. Then, just as she was turning away, he leapt forward, wrapping his arms about her. "Changed my mind," he explained to the surprise in her eyes, as Ryes pulled them both back to her own time, feeling the wrenching feeling much more than ever before, holding firmly onto Rhodi and Maren to anchor her and bring them home. She protected him as best possible from the wrenching of the shift in time.

"Made it," she breathed, then her eyes closed as she suddenly went limp in the man's arms. He was shocked but managed to hold onto her. Monty immediately turned, taking Ryes from him.

"Come on, Boss Lady. Don't do this to us," he urged. He realized she was barely breathing. "MAREN!" he shouted. Ted stepped over, taking her from him, seeing the panic in his face. He laid her out on a cart they had ready, just in case, and began to check her, noting her breathing was shallow and her skin temperature was extremely low. She was icy to the touch!

"Man, get a look at what's left of the Quest!" Tuppins declared, shading his eyes against the late morning light. He saw they were in the middle of a square of some kind, beside a fountain with a big statue of a Phoenix in the middle. But, rising nearby was the dark, sad wreckage they once knew as the Star Quest. It'd been torn to shreds. He hoped to get the chance to go give her a good, once over.

"You're sure that's her?" one of the women questioned.

"We're very sure," Ivan stated, stepping closer, now that it looked like they were finished. They noted that the area near them was filling with people, both the catlike ones and humans. There were even children running around, playing.

"Come on, Chuck's holding up lunch, until you're done," Neil protested with a grin. "Marc? Is that you?" he suddenly asked, stepping closer as he saw his old friend.

"Sure is, Neil, but where are we?" he demanded, shocked.

"Back at ol' Amitell station ten thirty-three," Bethany assured him, "Only we now call it Winterhaven and are busy trying to build a city on this site."

"Heck, we're out to change the whole planet and rescue the Earth, to boot," Neil corrected her with a laugh. The Talents were finally starting to let go of each other, smiling at their triumph. Maren rushed to Ryes' side, ready to check her over.

"Who is she, really?" Jake asked Neil, indicating Ryes.

"Actually, she's our Chief Executive Officer and even if she's young, she's a damned good one, at that," he replied.

"Will she be all right?" Bitty questioned, concerned.

"Looks like it," Torr replied, having joined the small circle of humans. "Maren wouldn't let anything happen to her, if he could help it. See, she's coming around."

"Is she his wife?" Jake asked, curious.

"No," Neil replied as he and the other Winterhaveners laughed at hearing his question. "He's her cousin. Garth's her husband, but he's up in one of the shuttles, setting up some advance warning satellites and rescuing some stranded crewmen from off one of the nearby moons," he explained.

"Oh," he responded in a low voice, as Maren helped his cousin to her feet, looking relieved. A pregnant, blonde-haired woman was immediately beside them, throwing her arms around the cat-man.

"Well, I'm starved. Let's go to lunch!" Torr suggested, smiling. Dodi stepped over to him with Tobin in her arms. He draped an arm around her shoulders, leading them off.

"We'll do introductions after lunch. Dr. Cruthers is off with Garth and Sabin, so that leaves Ryes to head the place, with Torr as her second. Maren is the Chief Medical Officer," Neil informed them, seeing the new humans grouping tightly around him and Monty. Denas stood apart, but Monty gestured for her to join him, smiling his assurance. She did so, shyly. He put a possessive arm about her, smiling proudly.

"Marc, I'd like you to meet my unofficial wife, Denas of House Clenons. When we head out for the Great Spring Gather next week, we're going to have Darman make it official," he informed him. "Denas, this is an old friend of mine, Marc of House Kline."

"Pleased to make your acquaintance," she offered, smiling.

"And yours, as well," he returned, curious. Monty marrying? It was an interesting thought, but somehow didn't surprise him that it was a cat-woman. He was too shy around other women! Brenda passed Neil Samantha to carry, while they, Monty and Denas led this newest group of humans off to the dining hall, with Ivan trailing them. Other Winterhaveners followed behind, heading down for lunch, too.

"Phil and Kovin are going to throw a fit," Brenda commented, smiling, as they reached the main doors to the lower facility. Neil chuckled his agreement.

"And we still have the Boodans to face tomorrow," he reminded her. Bitty listened in on them, wondering.

"Why would someone be upset over us? And what's a Boodan?" she asked. Brenda laughed merrily as they turned down the main corridor, then went down the stairs to the second level.

"Each time Phil and Kovin think they've got their building projects set; something happens to disrupt everything. We're going to have to add in new apartments for the Boodans, so it's not too much more to add in ones for all of you," she explained.

"Whoa! You mean we'll each get our own place?" one of the men questioned, astounded. "We just got here!"

"Well, you'll have to wait until they're built, but yes, you'll get your own place," Monty assured him. "And the Boodans are the people we discovered upon a moon of the third world of this system. There were some starmen, our cat people, who'd crashed there generations ago, and some humans, who're descendants of ones who crashed there some eighty years ago, Earth reckoning from the Star Quest."

"And a few crosses," Denas added, as Monty gave her a nod of his head.

"Crosses?" Bitty questioned as they stopped outside the dining room. Marc realized it still looked much the same, down below, just some added script to the signs.

"Human - starmen, mixed children," Monty explained. "We're only starting to see some natural occurrences."

"You're kidding?" Tuppins demanded, astounded.

"Nope. In fact, my dear lady here is going to be having our son by the end of this coming winter, or so," he assured him. They then turned to the dining hall, not waiting to see their reaction.

"He's changed. Not as nervous anymore," Marc commented to Neil. He laughed, nodding his head.

"He's settled down and grew up a little," he replied. "Come on, we're all starving."

"But I don't feel like lunch," he protested, stepped into the dining hall with him. He stopped. "First kids, now highchairs? How long have we been gone?" he questioned, astounded.

"We were in the suspension tubes for almost eighty Earth years," Brenda told them all. "You got to take a nice shortcut if you ask me. But we've been out of the tubes since last fall, not even a year, yet."

"And in that time, we've all been busy building Winterhaven," Ryes finished for them, crowding in through the press of the people blocking the doorway. "Come on, everyone grab a tray and we'll discuss this over lunch!" she ordered with a grin on her face.

"Yes, Ma'am," Monty returned, playfully saluting her. She blushed as she swatted at his hand, then turned to go grab her tray. She had Sayer and Raby bringing the horde in with them, so knew she'd just have time to get settled before she'd have her hands truly full. What to do about their new humans would simply have to wait until her cubs were fed. But it worked! She'd left out Rhin to see if she could do this without him and realized he'd be vital for their real, future rescue. His Focus Talent would be a vital resource! But she brought these people out of the past and could now hope for her Great Aunt and Hadu!

248

New Arrivals
Chapter 20

"They did what?" Garth demanded, wanting to be sure of what he was hearing, sitting up in his chair.

"Brought some humans out of the past, into the present. It was supposed to be a practice of some kind," Torr repeated himself, grinning as he saw the expression on Garth's face, as he appeared to be struggling with his inner reactions.

"As soon as she reaches her office, have her give me a call," he finally ordered, calming himself down a little. "But it did work?" he pressed, anxious now.

"Oh, yeah. We now have seven new humans from off the Star Quest. Four women and three men. She's going to have Raya assist her with their orientation, shortly. The horde always comes first," he reminded him. Garth grinned to himself, wishing he were there to help with the cubs. It was funny, he realized, but he missed both his wife and cubs, so very much. Even if there were plenty of children here with him to keep them all distracted, they weren't his children.

"Yeah, I miss them all," he replied, then sighed. "So, other than that, everyone's fine?" he asked, still needing to hear it.

"Same as normal, cousin," he assured him. "So, we'll see you all tomorrow?"

"That's what it looks like," he agreed. "We're putting a little more haste into our home journey. Look after things for me, will you? And sit on Ryes, if you have to."

"You bet," Torr promised, grinning.

With that, Garth cut the com. He sat thinking for a few moments, then called up Sabin on a private channel, to pass on this news and get his feelings on the matter. A walk into the past, a retrieval, and it worked!

"Well, we're getting everyone checked-in," Torr informed Ryes, seeing she was just finishing with using the com. "What's up?"

"Garth ordered all ventures into the past are now strictly off limits without his physical presence and prior permission," she sighed out, pouting. "Other than that, he requested for me to bring Maren and the other Healers up to double check on everyone, in preparation for the landing."

"That's a good idea and a great way to check up on everything up there," he agreed, smiling. "But won't you be spreading yourself and everyone else too thin, after what you were up to a couple of hours ago?" He realized the pool of power she and the rest drew upon, never seem to diminish, but then he never knew how a Booster truly worked.

"I'll be fine," she said in denial. "And I would hope with the link earlier, it would've helped with it being a shared burden. How do you feel?" she questioned. It was a valid concern after all. She knew Maren would never complain, nor decline her request, but wanted to be sure she wouldn't be putting Torr too close to the edge.

"I don't feel tired, at all," he admitted. "I've got Healing, too. Do you want me to help?"

"Oh, yes, I forgot. It's fine with me if you want to lend a hand, but the final approval will rest with Maren," she reminded him, smiling.

"It'd be more training," he returned, "I'll go ask. Want to come along?"

"Sure," she agreed, standing up. "We might as well take care of it now, so we can rest up for tomorrow. I can't wait to see him, Torr! It's seemed like he's been gone for so long."

"Not anywhere near as long as the last time," he reminded her, with a touch of mischief. She nodded her head to this, relieved. "Should we take one of the shuttles to the Gather? It'd sure impress the heck out of everyone - even Darman," he asked, with a laugh.

"We'd better. By the time Ethan and Rowan have told the tale of their adventure to Booda to Darman and the other elders, we'd be in trouble if we didn't have one of them there so they could take a quick flight!" she declared, as they laughed, they walked from her office to medical. "But with the shuttle we're severely limiting the trips to one or two, at the most, per person," she decided and informed him, thinking they weren't leaving it open for just anyone. "Let's see what Maren and Ted think?" Torr nodded his agreement, seeing her point.

"You may be right about limiting it, but it'll be good to have if we need to run things back and forth from Winterhaven, too," he replied, as they entered medical, stopping at the front desk. Cliff was watching things today. He and Scott rarely pulled this duty, unless their own work in the labs was truly slow.

"Is Maren busy?" Ryes questioned him, smiling.

"He and Ted are just finishing the evaluations of our new arrivals," he told her. "I don't think they'll mind if you step back there."

"Thanks," she replied, giving him a nod of her head. Torr followed her, as they went back to the large examination room. She stood in the doorway, observing the others within. "What do you think?" she asked Torr in a low voice.

"They don't seem truly different from our other humans. I think they'll be fine. I was thinking, though. Let's give them quarters down here, then put up some of our outdoor shelters for the Boodans to use. That way we won't have the Boodans running around freely down here, and possibly getting into things," he suggested.

"I agree," she replied, "and I was thinking of creating more permanent shelters at the gather site, so we'll all feel more at home." He nodded, smiling his agreement. Maren noted them at the door and waved them on into the room.

"So, what's the word?" he questioned as he finished with Cassandra Reddin. The others were already finished, quietly talking with Ted about what had happened here, between times. Cassie blushed as she jumped off the exam table and stood uncertainly at his side.

"No more Time Walking without Garth's prior permission and presence," she sighed, looking unhappy. He chuckled in response as Cassie smiled, her eyes merry at hearing it.

"You knew he wouldn't approve," he scolded her. She nodded her head. "Cassie, you're free to go, if you don't have any further questions," he told her.

"Where will we be staying?" she questioned.

"Unless someone wants to take you in as a houseguest, until your own apartment is finished, you're more than welcome to choose from one of the old rooms down here," Torr informed her, smiling. "We've decided to put the Boodans up topside in some of the outdoor shelters, so we won't have them running around down here, freely."

"That's a good idea," Maren agreed, nodding his head to this.

"Garth also asked that you and all the Healers check up on everyone topside, before the landing tomorrow - just in case," Ryes told him.

"I planned on it anyway and was glad you showed up," he replied, smiling at her surprise.

"Can I come along?" Torr questioned, hoping for the chance.

"Sure. I'd be good practice for you to use your Talent," he agreed.

"What's this Talent stuff, really?" Cassie dared to ask.

"What you people call psi ability. We have fourteen distinct Talents bred into our families for tens of thousands of years. They are: Healer, Visionary, Mind Voice, Catalyst, Time Walker, Dreamer, Booster, Manipulator, Empath, Inner Sight, Storm Caller, Water Shaper, Flame Shaper and Earth Shaper. Mostly, here in Winterhaven, we have Mind Voice, Healer and Visionary," she informed her. "Most of the Talent names are pretty descriptive, for the better part. But Inner Sight is like Empath, only with machines and other types of devices." She saw three of the other humans had stepped over to listen to her explanation.

"But some of the ones gathered in your circle were humans," Bitty pointed out.

"Yes. I've discovered some of our humans have psi abilities, too. Monty and Scott have Mind Voice, Sadie has Booster and Healing, Wren has Healing only, Max is a Dreamer and Leon has Chameleon. I'll have to check the rest of you, too. But it'll have to wait until after the shuttle puts down, tomorrow. If I overdo things, I'll only get Garth upset with me," she admitted, smiling. There were chuckles of agreement out of Ted, Torr and Maren.

"Oh, yeah he would," Ted agreed. "I believe our new arrivals are ready for their quarters assignments and to check in on what duties, or training, you'll have them begin with, whenever you feel they're ready, Ryes."

"Great, but we'll have to run a check on the others up in the shuttles, first. If you don't mind?" she asked their new humans. There were smiles and nods of their heads, as they weren't used to having someone of higher rank asking their permission for anything.

"Mind if I tag along? I'd love to see space again," Ted requested, hoping.

"Absolutely, you're more than welcome to come. I'm sure we can use your wisdom and advice," she assured him. It was rare for him to ask, so she felt it was his due.

"Tayna from the way she sees it, is a feast for the senses," Torr agreed, nodding his head as Maren laughed agreement.

"We're just sensation junkies," he admitted, as Ryes nodded, a big grin upon her face and lighting up her eyes now.

"Could I see it, too?" Bitty asked, as the remaining people gathered closer.

"If you're sure you want to try," Ryes pressed, not knowing the way she thought, yet. She smiled in response.

"Yeah, I'd love to give it a try. I want to see more of these Talents of yours."

"We'll use the waiting room. There's more room and the chairs are more comfortable, than the ones in our conference room," Maren suggested. Ted and Torr gave him a nod of agreement. "You go get situated, while I go gather our Talents." Ryes nodded as he turned to leave.

"Let's get ready," she urged them, leading the way.

They rarely used the waiting room, so it made sense. Torr and Ted, with Marc, Jake and Logan helping, pulled some chairs into a circle formation in the middle of the room, once they saw what they were doing. Ryes saw there were too many and realized the rest of their new humans were intending to come on this adventure, too. She was glad she'd have the rest of this day and evening to rest up for tomorrow morning! Maren appeared shortly, with the other three Healers. He huffed at the added chairs, but decided since Ryes didn't protest, he'd do his best to support her. He, Tennan, Minya and Ruan all took seats, as did Ryes and the rest.

"Such a large gathering for being a work outing," Ruan commented, mildly scolding, smiling at Ryes as she spoke.

"They need to understand what Talent is. This is a good way to show them," she explained in return, meeting her eyes.

"Hey, I'm here to help," Torr protested.

"Ah, that is true, you do have Healing, which must be helpful in case of an emergency," Minya returned while the other Winterhaveners laughed. Torr was usually too busy running Security to spend time helping in the clinic.

"It is, very useful," he agreed with a proud smile.

"Let's get started," Ryes intervened, smiling as she extended her hands. Maren clasped her one hand, while Bitty grabbed her other. Everyone joined hands all around, the humans were a mix of excitement and curiosity. "I want everyone to close your eyes and relax, while I establish the inner meld, then once we're all ready, we'll begin." The ones who'd been through this before, quickly complied. The newcomers were a little slower, except Cassie, who instantly obeyed, smiling as she took this with a spirit of adventure.

Ryes reached out to all the minds in her keeping, forming up the inner weaving of their thoughts and emotions. It took a few moments to get everyone settled, then she unleashed Empath and reached outwards. She pulled them upwards a little bit, to feel and know the life all about them here in Winterhaven. They lightly brushed the minds of the caged birds, as they dozed in the sun, or tended their chicks. They found a scatter-chase as she lay in her den, cleaning and nuzzling her newborns, having just finished giving birth. A windracer was galloping freely in the field, running for the pure joy of doing so. She pulled them upwards, further away from Winterhaven, so they could look down upon it from up above. Their apartments and other buildings were so small, compared to the twisted remains of the Star Quest. Further up into the sky, she reached, until all of Tayna passed below them, filled with a life of her own.

"I will never tire of this!" Ted sent out into the matrix of their joined minds. There was a ripple of amusement and agreement.

"Well, we do have work to do," Maren reminded them. Reluctantly, Ryes turned outwards, connecting with the dance of life of the planets and stars. This amazed and shocked the newcomers, as well as Ted. They'd never viewed space as having a life of its own! She reached outward, looking for their shuttles, finding them very quickly; they were much closer to home than she expected. She found Mitt first, to see if everything were truly all right.

"Just bored is all," she returned, amusement in her mental voice. "Garth told me you'd be checking up on us, later."

"Just give us a few moments to check on the others in your shuttle, first," Maren returned, smiling to himself with her attitude toward space travel being jaded, already.

"How's the Flutter-wing holding up?" Ryes asked, while the Healers were working. She was granting them her Booster to draw upon, and Ted was freely tapping her Healing Talent, being an old hand at using it by now.

"There's no way I'm even trying to land her. If it weren't for you, we'd still be back on Booda. I heard what Garth and Sabin were discussing about it. They keep forgetting I have Mind Voice and will use it, too. Axel thinks we'll just go ahead and leave her up in a geo-synchronous orbit over Winterhaven and ferry down my passengers," she informed her, disgusted. "I don't know if we'll ever be able to retrieve her, or not."

"Why not build a platform up here, using this shuttle as part of the base material? That's what they did at Timberland colony. Lone Pine wasn't much of a starport, but it's usable," Jake suggested.

"That's an idea," Marc agreed, "At least it'd be useful."

"Then we'll call our first starport `Flutter-wing,'" Ryes teased.

"I don't think much of her name," Mitt returned, amused. Who were these new minds? The ones she retrieved off the Quest from the past?

"You're right. We should let everyone have a say in naming the platform," Ryes agreed. "We'll have a `name the starport' contest."

"That sounds better," Mitt agreed, happier about it. Then she felt Maren's touch, as he gave her a check, too.

"You're getting close to your season," he informed her. "Maybe soon after we get back from the Gather."

"Great! At least we'll have time to clear both of our workloads," she sent, sighing in relief. "Isn't it going to be early?"

"A little, but then I never claim a hundred percent prediction on something like that," he returned. "I'll let your brother know."

"No. Let me tell him and Axel, both. They'll just have to deal with it."

"Alright, time for us to hop over to the Sand Burrower. See you tomorrow!" Ryes told her, feeling the Healers were done.

"I can't wait to get home," she admitted, her relief plain in her mental tones. This brought out amusement from the others in response. "See ya, Sis!" Ryes gave her love and an acknowledgment, then let her go to reach out to Sabin.

"Hello Sabin," Ryes greeted him, as she brushed his thoughts. He'd been on the com with Garth, talking about something. He turned his attention to her and the others, amused as he used his Mind Voice to link in now. "We're just conducting the checks, as Garth ordered," she explained.

"That's right," he agreed. "Better get to work as you must be tired after all you've been doing today," he advised. She checked him, herself, as Maren and the others began checking the starmen on his shuttle.

"Where's that one Talent of theirs?" she suddenly asked as she was finished. She realized she hadn't felt her presence upon this shuttle, nor on Mitt's.

"She's riding with Axel. She said something about having to help protect her little niece, or something. We've got Rowan keeping a close eye upon her."

"I'm not sure about her. I think Nesa is playing some kind of game."

"Mitt claims she's on the up and up, as the humans say and I didn't see anything else, either. She's merely realized it was a losing play, with believing humans were nothing but fodder and our holding our own group as sacred," he returned. Ted was amused at this, adding in his agreement.

"Was it really that bad?" he asked Sabin, directly. Sabin was surprised, and yet not so, that Ted was along for this visit.

"Far worse than I imagined, even having what Ryes showed us before. If these ones wish to migrate out of Winterhaven, I'm not going to stop them, but if any of them even tries to touch anyone at home, either starmen or human, they'll answer to me," he responded.

"Better you first, than Ryes," Maren spoke up, joining into the conversation. "I'm sure she'd do something more drastic than just gluing them to the walls." Ryes was embarrassed, but knew he was right.

"We'll see how things go. It might not be so bad," she offered in hope.

"And what's that other saying the humans have about barnyard animals being in the air?" Sabin quipped back, amused.

"When pigs fly," Bitty supplied, smiling to herself. This little bit intrigued her. "What did these people do?" she asked, curious.

"Had the humans cruelly enslaved," Sabin told her straight out, feeling she was new to his senses. "Who are you?" he asked.

"My name's Babette Parleer, but everyone's called me `Bitty' since I was a kid," she introduced herself, "And you?"

"I'm Sabin. I get the honor of serving as the Executive Officer of Winterhaven, thanks to Dr. Cruthers," he returned merrily. "Welcome to the colony."

"Thank you," she replied, smiling to herself. She'd never been welcomed anywhere, personally, by any Exec before!

"We are finished here," Minya informed them.

"Good. We've got two more to complete," Ryes returned. "See you tomorrow, Sabin. Ardis is going nuts with all this waiting," she added.

"You think this is driving her nuts?" he said, amused, then let go of the contact, so they could finish what they were here to accomplish. He turned back to the com, just hearing Garth and Mitt already talking about their visit.

Ryes next drifted over to the Defender, touching both Axel and Rowan's minds, finding they weren't surprised.

"Ah, finally," her grandfather scolded. "What took you so long, child?"

"Just chatting," she returned merrily. "What do you think of space travel now, grandfather?"

"Now having a small taste, I want more," he replied. "You'd best get to work, while you still have the energy to do this. Weren't you Time Walking earlier?" he pressed.

"Yes, you must be tired, by now," Axel agreed.

"I'm a little winded, but I think I can manage this, just fine. We're thinking of leaving the Flutter-wing up here as a start to our space platform," she told him, wondering what he thought of the idea.

"At least it'd be useful," Axel agreed. "We could store emergency supplies for the other shuttles, against need."

"Axel, is that you?" Marc questioned, amazed.

"Yeah, who's this?" he returned, puzzled.

"Marc Kline," he told him.

"Marc? I thought you were lost?"

"I guess I was, until this morning," he said, humor in his mental tones.

"You two can talk later, when you're back home," Ryes urged, feeling Nesa questing upon the edges of their contact, unsure of her welcome. "Hello Nesa. How're you doing?" Ryes finally asked, allowing her full contact with the group meld. It shocked her, but she quickly recovered, feeling the others greeting her openly here.

"I had trouble, at first, but have gotten used to this light feeling," she replied. "I'll have to adjust all over again, once we land, won't I?"

"Yes, you will," Ted assured her, merrily. "But I think you'll love Tayna, once you get used to the higher gravity."

"It looks so pretty and green and blue from up here," she stated.

"You'll be fine. What was this about having to help with your niece?" Ryes pressed, glad Rowan and Axel were here to listen in.

"Since my brother was behind her getting, and he's chosen to ignore her existence, I felt it was my duty to help provide for her. Is this all right? May I hunt upon your lands to help provide her with food?" she requested. This took Ryes aback for a moment.

"We usually conduct our greater hunts in Hailys, but don't have any scheduled until after the Great Spring Gather. We have plenty of food for everyone in Winterhaven. But, if you feel you must hunt on your own, you'll be a resident of Winterhaven and have the right to hunt, at need, on our lands. Many of we starmen were merely hunters, until we found the deserted Amitell station and began to reach for more, than what it was just being simple hunters. You're welcome to explore your new potentials. We do require cross training, so we'll all have some familiarity with the equipment and professions available here." While she was explaining all this to Nesa, she felt Abbra's timid contact and added her in, too.

"I look forward to this," Nesa returned, wanting to think over all she told her. She didn't have to hunt? It was an amazing thought. Then she realized Abbra was here in the mind meld, too! That shocked her, deeply. She had Talent?

"I can't believe the size of that bounder Monty took down, the last time," Maren sent with humor. "We're finished here. Time to move on, cousin."

"How can you do this, Abbra?" Nessa questioned directly, needing to understand.

"I knew I could always hear the thoughts of others, but since you were so much stronger, I didn't want you to know about it, before," she told her. Fear still coursed through her emotions, upsetting Ryes.

"Humans can hold Talent, just as starmen. They just haven't bred for it, as long as we have," she gently scolded Nesa.

"Does this mean that my niece might hold Talent, too?" Nesa returned, practically holding her breath.

"The possibility definitely exists," Maren answered her.

"All the more reason for me to stay near and help provide for her," Nesa responded, somehow relieved. There was more to this human than she ever believed! At least they had a little time to learn more about each other, before they landed. Language wouldn't be a barrier now, since they could speak directly to each other's minds and hearts!

"Alright. We do have limits, today. I'll talk with both of you later, Nesa and Abbra," she told her, then gently let go of them, Rowan and Axel. She reached out to Garth on the Avenger, her heart filled with joy to feel him, again.

"What took you so long?" he asked, merry at having been left for last. He could understand why. But he was so very happy to feel her again.

"Well," she returned, "got to save the best for last."

"She just doesn't know when to stop chatting," Maren added, mischievously teasing her.

"YOU!" she sent, flustered but happy, "Can't get any privacy here!"

"How're the cubs?" Garth sent, feeling a tightness in his throat, as his emotions spilled through their link.

"They miss you," she replied, trying to keep the longing for him from her mental voice, but it was hard.

"How are you holding up?" he pressed.

"I can't wait to see you, tomorrow," she admitted. "Ardis isn't the only one who's chaffing at this separation. Next time, we get to go out and the two of you can stay home with the cubs."

"Now that's something I'd pay to see," Ted supplied merrily.

"Me, too," Tennan agreed, laughing to herself at the vision it conjured in her mind.

"You'll all get your chance, later," Garth assured her, chuckling to himself. "Get to work," he advised. Minya, Ruan, Torr, Ted and Maren were already doing so. Ryes reached out to him herself, making sure her husband was fine and giving him her love from her heart at the same time, shielded from the rest. She felt his love for her ignite and fill her being for a few short moments.

"Just a few deficiencies, but otherwise all right. We'll have to figure out the ideal starman, spacefaring diet for the next trip out and away," she told him, pulling back reluctantly now.

"That's another thing I should've thought of," Maren said, speaking up, as Tennan started her rounds of checks, too. "Ted? Please remind me to add it to our list."

"Yes, sir," he answered, amused. It was something they'd forgotten to investigate.

"How are my assistants holding up?" Dr. Cruthers asked, having floated over to grip Garth's wrist, so he could join in the commune.

"They seem to be just fine," Ryes replied.

"They aren't slacking off?"

"No," Maren assured him, laughing to himself. "Dotti thinks they'll just be finished with the work you assigned them, right before you land."

"Fine. Let the ladies know I have faith in them. Now, what was this about some new human colonists in Winterhaven?" he pressed.

"I decided to try bringing forward a person from the past to here, using my Time Walking. The point was that it wouldn't be as far back in time, as the one will be when we try to rescue my Great Aunt Adina and Hadu," Ryes explained. "We now have seven new people added to our roster." There was a ripple of amusement from the new humans, as they realized they were the subject of the discussion.

"You do tend to reap more than you originally plan, m'dear. Just be careful," he advised.

"Garth's already forbid me to do it again, unless he's present."

"And with my permission, prior to the attempt," he added, still unhappy with the risks she took when he was away.

"We're finished. Everyone's fine and fit for the landing tomorrow morning," Maren informed him, knowing he was interrupting the upcoming lecture, he knew Garth wanted to give Ryes.

"All right," Garth replied, knowing she did have limited energy today, if she'd been Time Walking earlier. "See you tomorrow," he promised.

"I'll be waiting!" Ryes promised. She let go of him and Ethan, pulling them all back to Tayna, then down to Winterhaven, itself. When they opened their eyes, having been released from the meld, there was wonder on the faces of their new people.

"That was a trip!" Logan declared, feeling like he wanted to jump and shout.

"I've never imagined," Selena added, grinning happily, wanting to go back to see more.

"I'm ready for a nap, more than anything else," Ryes stated. "But we've still got a million things to do, yet. Let's see about getting you folks settled into your quarters, first." She stood up on unsteady feet. Maren jumped up and quickly added his arm to support her.

"Why don't you leave the quarter's assignments to Torr, and you go back to your office to rest a little?" Maren suggested, worried.

"I'll be fine," she replied, irritated.

"Don't cross me, cousin, or I'll put you to sleep for a few hours," he threatened.

"No, you can't. I won't let you!" she quipped back, merrily. Suddenly, she slumped into his arms. He smiled his triumph to the others in the room.

"I was ready, before she could defend herself. Teaches her to go against her doctor's orders!" Ted, Torr, and the women Healers laughed at this, nodding their heads.

"She has the family stubbornness," Tennan put in, supporting her brother.

"How long will she be out?" Minya asked, wondering.

"Only a couple of hours. She needs the rest far more than she'd ever admit," he informed her. "I'll go put her into one of our recovery beds for now. Torr, if you could take care of our newcomers, for the time being?"

"Not a problem," Torr replied, still smiling at Maren's craftiness. "This way, folks. And we'll see if there's anything left of your things on the Star Quest later, after dinner." He gestured for the humans to precede him out the door. Marc hefted his duffle to his shoulder.

"I already have my more-important stuff," he told him, as he passed Torr, smiling. Torr nodded his head in agreement.

"I'll send a message to Raby and Larisa, so they'll know," Tennan offered as Maren held Ryes in his arms.

"Thanks Sis," he replied, then turned for the clinic beds, glad he'd been quick. She did need the rest, far more than she'd ever admit - even to herself!

A Look Ahead

Chapter 21

Late the next morning three of the shuttles landed, loaded to capacity. They'd taken most of the starmen off Flutter-wing, leaving only Mitt and a handful of others for the last trip. As soon as Garth's shuttle was unloaded, he took off immediately, to go get his sister and the remainder of the Boodans. The Talents were relieved they weren't needed for this operation, after all.

"You still have to wait," Maren commented, seeing the sad look in Ryes' eyes. Ardis and Sabin were laughing and kissing; happy to see each other again.

"You were still mean, yesterday," she returned, teasing him as a distraction.

"What do you mean? You deserved what you got! Besides, how can you think you could withstand an unexpected Talent attack, if you can't even deflect me?" he pointed out. "We have the Great Spring Gather ahead and the gods only know what we'll be facing there!" She looked to him with shock in her eyes, seeing he was right.

"I forgot all about the last one, already. You're right, we'll need to be on our toes," she returned, relieved he was thinking ahead, after all. Maren smiled as he nodded his head, then stepped forward to greet their newest newcomers. He'd come up with that defense last night, as he and Dotti discussed it. He was glad that it worked, and even better than he thought! And he knew she didn't casually "snoop" with her Mind Voice. Ryes stepped up to walk beside him. "Here we go again..."

"They'll settle in fine," he assured her. "It may take them a while to get used to things, though."

"Ryes?" Nesa questioned, stepping forward, out of the crowd. Ryes nodded her head in response. "I'm honored to meet you, at last."

"Ryes?" another voice called out from the crowd, as Abbra worked her way out and ran toward them with a huge smile upon her face, and infant daughter in her arms.

"I'm happy to see you both, finally," Ryes responded, laughing. Abbra threw her free arm around her, laughing and crying at once. "And this is Maren," she introduced him, after she let her go. She hugged him in a similar fashion, relieved they were both real! Nesa merely stood back, smiling. She wasn't quite that trusting of these strangers, yet. Rowan and Ethan approached them, smiles across their faces.

"Glad to see the two of you back upon solid ground, again," Maren told them in greeting. Ryes laughed in agreement as they stepped over, giving her hugs and kisses in turn.

"Now we're my two girls?" Ethan teased, winking to Rowan as he smiled broadly in response. Maren laughed, catching on.

"Well, I believe if you turn around, you'll have your answer," he advised. Bethy and Dotti were right behind him, having just emerged from the main facility. It took them this long to get the last of the project completed! He did and was pleasantly surprised. He laughed as he threw his arms about them in a grand, group hug. They were laughing right along with him, with tears in their eyes.

"This place is so exposed," George commented, having come over to join his sister.

"So many other people!" Nesa returned, frowning as she saw more emerge from some heavy, underground doors. Ryes, Maren and Rowan laughed at hearing this, forgetting the way they grew up.

"You'll get used to it," Ryes assured her. She pointed to the newly erected shelters, sitting just west of their apartments. The first new section was going to be going in on the southern side. "We have some shelters all ready for your use. We have eleven apartments still available, but we're planning on letting only families with small children draw lots, to see who'll get them. The rest will have to wait for the new apartments to be built."

"What is this, `draw lots?'" Abbra questioned. Ryes had spoken the last first in Dolbith, then in English, so they'd both understand. It appeared the inhabitants of this Winterhaven spoke a combination of both languages, as a matter of course. She was having a hard time following them, at times.

"Oh, I forgot," she returned, then closed her eyes. "I'll need you, Raya, Rhodi, Denas, Dunn, Poli and Sayer. We need to do a quick instruction of languages for these people," she sent out, to the individuals she'd need. She quickly got affirmatives from all the women.

"What?" Maren asked her, feeling left out, not knowing what, or to whom she was speaking.

"We need to teach the Boodans our languages," she told him, smiling. "I merely asked a few ladies to step over, so we can get this done more quickly."

"A very good idea, my dear," Ethan commended her as he pulled out his pipe, at last. He truly was home!

"What does that say?" Nesa asked, indicating a colorful banner which Phil had hung up across the two closest shelters.

"It says welcome in both Dolbith and English," Dotti replied, wondering. "Can't you read, dear?"

"No. Reading was only for the men," she replied, fascinated with her long, curling, golden-blonde hair.

"WHAT?" Ryes demanded, absolutely insulted by the thinking behind such limitations. "Reading's not just for men, it's for everyone! This is absolutely ludicrous!"

"Calm down, Boss Lady. You can't change the whole universe in one day. Just take care of the little bit you can," Jim advised, having followed Raya over to them, knowing Bethy would be nearby.

"What would you like us to do, Mom?" Sayer asked, having just heard her. Ryes turned to see her eyes were round, then regretted her outburst of anger.

"We're going to need your help to teach these new people how to speak and write in both languages. I'm sorry, honey," she finished as Sayer stepped over to her and threw her arms about her.

"That's all right, Mom. I think I understand why you were mad," she replied, as Ryes kissed the top of her head and sighed.

"She's your daughter?" George questioned. Ryes looked up to him, smiling merrily at this question.

"You bet she is," she assured him. Sayer and the others gathered near, laughed in agreement. "Let's get all the women and children collected over here, first," she suggested, seeing the rest of her stronger Mind Voice Talents were now present.

"Human or starmen?" Nesa questioned, thinking she'd understood her, this time.

"Both," she returned. "We're all just PEOPLE," she emphasized. Nesa nodded in turn, blushing. She forgot how different things were here, already! She saw they did treat each other as equals, after all... men, women, humans, starmen. Only the children were occasionally curbed, and that wasn't for what they were, just for their energetic displays and occasional, inappropriate behaviors. This would take her time!

"Let's gather in a circle," Raya suggested, now understanding what was needed of them. It wasn't simply an understanding of both languages, but of the basic tenets by which they lived here in Winterhaven!

"I'll provide the power base for the meld," Ryes offered as the women of both the humans and starmen came closer, with their children.

"Thank you, cousin," Denas told her, smiling as she took Dunn's hand. Ryes took her hand and Sayer's, giving her a nod in return.

"May I help?" Abbra asked, feeling power in the air, emanating from these women.

"And I?" Nesa added, realizing it was important to be included from the start.

"Yes, you may," Raya granted, leading in this exercise. She, Rhodi and Dunn were the strongest of the Mind Voice Talents, Ryes aside, and they now took turns leading such forays. Abbra took her hand, as Maren took her daughter. She smiled her thanks, then took Nesa's hand. At least they'd known each other, all their lives! Poli finished their circle, making it complete. Ryes delved down within, joining the inner commune Raya formed. Then she opened up her pool of power for the others to use for this task.

It seemed to take forever but was only a few minutes. They quickly reached out to every woman and child around them, giving them a full understanding of both languages, as Ryes insisted, both the spoken and written forms. Then they instilled an understanding of the way they lived here in Winterhaven. It wasn't just the sense of equality between the two peoples, but of both the men and women, with the women having a slight edge in some instances. Nesa and Abbra were caught up in this, finding the direct feed exhilarating, and the power granted out by Ryes as phenomenal. Once the women had been encompassed, they next reached out to the men, doing much the same, without as strong an emphasis of the edge the women held. They all agreed they'd come to understand this very shortly, anyway. They released their meld, opening their eyes, just as the last shuttle was landing.

"Oh, we forgot them!" Poli exclaimed, chuckling.

"Dunn and I can take care of the last ones," Raya offered, smiling. It was the way things usually worked around here, anyway.

"Oh, Garth!" Ryes exclaimed, then rushed back to where Raby stood waiting with the cubs napping in their stroller. "Come on, Dad's here!" she urged, grinning as she took over the stroller and started walking toward the last shuttle. She heard the fussing, as the cubs started to wake, protesting such rough treatment, as she rushed over the rough surface with the stroller.

"Dad! Aunt Mitt!" Sayer yelled out, running ahead of her with Raby. Ryes laughed, not quite as daring with the little ones in this contraption upon the rough ground; she'd have to adapt the wheels. And she knew she'd get her turn soon, anyway. Garth and Mitt had already given out hugs and kisses to the girls and Sernn, by the time Ryes arrived. Minn stepped up to claim his wife too, a huge, happy grin upon his face as he wrapped her into his arms.

"I don't move as fast with the cubs to push around this way," Ryes told Garth as he laughed and threw his arms around her. He kissed her passionately, his heart relieved they were together, once again. When they finally could release each other, he bent down to check on each of their cubs, in turn.

"I couldn't fly this thing fast enough," Garth teased, as he stood back up.

"We're just going to have to build a bigger, faster ship," she told him, teasing.

"How about we see if we can excavate anything useful out of Hailys starport?" he countered. She stopped, realizing he was serious about it. "After the Gather, why don't you and Mitt try to see if any of the ships survived the attack? Or maybe find something we could marry onto the human technology?"

"I'm at your service, O'Great One," she replied, bowing with a mischievous smile upon her face.

"It's a good idea. We could give it a try," Ethan spoke up in support. He knew they had to gather what forces they could, still. Earth and her inner colonies needed them.

"We could see what's there," Axel agreed, his arm securely latched around Kerry, as they joined them. "If nothing else, with enough metal and parts, we might be able to see what we could shake together."

"It'd be better to have something we could run against the Snagospin - just in case they decide to notice us, here," Sabin added.

He was holding both Dale and Adris, with Ardis and Katas hanging onto his elbows.

"And let me guess who gets to do the excavations?" Ryes questioned, merrily.

"Who else? You're the one with Earth Shaper and Manipulator, not to mention that pool of power you have to draw upon," Garth reminded her, grinning. "Not to worry, my wife. We still have to finish getting ready for the Gather and head out in a few days. We'll worry about it all when we get back."

"The satellites aren't much, but they're better than nothing," Axel commented, smiling at their boldness. They might end up building that starport for real, in time!

"Let's get everyone settled, at least. Tonight, we'll have a drawing for the few, open apartments after dinner, then we'll have the next few days to pack for the Gather and talk all we want about a starport and fleet of fast armed starships," Ryes teased, reminding them they still had priorities to attend to. The Boodans stood among them, smiling at how easily they were accepted among these strange peoples, as if they'd been born here.

"Right!" Torr agreed, then raised his arms and shouted out, "I need all the Boodans to follow me to the shelters we erected for your use, for the present. We'll have more permanent homes available for you soon, but for now, let's sort out where everyone will be staying and the available facilities. And anyone who wants to join the work crews to help build your new apartments, will be more than welcome." He and Wren lead the Boodans toward the shelters.

"Time for us to take a break," Garth insisted, smiling down at his wife.

"I already had this day declared a new holiday, Boodan Day," she informed him. "And the only ones who didn't listen, besides Bethy and Dotti, were Chuck and his crew. They're preparing a special feast in honor of all our new additions. So, there's nothing going on until dinner time," she assured Garth, smiling up into his eyes.

"See Ethan, I know how to pick an efficient staff," he stated, grinning. The others around them were chuckling at this, in agreement. They all turned for their homes, relieved everyone was back, safe and sound.

"Who's that?" Ryes asked, frowning, as she thought she saw someone, who resembled her mother, standing and looking over each of her cubs. Her hair was red, short on top and the rest pulled back into one large braid.

"Who, where?" Maren asked, having just emerged out of the kitchen area with his tray in hand. Then he spotted her, too. "I've no idea, but she sure looks a lot like you." Garth stepped out behind them, noting the stranger. Ryes walked directly over to their table, ready to confront this stranger.

"Who are you and what do you want?" she demanded. The young woman looked up to her, startled, then smiled merrily.

"Great-great grandma Ryes?" she questioned. "I only wanted to see what my great grandma looked like, when she was little." Ryes took in a deep breath in shock, then frowned. Had she heard her correctly?

"You're my great-great granddaughter?" she pressed, wanting to make sure she heard what she thought she heard. Garth and Maren had stepped up behind her, curiosity in their eyes. The young woman nodded her head in response, grinning merrily.

"Ah! Great-great granddad Garth! And you must be Cousin Maren," she added, then shook her head in obvious merriment.

"But, what's your name?" Ryes pressed, wanting to know. Her curiosity was peaked now. She was wearing a long, colorful tunic top and loose, comfortable-looking pants. Her boots looked well-made and expensive. Then she noted she wore the necklace of opals and diamonds her own mother had granted her, after they buried her next to Ronn! She had to be who she said she was!

"Nope. You'll figure me out and will leave messages to guide me, later," she replied. "Oops, time for me to go." With this she faded and disappeared from sight. Maren laughed heartily at this.

"You're going to be a great-great grandmother," he teased as he put down his tray. Garth was grinning, too.

"But how?" she asked, still not sure of this whole thing.

"Look, you can Time Walk, don't you expect you've already passed down that ability to your children? What's so far out of line with thinking that some of your and Garth's descendants won't try to sneak back to see what things were like in the beginning?" Maren asked, as she placed her tray down upon the table. She playfully frowned, turning to her cubs.

"Okay, which of you is going responsible for our mystery girl?" she demanded, playing along, seeing Maren's point. There was nothing she'd ever be able to do about it, anyway!

"It looked like she was more interested in either Shaysa, or Jann," Garth told her, chuckling, "and she did say, great grandma." He sat down his tray and wrapped an arm about her in support. "Don't worry about it. Kids will always be kids and she did look young. I'll bet she hasn't even had her first season yet," he assured her.

"I hope she has someone looking after her," she sighed in return, recalling her own first Time Walking forays.

"If she's anything like you, no way. But at least this isn't as far back as Hailys," Maren told her, as he sat down now.

"See? Now I'm going to have to figure out who she is… or rather will be!" Ryes returned, then smiled up into Garth's eyes. "But not until after dinner," she added. He chuckled, nodding his head in agreement, then gave her a quick kiss.

"Hey, hey. You two can save that for later," Gann teased his brother, as he and Saree stepped out of the kitchen to join them. Dotti, Bethy and Jim were right behind them, with Rowis, Karis and Tars trailing them. It looked like Sayer, Katas and Raby were talking about something nearby.

"I'll remind you that I'm base commander around here," Garth returned, grinning, glad to see his brother looking happy. He'd worried about him while they were gone. He released Ryes, so they all sat down, ready to eat. Ryes turned to take care of their little ones.

"Mom, who was that?" Sayer asked, as she, Katas and Raby finally approached the table. "A ghost of some kind?" They'd waited until she left, having spotted her before Ryes. The way she just faded out scared her. Ryes laughed, shaking her head in denial.

"Just another Time Walker in the family, stepping back to see how we used to do things," she assured her. She gave her a grateful smile of pure relief. Garth took the plate from Ryes' hand, while she was distracted. She looked at him in surprise.

"You've been taking care of them all alone for the last several days. It's my turn, now," he told her, taking the smaller spoon from her hand, too. She grinned at this, then gave him a nod of her head.

"Not quite alone, but I'm sure they've missed you as much as the rest of us," she returned, surrendering the duty gracefully. She sighed as the girls sat down, wondering about their mystery girl, again. Who was she? And why did she need her guidance? She said I'd figure out who she was, in time. Ryes found she wanted to know now! But how?

"What's the matter?" Maren asked, seeing Ryes looked distracted.

"Still puzzling out our young mystery," she replied, smiling.

"You're just going to have to get used to the idea that your children will have children, who'll have children, who'll have children," he returned, merrily.

"It boggles the mind," Bethany stated, placing a hand to her own stomach as she smiled at the thought.

"That's how you truly become an immortal. You live on through your descendants," Dotti added, smiling. She knew there'd been a small commotion but hadn't been quick enough to see her.

"She did look just like you, Ryes," Maren agreed, as he picked up his mug of tea. Ryes shook her head in denial.

"She looked just like my mother," she refuted him.

"And whom do you think you resemble?" Rowan questioned as he and Ethan stepped over to their group of tables.

"He's right," Mitt agreed. "I've met her ghost, too."

"Alright, she looks like me," she surrendered with a sigh. She started to eat, still trying to work the problem out in her head. She couldn't use her Time Walking for this, as she didn't know the consequences of trying to walk ahead and wasn't going to risk everything she knew and loved for the sake of curiosity! Her Visionary Talent was nowhere as strong as Sabin's, and the only Visions she had was when she and Maren were in direct physical contact. She also realized they'd both been emotionally upset at the time when they occurred. She wondered if she could "drive" a Vision, to look forward? And would the future she saw be the same one which would happen? There were still too many chances and questions.

"What's this?" Mitt asked, pointing to a small custard cup set upon her tray. Ryes smiled, her eyes lighting up with humor.

"Raya and Chuck came up with bubblenut custard for dessert. If you thought plain ol' bubblenuts were good, then wait until you taste this! Usually, Shadd and Maren grab two or three cups each, so you've got to be pretty quick around them," she explained. Mitt tasted it, then a smile blossomed across her face.

"When you're right, you're right! This stuff's great!"

"But it's for dessert," Garth teased her, having taken a quick taste of his own, finding it a delightful surprise. Maren was laughing and nodding his head at this.

"Dotti makes me wait, too," he assured Mitt. "She says I have to set a good example for my younger siblings."

"That's true," Minn responded, stepping over to the table. Sana, Justin, and little Fane were behind him, moving to sit next to Sabin and Ardis. "You don't need to set a bad example for Sernn." Mitt chuckled at this, grinning.

"Ooooh, has he got the wrong mom, then," she teased, seeing Sernn joining them, laughing as she said it. "I usually set the most reasonable example, I can."

"Define reasonable?" Maren challenged, grinning.

While the others were chatting and Garth was feeding the cubs, Ryes finally decided she couldn't wait and tried to purposefully call up her Visionary Talent. She thought if she could direct her Time Walking when she ventured into the past, why couldn't she also direct her Visions? She closed her eyes, wrestling with it, trying to direct it forward, far into the future. She was seeking a girl, who called her great-great grandma... She suddenly found herself standing in a tiny clinic room. A woman lay upon a birthing bed with a Healer in attendance. Two cubs had already been born. They'd been cleaned and were wrapped in birthing blankets, and were lying next to their mother, as her face shone with pride. Her face greatly reminded her of Mitt. Finally, as the last cub was coming, the Healer's face took on a look of wonder.

"She's a Booster," he announced with a laugh as he held her in his hands. The pride on his face was plain to her eyes. "And our daughter's strong!"

"I'm naming her Manda. What do you think, dear?" she asked as he was busy healing her umbilical cord.

"Perfect," he agreed, smiling. He delivered her afterbirth, then spent a few moments healing his wife, all the while cradling his youngest cub in his one arm, protectively. He then strode over to clean, weigh and measure her. Ryes got a good look at her as he went to make his computer entries. Yes, she was sure this was the child she sought. Satisfied, she decided to move onward, to make sure, by checking to see what she would look like when older.

She found herself standing in a tight, metal-walled room, with two women arguing something. The child looked about a year and a half old and was playing on the floor with another girl cub her age; most probably her littermate, Ryes thought. She had a head full of ring-curls all in red hair and bright green eyes! Her sibling appeared to have reddish streaks through her curly white hair. Both looked so beautiful and unique.

"You're not keeping Manda as her name!" the older woman insisted, her face darkening with anger.

"She's my daughter and that's what I decided to name her. I'm not backing down on this, mother, and that's final." The young mother's face was set with a well-known, family-related stubborn look, as she faced her mother off.

"Time for us to lift off, Gram," the Healer said, stopping by the hatch-shaped doorway. Suddenly, Ryes realized she was on a starship of some kind! "We've got a fast run to make to Kisteela." The older woman met his eyes, realizing he spoke the truth. She huffed, then turned and edged around him, leaving quickly.

"Still that same, old argument," his wife explained, with a sad sigh. He stepped forward, wrapping her in his arms, kissing the top of her head.

"She'll get through it. Just give her a little more time," he tried to reassure her, as her tears started to quietly flow.

"I know," she sobbed out, clutching him. Ryes decided she had to understand why her mother so objected to her naming the child Manda? She then called up her Catalyst Talent and clearly saw a dormant reflection of herself! This tiny cub was a Talent of One Plus! Both cubs carried Talent, but Manda's was her own. With this discovery, she left to try to find the mother.

She found the older woman, as she sat upon a bench, to one side of what must be some type of starport. It had to be on a planet, for there was bright sunlight coming in from a bank of windows, nearby. She sat down next to the woman, who was quietly crying, too.

"What's the matter?" she asked, willing herself to be seen, as if she were merely Time Walking. The woman looked surprised, then her eyes were suddenly filled with such deep, heart-ripping longing. It shocked Ryes, but she smiled encouragement for her.

"Oh, grandma! It's been so exceedingly long," she whispered as she visibly fought the urge to hug her. "I've missed you, so much!"

"It's all right," she crooned in comfort, clearly seeing her need for her presence. "Why do you fight over Manda's name, Gram?" she questioned, recalling her name. She wasn't sure if she could cover any faux pas she might make with this woman, who was her own granddaughter!

"Then she is THE MANDA? The Talent of One we're supposed to be on the watch for?" she demanded, needing to know, so to ease her own heart. Ryes smiled grandly for her, nodding her head.

"Yes. She's a Talent of One Plus, like myself. Just take as good a care of her as you can, and things will all work out," she assured her. She sighed, happy and relieved to hear this news.

"Thank you, Grandma Ryes. I'll make up with Shea, when they next land back on Tayna."

"Good. I wouldn't want you to fight with your daughter, after all. She kind of reminds me a little of Mitt," she admitted, smiling. Gram laughed merrily at this, her eyes shining.

"No wonder she's such a headache, at times!"

"I must go as I don't have much time. Take care of yourself, Gram," she replied, then drifted onward. She still hadn't found how Manda looked when she got older - to be sure! But she comforted herself that she helped her future family settle a dispute peacefully. She finally settled, finding young Manda in an eatery, at what looked like late at night. She did look, as she had when she visited, except now she was wearing what looked like a shipsuit. There were patches upon her shoulders, proclaiming both the company she worked for and the ship she was attached to. She and her cousin were talking with a human-looking man, who they named as their cousin to a human companion of his. They seemed a close trio to her eyes. She finally let it go, not wanting to push things for now.

"Ryes?" Ardis questioned, seeing her eyes closed and that she just dropped the fork she held in her hand. It clattered on the table where it fell. What could she be up to now, she wondered? Garth turned his attention to his wife, hearing a strange note in their friend's voice.

"Ryes?" he demanded, putting the now-empty plate down, from which he'd been feeding the cubs, and grasping her arms. Her eyes were closed, her body slack and her skin was cold to the touch, but there wasn't the feeling of great power surging around her, like when she went Time Walking. What was she up to now?

"Let me see," Maren offered, already having his Healing Talent active, to see what the problem could be. But, as he touched her, tapping her Mind Voice, he felt her presence returning. "And where have you been?" he sent, directly mind-to-mind.

"Looking ahead," she returned, merrily. "I had to find out our little lady's name. And I found her! And you won't believe what it was like!" she exclaimed, delighted.

"Well, I'm sure Garth's not happy with you right now. So, we'll save this for later," he advised. "Better adjust your body temperature back to where it's supposed to be." With this he withdrew, grinning as he gave a nod to Garth. "All's fine. She was just out `gallivanting around', as the humans say it."

"What were you doing, now?" Garth questioned Ryes, as soon as she opened her eyes. She smiled for him, seeing Maren was returning to his own seat.

"I wanted to know our mystery child's name. Now, I know who she is, and I think, understand why she'll need my guidance," she replied.

"You were Time Walking ahead?" he pressed, unsettled that she'd do something so foolish!

"No. I was trying to use my Visionary Talent with the same kind of focus I use when I go Time Walking," she explained. This instantly caught Sabin's attention.

Small Things

Chapter 22

"You were doing WHAT?" Sabin demanded, hoping he hadn't heard what he thought she said.

"I was using Visionary Talent to look ahead, so I could try to find our mystery child," she explained, wondering at the odd expression in his eyes. The sudden sternness on his face puzzled her.

"Oh, my," Senna commented, as she was about to sit next to Sela and Justin. She bit her lip in shock at such a concept. "You never use Visionary Talent like that, my dear!" she gently scolded.

"No fool would ever do such a thing! How do you know, if you drive the Vision, that it's the right course the future will be taking, and not some whim of your own, or some side trail, which will never be?" Sabin sternly questioned, trying to get her to see reason, before she caused herself, or others, harm.

"How could I ever create these people, if I never imagined their existence, before?" she questioned in return. She couldn't understand why they were so upset when all she did was track down her great-great granddaughter. It didn't concern them.

"You just met her, so you can imagine where you'd find her," he refuted, starting to get angry with her stubbornness.

"I couldn't have imagined where I found her!" Ryes returned, meeting his eyes squarely. Her anger was rising. "How do you know, unless you've ever tried it?" she pressed.

"I did when I was young and caused all kinds of headaches for everyone then. I don't want you trying to direct things now, as you thought you saw them in your imaginary future!"

"So, you let your Talent work fully on its own whim? It rules when and what you always see?" she questioned. "Your Talent's supposed to serve you, not you it! So, you messed up when you were a cub, have you even tried to use it so, now?"

"You don't understand! Visionary doesn't work that way!"

"How do you know, unless you try?" she snapped back.

"Hey, you two are getting too serious about this!" Maren interrupted them. "Give it, and the rest of us, a break. It's not that important," he urged, trying to get them to see reason.

"Why don't you and Sabin discuss this tomorrow morning, after breakfast?" Garth suggested, thinking his blood-brother might have some valid points, but then so did his wife. Ryes seemed to relax a little at this, giving him a nod of her head in agreement.

"Sounds fine with me, if you have the time, Sabin?" she replied, turning back to him. He gave her a nod of his head. Neither of them was smiling.

"I'll have Wren let Larisa know what openings I have on my schedule," he told her, smiling a little tightly now, not quite free of his anger. He realized he still had problems sometimes with the thought of having a secretary and a schedule to keep track of, too.

"All right," she replied, then turned back to her dinner, as Garth was cleaning up the cubs. She still felt guilty leaving their care all up to him, but he looked like he was enjoying it, as he was teasing and tickling each of them in turn. Torr and Dodi emerged from the kitchen, carrying their trays and Tobin. As he stopped, he nodded for Dodi to keep on walking toward their own table. The expression in his eyes had Ryes instantly on the alert.

"What's up?" she asked. He waited until everyone else was out of easy hearing. This had her frowning, knowing it had to be something important. Garth noted this, too, granting him his attention, having handed the cubs some hard biscuits to chew upon as a dessert.

"Is there something the matter, cousin?" he asked, in a lower voice. Torr gave him a nod of his head, then said,

"I don't know what to do about my mother," he started, talking so low only Ryes, Garth and Sabin truly heard him.

"What?" she prompted, also in a low voice, as she frowned wondering what could be wrong with Rein? She was always such a cheerful, gentle person!

"She's hooked up with Ivan," he informed them.

"And?" she pressed, not understanding the problem at all. There was a strange, shadowed look in Garth's eyes as he thought he suspected where the problem may lie.

"Her next season's due this coming winter," he started, unsure of how to voice his feelings about this, even to the people he felt closest to here. "I'm not comfortable with Ivan fathering any cubs with her," he finished, sighing. Hot anger instantly flashed in Ryes' eyes, as his comment registered in her mind. She would've never, ever suspected such an attitude from him!

"How can you say such a thing? It's HER CHOICE, Torr, not yours," she admonished, keeping her voice low with tight effort.

"But, a human?" he continued, seeing her anger, still feeling like he had to press on.

"If you feel that way, then when her season comes, just drive her back over to Matlowe and let Korman have at her, again," she challenged, still speaking in a lower tone of voice, as it dripped venom. She saw the color suddenly drain from his face at this, and she mentally kicked herself for being so crass. She'd let her temper get out of hand and had struck out the wrong way, with the wrong person!

"I..." he started, still in utter shock.

"I'm sorry, Torr. I should've never said such a thing to begin with, especially to you," she apologized. Then, as tears threatened to blind her, she stood and rushed out of the room, heading for the outside doors.

"Ryes?" Maren questioned, seeing her anger, then tearful departure. He didn't know what the problem was, but saw she needed him. He stood to go after her, but Garth grabbed his wrist.

"Let her go," he advised in a low voice. "She'll work it out."

"But," he started, then saw Sabin shake his head, too.

"She's had a long, hard day," he told him. "She just needs some fresh air," he advised.

"You can talk with her tomorrow," Garth suggested, sighing. "Sorry, cousin," he apologized to Torr, who now was sitting, his face still displaying his inner unease. Maren sat back down, thinking they didn't understand her as well as he did, but since they were his closest friends, he had to do as they directed.

"What set her off?" he pressed, needing to know.

"Nothing," Garth assured him. "She's just a little tired, is all. We haven't even had a quiet moment together since I got back this morning. I've been answering messages and getting issues settled, it's no wonder she's on edge. I'll talk with you after dinner, Torr," he added, giving him a nod of his head. Torr nodded in response, then stood back up, recalling he should probably be with Dodi and Tobin right now, anyway.

"Yeah, later," he replied, then left. He'd forgotten what Ryes had once seen the night his father died. She did have a point, that there were far worse men for Rein to mate with, than Ivan. He realized he'd have to talk with his mother about it later, too. In Winterhaven, it would always be her choice.

Ryes rushed outside, into the cool air of the evening. The sun was low to the horizon, just starting to set. She didn't want to be cooped up in her apartment, no matter how spacious it was, she wanted… She fumbled within herself, looking for what her soul craved, then realized it was the forest! She stood for a few moments, uncertain, then instead of heading to the garage for one of the vehicles, she turned for the windracer paddock.

She had finally gotten where she rode on Honey once a week. She was having to leave most of her care up to others and it made her feel guilty. Honey was her special responsibility; Darman having entrusted her to her over three years ago now. She'd fully intended to carry out her vow to Darman, to always watch after Honey and care for her each and every day. But, with having to run Winterhaven, her time had become premium, and she wondered when things had all gone so nuts?

"Honey," she called as she stepped up to the fence rails. The mare perked her ears forward, then trotted quickly over to her. Ryes pulled out the carrot she snagged for her earlier, it now being her habit to give her little tidbits in the evening, before going home and to bed. As she ate the offering, Ryes gave her a good scratching, noting her coat looked well-tended. That was a relief, at least! She walked toward the supply shed and emerged a few moments later with a headstall and reins. She let Honey out of the pen, then secured the gate. She put the headstall on her, then secured the reins. She hopped up onto her back, riding bareback, then slowly walked her clear of the site. Once they were across the creek, she let her have her head, even with the sun so low to the horizon, she knew she could keep them both safe.

"Took you long enough," Garth teased, as he found her sitting near the creek, letting Honey get a last drink of its cold, clear water.

279

She grinned, nodding her head at this. She'd been looking up to admire the blazing stars. Shaysa was dark, in her new moon state, Menna wasn't even up yet, and small Porr's light couldn't compete with their glory. She treasured the night sky, missing being outdoors now that she had so many other things to keep her in all the time.

"I had some thinking to do," she replied, her voice low and thoughtful. "Is Torr all right? I didn't mean to snap like that."

"I know. First the Boodans, then Sabin, and poor Torr just caught the buildup you had ready for the next person to cross you. If it hadn't been him, I'm betting I would've caught it before bedtime." She chuckled at this, as he sat down next to her in the tall, green grass.

"I'm not that bad," she protested, smiling to herself.

"I've heard some of Rowan's stories," he teased in return as he put an arm around her. "This reminds me of when we were out on the trail," he said, as he stretched out his legs, looking up into the night sky. "They look so very different from up there," he sighed, then turned back to his lady. She snuggled in against his side, sighing in pleasure, too.

"I bet they're really spectacular, up close," she replied. He bent to nuzzle her ear, causing shivers of excitement to travel up her spine.

"They would've been even more so, if you'd been there to see them with me," he told her in a low voice. She chuckled merrily.

"Next time," she promised. "What is weightlessness truly like?" she asked.

"You'll find out," he teased, as he took her into his arms, pulling her down into the grass with him. She laughed outright as she realized he wasn't just playing around. It'd been such a very long time since they free mated beneath the stars.

The next morning the Boodans gathered, after an early breakfast, in the Village Circle. They were amazed by the foods available and the quantities they could freely eat with no protests ever raised. And even if the shelters seemed flimsy at first, they had each slept in wonderful comfort. This new life just starting had both the humans and starmen excited for what would be happening next. They came to this vast comfortable cavern, sitting near the stage, as they were urged, wonder playing in their eyes.

Torr covered customs and safety for them, having a big screen display that took the Boodans several minutes to get over its existence before they could listen to what he was saying, or explain what they were seeing. Nick chortling gleefully for at least ten minutes didn't help. It took time, and clearly taxed Torr's patience. Still, he finally got some participation and understanding, even if it was due to Nick, Terry, George and Nesa leading the rest into trying to become new citizens.

It was everything Ryes could do to not laugh out loud, herself. She did note that while they were mostly separated by a seat between the adult humans and starmen, the children were intermixed, as well as Abbra and Nesa being a solid presence, sitting together, taking turns holding little Misti. The others on both sides were at first uncomfortable with it, but as they forgot themselves during the classes and lectures, they started to fall into being more accepting of each other. That gave her hope.

"How long will we be living in the strange dwellings? They seem thin and not secure," Huras asked, worried. Ryes had stepped up to the main podium, standing next to Torr, giving him a break. She gave Huras a nod as she took the microphone.

"I know Torr said it earlier, but I'd like to say it again, welcome to Winterhaven and Tayna," she said, first. "If you would like to help build your new homes, they'll be ready for all of you much faster," she invited with a big smile upon her face. "We all contribute here in Winterhaven, to help each other as well as ourselves. We do expect all adults to learn how to use the travelling machines, so in case of an emergency you can get yourself and others to safety." Nesa raised her hand, learning that was how to get noticed, and her questions answered.

"Nesa?" she asked, wanting to hear her question.

"When does this training start?" she asked, appearing uncertain. "And will we need to learn to fly the great flying machines, too?" Ryes smiled giving her a nod.

"You'll have some basic classes for a few weeks starting tomorrow, so you can learn our ways of doing things here, first. Then we'll start the advanced classes after that so you can find your place – what you like to do, or are truly good at doing," she explained.

"The children will have to attend classes, too. They'll be learning basic ideas, as all our children are learning," she followed-up quickly, before more questions could start. Hands now shot into the air. She pointed to the first one, which had gone up.

"How do you gather your food?" Belens, one of Nesa's hunters, asked, appearing concerned. Nesa turned her head to see him sitting behind her in these incredibly comfortable chairs and gave him a nod.

"We have fields planted and growing our fruits, grains, and vegetables. We have a handful of farms, just established, away from our main village here, which will supply foods, and allow proper animal management and care. We have hunting forays and other gathering forays that happen regularly in Hailys, the great ruins of a wonderful city that once existed for hundreds of years. You'll be welcome to participate in any of these areas, if you feel you must provide food," she informed them. This seemed to relax many of their newcomers, as she realized gathering food had been one of their main concerns on Booda.

"But consider, what else can you do? You won't know until you try. Maybe one of you could be a great new pilot? Maybe good at teaching children? Maybe making new furniture is what you love? Maybe you'll find that planning and building new structures is more fun, than you ever thought before? Maybe you'd enjoy being a peacekeeper? Maybe you'll just thrill to riding on a windracer and hunting with a bow? Or you might enjoy running your own farm? There're endless possibilities around you here in Winterhaven. We want you to find what makes you happiest and you enjoy doing best."

"But what do your elders do?" Huras asked, concerned. It all sounded too active. She had to resist laughing, again.

"We have several here among us and honestly, we younger ones are hard-pressed at times to keep up with our elders. They don't sit around and discuss important matters, they're very active members of our community. Elder Ethan is head of our Research branch and actually holds equal rank to Garth, our base commander. My grandfather, Rowan, was a cloth weaver before. He does teach weaving techniques to others, but he's busier making sure many things flow smoothly here in Winterhaven and works closely with Ethan. Elder Metta from Matlowe Village is helping to shape our future too. He's working out detailed plans for managing the College of Matlowe and preserving the great library Prince Callas left for all of Tayna. We have quite a few other elders here too, who're all busy performing various endeavors, doing things they want to do to help Winterhaven grow." Huras, Pak and Nick all took this in with Nick giving her a nod and smile in understanding.

"When do we begin?" George asked, feeling bold in the following silence. Ryes smiled and gave him a nod of her head.

"Very soon. I want Maren and his team to give each of you a good check, once more, then I'll take you to our classrooms to acquaint you with where you'll be learning a lot of new things, then a tour of Winterhaven, so you'll know where to go for important things," she replied, still smiling.

"All this in one day?" one of the other Boodan men asked, astounded. She laughed and nodded her head again.

"But first, I have an important message for you to view. It was found beneath Matlowe Village, but I feel this one is very important for all of you. The starmen were once a part of Prince Callas' network to bring messages and supplies from the outer colonies. The Snags, or Snagospin, were the enemy who brought the ship, or ships down on Booda and left your ancestors there to die. The humans' ship, the Star Quest, which I know you saw yesterday. It's sad what was left of her, but some of those who survived the battle with the Snags ended up upon Booda, too. So, this is important that you all understand our true enemy. It was never each other; it was always the Snagospin who're the ones we need to turn our wills to force them away from all good peoples – back to their own worlds for all time!"

She saw surprise on the faces before her and some worry, but before allowing their questions to slow things down now, she waved Torr off the stage, signaled the podium to descend below and stepped off the stage herself, and the lights dimmed as she activated the recording from the crystal. She was only going to show them the first part for now. The rest could wait until later, when they could realize their true part in this new life. The lights in the room dimmed as she took a seat, herself. She found she never tired of this recording.

"You don't have to come out to the Gather, if you don't want to, Lissel," Ryes assured her, having heard her telling Almas that she didn't want to attend the Gather. Both women turned around, surprised to see her standing behind them. "We don't force attendance upon anyone," she finished, smiling encouragement for them. She'd stepped into the dining hall to get her and Larisa some fresh mugs of tea. They usually took turns at it, it being hers this time. Then she overheard them talking in fearful voices and had to find out what the problem might be; concerned for them.

"The way everyone was talking about it, we thought attendance was required," Almas replied with a small smile and a bow. Ryes laughed merrily at hearing this, shaking her head.

        "No, never! We'll have some booths, to sell some of our own
wares and crafts, but we already have the staffs for their operation
set up. We'll have people along for security reasons, but unless
you're assigned to a specific detail, and are just out to meet the other
peoples of Tayna and party, or shop, or watch the varied
entertainments, you don't have to come along." Lissel looked
instantly relieved to hear this from her. Almas was frowning in
thought.

        "This gather is widely attended?" she questioned, wanting to
better understand what it was about.

        "It's one of two official gathers held annually: one in the
spring, one in the fall. We'll have the Caravaners, the Mountain
tribes, the Plains people, others from nearby cities and villages,
including some Ruskins and other peoples. There'll be an exchange of
news, settling of treaties, gathering of merchants and crafts people
from all across this continent, and maybe even some of the trading
ships' captains. According to Darman, who attends can vary from
year to year, but it's never dull. Everyone's been isolated by the
winter snows and are anxious to meet others and party, before the
true heat of summer settles in," she explained, grinning
mischievously.

        "How long is this gather?" Almas added, artfully frowning and
curious. Her rich, dark skin gave her an exotic appearance.

        "At least two weeks long, and I heard it can run up to a
month, if there's a lot of disputes to settle, or treaties to finalize."

        "And how long are you planning on staying?" she pressed, her
eyes telling her little. Ryes sighed. It was the one and only sticking
point between her and Garth. He thought they should stay until it
was over. She felt they should have an established calendar and stick
to it, making it only for the two-week duration.

        "At least the two weeks, but you don't have to stay that long.
We'll ferry people back and forth with some of the larger helicopters -
for the Winterhaven residents only. I don't want strangers sneaking
back here for their own purposes, without our knowledge, or
permission," she explained. Lissel sighed relief at hearing this, her
happiness showing in her golden eyes, nodding her agreement.

        "But what about our weekly practices?" she asked. Ryes
smiled, nodding her head, understanding the importance of the
sessions.

        "If I can, I'll get back to join in, otherwise the remainder of
the group here can continue as normally scheduled. At the last
gather, we had a group of Talents out of the Southern continent

challenge us to an inner duel. We triumphed, but it was amazing to think they were actually attempting to kill me with their attacks. Truly, they had nothing on Doran! And I'm hoping we won't see any more of that, but if you do come out, remember to stay aware - just in case," she warned them. "Well, I've got to get back to my office. Got a lot of stuff to finish up, before we leave. If you have any more questions, please feel free to stop by my office after another couple of hours," she invited, giving the ladies a nod. With this, she walked over to the huge pot, which held fresh tea, and filled their mugs from the spigot, then left after giving the ladies a happy smile. She wondered what the problem truly was, facing the crowds of unknown peoples, or leaving their new safe sanctuary?

"Let's go tell this news to Rhodi and Poli. I'm sure no one's ever let on about what happened the last time, and that Talent battle," Almas suggested, standing with her half-empty cup. She didn't even wait for Lissel but turned for the pot to refresh it.

Lissel stood for several long seconds, her heart and mind unsure. She wondered if she actually had the courage to go out among strangers, again. It was odd, she thought, that she no longer thought of the people of Winterhaven as strange at all. They were all perfectly normal and almost like a large family; humans and starmen. She felt safe, warm, and welcome, as if she'd grown up and lived here, all her life. She could even understand Saree and Denas finding mates. It somehow didn't feel strange to be with a man. After all the years of darkness and madness, it was like waking up and walking out into the light - free. Still, she was the last living Forester and should see what can be learned of the rest of Tayna.

"Coming?" Almas questioned, seeing her friend was lost in thought. Lissel smiled, giving her a small nod of her head, then went to fill her own mug, and following her out the door.

Early Visitors

Chapter 23

"We're about ten minutes out, if what Darman said was true," Ryes said over the radio. This time she was piloting one of the choppers, instead of driving. Garth teased her, saying it'd prevent some people from having heart attacks over her driving. It was a different location than the Caravaner's Gather site but laid out in similar fashion, from what she saw when exploring it last month in preparation. It was far larger, and from Darman and Rinna, far more widely attended. She had again repaired, expanded, and improved the roads between to enable their vehicles easier access, as well as for other Taynans attending.

"Fine, we're just on the other side of the hill, from the gather site. We'll stop here and wait for you," Garvin replied, still smiling to himself over being in charge of the rovers. He signaled for a halt, and the six vehicles in the convoy braked to a stop behind him. There were two vans coming up behind, who stopped with them, rather than pass up these strange metal vans. They seemed calm, so had probably seen them at their gather a few months ago.

"I'm ready for landing, as soon as you signal," Garth reported. He was piloting the Avenger, while Axel and Sabin were in the Stinger, one of their fighter spacecraft.

"Let's fix your landing site, first," Ryes teased, smiling to herself. She hoped they had their camp site ready, as Darman promised. Of course, he didn't know they'd be bringing along a shuttle and a fighter and would need a little additional room. Still, she figured she'd find a way to make it all fit, which is why they only used two of their biggest rovers this time.

"Alright, we're coming up on your position, Garvin," Ryes finally told him, catching sight of the line of rovers ahead. She saw him wave to her out of his window and smiled to herself again, then eased back so they would all arrive at once.

"I see ya," he replied, then gunned the engine of his vehicle back to life. Overall, this trip hadn't been bad, and he enjoyed seeing more of Tayna than he ever imagined. He'd never seen Marla happier, either. Little Myran was pointing and making baby noises at anything which moved on the road before them, tickling both her parents. They eased around the hill, then went down the winding road toward the shallow, open-ended valley ahead. Ryes had previously cleared the trees for the vans, so they had a clear path now that was wide and high enough for safe passage.

"I think I see where we're supposed to camp," Ryes announced. There were some white-painted rocks placed out in the symbol of the Phoenix, at the far side, near the river, which emptied into the large, nearby lake. "It looks like there's plenty of room for the shuttle, too." She and the other helicopters now had a clear view of what lay below, as the people below now had a clear view of them. She internally debated about flying on ahead of the rovers, then remembered to stick with their original course of action.

"Hey, let's go on and set down," Mitt insisted, over her headset.

"No. We'll all arrive together as planned," Ryes responded, "Let's show them unity, no matter what one kind of vehicle can do, which any of the others can't. It'll show them we're not easily divided."

"That's right," Rowan agreed, "Never expose your throat to strangers." Ryes chuckled to this, nodding her head to herself.

"And we're not going to do that," Garth agreed, "Stick together. We can see you and we'll land, as soon as you're all into position. This is part show, part bluff. Let's put our poker faces on. We're not among friends and family, except for the few caravaners we already know and trust," he warned them all.

"Yes, Sir," Ryes replied. There were other responses of acknowledgment from the rest in their mixed convoy. So, they slowly wended their way down to the valley, then across to their campsite, now followed by running children, who were laughing and waving. There was a party of elders awaiting them, so the rovers first pulled up, forming a line of three across and two deep, with the big ones in front. The choppers now landed with the two larger ones in front, the two smaller ones behind, and finally, the shuttle landed next to the choppers, but slightly to the back, leaving room for the fighter to land in front of it. It dwarfed the choppers and Ryes noted the shock on even Darman's face, as she was still finishing her shutdown procedures. The elders had been holding their ears with all the noise from the machines – especially the shuttle and fighter.

"I think we got their attention," she commented over her headset. There was laughter in response from everyone else, as Sayer gave her a thumbs up, from her copilot's seat, a big grin on her face.

"Stick to what we planned," Garth warned, unnecessarily. Everyone was, and most were still busy with shutdowns and getting ready to emerge from the various vehicles.

"Gotcha, boss," Axel replied, as others added in their agreement. As soon as Garth sent the ready signal, they all opened their doors and assembled as a group, in front of the vehicles. As soon as they assembled, Garth turned back to his dear family and friends.

"I've reconsidered. We'll use a physical wall like Ryes raised at the last gather. I don't want anyone to casually view us, or what we're doing out here. The less they know of us, the better," he addressed in English. "Let's be a mystery, don't explain things in any detail to anyone," he ordered. The people assembled before him gave him a nod in unison, bringing a smile to his lips.

"Let's show them what Tayna should be, a united people!" His people cheered.

Then with Garth, Ethan, Ryes, Metta, Sabin and Rowan leading the rest, they walked over to greet the waiting elders, formally. Ryes noted there was understanding in both Darman and Kyma's eyes at seeing this small display. At the last gather, it was obvious this was a close group, now at this one, they strove to make sure everyone saw they were united in not only what they believed, but in their behavior and leadership, as well. Garth smiled as he, Ethan and Rowan stepped forward from the others to greet them.

"Early, as always," Darman commented, as he hugged Garth happily, chuckling at his savvy in their arrival display. Garth was chuckling, too.

"Wouldn't want to disappoint you," he replied, as he pulled back to look in his eyes. "Have things been faring well?"

"It's been a good year. Not great, but far from the worse," he informed him. "And anything new happenings back home?" he pressed in return, glancing toward the spacecraft.

"We got the warning, communication, and navigation satellites set up, rescued some years ago survivors from off a moon of Tyssen, and even found some `lost' humans from off the Star Quest," he told him, "Not truly busy, but never dull," he finished. This had Darman, Dastin and Kyma all laughing heartily, shaking their heads in disbelief.

"I fear to think what will've happened there, by the time the Great Fall Gather arrives," Kyma commented, as he stepped forward to give Garth a hug in welcome, too.

"I do hope we get a trip on this big new machine of yours," Dastin prompted, hoping they could at least see it.

"We do plan on taking up a select number of elders, only," Ethan replied, smiling merrily at seeing the way Garth was holding his own with these men of power on this world. After having been placed into a position of responsibility for some months now, he was coming into his own and understanding more of what his leadership encompassed, even if he was still very young.

"Once we have an understanding of what the order of business is, we'll let all of you know when the first trip will be scheduled," Ryes assured them, openly supporting Ethan's response. Dastin let out a sigh of relief.

Then, once these three elders had greeted them, Darman began the introductions for the remaining group of elders. There were now over fifty gathered behind the leading three, most looked very interested in all of them; some looked wary and unsure. Ryes had reached a point where it didn't bother her anymore. They would think what they would think. After the introductions were finished, Sabin turned and dismissed the rest of the Winterhaveners, so they could begin the process of setting up camp. There was relief in the eyes of many of their people at this. After travelling so far, it was a blessing to be able to set up their shelters and take a break, to unwind at last. A woman and two men, whose dress looked different to her eyes, as well as a plainsman elder, approached Ryes, as the rest were breaking up and Darman, Kyma and Dastin were leading Garth, Rowan, Metta, and Ethan off elsewhere. Sabin was busy organizing the camp set-up.

"You are Ryes, the wife of Garth?" the woman questioned. She nodded her head in acknowledgment, wondering what she could want?

"Yes, I am," she assured them, a small smile upon her lips.

"I'm the new Chieftess of Menna's Hold. My name's Ross, and my former chieftess gave my niece to your husband, in exchange for her son stealing his windracer," she told her. "Kyma said she's being well cared for, but I wondered if I might see her for myself?" she requested. In truth, she could rightly refuse this visit, but she still hoped to see her tiny niece, anyway. Ryes' smile widened and her eyes took on a merry look, relieving her fears instantly.

"It'd be my privilege and honor to present her for you to see," she replied. "I hope you don't mind, but I've renamed her Shyla, as I'd already named my own daughter Shaysa." Ross blinked at this, surprised, as white-haired cubs were fairly uncommon, even if she was red-haired and rare, herself.

"I don't mind at all, as long as she's raised well, with love," she assured her, smiling at last.

"Lady Ryes," the elder now addressed her, getting her attention. "My name is Dyan and am the chief of the Moondance Tribe. I've come to see how the women, who were sold to your husband and Sabin are faring? They were once members of my tribe and I've been concerned."

"We don't allow slavery, nor for people to be owned by others as property. They're now free women, except we felt that with Sayer, Katas and Raby being so young, we've adopted them into our families, until they're old enough to live on their own," she explained. "Garth and I have adopted Sayer and Raby, while Sabin and Ardis have adopted Katas. Dodi has settled down with Torr, and she seems very happy with that arrangement," she explained. "You're also welcome to visit, but I have to warn all of you, it's a little nuts right now, as we're getting things set up." Dyan laughed at this; his eyes merry as he gave her a nod of his head.

"That I well understand, but I'd still like to check on the women," he replied. He wondered at this; that they didn't keep any slaves? The women were now free? It was an incredible concept! And they lived far too close to the Moondance Tribal lands! Ryes gave him a nod of her head, then turned to escort them.

"Please follow me," she invited. She walked back, skirting the unloading of the rovers, as Maren joined her, a curious look in her eyes.

"Someone has to play bodyguard for you," he told her in English, in explanation to the interest in her eyes. She smiled at this, nodding her head. These people were still strangers after all!

"We have some visitors who wish to check up on our new girls; Shyla and Sayer, Katas, Raby and Dodi," she explained in Dolbith. Maren nodded his head, smiling at this in understanding.

"Ryes?" Rhodi called out as she hurried over, having finally found her. Ryes stopped to see what she needed. "Sabin told me we will be escorted if we leave the camp. Is this truly necessary?"

"Rhodi, I'd like you to meet Dyan, who is the Chief of the Moondance Tribe. It's their custom to own women, as if they're property. The idea of the escort is only for your own protection," she assured her. Rhodi's face blushed darkly, as she realized she had a point. Then she stepped forward, offering Dyan her open hand.

"I would hope that in time your people will come to see things differently. My name is Rhodi of House Klark of Kahmarr, and I am still honored to meet you, elder sir," she said, all her courtly manners in full operation. Dyan smiled in return, crossing her hand with his own, not sure if he'd been insulted, or not. There was some low chuckling from the two men accompanying Ross. She merely stood with a smile upon her lips, observing everything around them. It was busy and looked like chaos but was still far better organized than any camp set up, she'd ever seen, and they'd just arrived!

"It's why I also have an escort with me here, at all times," she told Rhodi. "My name's Ross of Menna's Hold. I've been newly appointed as the Chieftess of my hold." There was real pride in her voice, tinged with a trace of uncertainty, but the smile upon her face was genuine.

"I am pleased to make your acquaintance," Rhodi replied, as she offered her, her palm also. Ross crossed it with her own, smiling grandly.

"Please feel free to visit our camp, at any time," she encouraged her. If she truly came from Kahmarr, she wondered how she managed to get here to Tayna? She had many questions for her. Rhodi smiled broadly at this, giving her a small bow of her head, then bowed to Ryes and left. Ryes sighed, watching her until she'd gone around one of the shelters, which was almost fully raised.

"She's finally starting to step out of the dark," she commented, mostly to herself, as Maren chuckled, nodding his head.

"That she is," he agreed. With this, Ryes continued toward where she knew her own shelter was going up, finding it almost ready.

"You didn't have to rush ours, Sabin," she scolded as she smiled in appreciation. He turned and saw who was with her, surprise in his eyes as he recognized them all.

"Sabin!" Keen declared as he stepped forward quickly, throwing his arms around him in a hearty hug. "It's good to see you're well, my friend!" Sabin was laughing as Ardis stepped over, her curiosity aroused, with Dale in her arms. Katas followed with Adris in hers. Then Katas recognized Dyan and the color left her face. She quickly ducked behind Ardis; afraid he'd come to try to take her back. Ardis was shocked by her move, wondering what was wrong? Her eyes met Ryes', seeing she looked to have expected this, to some degree. Maren shifted to stand between her and Ryes, hoping to assure her that he would protect her, too.

"It's good to see you, too," Sabin replied, laughing. They let go of each other, grinning like two fools. "So, what's been happening up in Menna's Hold?" he asked.

"What's wrong Katas?" Ardis asked, just loud enough for Sabin to hear her question clearly. He suddenly looked over to see her trying to hide behind Ardis.

"What's the problem, dear?" he questioned, turning to note her fear clearly written on her face.

"I'm not going back!" she told them both in a low voice, trembling now.

"Of course not," Ardis laughed, "you're our daughter!"

"Yes," Dyan told her, stepping closer. "I only came to see how you're doing, because your older siblings were worried."

"Dyan?" Raby breathed out, almost frozen in her tracks. She'd seen Ryes and had rushed over to ask her a question. Suddenly, she found her throat dry, as her mind screamed at her to run and hide.

"Let's get this settled right now," Ryes declared loudly, noting her terror. "You're scaring the girls, Dyan," she mildly scolded. She then used Mind Voice to call Sayer and Dodi to them, too. She assured all four of the girls that none of them were going back to Moondance - ever. And if there were any problems, she'd personally escort them to Winterhaven in the shuttle, if she had to. This calmed both Raby and Katas, as Raby stepped over to her side.

"I don't mean to get them so upset," Dyan replied, seeing his mere presence had frightened the two girls with them now. Sayer appeared with the stroller and the five squirming cubs within. She stepped over to stand near Ryes, too.

"It's that they've all settled so well into their new lives that this might be painful for them, to some degree," she explained, smiling to take the edge out of her no nonsense demeanor. She put an arm around each of her older daughters, as Dodi appeared with little Tobin in her arms.

"You've had a cub?" Dyan stated, unbelieving, as he saw her approaching. It hadn't been a long enough time! She smiled as she shook her head.

"He's Torr's son by Shadd. She decided she didn't want either of them anymore, so they're both mine now," she explained, smiling merrily. She realized she had no fear, as she spoke to him. He no longer had a say in the course of her life. Raya and Mitt appeared, with Sernn trailing them. They'd heard Ryes and what she'd said to the former plainswomen and came to help, if needed.

"It's her loss, after all," Raya stated, supporting her friend. "Elder Dyan, how do you fare?" she asked, stepping closer to join them. The other man with Ross immediately recognized Sernn and gestured him closer. He did, knowing his present mother and Aunt Ryes would never let anything happen to him. Mitt watched them with sharp eyes, not quite trusting people she didn't know!

"I've fared better, but am fine for now," he replied. She realized how old he seemed to be getting.

"If you ever have need of a Healer, we have several at our disposal," Ryes offered. "Sayer, could you please set out the cubs' groundcover and blanket?" she requested in English. "I think it's time for them to get a little exercise. Ross is also here to see Shyla. Let's see if she can tell which one is which," she suggested. Both Raby and Sayer giggled at this, as Sayer went to fetch the requested items from their things. Ross heard her and her niece's names being mentioned, as she stood and watched everything, seeing five cubs in the wheeled contraption, two with snowy-white hair. She wanted to see them more closely, but knew an elder held higher priority, still. And this was sounding so very interesting. They kept no slaves!

"Maybe later," he declined, not sure if he truly needed to see one, but Maren stepped closer.

"It would only take a few minutes," he offered. "My name's Maren and I'm a Healer," he said, introducing himself.

"I highly recommend it," Raya insisted, smiling, "Maren's strongly Talented and well trained."

"You always were such an opinionated woman, since you were a cub," he stated with a smile, missing this one niece the most, then nodded his head, granting his permission as he turned back to Maren.

"Let's get some chairs here," Ardis ordered. "Raby, Katas, if you could, please?" she requested. Katas smiled as she handed her Adris.

"You bet, Mom," she replied as the two girls ran off to find some chairs. Ardis was chuckling as she watched them disappear.

"You must be Ardis," Keen stated, smiling.

"Right. Let me introduce you, Ross and Dyan to my lady wife, Ardis, and our two sons, Dale and Adris, and our oldest daughter, Katas, went to help bring some chairs," Sabin said, realizing he hadn't introduced them, yet. The pride of his family was in his eyes and plain for all to see.

"Pleased to meet you, Lady Ardis," Keen told her as he bowed to her. She laughed merrily and blushed at his display, dipping her head in return.

"I could swear you've grown, Sernn," Koras declared, as he hugged his own son. "You look good, son."

"Maren healed me, so I don't have to worry about dying," he told him, smiling as he blushed darkly. "I want you to meet my new mother, but my new father is busy helping to set up some shelters over there," he told him, pointing to where they'd left Minn.

"I'm sure I'll have time to meet him," he promised. He stepped over to Mitt, extending his hand to her. She looked surprised, then crossed his with her own.

"My name's Mitt," she told him, smiling at last. "Garth's my older brother," she added. "My true-mate, Minn, will join us as soon as he finishes with the shelter he's helping erect now," she promised, having already requested his presence via Mind Voice. This was too important to all of them! If this man was Sernn's father in truth, she wondered if he'd come to take him back?

"My name's Koras. I'm husband to my Lady Ross. Have all of your people spoken true-mate vows in this Winterhaven of yours?" he questioned, smiling at such a concept. There was laughter out of the Winterhaveners in response.

"It might seem that way, but in truth, very few couples have done so," Mitt denied. "Still, you've got a sampling of most of the ones who have, right here. Ryes has with Garth, Maren has with Dotti, Sabin and Ardis have, as well as Raya and her husband, Kovin. We just seem to have found the right people and knew it."

"Sana and Justin are now added to the list," Maren told her. "I'm not sure of anyone else, though."

"Monty and I are thinking about it," Denas admitted as she came over to see who these strange people were, here in the middle of their camp so soon. Sayer appeared with the groundsheet and blanket for the cubs.

"They had these buried," she explained, as she handed them to Ryes. She nodded her head to this, as she and Maren spread it out upon the ground near them, adding the blanket on top. Ardis immediately set down her two sons, as Dodi put down Tobin. Ryes bent to release her cubs from the stroller, seeing them all unhappy and squirming; wanting to get out, now.

"You must be very sure before making such a deep, lasting commitment," Maren cautioned her, worried for them.

"Yes," Ross agreed. "It binds the two souls together for eternity," she warned. Denas smiled at this as she nodded her head in agreement.

"Remind me to tell you about what Dotti and I went through. We know we're true-mates from before this life, and from what we had to endure to find each other in this one..." he finished, practically groaning in exaggeration as he smiled. Ryes chuckled as she nodded her head, knowing their history.

"Ross, would you like to see your niece?" Ryes offered, having put all five of her cubs down on the blanket. They were immediately trying to crawl off. She extended Manipulator to help contain them.

"Ryes, you have a distinct advantage over the rest of us," Dodi playfully scolded. She laughed as she nodded her head.

"I call it an equalizer. I'm outnumbered here and they're getting so active now!" she protested. Ross sat down on the blanket with her, as she looked at both white-haired cubs, trying to see her sister's features in either face. Trouble was, they both looked like her, while neither looked like her, she was filled with mirth and frustration.

"I can't tell them apart," she admitted, looking to Ryes. She laughed lightly, as she nodded her head. The others were laughing in agreement. The fact that she was a Talent, put her a little in awe of this woman. She recalled Garth's steadfast devotion to her and didn't think he could be that way, if she weren't someone who could be that way toward him in return. Raby and Katas returned with several folding chairs, as well as Minn, with his arms full of them, too. They started setting them up for everyone to sit upon.

"Few can tell them apart," she admitted, "This is Shaysa, my daughter by birth, and this is Shyla, your little niece, and my daughter by choice," she told her. Ross noted that all the cubs were healthy, active and of a good size! Her own son was several months older yet was about the same size as her niece was now.

"May I?" she requested. Ryes thought she knew what she was asking, so nodded her head in agreement. Ross picked up both Shaysa and Shyla in her arms, as she sighed in happiness. "They're so big and heavy!" she commented, realizing they were each heavier than her son, too.

"They're all bottomless pits," Ryes assured her, laughing. It made her feel a little uncomfortable for her to be holding two of her cubs, but she did her best to quash her anxiety.

"That's the truth!" Ardis agreed, smiling. "It's a good thing you finally got them past the nursing stage."

"You don't nurse them?" Ross questioned, frowning and surprised, thinking they weren't ready for real foods, yet.

"They started biting, as their teeth came in, and with my schedule, I've resorted to a formula preparation and feeding them some finely pureed foods," she explained. Ross looked around and realized only Dodi looked to still nurse her cub, while the other two women were already dried up, the small rounds of their breasts marking them as having had cubs already.

"It's nutritious for them," Maren spoke up in his cousin's defense, seeing her disapproval. "It's similar to what the humans feed their children."

"The other people here with you?" she asked. This got laughter and nods in response to her question. "And is that their language you sometimes speak?"

"Yes, it is," Dodi replied, smiling merrily. "I've found that even if I've spoken Dolbith all my life, there's still much about our own language to fully comprehend. It's why I'm taking both Dolbith and English classes, so that even if I can already speak both languages, I can better understand them."

"We've gotten to where we usually speak a blend of both languages," Ryes added, seeing Dyan and the two men who'd come with Ross, were all paying them strict attention. Maren closed his eyes and began his examination of the Moondance Tribal Chief, with Raya paying this close attention.

"So, you're Sernn's father?" Minn questioned Koras, as he took a chair next to him. He smiled and nodded his head.

"I was barely of age to mate, when Senah decided to take me to her bed, in hopes that my youth would overcome her curse. Sernn was doomed to die, my youth not being strong enough, after all. It's good to see him with good color and strength. I've never seen him so happy, even if I was never allowed near him after he was born," he explained. There was shock in Minn's eyes as he heard his brief tale.

"How could she do that to you?" Denas demanded, frowning as she took a chair near them. She saw Sabin's eyes were shadowed, as his eyes met Ardis'. She smiled for him and stood up to lean over to whisper something in his ear, while giving him a light kiss on the cheek. This seemed to lift his shadow a little.

"She did practically whatever she wanted. She had the support of the strongest warriors, as many had been loyal to her father, and many she openly invited to her chambers, any time they felt the need," Keen informed her, looking grim. "A handful held back from her, only coming to her chamber under orders - those being reinforced by her personal guard. Luckily, I never fathered anything on her."

"Did anything come of this last winter's?" Ryes suddenly asked, needing to know. Then she realized she should've never spoken it aloud, as the color suddenly drained from Sabin's face. "Forget it. I'm sorry Sabin. I didn't think..." she apologized. He gave her a nod of his head at this, knowing she'd forgotten there were others gathered with them, who had no knowledge of their travels of last winter. And that there were some things they didn't speak of openly before them.

"Did Sabin father any cubs on Senah?" Ardis suddenly pressed, needing to know, being direct. Ross carefully put down the two cubs and stood up, facing them both.

"Maybe, but it's not certain the cubs are his, and we won't know until they're born later this year. Kyma wanted to have his Healer woman check your life's pulse, if you were agreed, to verify if they are truly yours when they're born. Senah's life is forfeit for the many crimes against the Mountain Tribes she committed, including hindering, and using two Bearers of a Badge of Passage in the manner she did. She only lives long enough in Kyma's hold to give birth. If the cubs are yours, it'll be up to you, Sabin, to determine their fates," she told him, knowing she had to discharge this duty sooner, or later. She'd hoped to be able to do so in more privacy.

"If they're Sabin's, we'll take them to raise as our own," Ardis declared, not looking to see if he agreed to this, or not. She felt him take her hand, giving it a light squeeze in response.

"I'll tell Kyma," she replied, obviously relieved. She knew whether, or not, Sabin agreed to take in the cubs, it still lay with his mate, especially if they were true mates. Ardis was young, as was Ryes, but determined and knew her own mind. There was a general release in relief from those gathered around her.

"You may have your own horde to look after, Ardis," Ryes teased her, smiling. She laughed in response, nodding her head as she imagined holding little ones, once again. She found no fear and was actually hoping they were Sabin's, as she knew they'd grow up in Winterhaven well, and Maren would be able to heal them, if they carried Senah's curse.

"We'll see... It might be interesting, and I've had a chance to watch how you manage your own, so we'll be all right," she assured Ryes, beaming. Katas laughed lightly as she nodded her head in agreement, ready to help.

"So, are you going to leave Sernn with us?" Minn asked straight out, wanting to see where this man's interest lay. Koras met his eyes, evaluating him. The woman he named as his new mother didn't look to even have had her first season, yet the man who now faced him looked far older than her but was still younger than himself. He sighed, looking to Sernn. He saw the anxiety in his eyes and tension in his body. He moved to practically meld into Mitt's side, if he could, not wanting to leave her.

"Yes. He wants to be here with you. But, if it's at all possible, could I visit the three of you in your home later this summer? I'd like to see for myself this Winterhaven of yours," he replied. Minn smiled, nodding his head in concession to this simple request.

"That's agreeable," he replied, then extended his hand to him, palm flat, claws retracted. Koras chuckled as he crossed it with his own.

"Finished," Maren breathed, opening his eyes. There was a look of utter delight and amazement in Dyan's face. He moved his shoulder and suddenly stood up, jumping about, as if dancing in joy.

"There's no pain!" he happily declared. Then drew the Healer to his own feet and threw his arms about him in a great hug, as tears were in his eyes. Raya was laughing at seeing this display, having never seen her uncle so joyous before.

"My finest mares are yours," Dyan told him, pulling a laughing Maren back once more, to look into his eyes. Maren shook his head in denial.

"We have more windracers around Winterhaven, than we know what to do with," he replied. Then saw the pain in the old man's eyes. "But, if you will, your finest, strongest filly, as soon as she's old enough, for my daughter, who won't be born for some months yet."

"You shall have her," he agreed, giving him a nod of understanding, vowing to breed the finest mare possible for him. He let him go, smiling to Raya. "I'd best go see to other matters," he told her, then turned to nod to each of the women he'd come to check upon. "I'll tell your families of your health and happiness," he said, then turned, striding back out of their camp, needing to catch up to Garth, to speak to him about how Healers were addressed in this treaty he was proposing to Dara.

"Another happy customer," Maren commented with a smile. Raya nodded in agreement.

"I'd best get back to helping Chuck with the kitchen setup. He's heading back home tomorrow, leaving the whole thing in my hands," she told them, then turned, heading back the way she'd come.

"And if you'll excuse me, I have an encampment to finish organizing," Sabin told Keen. "But you're welcome to drop by here to visit anytime, later."

"I'll do that," he agreed, "got a new set of cubes made. You can help me break them in." Sabin laughed at this, nodding his head.

"And now we can play in the sunlight," Sabin teased with a huge smile, looking to delight Keen, too. With this, he turned to deal with Spann, who'd run up and looked like he needed to talk with him, leading him off as he listened to his complaint.

"So true, my friend," he breathed out, so happy he'd survived that dangerous winter storm.

A Call for Help

Chapter 24

"They're starting to drop off, Mom," Sayer pointed out to Ryes, who watched Sabin leave, wondering how things would work out. Of Ardis, she had no doubts in her mind at all.

"Then let's get them settled," she agreed, smiling down at her smaller children. She lifted them back into their stroller as she wondered if their travel cribs had been found yet? "Do you know if," she began as Nicos and Anders appeared with their arms full of familiar, baby furniture.

"Mason thought you might need these," Nic told her. She laughed and pointed toward her shelter.

"Right in there," she directed, as Raby and Sayer moved to help with the setup. "The first day seems to be the worse," she commented to Ross, as she held both Shaysa and Shyla again, smiling down at them, as she sat on the edge of the blanket.

"I can't get over both girls not only having white hair, but looking so very much alike," she commented with wonder, in a low voice.

"What was your sister like?" Denas asked, curious.

"She had very light-colored hair, almost like Dodi's," she told her, looking up and seeing the thoughtful look in Ryes' eyes. "Do you know how rare, white-colored hair is?" Ryes smiled, nodding her head, understanding the implication.

"More rare than red-haired. The only one I've met so far, is Saree," she agreed, "And my cubs, of course. Please tell us more about her?"

"Rona was always a little wild and did things her own way. She knew her first season was due and was determined to have a man Senah had never touched. She came out to last year's Great Spring Gather and found a plainsman, who suited her fancy. They spent most of the gather in her tent. She was prone to laughter, singing, and dancing, whenever the whim took her. She was a good little sister and I still miss her terribly," she replied, putting first Shaysa back into the stroller, then Shyla. There were tears in her eyes, as she turned back to them, wiping at them with a sad smile.

"I hope Shyla grows up like her," Ryes said, reaching out a comforting hand to this woman, gripping her shoulder momentarily. She leaned over and kissed both cubs, then sat back down on a chair.

"I think she will," Keen agreed, placing a hand to his cousin's shoulder in comfort too. He noted there were no words spoken in anger, nor voices raised in disagreements here. There were smiles and laughter around them, as these busy people were already, almost finished raising their campsite.

"What about her father? Will he try to claim her?" Maren questioned, knowing it needed to be voiced.

"I spoke to Rona before she died, giving Shyla birth. She knew of Senah's heart, even then. She told me, she'd had a Vision that she'd survive and grow to be a fine healthy, happy woman. She told me to let her go when the word came down. I know she saw her own death, but she only wanted her daughter's freedom from Menna's Hold. I don't think she'll have the future Rona saw for her out among the plain's tribes. And I'll fight any claims he tries to make against you, for her. She and your daughter belong together, I believe it with all my heart," she said, looking to Ryes at the end. Ryes gave her a nod of her head, understanding and appreciating her support. And now she knew why Shyla held a sleeping Talent!

"I'll raise her the best I'm able," she vowed. Then saw Sayer waving from the shelter doorway. "Excuse me, while I settle them down for a nap." With nods and chuckles of agreement, she pushed the stroller, with the sleepy cubs, toward the shelter.

"You can tell Kyma that I'll be able to give Aina Sabin's life pulse, so she won't have to bother him about it," Maren offered. Ross looked to him, surprise in her eyes. "I am a Healer after all and know Sabin well. Here, let me give you a quick check," he offered. She looked to Koras, then gave Maren a nod as Koras looked to approve of the gesture. She sat down upon a chair next to Denas.

"I don't even know your name, Healer," she commented, as he sat down next to her. He smiled as he gave her a nod in understanding.

"My name's Maren and I originally came from Matlowe Village," he introduced himself, "And may I present Denas, who's a cousin of Ryes' and came to us from out of the past, Dodi, who came to us from the plains, Ardis and Mitt, who came from Matlowe as a part of our original group, and Minn, who originally came from Matlowe too, but after we'd established Winterhaven as our new home." Ross smiled at this, giving him a nod of her head.

"And I'm sure you've already heard that Koras is my husband, and Keen is my cousin and a friend to Sabin and Garth," she told him. He smiled and nodded to this.

"And Ryes is my cousin, now, may I?" he requested. She gave him a nod, so he closed his eyes and extended a hand toward her arm, latching on gently. The first thing he noted was she was suffering from two types of parasites, which he quickly eliminated, then, began repairing her damaged organs and taking in an estimation of the rest of her health.

"That should keep them for a couple of hours," Ryes sighed as she joined them, once again. Suddenly a man ran up to her and grabbed her, lifting her up in the air and spinning her around as he laughed merrily at the surprise on her face.

"You're back!" Shams declared, realizing he was acting like a cub again. "I wasn't sure if you'd come."

"You can put me down, now," she calmly told him, smiling, and blushing at his display. Mitt laughed as she and Minn had stood up at his running into the immediate area and grabbing Ryes.

"Good to see you, Shams," Mitt said. "Ah, I'd better go see if there's anything else I can do to help finish getting our shelter up. Coming Sernn?" she questioned as he was instantly beside her. She ruffled his hair, then draped an arm over his shoulders as they walked off.

"Is this where our shelter will be?" Saree asked, having come over to Ardis, to show her the small map she'd been given earlier. She laughed and nodded her head.

"Gann and Garth are pretty close, so Garth wanted you two near the rest of us, here," she assured her. Shams finally let Ryes back down. She stood a few moments as she straightened out her tunic top and regaining her composure.

"Now, why wouldn't Garth and I be here?" she questioned him, gesturing him to sit in a chair. He turned and stopped as he caught sight of Saree. Ryes chuckled as she noted his interest. "Her name's Saree and she's already mated to Gann," she mischievously whispered in his ear.

"All the finer ladies are always taken quickly," he returned in comment. Ross frowned at this exchange, wondering.

"You're just fond of ladies with different colored eyes," Ryes teased, as they both sat down.

"Not true," he quipped back, "Grandfather had originally planned to introduce me to you the winter before last, but my mother desperately needed my help that year. I had no idea you had green eyes at the time and was only planning on offering to mate with you solely for Darman's sake," he replied, seeing he had everyone's peaked interest as he told her this news. Ryes blushed, shaking her head. "But, after meeting you at the last gather, I've been kicking myself for not making that trip out to Matlowe with him far sooner."

"And now it is too late," Denas stated, laughing lightly. She saw Ryes was tongue-tied and unable to come up with an immediate retort.

"Ah, that's the truth. True-mate vows are far stronger bonds than just a mere husband and wife relationship," he replied. "I don't believe I've met you, m'lady. My name's Shams." He bowed to her as he introduced himself, smiling to note the white-haired lavender-eyed woman was watching him too.

"I am pleased to make your acquaintance. My name is Denas of House Clenons. I am a third cousin to Ryes," she explained, blushing as he smiled into her eyes.

"You're such a rogue, Shams!" Ryes told him, swatting at his arm to distract him from Denas. "She's already mated, too."

"Ryes? I need you to see this," Maren requested in English, as he sat with his eyes open, looking to her. She turned and saw the look in his eyes, so quickly went to his side, calling up her Healing Talent, too. She knelt beside him, closing her eyes.

"What is it?" she questioned directly, using Mind Voice.

"Her arm looks like it was deliberately broken, and it healed poorly. It's a years-ago injury, but I thought you should see it," he explained, before he set himself to heal it. She tuned in to where he indicated, seeing it for herself. It shocked her that anyone would do such a thing to another. And he was correct, from the way the break had formed, it was deliberate! She helped him heal her, then did her own check, noting what he'd done for her.

"What's the problem?" Ross questioned, after they opened their eyes. Maren smiled his reassurance.

"It looked like someone broke your arm deliberately, long ago," he explained. "I'm still teaching Ryes a few things about using her Healing Talent and wanted her to see it for herself." Ross appeared shocked at this, realizing she could move her left arm freely, as she'd been unable to do for too many years!

"My older cousin, Senah, broke it when we were young. She didn't like the way I looked at a boy she liked then. She was vicious, in many ways," she replied, sighing as she recalled that time, once again. She had no idea how she survived her childhood!

"Since you were infested with some parasites, I'd like to check the others with you. It's odd, because from my studies of the human's parasites, it looks like one you would pick up from eating slimers," Maren commented.

"But we do eat them. At our spring festival, we eat raw slimers to honor Ricmon," she explained, blushing.

"Well, they're slowly killing you and probably your people," he warned her, looking her in the eye. "Isn't there something safer you could do to honor Ricmon?"

"I don't know. I'll have to consult with the elders and Great Chief Kyma," she replied, feeling at a loss with such news. How could this be? But then, there was the high infant mortality, the frailty of the elders and the sometimes listlessness of the rest of her people. Could this tradition truly lie at its roots?

"Please do so," Ryes urged, hoping she'd realize the importance. Ross gave her a nod.

"Do I have your permission to check the rest of the people from your hold and treat them?" Maren requested.

"We have nothing of any value to pay you for such a service," she replied, knowing this for a truth. They had far more here around them in this temporary camp, than they had themselves, back in Menna's Hold.

"Yes, you do," Ryes stated in denial. "We would ask to borrow of your craftsmen, artists and singers to teach our people and children back in Winterhaven in return, for a length of time which Garth, you and your elders can agree upon," she proposed. "We mostly have only the tales and songs we grew up with in Matlowe and want our children to know more of the world, than we were taught."

"You would want to know our songs and legends?" Koras questioned, thinking this was a silly little thing to ask, for such a great service.

"You'd better believe it!" Ardis piped in, taking a chair as Katas and Raby were taking her two cubs to lay down for their naps, too. She grinned as she saw the clever way Ryes found for them to pay for such a service, without putting the whole tribe into deep financial obligations, which would only create further hardships for them.

"And they don't all have to come to teach us at once. We can stretch this out through time, so they're not so far from their families, for a long time," Ryes added. She saw Riss run up to the doorway of her shelter, probably looking for Sayer. "Riss, come here for a moment, please?" she requested. He looked like he'd been caught doing something wrong, causing the gathered adults to chuckle as he reluctantly stepped forward.

"Yes ma'am?" he questioned, looking down. "I was only seeing if Sayer wanted to play." Ryes smiled for him, nodding her head.

"It's all right. I just want you to tell these fine people how many songs about the mountains you were taught, back in Matlowe Village?" she encouraged him. He looked up; surprise written upon his young face.

"Mountain songs? I don't know any mountain songs," he admitted, seeing her guests were dressed strangely.

"Would you like to learn some?" she pressed, smiling to see the curiosity in his eyes.

"I don't know. Is there much to learn about mountains?" he asked, not understanding her question.

"There are many wondrous things in the world to see and know, and you are only shorting yourself by not looking further out into the whole of Tayna," Denas told him, smiling to see the puzzlement in his eyes.

"Thank you, Riss. You and Sayer may go on and play, but if you want to leave our encampment, you must have an adult escort," she reminded him. He gave her a quick nod of his head, then dashed back to see Sayer already waiting for him. She laughed as he grabbed her hand and the two of them quickly disappeared. "You see, our need exists," Ryes said, turning back to face Ross.

"This was a token we never considered to have such deep value," she replied smiling, as new ideas awoke within her mind.

"Then, for the moment, may I please check Koras and Keen? We can later discuss the exchange for the care of the rest of your hold," Maren offered.

"For now," she agreed. Koras shifted over to a chair next to Maren and relaxed as he bent to his work. Ryes moved next to her cousin, to offer him her power, to Boost his efforts. She'd just finished the wall around the campground as they spoke, putting even the final touches to the great Phoenix next to their main entrance. Tonight, she planned upon adding in some permanent shelters for everyone, if she could. She realized wasn't tired at all and had plenty of energy to lend Maren.

"Now, you're giving me ideas!" Shams declared, grinning.

"It's what you've done all your life," she responded, opening her eyes to smile at him. "You travel and entertain peoples, as well as trade and provide an avenue for news."

"Ah, but how many songs about mountains do we sing?" he returned, "And how many songs about the Yuri do you think I know?"

"I would think quite a few about the Yuri, and if you don't sing many songs about the mountains, you'd better start trading to learn some. You never know when they'll be in vogue," she teased.

"I would rather the songs I heard Monty playing about the calling-longing from out of the depths of space. If you have never traveled long in the space lanes, you never truly know what those songs mean. For being from such different people, we have much in common with the humans," Denas commented. Saree laughed lightly at hearing this, coming to sit near her friends.

"But we are not truly two different people as you, yourself, have discovered," she returned, teasing her friend.

"What do you mean?" Ross pressed, curious at the hint, thinking she could guess what she implied.

"That I now carry Monty's son," Denas replied, not sure if they were going to discuss their crosses, so soon. But they did have a few of the ones from Booda with them here.

"Naturally?" she returned, not quite believing her. Denas nodded her head to this, smiling brightly.

"Yes, and quite an unexpected surprise. There is still some controversy about our crosses, but overall, most of the people have decided it is not an important issue," she explained.

"Oh, I wouldn't say that," Maren disagreed, as he opened his eyes, having finished with Koras, giving him a nod of his head. "You wouldn't believe the yowling I've heard, and the starmen are the worse of the two peoples." Keen changed places with his friend, smiling as he could imagine such a thing. A crew of humans and starmen appeared, readying to set up Saree and Gann's shelter, near them. Minn got up to lend them a hand.

"Change is always hard to bear," Dodi spoke up, a sleeping Tobin in her arms, even with the racket.

"But this one's just a part of life," Ryes agreed with her. "I'll see what I can do to get the heat off you, Maren," she told him.

"Why would they be upset with your cousin?" Shams questioned.

"Because his own wife is pregnant with his daughter," Ardis replied for Ryes, seeing Nesa and Abbra approaching them. "Headache at four o'clock," she warned.

"Oh, what now?" Dodi questioned, sounding annoyed and so out of character for her. Ryes smiled, knowing Nesa tried everyone's patience, and the way she loved to badger Torr, overall.

"I wonder what kinds of songs the Boodans know?" Saree questioned, smiling, once the ladies were in earshot.

"Why would you want to know of our songs?" Nesa asked, stopping before the impromptu gathering of people.

"To expand our understanding of others," Ryes told her. "How can I help you ladies?"

"Torr has ordered us to remain in the campsite, unless we have a male escort. Is this necessary?" Abbra asked, before her friend could voice it, with her own version. She found it did no good to try to antagonize Ryes outright.

"Yes," Ross replied for her, gesturing to indicate her own husband and cousin with her. "There're many plainsmen here and they regard all women as property. The escort is only to protect you," she explained.

"It's the truth," Ryes added, seeing the doubt in Nesa's eyes. She had to smile to herself. They hadn't even been on Tayna very long and were already chaffing at being restricted to an area which was far larger than their whole, original settlement!

"But, what about The Laws?" she questioned.

"That's what we're trying to work at getting enforced," Ryes informed her. "Garth's meeting with the elders here, for the next two weeks, to work on getting them reestablished."

"What Laws?" Ross asked, not knowing of this, at all. She wondered if Kyma knew?

"The Laws set forth by Prince Callas of House Ladearis, who was the heir to the throne of Kahmarr, who chose to stay on Tayna to establish Law and order, the Caravans, the trading ships and trade agreements, in the wake of the Snagospin's attack, which wiped almost all civilization from Tayna," Ryes told her. "We've found an old holo he left, to explain what he did and why. As a Chieftess, I believe you should have access to this holo, too."

"I'd like to see it, yes," she agreed, as questions danced in her eyes.

"Give us a day to get everything settled and sorted out, and I'm sure I'll be able to locate it among our things, and show it to you, so you can see it for yourself," she offered, knowing she might be going against Garth and Kyma by such a move, but still felt Ross deserved to know.

"How can we be sure that it's genuine?" Koras demanded, not wanting to be saddled with some alien laws in Menna's Hold!

"I could show you the recording of what happened, when we found the vault and library beneath Matlowe's Village Circle," she offered, calmly meeting his eyes, understanding his discomfort.

"May I see it, too? The recording, as we did see the whole-oh," Nesa requested, not wanting to be left out. Abbra nodded her head in agreement.

"Yes, you may. We've barely gotten your people settled but had planned on showing you all the full message since you only saw the first part," she replied, smiling. Nesa gave her a nod of her head, believing her. She was one of the very few people she found she truly believed. "Do you mind waiting for tomorrow?" she asked.

"No, I don't mind," she replied, mollified a little. She sat down, taking little Misti for Abbra, as she went to bring a second chair closer. "I just can't get used to the huge, bright, sunny sky!" she complained.

"Where're you from?" Ross queried, wondering at her manner and unknown accent. She noted both women appeared so very thin.

"Booda," Nesa replied, grinning. "It's one of the two moons of the third planet you call Tyssen." She watched to see this woman's reaction. She'd wanted to bait a few of these Tayna natives, and the truth was always so much more fun than any fabrication!

"I discovered them there, by accident. And since Garth was out placing the warning satellites, he decided to stop by to check up on them. We couldn't leave them there, in those harsh conditions,"

Ryes admitted. Maren opened his eyes feeling a little winded now.
He smiled as he gave Keen a nod of his head. Keen laughed as he
realized he felt better than he ever had, in his whole life!

"Thank you, Healer!" he declared, "I'll write a new song, just
for you!" Maren laughed at this, nodding his head.

"Just don't be trying to sing it. We'd all like to be free of
headaches," Ross teased, smiling. She realized she felt much the
same. It was incredible how poorly she'd felt before and never knew!
She turned back to Ryes. "We truly must go. I have other matters to
attend to today, but will be back about this time tomorrow, to see this
whole-lo of yours," she promised, standing up. Koras stood, too. Ryes
stood, extending her hand her, feeling they did have family ties
between them.

"Until tomorrow," she replied, meeting her eyes as she spoke.
Ross smiled as she crossed it with her own hand. Yes, she realized,
she did feel a kinship with her, after all. She then bowed and the
three of them quickly left their camp. They had much to discuss with
both their own elders and Great Chief Kyma! She wondered if he
knew what a whole-lo was?

"Sorry to have so much work for you, right at the start," Ryes
apologized to Maren, noting Dotti approaching, with Karis running
ahead of her, laughing. "And it looks like you might be needed," she
teased. He turned, seeing them and smiled, as he let out a sigh.

"My siblings are a handful, at times," he agreed. "I'm
surprised she hasn't thrown the whole lot of us out, already."

"After all the troubles the two of you went through to find
each other?" Ardis teased, grinning impishly.

"Our shelter's all set up, it's right behind Ryes and Garth's,"
Dotti informed him, smiling as she took a vacant chair next to him.
"I've got Tars entertaining Rowis, but I don't know how long that will
last!" He gave her a quick kiss as Karis came over to stand near
Ryes.

"Can I help?" he asked, meaning it. She thought on it for a
few moments, then nodded her head.

"We can use some stones set up in a ring, where we'll be
building our central fire. Would you like to help gather some stones?
Just put any you find, over there," she suggested, pointing to a spot
near their chairs and out of traffic in the area.

"In a big pile?" he pressed. She nodded her head to this, so
he bent to pick up the first two he saw and went to place them where

she requested. Some of the younger cubs were running through the area, so he called them over and enlisted them in the project, too. There were screams of delight as all the children got into the game, almost as if they were hunting for treasure. This got the adults laughing at their pranks.

"Great idea," Dotti commented, smiling. "It's sure to keep them busy for a little while." Jons was struggling to lift a large one, so Aldin rushed to her side to help. The two of them discovered some tiny scaly scampers beneath the rock, so as soon as they added it to the pile, they rushed back to catch what they still could.

"And it's something constructive," she replied. She noted Maren was doing a quick, unobtrusive check on his wife and developing daughter, as usual. He was afraid to let anything ever happen to either of them. Damian and Eric walked into view, spotting them, and coming straight over. The cubs spotted Damian and immediately ran to him, to give him hugs and kisses. They greatly missed him as their teacher.

"Well, it was working for a little while," Ryes added, as Eric joined them, laughing. He couldn't believe how good it felt to see everyone again! It was like coming home, even if his own, original home lay light years away.

"Eric!" Ardis cried out as she jumped up, with Ryes, to give him a hug and kiss in welcome. He laughed at this, knowing tears were threatening to start.

"It seems like it's been forever," he said, as Ryes hugged and kissed him, too.

"Now why doesn't she greet me like that?" Shams protested, teasing, even if he meant it deep within his heart.

"It is a little hard to give someone a kiss in greeting, if you are being swung about in the air," Denas quipped back. She didn't know this human but saw both him and the other man were well loved. Even some of the work crew stepped over to fuss over and greet them, too. She noted they'd dropped to using almost pure English, as Ryes was filling them in on some of the things which had happened, in the last few days. Monty suddenly appeared out of nowhere, running straight up to Ryes, handing her a headset.

"You'd better listen to this, Ma'am," he advised. The look on his face and manner of address, let her know it was very important. She took the headset and put it on, activating it immediately. A frown instantly alighted her face as she heard what the problem was, herself.

310

"Mitt! I need your help," she immediately sent, using Mind Voice, then debated about informing Garth and his party this way, or not. "Get Sabin," she ordered Monty, aloud. He gave her a nod of his head, but she placed a hand to his shoulder first, invoking Empath to quickly locate him. He suddenly understood what she was implying. That he needed to start utilizing his Mind Voice, especially in such situations.

"Winterhaven, this is Ryes. We'll respond to this call. Relay to Polas that we'll be there soon, and to hang on," she ordered over the headset.

"Yes, Ma'am," was the response, "We'll relay and stand by."

"Good. Over and out," she said, setting the headset to standby, as both Mitt and Sabin appeared. She looked up to them, then gave them the full story directly, mind-to-mind. "I'll need one of you to stay here to keep an eye on things and one of you to pilot the shuttle, since I haven't had enough time to learn it, yet."

"Aren't you going to tell Garth?" Sabin pressed, knowing he needed to know what was going on, too.

"You don't think I'll be disrupting things by telling him what's happening - directly? I don't want him distracted from something important," she stated, needing his advice in this matter. He looked thoughtful for a few seconds, understanding what she meant.

"Use your Empath to check in on him, first," he suggested, thinking she should've seen this by now. She grinned, giving him a nod, as she realized he was right. She closed her eyes and extended herself out, finding him and the others very quickly. Sabin joined her in a commune, seeing the scene for himself. Garth seemed to note their presence, so closed his eyes to open up his own Talent and allow their contact with him. Sabin quickly filled him in on the situation.

"Leave Torr to watch the camp. Take Maren and an armed escort along with the three of you, and report back to Torr, as soon as you can," he advised. "Be careful!" he added in warning.

"We will," Ryes promised.

"Also get me a headset, so Torr can keep me up to date," he added, then let them go. Darman had asked him something, then noted he was preoccupied. Ryes and Sabin withdrew to let him get back to what he still needed to do.

"What was it?" Darman asked in English, as Garth opened his eyes again.

"Trouble. Gracie was taken by an elder in Wicker Village as a hostage. Something about a trade agreement had broken down and he decided that he was entitled to her, as part of a payment he was due," he replied. "Sabin, Ryes, Mitt and Maren are going to take the Avenger to deal with the situation. They'll be able to get out there and back, quickly."

"I should be there for this one," Darman stated, standing up. He wondered how things had gotten out of hand, and why a Wicker elder would feel Gracie was his to take as he pleased?

"There may not be enough time," Garth cautioned.

"We'll see," he returned, as he rushed out of the tent, startling the other elders with his hasty departure.

"You three remain here for me," Garth told Ethan, Metta and Rowan. They gave him surprised nods of agreement, knowing this was an important situation. He rushed out after Darman, but saw he stopped and was talking with one of his own people. The woman held protest in her eyes but bowed to him and closed her eyes to concentrate.

"I'm having Tova contact Ryes with a request to pick us up," he informed him, smiling. Tova opened her eyes, looking to see both men watching her closely.

"She said they'll be here, shortly," she stated, then sighed as she walked away. In a very few minutes, the Avenger had taken to the air and came to hover over their location. The hatch opened and Ryes looked down to them and waved. She extended Manipulator and pulled both men up into the shuttle with her. Then floated down three headsets to Ethan, Metta and Rowan, as the whole group of elders had emerged to see the shuttle for themselves. She sealed the hatch and the ship quickly rose, heading upwards, toward the east.

"She moves so fast!" Dastin commented in a low voice. Ethan chuckled at this, nodding his head, as Rowan and Metta were laughing.

"She does, at that," he agreed.

Saving Grace

Chapter 25

"What's wrong?" Eric and Maren questioned at the same time.

"An elder's taken Gracie hostage in Wicker Village over a trade agreement having fallen through," Ryes explained, as Sabin had Mitt call Torr to them, since he hadn't been practicing his Mind Voice very much. "Garth thought you should come with us," she told Maren.

"Wait, if it's involving a trade agreement, I should be there to negotiate on my grandfather's behalf," Shams stated. Ryes met his eyes and realized he was right. He'd have an understanding about the base situation.

"Alright, but only to help defuse the situation," she agreed. Sabin looked unhappy about it, but realized he did have some leverage to help, so gave his nod of agreement.

"Let's go," he ordered.

"Ardis," Ryes said, as she paused to meet her eyes, her heart wrenching now, but needing to ask.

"I'll watch after the little ones," she promised, knowing what she was going to ask, as she waved her onward. She prayed in her heart that Gracie would be all right!

"What's the matter?" Torr asked, as he appeared. They were now heading as a group toward the Avenger. And it wasn't even lunch time, yet! Ryes quickly filled him in, using Mind Voice as she walked, not wanting to waste time. "Oh. I'll keep an eye on things," he agreed, as he caught the headset, she threw him. She gave him a wink as she turned to jog, to catch up to Sabin, once more.

"At least we do have the speed the Avenger grants us," she commented.

"We do have this one small blessing," he agreed, chuckling as he thought of the scramble they would've had before with only the choppers. Ryes quickly opened the hatch and jumped in.

"Chief Exec onboard," she called out to the computer.

"Acknowledged," it responded, standing down the inner defense system to standby. They'd set up the computer to respond to only a handful of voices, as a security measure, to help prevent others from harming themselves, or their precious vehicles.

"It knows you?" Shams questioned as he followed Mitt into the ship. Ryes pointed to a seat, then sat down with her eyes closed. After a few seconds, she opened them again.

"Darman insists upon us stopping to pick him up," Ryes told Sabin.

"It'd be best if he were with us," Sabin agreed. "Go ahead and head toward the center of the Gather. That large tent, next to the great fire," he ordered Mitt, then turned back to Ryes, curious. "Whom did he use?"

"Tova. She's not too fond of me," she replied grinning, then turned to Shams, as Mitt was powering up the systems. "Of course, the Avenger knows me! I helped program her," she told him, a big grin upon her face.

"At least Tova and Gurri are no longer together," he let her know. She gave him a delighted look, then sighed.

"I hope they both find better, new lives," she mused. "I've haven't had the time to finish my piloting classes, or I'd be flying the Avenger now," she said. Shams laughed, shaking his head.

"With everything else you've been doing?" Maren agreed, seeing four humans crowding in with them, too. Ryes got up from her seat, as Mitt lifted off, indicating Sadie take it. The shuttle only had it configured for ten seats total, with straps anchored, which could be gripped by another ten who would be left standing.

"I can stand," she refused, embarrassed.

"I have to bring Darman aboard, and I'm sure Garth by now, too," she told her, smiling, "Sit, and that's an order, my friend." Sadie grinned as she nodded her head and sat in her place. Ryes moved over to the inner hatchway, as Mitt gently took off, grabbing a strap. Shams started to unbuckle so he could stand with her, but Maren grabbed his arm as he shook his head no, understanding Ryes.

"Leave it be," he whispered. He looked rebellious for a moment, then saw Ryes never even noted him and knew he was right. Maren helped him buckle up again - properly this time.

"I see him below us," Mitt called out to her. Ryes had just opened a storage locker and removed four headsets, putting one on, then cycled the inner and outer hatches.

"Now, I see them," she replied, over her headset. She leaned out and waved to the two men, then gently lifted them up to the shuttle. Darman took a seat next to Shams. Before she sealed the hatches, she dropped headsets down to her grandfather, Metta and Ethan then closed the hatches. "All clear. Let's get moving!" she ordered. Garth wrapped an arm about her, as he held onto one of the straps. Ryes wrapped both her arms about him and laughed, as the thrust pushed her tighter into his body. His smiled widened, as she happily sighed.

Polas sat worried. It was so unlike Old Trinkas to act in such a rash manner! It was a good thing Gracie had the communications gear, so he could call in for help. And it was true that those back in Winterhaven were confident about when Ryes said she'd be here, as fast as possible, it would be soon. But it could still take days by chopper, and he knew it. It was how to help keep the rest of the Wicker Village elders calm and somehow get them on his side. There'd been more and more tension as they approached Cootain, but no one had ever threatened violence before! And for Trinkas to actually carry Gracie off, as if she were no more than a sack of finely ground grains, was more than he could bear! But he feared to move against him, as he might feel compelled to harm her. He tried to calculate how many days it'd take for the choppers to reach them from out of the Great Gather. At least three or four days. He had to stall things for at least three days... How?

"You know Ryes'll never tolerate anything happening to any humans," Didas said, trying to comfort her husband. "Maybe we should stress to the other Wicker elders that to cross her is to invoke the worse thunderstorm ever imagined? They might help us free her."

"IF they choose to believe us," he replied with a chuckle, then heavy sigh. His brother and littermate, Ponti sat near them, nodding his head in agreement.

"I don't understand this problem with the exchange rates. What could be happening in Cootain, to cause such disruption this far away?" Ponti questioned. "Let's get dinner made, then see if we can invite some of the elders to share a few drinks at our fire later," he suggested, hopefully. "We have to find a way to leverage their help."

"It shouldn't take them more than three or four days, from out of the gather site," Didas commented, looking to see the pain in her husband's eyes. He nodded his head in agreement.

"Why is the yellow light flashing every now and then, on the communicator?" Mella asked, as she came out of the van to join the others. She'd finally gotten her son to sleep.

"It's so they can find us," Ponti explained to his wife. He stood up to help her with dinner preparations, moving the flat rock more directly over one side of the fire, so they could cook on it. She placed a fresh pot on it to brew their tea, as Ponti went to slice the fresh bounder meat. It was a blessing Mella was good with her bow and arrows. They were far better fed this year than in the years before, even with having to feed Gracie!

"It's all my fault," Tossin groaned out, still replaying the event in his mind, again. "If I hadn't been so trusting..."

"None of us expected it," Mella scolded as she put her sliced up tubers into a pot. "I'm only glad it wasn't me he grabbed!" He nodded in agreement, giving her a relieved, guilty smile, agreeing with her in his heart.

Suddenly, a loud noise filled the air as bright lights came on high overhead. The small group was startled, as they jumped to their feet. They saw the large, strange craft lightly descending toward them, landing in the clearing next to their van, which sat just outside of the village proper. Oddly, their windracers were calm through the landing, as if it happened every day. Their time in Winterhaven had inured them to the racket of large machines coming and going all the time.

"They got the shuttles operating!" Polas declared, joyous to know they had others who'd be better able to resolve this, already at hand! He ran toward the opening hatch as Garth and Ryes appeared in it, warily stepping down the stairs. Darman was right behind them, and Polas smiling in relief to see him, so quickly arrived.

"Thank goodness; we thought it'd be days!" Ponti said, having run up behind his brother. Ryes grinned now, as she nodded.

"Aletagga can favor us, at times," she told him, as Garth nodded his head. Darman stepped forward, confronting both men.

"What happened?" he demanded, right off. Both immediately launched into a full telling about the meeting, which ended with Old Trinkas carrying Gracie off over his shoulder. As Polas and Ponti told the tale, the rest of the passengers got off the shuttle to stand and listen to it, too. Ryes quietly made sure everyone was armed with either stunners or pistols, or both, just in case, with Sadie and Jake now bearing rifles, too. She quietly handed Mella, Didas and Tossin stunners, seeing they might need them now, and on the road. Darman refused the pistol, but took a stunner, as did Garth. They were as ready as possible. She only wished they had more light. The sun was quickly setting in about two hours.

Darman, Garth and Polas led the way into Wicker Village, going straight to their village square. They were met there by a lot of very nervous elders and villagers, who'd seen the landing of their ship, out of the very air.

Garth noted this village seemed so vastly different from the one of his birth. The houses were larger and in far better upkeep, and there were many more villagers, so that they almost overflowed the village square, which was again larger than Matlowe's. The people looked well fed and were better dressed, than the ones in Matlowe. A clear trickling stream ran its course through the village itself, with bridges providing a way across. The water looked inviting, but he saw an old woman dumping out a pot into it and knew it was a deception. How could they do this to their own drinking water? Darman saw where he was looking and gave him a nod of agreement. He appeared to wonder the same himself, years ago. Sabin, Ryes, Maren, Sadie, and Jake were off on their own errand, with Mella leading them. They were going to confront Trinkas directly and would join them as soon as they had Gracie safe and secure.

"We have come for the return of our own!" Garth declared in a stern voice to the gathered elders before them. Their platform was larger and looked in far better upkeep, but the old men and women sitting in their seats seemed no different. And they practically jumped at the sound of his voice. It made him feel bad, as he'd never intended to scare them, but he wasn't going to back down now. "How do you intend to make amends to us, for what you've done to Gracie?"

"O'Great One, we never intended to offer you offense," one of the elder women spoke up, bowing as she did so. "We saw your great air machine and knew the strange woman, who was taken, must be important."

Garth almost smiled at this, for this was what Ryes had fallen into calling him, when she was teasing him since they'd seen Prince Callas' ancient message. He realized with his mode of dress of the comfortable blue shipsuit he'd fallen into wearing most times now, the Badge of Passage upon his shoulder, his strange ornaments like the headset with blue and green lights upon his head, watch upon his wrist, small hand lantern and other items hanging from his utility belt, and his mix of followers, he must appear to be someone of some importance from a far land.

"No offense will be taken if she's unharmed and immediately returned," he replied, assuring them.

"That may be impossible, Sir. Trinkas has gone mad and took her inside his home. He won't come out, nor speak to anyone. We don't even know if he, or any of his family still live!" another elder related, as he dropped to his knees, as if to beg for Garth's mercy.

"Then, we'll see to it ourselves," he replied, then urged the man back to his feet.

"Tell me, what is this problem with the trade exchange rates? What are you basing this whole matter upon?" Darman asked, stepping forward to stand next to Garth.

"There's madness in Cootain, itself. The people are burning their things in the streets rather than give them over to the ruling family, who're raising the taxes and bleeding them all dry," the original woman told him, feeling more comfortable speaking to him, than to the young leader with him. The younger man's eyes held steel in their bright, honey-colored depths and it greatly frightened her. This gentle elder was familiar and one she didn't fear.

"Trinkas went to find out what was happening there, and returned with a madness about him, too. We've all been afraid of him since he returned last week," another woman spoke up, supporting her friend. Others were nodding agreement while the people gather nearby were talking in low voices in full support of that explanation.

"He said the crowns in Cootain now claim us and Berrals as a part of their domain and will be sending tax collectors and soldiers to enforce their will," the one man related, panic in his eyes. "We can't stand against Cootain's armed soldiers! We're doomed!" Darman and the others were shocked to hear this, but he briefly met Garth's eyes and saw the anger residing deep within. He wasn't going to stand by and let this village suffer due to the whims of some distant aristocrats.

"Did he say when these soldiers and their tax collector are due?" Garth questioned.

"No, only that they'd be on their way here, soon. There're four other villages which lie between us and Cootain, so it's hoped they're delayed somewhere between," the first woman replied, seeing the fire alight in his eyes. He didn't know them yet was personally insulted by the plight they were about to be beset. She was shocked and amazed, and realized why these strange people with him followed his lead. She saw she might do so, too, with his fiery passion.

"I'll have Ryes check their location for us, soon," he replied. A commotion started up at the back, and to one side of the gathered crowd. People gave way to allow a small party through, astounded at their presence, most were strangers to them.

"It looks like we won't have long to wait," Darman agreed, smiling as he recognized the rest of their group.

"That's a relief," Shams commented, mostly to himself. Garth glanced at him, curious. He noted his eyes were still glued to his wife's form. He'd hoped they'd settled this at the last gather, but it looked otherwise, and explained why he'd been aboard the Avenger, when they stopped to pick them up. He realized he was going to have to do something about it, but not now.

"I say it'll probably be easier if we just walk in and take things from there," Ryes suggested. Mitt gave her a nod of agreement, but Maren appeared thoughtful.

"We'll do it my way," Sabin ordered. Even if Ryes outranked him in Winterhaven, he outranked her away from it, by Garth's decree. She'd protested but knew there was little she could do about it. "Prepare yourself and follow my lead." She met his eyes, then gave him a nod of her head, leaving it in his hands.

They continued openly walking through the paved streets, until they reached the house Mella indicated where Trinkas and his family lived. He didn't want them to try to sneak around. He wanted the villagers to know they were here, and unafraid. The villagers and carts they passed paused and stared, knowing they were strangers, but no one stopped them. As they approached the house, they saw there was a small crowd already in front of it. They were demanding Trinkas to come out and talk with them, with no visible response.

"They're trying your way, with no results," Mitt pointed out, smiling. Sabin gave her a shake of his head at this, then led them up to the front of the crowd, a few realizing they were strangers, just as they stepped up in the front. Mella stepped up behind them, ready to help, if needed, and ready to inform the villagers what was happening, if they asked. Maren noted Jake and Sadie looked nervous, but held themselves steady, and at the ready.

"We've come for our Gracie, Trinkas. Let her go, or else!"
Sabin loudly called out, facing the house with his hands upon his hips.

"You can't hurt me. No one can hurt me, now," an old voice
called in response from within. "They're coming to kill us all. Best
seek mercy at your own hands!"

"Ryes?" Sabin requested, turning to her. She gave him a nod
of her head, then closed her eyes.

She reached out with Empath, searching the structure before
her. She clearly saw the old man, sitting on a chair in his living room
with a mug of ale and the body of an old woman lying across his lap.
Ryes saw she'd been murdered, with a long slash across her throat,
and he and the chair were soaked in blood. She searched further, her
heart trembling in fear for her friend. She found three cubs of varying
ages, the oldest one dead, the other two just barely alive. She
extended her Healing Talent, granting them enough to stay alive for
Maren to fully treat. She had to find Gracie! She discovered the cubs'
parents, lying in pools of their own blood outside the cubs' room,
having died violently, too. She'd now covered all the rooms of the
house, itself, with no sign of her. She delved deeper, recalling
Darman telling her some of the homes in the east had food storage
cellars beneath them. She found Gracie at last. She was bound and
gagged, lying in the darkness, next to a barrel of tubers and roots.
Using Manipulator, she freed her of the bonds, but left the gag on for
a moment. She then extended Mind Voice.

"Gracie, we're here. Stay quiet. The old man's mad and
already killed most of his family, so don't attract his attention right
now. Let me tell Sabin what's going on and we'll be in to get you out,
pronto!" she told her. Tears of relief flooded Gracie's eyes as she
quietly sobbed, knowing she'd be safe, as she sat up and nodded.

"I will. Please hurry," she pleaded in return, trying to focus on
the words she wanted to project, as she fumbled to remove the gag.
Ryes returned her attempt with a wash of love and support, then
withdrew. She returned to the old man, extending Healing to put him
into a light sleep. She opened her eyes to meet Sabin's.

"He's truly mad, Sabin. He's killed most of his family, but I
managed to sustain two cubs, so Maren can Heal them. I found
Gracie in a cellar, beneath the kitchen. I think she's all right, but we
need to get to her, as her courage is failing," she told him, speaking in
English. "I put Trinkas into a light sleep. I'd like Maren to look at him,
as it seems as if he's highly fevered," she added.

Sabin gave her a nod of his head, then motioned for Jake and
Sadie to open the door. It was locked, so Jake kicked it in, while
Sadie covered him, then both stopped as they saw the elder

unconscious with his dead wife lying on top of him on his over-stuffed chair, at the far end, in the large room before them.

"He's out of it," Sadie reported to Sabin, in Dolbith. "But you're not going to believe this!" She quickly turned away as the stench of death rolled out to them. She started to gag, but managed to keep some level of control, as Maren walked up to extend his Talent to both her and Jake. Sabin, Ryes, Mitt, and Mella, with the other villagers crowding behind, stepped up to see it for themselves.

"I'll go find Gracie," Sabin told them, stepping into the room, heading for the back to look for the cellar door, hoping the kitchen was that direction.

"Where are those cubs?" Maren questioned, looking to his cousin. Her color was washed out, but there was determination and compassion in her eyes.

"I'll take you there," she said, then stepped into the room, leading him to the right and the back rooms, where she knew the cubs lay. Mitt hung back, reluctant to enter. The smell of death didn't cause her to pause as much as the body of the woman.

"Is he dead?" one of the villagers asked, standing near her.

"No. Ryes merely put him into a resting sleep. She thought Maren should examine him first, to see if the fever he has could be at the root of all this. If it is, we'll have to have Maren and Ryes double check everyone he's been in contact with. You wouldn't want something like this to spread," she advised. There was renewed panic in the man's eyes as he realized what she was telling them. An epidemic of madness? It was a terrifying thought for her, too! She shifted back from the open doorway, as did Mella.

"We must take this to the rest of the elders!" a man declared.

"We'd better see to the dead, first," the first one returned. "Get some shrouds prepared," he ordered, turning back to his friends.

"How many will we need?" a woman asked, her face grim as she peeked within. She saw a man emerge with the strange, dark-haired woman in his arms. She was crying, as he carried her past the carnage. They came outside, and he put her back upon her feet.

"It's all right, now," Sadie assured her, still keeping an eye to the small crowd gathered around. They seemed more in shock.

"I know. I was never so happy as when Ryes assured me you were all here," she told them, smiling through her tears. She wiped her face as Mitt put an arm around her, in comfort.

"We'd never desert you, you know that," she assured her, smiling. Sabin turned and went to see what was keeping Ryes and Maren when he saw them coming toward him, each bearing a young cub and somber expressions.

"These are the only two who're left alive," Ryes told him, tears in her eyes. It'd taken a lot of effort to save them both. Now they had no parents of their own, anymore. Maren passed the child he bore to Sabin and turned back for the mad elder. Ryes had shown him what she'd noted earlier. He bent to examine him, seeing what she saw. There was a high fever and raging infection of his brain! Ryes passed the cub she carried to Mella, then stepped over to Maren, boosting his efforts as he tried to save Trinkas. After several long moments, Maren opened his eyes, knowing he was at the limits of his energy, now. He took a vial from his lab coat pocket and put it to a place where he extruded a small sample of the microorganism for later examination, then capped it securely. He also took pains to make sure the contagion wasn't present in the room around them.

"Sabin, we're going to need a medical team scrambled to help screen for the vector of this disease. If this spreads any further, all of Tayna could be at stake," he said, standing to face his friend, as he said it. "We're going to need all of us, as well as the villagers examined. This is an official quarantine."

"Will Trinkas be all right?" a villager asked.

"He'll need to rest to recover his strength, but once he knows what he's done, I don't know if he'll ever be all right again," he replied, looking grim. She gave him a nod in understanding.

"Let's go tell Garth," Ryes urged. "This is too deep to merely relay by radio." Sabin gave her a nod, then turned to the villagers.

"We'll need a few men to carry Trinkas to your village square. We'll get a medical team in here to make sure this spreads no further," he assured them. There was hope behind the panic in their eyes. Strangers they may be, but miracles they seemed capable of working, and they believed him. Sabin was merely glad of the instant cooperation.

They gathered the dead into the living room, lying them out in a more fitting pose, then closed the door, carrying Trinkas in the rug, which had lain upon the floor, in front of his favorite chair. The group turned toward the village square, relieved it was over, but knowing there was still much ahead of them tonight.

Quarantine

Chapter 26

"I've declared this village officially under quarantine," Maren informed Garth and the village elders, as the rest of their party came up behind him. "Trinkas had a disease which caused a swelling in his brain, a high fever, and his madness. I've eliminated it in his body and repaired the damage, but we've got to find out how it's spread and where he got it to begin with."

"Where's the rest of his family?" one of the elders questioned, seeing only Trinkas and two of his grandchildren with them.

"They're dead," Sabin informed them all. "The fever drove him to madness, and he'd killed them all. He thought he was saving them from being tortured by Cootain soldiers."

"Ryes and Mitt, could you please use your Talents to look through his memories and see if you can find the root of this disease? He might've picked it up in Cootain," Garth requested. "Since Maren declared a quarantine, we're all stuck here until we eliminate this threat. And Darman and I still have serious work to finish back at the Gather." He chaffed at the delay, while understanding the importance, at the same time.

Ryes gave him a nod, then signed for the men carrying Trinkas in the rug to place him upon the ground near them. Fresh blood still darkened his clothes and was smeared upon their hands and clothes, as they gently placed him where she directed. Ryes and Mitt then knelt to either side of his shoulders, as if they'd rehearsed it all earlier. Mitt smiled as her eyes met Ryes', then they closed their eyes, ready as could be to begin.

They melded their minds and hearts, then delved through his memories, looking beyond the madness, back to when he journeyed to Cootain. The long walk to reach the city was very normal. But Cootain, itself, was frightening with the way the people acted in such bizarre behaviors, all as if it were perfectly normal! Mobs of people wandered aimlessly through the streets destroying everything and laughing about it. Bodies littered the alleys, too, people who'd been too slow to evade the mobs. They saw madness reined there, through his eyes. Ryes noted the one thing he kept complaining about, which no one seemed to listen to him, was the bad taste in the water. They both withdrew, relieved to only have experienced what he'd done to his own family here.

"I think it was something in the drinking water," Ryes told Garth, as the crowd looked to them with questions in their eyes.

"He kept complaining about the water," Mitt agreed. "And if you think what he's done here is bad, you should've seen what it was like in Cootain! It's driven everyone mad!" Maren didn't look happy at hearing this news. He didn't have enough staff to handle a city the size Cootain was reputed to be.

"We'd best get Dr. Cruthers and Dr. Turner in on this as consultants. They might have some ideas about approaching the problem," Garth suggested. "Mitt, bring the Avenger in to land here in the village square, so we have access to her resources," he ordered. She gave him a nod of her head, then headed off with Mella, Polas and Sadie in her wake. The Village Square was more than large enough to accommodate the small space shuttle, without crowding.

"We're going to need a cleared area, large enough for the Avenger to land," Sabin ordered the villagers, indicating they clear a wide area. They readily followed his directions, as if he'd grown up here and knew them all.

"Winterhaven, this is Garth," he spoke into his headset. He got a response immediately, as the computer on the shuttle relayed his signal automatically. "Maren has declared a quarantine in Wicker Village and will need a medical team scrambled to support him. Exclude Dr. Turner for now, to continue to head up the treatment team in Winterhaven, in his absence. I also want a relay set up so I can speak with Dr. Cruthers," he ordered.

"The AI's going to have an electronic coronary over this," Ryes teased Garth, smiling as she stepped up to him.

"I only hope it's something in the water. If it is, it'll be easier to track down and eliminate," Maren commented, feeling tired. He didn't even want to think of all the work still ahead.

"Let the guys from the lab have their fun," Ryes urged. "You need to get some rest. You've been on the run all morning long and it's just past lunch time where we came from. Plus, we both need to take the time to wash up," she added, noting they were covered in dry blood.

"Wait until the shuttle gets here and use the showers on her," Garth advised in English, having deactivated his mic once more. "We don't want to further contaminate their drinking water." Ryes made a face at this, then nodded her head in understanding.

"A nice, hot shower does sound inviting," Maren commented in Dolbith, smiling as he saw the intense curiosity in Shams' eyes. It irritated him not knowing what they were saying when they used English, and he knew if he snooped, they'd know he was doing it. Maren bet himself he'd find some way to start learning English before the end of the gather.

"You're all right, Gracie?" Garth asked, glad to see she looked well, if appearing shaken, with puffy, blood-shot eyes.

"Mostly," she replied, putting on a brave smile, as she tucked back her long dark hair back behind her ear. Maren mentally kicked himself, as he gestured her over to his side.

"Let me make sure," he ordered. She smiled more genuinely as she complied, knowing he'd know for sure. He closed his eyes as Ryes closed hers and placed a hand to his arm to boost his Talent and grant him hers to utilize, if needed. He opened his Healing and began to examine Gracie. After several long moments, he finished and opened his eyes again, an odd smile upon his lips.

"Who?" he whispered in English, as it seemed everyone, but Ryes and Shams were busy watching the Avenger begin her landing. Gracie blushed and nodded her head.

"I didn't think it was possible," she began, still doubting, shock in her dark brown eyes.

"We've had two natural crosses show up in Winterhaven and eleven crosses from the families we retrieved off of Booda," he informed her. "I've made a few adjustments because he's not quite `right' and will need to make a few more as your pregnancy progresses," he warned. She blushed deeply, then smiled shyly.

"Tossin's the father," she admitted. "We started talking and spending a lot of time together, then realized we both felt the same way. I just didn't think something like this could happen."

"Life's always full of surprises," Ryes teased her, smiling as she spoke Dolbith. "I don't think Garth will let you travel with the caravan any further, but we'll wait to see what he and Darman decide."

"If there's madness in Cootain, I don't think he'll let anyone go there," Shams commented. "Let's see where this started and how far its spread."

"That we'll find out for sure," Maren assured them, as Mitt set the shuttle down, light as a feather. "She's one fine pilot," he added, then stepped forward, as soon as the hatch opened and Polas waved to them, grinning happily. Maren laughed in understanding the thrill of a first flight, then headed up as soon as Polas, Mella, and Sadie came down. He needed that shower first, then to talk with Ted, who was back in Winterhaven.

The Defender set down in the village square in the early morning hours, well before dawn, piloted by Shawn Winter, who'd just finished his training. The Avenger flew back near the caravaner's small campsite, but this time Mitt set her down, so she blocked the road which ran into Wicker Village from out of the south, to help prevent anyone from casually entering the village. They posted two of their own guards, to further enforce the quarantine. Garth had two of the villagers guarding the road which ran into the village from out of the north, then two more at the wide path, which was out of the east. They were to let no one in, nor out, until the ban was lifted.

Maren had tables set up with Gracie and Sadie taking names and blood samples from each and every villager, while asking them questions about their health, and taking their temperatures. Sadie practiced her Healing Talent, taking care of minor matters on the spot. Maren showed Ryes what to look for in the samples, then had her helping him screen them, using her Healing, until they both were exhausted, practically falling asleep over them. With the arrival of the second shuttle, there was relief as the medical staff took over, double checking their results and seeing to the rest of the samples, giving them all a break. Anders and Ivan were also here to help screen the villagers. So, Ryes, Gracie, Mitt and Sadie retreated to the shuttle to get some sleep.

Scott, Jon and Cliff were in their element, reveling in the challenge of isolating the vector for this contagion. They found a waterskin Trinkas used on his journey and discovered it was teaming with their newfound foe. Sampling began of all the water supplies in the area to screen for the bacterium, using drones to gather the samples. By dawn, they isolated the people who'd been infected, or exposed. And they declared the stream running through the town a biohazard, with discussions opening with the village elders about correcting the problem, which originated from constant dumping.

Maren, who was finally at the end of his strength, collapsed across his table and was sound asleep before his head touched the wood. Scott smiled as he helped Ivan carry him into the Defender to sleep. Ryes, Mitt, Sadie, Gracie and Shawn were already sound asleep, having helped all night, but Garth, Darman and Sabin had slept while the others worked, so were just awakening and starting the day.

"How's Trinkas?" Sabin asked, as he and Scott emerged from the ship.

"Awake and is doing better. His grandchildren are afraid of him, though, but are being cared for by an aunt of theirs. He's been crying off and on this morning. Even if he knows it was the disease, he still can't forgive himself," Scott told them, a sadness in his eyes. "They're going to have a funeral pyre for the family before dinner tonight and Maren has already cleared the house of all contagion." They paused as Shams stepped up to them looking exhausted. He'd been helping with the villagers to keep them calm and informed.

"Can I sleep in there, too?" he requested, knowing he wasn't entirely welcome with this group.

"Sure, but it looks like all the seats are taken, already. Do you mind sleeping on the floor?" Sabin asked, a smile upon his face.

"As long as it's a place to lie down," he responded, tiredly grinning in relief.

"Help yourself. There're air mattresses you can use to be more comfortable. Scott, could you get him one, please?" he asked. Scott nodded his head, then showed Shams into the shuttle, getting out an air mattress and inflating it for his use.

"I was wondering how a mattress made of air could be used," he commented with a surprised smile, while Justin inflated it.

"They're very useful," he replied, chuckling, "and far better than sleeping on the ground." Shams took it and the offered blanket, then set it down near Ryes' reclined seat, he got as comfortable as he could, as Justin left the ship. Very soon, he was fast asleep.

Ryes woke up, feeling out of place. She reached out for Garth, but found her hand encountered an arm rest. She opened her eyes and saw she was sleeping next to Sadie, in a seat, inside one of their shuttles. Suddenly, she recalled what happened yesterday! She sat up to get her bearings, noting everyone else sleeping in the cabin, including Shams, who was practically right under her chair. She closed her eyes and reached out with Empath, searching for her husband. Once she found Garth, she could relax. She wanted to check on her cubs, so opened her Talent more fully, extending outward toward the Great Gather site.

Tayna turned below her, as her spirit traveled across the continent to reach the place she sought. She found their encampment and the people there just starting the day. She lightly touched Ardis, Saree and Denas, to make sure they were all right and that everything "felt" right with them. Denas noted her immediately.

"Are you all right?" she questioned, closing her eyes, glad to feel Ryes' spirit at least.

"I'm fine. It may take this village some time to get over this, though. When I went to bed this morning, they were still trying to get things sorted out. I shudder to think what we'll find in Cootain from the memories we saw in Trinkas' mind," she told her. "Is everything there truly going well?" she pressed.

"For the most part. Ethan and Rowan were complaining last night about being left behind," she sent, humor in her mental tones. "But we will manage until you get back."

"I wanted to be sure," she returned, amused to think of those two elders wanting to lark about, as if they were still young cubs! "I also need to check in on Sayer, Raby and the horde," she added. "It's too quiet without them here!"

"I can well imagine!" she returned. "Anything you want to pass on to anyone else?"

"Nothing I can't relay by radio," she returned, smiling to herself. "I'd best go check on the cubs." She felt Denas' love and farewell, as she gave her, her own love in return, then reached for Sayer. She felt her surprise and joy at her contact.

"MOM!" she managed to calm down enough to send. "Are you on your way back?" she asked.

"I wish," she sent in return with unexpected longing in her heart. "We still have to check the other villages and farms around here, then see what the situation in Cootain is like. Are you all right? Is Raby all right? How's the horde doing?"

"We're fine. Ardis, Cousin Denas, Aunt Saree and Dodi are all taking care of us. Will you be there a long time?"

"It might be a few days. I miss you and love you. Tell Raby the same. I've got to go for now. I'll check in on you later," she promised.

"I love you and Dad, too," she replied, tears in her eyes. With this, Ryes broke off. She did a quick check on the cubs and Raby, giving each of them the love from her heart, then returned to herself with tears in the corners of her eyes. She sighed as she opened them, wishing she were with the cubs. Then realized she needed to use the facilities; seeing everyone was still soundly asleep. She crept out of her seat, over Shams, then into the bathroom, all without anyone stirring, so glad of her forest-inspired skill.

"Ryes, I need your help to check on the conditions in Cootain and the surrounding countryside," Garth told her as she emerged from the shuttle. She smiled sweetly for him, then gave a nod of her head in agreement.

"And good morning to you, too," she told him, an impish light in her eyes. He chuckled at this as he bent to give her a quick kiss.

"If it weren't so vital," he urged in English. She nodded her head once more, understanding its great importance. He led her over to a shaded table, near the elder's platform.

"She's your great Talent?" one of the elders questioned, as he eyed Ryes' petite form.

"Yes, and my wife," he assured him, smiling with a hint of grit. Ryes took the chair he indicated, looking to these people with some interest. Garth sat down next to her.

"I take it, I'm supposed to check the areas between us and Cootain, on the east coast?" she questioned merrily. These people all looked too solemn for her tastes! Even the medical staff from Winterhaven seemed too quiet, as they looked at her with hope.

"Yes, we need to know what's happening there," Darman urged. "Did you sleep well?" he added, smiling, seeing she looked like she was in a contrary mood today.

"Yes, Grandfather, as well as can be for sleeping in a reclined chair," she teased. "Alright, give me a moment," she stated, turning to meet her husband's eyes. He gave her a nod of his head, so she settled back into her chair, closed her eyes, and relaxed her body as best she could in a hard chair. She extended a hand to either side, in invitation for them to join her on this journey and felt her offer readily taken.

Sabin took up the chore of holding the inner meld, utilizing both their Mind Voice Talents to bring in the elders, who lacked Talent, as well as the humans. Scott fumbled a little with his Mind Voice but lent his to bolster theirs with the meld. Once everyone was settled,

Ryes unlocked her Empath Talent fully, extending herself upwards upon the wings of a hunting bird, flying high over the small mountains to the north of this quiet village. As the bird soared and dipped, she noted small farms below. She let the bird go, to swoop down to check upon the inhabitants. Everyone looked happy, as they were sharing a meal out in a field. She delved deeper, using her Healing sense, seeing nothing extraordinary in their health, other than some old, poorly mended injuries, which Scott noted. She let them go, reaching toward another farm, nearby.

After hopping from one small settlement, to village, to farm, for what seemed an eternity, Ryes finally took in an aerial view of great Cootain, itself. There were ships in the harbor, some carts moving on the cobbled streets, people coming and going, but no strange deeds depicting the madness she and Mitt had seen in Trinkas' memories. She found the inn where he stayed, when awaiting his audience, finding the scars of the burning, and gently touching the minds of those who'd either been witness to the craze, or had been involved in the bizarre behaviors. There was a profound sadness hanging over this town. She reached further, seeking out any Healers, to see if they had truly stopped the contagion.

"Who?" a mind demanded, seeking her out, in turn, sensing her intrusion.

"I am Ryes of House Li," she replied. "We're in Wicker Village, seeking to know of the conditions in Cootain. An elder brought back a terrible madness, which our Healer discovered was a symptom of an infection," she explained, feeling this woman was a Healer, also.

"How can you touch me here in Cootain, if you are in Wicker Village in truth?" she demanded, disbelieving her. Her ire was plain.

"I'm using my Empath and see, I'm in Wicker." Ryes opened her eyes and took in the buildings around them – letting her see where they were and who sat around her, then closed them again; having deliberately kept the shuttle out of her field of view. She felt her shock, but she calmed herself, once more.

"Then you know of the disease? We've barely contained it here and have yet to look to the countryside around us," she admitted. "I am Ketch of House Pippe," she introduced herself, too.

"I've checked some of the farms and smaller settlements between, and I didn't find any signs of either the madness, nor the disease itself," she informed her.

"How would you know it?" she demanded, "This isn't a game!"

"No, it's not a game," Ryes agreed, then opened up her mind to her to show her how she knew the disease, itself, and a brief sketch of her search, as she approached Cootain. "I was only doing a representative sampling, so may have missed some carriers," she admitted.

"You've done well, at any rate. We have a team heading out to Mergas, now. They'll verify your earlier search. Who are you? You have more than one main Talent," she pressed. Ryes smiled to herself at this, knowing better.

"I'm only myself," she dodged. "Did you find out where the contagion originated?" she pressed.

"Yes, from some contaminated fish. Some idiot cleaned them in the main town well, a whole shipload of contaminated fish. We're cleaning everything out, so it'll be usable again soon."

"We've got the source eliminated here in Wicker Village, so will be returning home, soon. Good luck to you, there," she sent.

"Where are you from?" she asked, still disturbed at not knowing this powerful woman.

"Winterhaven," Ryes replied, then shut out her contact. She returned them all to Wicker, briefly viewing it from above, before settling back into herself, once more. She gently released the others; glad it hadn't spread as widely as they feared.

"Lady Ketch is the Healer to the Crowns!" the same elder, who criticized her earlier, informed them after they opened their eyes. Most were still giddy from the journey. Ryes realized she felt winded.

"But it's good news, at least!" Scott declared, as he smiled at Jon. Now he understood what he'd meant, when he tried to explain an earlier journey, he'd taken with Ryes. In all reality, there were no words to adequately explain it! Cliff and Ivan nodded in return, relieved. Jon was still trying to grapple with this newer, amazing experience, himself.

"May I see about breakfast, now?" she asked Garth, stifling a yawn, which snuck out. He chuckled as he gave her a kiss.

"Go right ahead," he encouraged her. "We've still got a few issues to deal with here, then we should be heading back to the gather by this evening."

"That's good news. Sayer's feeling a little anxious," she told him, "And it's too quiet without the horde to look after."

"They'll be all right and you'll see them soon," he assured her, then nodded his head as she stood up. Darman stood as well, following her. When she reached the table set out with breakfast provided by the villagers, she turned to see what he needed.

"What's the problem, Grandfather?" she asked, wondering.

"Don't let Shams get to you. I've tried to convince him that whatever plans he thinks he has for you are wasted energy, but he won't be dissuaded. Garth's being fairly tolerant for now, but I don't know what to do about him, in truth," he admitted, looking down to meet her eyes.

"Don't worry. I've been ignoring him in part, and treating him as if he were a cousin, like Maren, at the most. He'll eventually get the idea. It's not healthy for him to chase me about. He needs a lady of his own to care for, who'll care for him in return," she said. She was getting worried about him, too.

"I know it and pray for it," he replied, smiling as he looked into her eyes. "Ah, if I'd brought him with me to Matlowe, years ago, he would've never left. So, I would think Aletagga has a will in this whole affair, and I only pray for the proper outcome, for Shams' sake."

"I'll add my prayers to yours, and we'll both hope for him," she said. Darman gave her a quick hug and kiss, then returned to the discussion table. They now had a few of the Wicker villagers wanting to come back to the Great Spring Gather with them. They suddenly realized there was more to the world, and they were only harming themselves by staying within the bounds of their own village. He wondered what the elders would think now that Ryes just gave them a quick view of only this small part of Tayna, herself?

Ryes was feeling restless, so after eating breakfast, she went back to the shuttle and got on the computer there to check on her messages and deal with other problems back home. After almost an hour's work, she realized she'd caught up, thanks mostly to Larissa's help. Mitt and Maren were still asleep, so she got out a pistol, checked the charge on her stunner, and found a collection bag. If nothing else, she could always see what new plants were out here to be found. It might please her Aunt Tanns and even tickle Wynne, to get some new specimens. She activated a drone to record things, as they were fond of now doing, when going on an outing.

"Where're you going?" Sabin questioned, as he saw her walking toward the bridge they crossed when coming into the village yesterday.

"Out to see about what's around for Wynne and Aunt Tanns," she replied, "I won't go far."

"You're taking an escort with you," he reminded her, as he met her eyes.

"Look, Maren's still asleep, but I should be relatively safe here in these woods," she assured him, smiling.

"You're still getting an escort," he insisted, not smiling now, so she'd know he was serious. She finally nodded her head.

"I'll go see who's awake, over at Polas' campsite," she replied.

"Alright, but I'll check on you, later," he threatened. She smiled at this, giving him a nod of her head.

"I'm counting on you to do so," she returned. She knew if she didn't take somebody, she'd get yelled at by Garth, later. So, she turned for the bridge, keeping an eye out to the plants around her as she went. When she arrived at the camp, she saw Jake, Shawn and Anders were awake, just finishing their late breakfast.

"So, boss lady, what's the word?" Anders asked, smiling to see it looked like she was set to venture out.

"Cootain's not going to be a problem. The Healers there already have the situation in hand. So, once we get things wrapped up here, we'll all be on our way back, again," she told them, receiving smiles of relief from them, as well as Polas and his wife. Tossin gave her a nod of his head in response.

"What about Gracie?" he asked, looking anxious. Ryes smiled as she looked at him.

"Well, mother and child are doing well, but it'll be up to Garth whether or not she'll be journeying on with you," she told him. Anders looked surprised at this, guessing what she might be implying.

"Can I see her?" he asked, uncomfortable with the acknowledgment of the pregnancy they had only suspected.

"Yes, but she was still asleep when I left. Give her about another hour, or so," she advised. "Right now, I'm going to need an escort, as per Sabin's order."

"I'll accompany you, Ma'am," Jake volunteered. He was serving in Security for now and was being cross trained to help pilot and maintain the remaining shuttles. He stood and put his dirty plate and cup into the wash bin for later.

"I'll take care of it," Didas volunteered. He gave her a nod of his head in thanks, then trotted to the Avenger to get his gear.

"We shouldn't be gone too long, maybe a few hours, or so. By then things should be settled and we can head on back to the gather, and Winterhaven," she told Shawn and the others.

"That's a relief," Polas commented, as Jake reappeared. "See you later and watch out for the forest demon," he warned her. She laughed at this, nodding her head.

"I will," she agreed, then the two of them set out for the nearby woods.

"Where's Ryes?" Shams asked, seeing her gone when he awoke. Maren was just rubbing the sleep out of his eyes as he shook his head.

"She's not one to ever sleep in. I'm sure she's outside, helping out," he told him, heading toward the shuttle's closet-sized bathroom. "Do you know how to use one of these?" he suddenly turned to ask him. Shams nodded his head.

"Sabin showed me how last night," he replied, yawning. He loved the conveniences they lived with every day. Maren nodded his head, then went in, relieved he didn't have to explain it for him.

Shams waited for Maren to finish before using it himself, then went outside as Mitt was waiting to use it next. He didn't see Ryes anywhere in the immediate area and wondered where she'd gotten to? He didn't think she'd go back to that elder's house, after what he saw of the mess inside last night. He spotted his grandfather, so went to ask him.

"So, if we have a standing treaty with Winterhaven, the troops from Cootain will have no legal claim upon Wicker. Are you sure this will work, Darman?" Trinkas questioned, now feeling more himself and needing this work to put off the emptiness he knew lay within his heart. He didn't want to think of his family, right now. He missed his wife, and her wise advice, horribly.

"You tell me another way to get a tax collector to leave you alone? You have no standing treaties with neither Cootain, nor Berrals, to spell out your obligations with them clearly, so why not have one with Winterhaven? They'd have to journey all the way out there to discuss the issue, and the command staff is out at the Great Spring Gather, so they'll have to either go further to talk with them about it, or wait until they return," he replied. "You're sure you didn't sign anything while you were in Cootain?" he pressed.

"No, I didn't even have to give my name to be announced at the lower courts," he told him. "Everyone was acting so strange when I was there." A deep sadness swept across his face as he recalled what he brought back with him, from that mad place.

"It's all right," he replied, placing a hand around his shoulders in comfort. Then Darman turned to his grandson, seeing him standing patiently beside him. "What do you need, Shams?"

"Ryes?" he asked. His eyes took on a look, as if having to bear a great burden, then he nodded his head.

"She had her gather sack and went out to collect some plants. She should be back pretty soon," he informed him, then waved a dismissal as he turned back to take care of Trinkas. Shams then saw a table set out with food, so headed that direction, seeing Mitt, Sadie and Gracie emerging from the Defender, too. They headed toward the table, noting the food. There were devices on the table to keep the cool things cool and warm things warm, and everything was so clean, which delighted and puzzled him at the same time.

"So, where's she gone off to?" Mitt teased, smiling as she grabbed a slice of fresh nut bread, adding honey on top.

"Into the woods to collect some plants," he informed her, as he got a plate and began to pile it with a sampling of the bounty before him.

"That's Ryes," she replied, laughing lightly. She snagged a piece of fruit, putting it into her pocket, then headed over to see how Maren was doing. It looked like he was already Healing the remaining stricken villagers. She bet herself he hadn't even stopped for something to eat, yet.

"Let's go sit down," Sadie suggested, grabbing a mug of honeyed tea. She had her plate already full and realized she was starved. Gracie nodded her agreement, so the three of them went to sit and eat their breakfast, first, not caring it was past noon now.

"What did he mean by that `forest demon' stuff?" Jake questioned, as he saw Ryes was fully absorbed in retrieving every other plant they came across. She looked up to him with a smile, realizing he was still new to Tayna, in many ways.

"I've no idea. It could be some animal, which would normally live in a different region, but might've broken free, and has claimed this area as its range," she replied, wiping her hands off on her jeans as she stood up, smiling. "Tayna was originally a hunting preserve and zoo, so there are quite a few interesting combinations of creatures here. We'll just keep alert to anything out of the ordinary."

"I'm not a woodsman. I wouldn't know anything out of the ordinary, until it came up and bit me," he admitted, uncomfortable with the endless green and brown surrounding them. And she moved with such surety through the woods, that it further set him on edge. Oddly, her drone gave him a little comfort.

"I'm using my Empath Talent to keep a sense of what lies around us. Don't worry, we should have plenty of warning," she assured him, hefting her now-bulging, carry sack. She refused to let him carry anything, for he had his rifle and was along to protect her. She was going to do everything by the book, so to speak.

"As long as you're sure," he replied. She gave him a nod of her head.

"We should be heading back, anyway, sunset's in another hour," Ryes told him. "They'll soon have things wrapped up and ready to return. But I want to do a quick check over in that meadow we passed, earlier." With this, she turned back, heading toward the Avenger, keeping an eye to the plants around her. She had Empath tuned to what lay about them, but unless it felt dangerous, she didn't bother with urging the animals away. There was a "sense" of something in these woods, but she had no idea what it could be. It didn't come close enough for her to get a fix on it and define it to her senses. It was shadowing their trail but keeping a good distance. It was another reason to go out into the meadow. She might be able to draw it out, so she could see it.

They arrived, so she strode quickly across the open area, heading for the middle; the drone flew above her, recording everything. There was a small mound, which might give a good view around them. She noted Jake reveled in the feeling of sunshine upon his face once more, and smiled to herself. She realized she spent too much time indoors lately. Being out at the gather was good for her and all their cubs. They at least got out in the sunshine every day.

"What's the matter?" Jake asked, seeing she stopped in the middle of this grassy area and was intently looking back the way they came. She nodded her head in the direction of the forest and he saw a tall man walking just within the trees. He didn't quite look right to his eyes, though. He appeared shaggy, or dressed in skins, but his walk was somehow bird-like.

"Be very quiet and alert. I've no idea what that is, but it's hunting us. It's cunning and I'm surprised it let us see it. Maybe its eyesight isn't as keen as its sense of smell?" she questioned, in a low voice. Jake slowly brought the rifle off his shoulder, now holding it at the ready. He thumbed off the safety, hoping it would choose to go elsewhere. It stopped and looked toward them, its nose trying to catch their scent.

"What's the plan?" he asked in a low voice, barely above a whisper.

"Stay put, until it makes its move," she responded, in return. It didn't look as if it heard their voices, but she wasn't sure. Suddenly, she felt Mitt above her.

"It's time to leave," she informed her, "Come on and hurry up," she urged, using Mind Voice. Ryes smiled as she looked up, seeing the Avenger overhead. The hatch was open, and Garth was waving to them.

"It's charging!" Jake warned, seeing she was distracted. He fired as it was crossing the meadow, far too quickly for his tastes. It collapsed into the tall grass as she lifted them up into the air, pulling them up to the shuttle and safety. The drone zipped up ahead of her.

"It looks like you got it," she commented, feeling its death. It almost caused her to lose her concentration and drop them back out of the air. She quickly shut down Empath. Garth pulled them both into the ship, then sealed the outer hatch.

"They're in," he told Mitt, over his headset. Ryes' color didn't look good, and he worried that she tried to push things too much for the last two days. "What was that?" he asked, once he got the inner hatch sealed.

"A forest demon. It was hunting us," Jake told him, grabbing onto a strap as the acceleration began. Mitt was a good pilot, but too fond of speed for his tastes.

"It's dead," she added, "and I think I need a nap, now," Ryes admitted, smiling.

"Why didn't you call us if something was stalking you?" he demanded, worried. She smiled up at him, shaking her head.

"If I can't take care of something like that..." she began but decided to drop it for the moment. The look in his eyes wasn't something she felt up to defying right now. She merely lay her cheek against his chest and sighed in surrender, closing her eyes. He was holding onto her tightly. This was enough for her, for the moment.

Cub-nabber

Chapter 27

Ryes returned to the campfire feeling utterly exhausted. Denas stood up to greet her return, a merry smile upon her face as she gave her a welcoming hug. Garth, Sabin, Rowan, and Ethan were trailing her, still arguing over an approach they just thought of, to try to get their point across tomorrow. The political connections and influences among the cities and regions were becoming more obvious as the gather meetings dragged on each day.

"How're the cubs?" Ryes asked her cousin, as Monty appeared from out of his own shelter.

"All asleep and dreaming peacefully," she told her, "How did it go?" Ryes sat down heavily upon one of the chairs, sighing as she reached for some fresh, hot tea.

"I can't believe how stubbornly some men will argue over one tiny, insignificant point, while the larger issues they dismiss with seeming little regard," she told her, a disgusted look upon her face. Denas laughed merrily at hearing this, knowing this was her first introduction to true political compromise.

"I can see why you do not usually go along with the men," she commented. Monty stepped over to them, smiling.

"Hey, I'm a man too," he piped in, teasing.

"But you've got more common sense than most of those elders, chiefs and leaders," Ryes assured him, smiling. "And smell a lot better, too," she added, wrinkling her nose up. "I'm glad we have our showers! I wish they'd spend a little time bathing in the lake, at least." Garth chuckled as he heard her protest.

"Wait another week," he assured her, as he sat down next to her. "At least with you along, there's fewer accusations of lies being made, all around. You'll just outright show them the truth. Your reputation is solid, Sweet One." She grinned in response; glad she was of some service.

"Those Wickers sure have things stirred up, with the threat of Cootain reaching out to claim whatever lands lay near them as their own property and being able to extend their rights to collect taxes from whomever they choose. I thought the elders from Berrals were going to have a fit over it, for sure. After all, Berrals is much closer to Wicker, than Cootain is," Rowan commented, grabbing an empty mug, filling it with some fresh, honeyed tea.

"I hope we're not going to be constantly called out to help drive off Cootain soldiers," Sabin added. "Are you sure we want to sign a treaty with Wicker Village? It's pretty far east."

"Yes. We need them as much as they need us. We must get recognized and established as a repository of information, technology, and resources; to gather the political power we're going to need to help reestablish the Laws across all of Tayna. We want to be the ones everyone turns to, as the center of order upon this world," Garth told him, noting the interest of the others, nearby. Rhodi's eyes were upon him, curiosity in their dark golden depths.

"You don't have too many aspirations, do you?" Ryes teased, smiling. He smiled in return, but she saw the fire which burned beneath.

"All I was looking for was a nice, safe place to call home, originally," Maren commented, noting his determination, too. "Away from my father, of course. Now, I understand what you mean, if we can't make all Tayna safe for everyone, no place on our world will truly be safe."

"That's correct, Maren," Dr. Cruthers replied, smiling as he lit his pipe, making sure the breezes would take the smoke away from the others, first.

"So, when we extend this philosophy out on a cosmic scale, we have a new Alliance, Union, Federation or Confederation, or whatever you choose to call it," Ryes stated, seeing what he meant.

"So that people don't have to live in fear of being indiscriminately bombed out of existence, while still being able to live governed by their own will and able to build, trade, or work as they choose, to their own, their families' and their communities' benefit," Garth replied, nodding his head. "That's what we all gain by an Alliance of Worlds. Peace and the strength to maintain it."

"Carrying forward what Prince Callas and the caravaners started into a governing body," Darman mused, nodding his head. Garth gave him a nod of agreement.

"But we have no standing army to enforce what we dictate to others, like The Laws, to make them behave," Minn countered, sitting down next to his wife.

"No, but we have the advantage of technology upon Tayna for now," Sabin pointed out, smiling. "We'll have our own troops, as well as a real fleet of starships, someday."

"Yes, we will," Ryes assured him in a low voice. He met her eyes, suddenly recalling she'd used her Vision Talent to look ahead. He recalled the brief scene she showed him in the starport, which was supposed to be situated over Tayna, herself.

"Your view of the future, aside," he replied, also in a low cutting voice. Those near them didn't miss their mildly heated exchange, though.

"What? You had a Vision without me?" Maren teased. Ryes shook her head, not wanting to be reminded of that particular evening, all over again.

"I'm going to bed. I'll be working with the other Talents, tomorrow, so you'll have to pick someone else to help. How about Dunn? I bet she'd love the opportunity," she suggested, as she stood up, mug of tea still in hand.

"I'll be in shortly," Garth told her, smiling. "I'll consider her, but do you think she'll be able to handle the stench?" he teased. Rhodi laughed at this, nodding her head.

"It will be good practice for her, in more than one way," she agreed. Ryes nodded her head to this, smiling. Dunn was one who was fond of cleanliness and a dust-free environment!

"Goodnight, everyone," she wished them. She got goodnight wishes in return as she turned for the door to her shelter, glad the day was finally over. Tomorrow would be far more relaxing. She turned on a small light to check on each of the cubs, then saw Shams fast asleep on an extra cot near the cubs. She sighed to herself at this, but realized she was too tired to care. So, she kissed each of the cubs and the girls, then turned for her own bed, extinguishing the light. Garth would be in soon, anyway.

"Our earrings are truly selling well. We might even sell them out in a couple more days!" Katas told Ardis, as she stopped by one of their booths, here in the merchant's area. All together they had six booths selling various wares. At the one selling bows and quivers, they were demonstrating how to operate them. That booth had a tent which hid a force field that prevented stray arrows from killing others at the gather. It'd also served as a safe haven, if needed, for the Winterhavener's protection.

Katas, Raby and Sayer had badgered Glyn into creating quite a few pairs of earrings for them to sell at the gather, but this time he took the time to teach them how to make their own, which pleased the girls to no end. They'd created some new styles. They enlisted Sadie, Wren, and Minya to help quickly heal their customer's piercings, as they were here anyway to man the other booths. Wren and Sadie assured the girls that it was good practice for them, as well.

"So, how would the two of you like to take a break and see a little more of the gather? I hear they have some good singers about to start their acts on the stage, near the food sellers," she invited the girls, as she chuckled at their instant enthusiasm. She would've never thought of doing something like this when she was their age. It amazed her at times to think back on her former Matlowe life and feel blessed for all she had now, and could look forward to in the future.

"I'd love it, Mom! There're some things I was thinking of spending my allowance on, too," Katas replied. Raby happily nodded her head. She had the horde by herself today, since Sayer was practicing with the Talents, and they were getting restless, being enclosed in the caged crawling space Minn constructed for them.

"The horde would love the change of view, too," Raby added. "They've been feeling confined without the trips back and forth to our camp, which Sayer usually does to distract them."

"We'll grab something to snack upon first, then listen to the singers. If they're not any good, we'll head back to do some shopping, before returning to your booth," Ardis told them, smiling. They gave her nods of their heads, as Dodi stepped up to join them.

"May I go with you?" she requested, having overheard her giving them the itinerary. She was bored with having to stick around the Winterhaven areas all the time but did understand why.

"Of course, you may," she assured her, understanding. She was starting to chafe at being escorted everywhere. She turned to Shawn and George, "Will it be a problem, guys?" she questioned, just to be sure.

"Not at all," Shawn assured her. He didn't mind playing escort for the ladies. Wren winked at him, smiling. "You're not coming, my dear?" he questioned.

"I'll be minding the booth for a while yet," she informed him, with a big smile upon her lips. "But we can always take in the gather, just the two of us, later," she suggested.

"That's a promise," he assured her, as they'd just started dating. Monty and Denas walked up to join them, having passed on the practice session today.

"What's up?" Monty asked, wondering.

"There's a good group of singers performing soon, over near the food vendors. Wanna come along?" Ardis invited in return. Denas smiled and nodded her head.

"It sounds wonderful," she replied, as Monty gave her a smile and thumbs up, too.

"Great, let's get the cubs packed up and head on over," Ardis ordered, loving the chance to head this small foray. She managed the housekeeping staff back home, but these were her friends, and this was far more fun than having to work. She found she didn't envy Ryes with all the extra work she had both back home and out here.

"Let's stick to our regular routines for a little while, then I want us to do a short demonstration of each of our Talents for the others. I think we're all growing stronger as we practice, but I want to see what each of you thinks. After all, I'm no judge of my own abilities," Ryes suggested to the group, as they assembled for their practice session. She was a little disappointed that Monty and Denas excused themselves today, wanting to merely relax and enjoy themselves, but she realized it was the reason to come to the gather in the first place. She was just too busy to get the chance, herself. There were times when it didn't pay being the wife of the leader.

"Is this where the practice is?" a man asked, smiling as he approached them. There was a group of twelve men and women with him. The fact that security let them through was interesting.

"Yes. We're holding our regular Talent practice session," she explained, sure they'd merely gotten lost.

"Great! What do you want us to do?" he questioned, smiling in relief. It was the right place, after all.

"This looks like it might get too crowded," Shams commented as he headed another group of Talents from the caravaner's camp. "Why don't we move this over to our campsite? We have a larger central grassy area with plenty of shade," he suggested, smiling to see the shocked expression upon Ryes' face. "The leaders thought all the stronger Talents should practice together at least once, at this gather." Ryes nodded her head, recalling Garth mentioning it to her two days ago. She'd merely forgotten.

"It sounds like an excellent idea," Maren agreed, seeing more people straggling into their campsite. Next Great Gather, they'd have to make sure they had an adequate, central meeting space, so they could accommodate a group this large.

"I'll let Torr know," Ryes added, sighing in surrender as the whole group got to their feet and were soon ready to go. Regular practice suddenly took on the air of an adventure, as there was laughter and delighted smiles all around!

"Torr," Ryes sent, knowing he was head of camp operations today. It was why he wasn't in their session when he'd normally be participating. She felt she had his attention. "We're moving our Talent practice session over to the caravaner's camp. They have more room to accommodate this larger crowd," she explained.

"I noticed how many were coming in for the practice," he replied. She felt his humor in response, his agreement, and acknowledgment.

As a group they headed to Shams' encampment, picking up more strays along the way. He and another person in his group chased off the other people, who were using the area he wanted available for the practice. As they settled into a large circle, Ryes lead them in introductions, as Maren, Rhodi, Raya and Mitt prepared themselves to serve as the ones to form the base and control the inner commune. Finally, all the stragglers appeared and joined in, and all was ready. Ryes sat down and took Mitt's hand, offering her own Talents for Maren, Raya, Rhodi and Mitt to utilize, to get everyone settled quickly.

"We were going to demonstrate each of our Talents for the rest, to gauge how each of us has progressed and grown stronger," Ryes sent out to the group. "But with so many, that could take a very long time. I propose this, why not have those who have some of the older, or more-forgotten Talents demonstrate them first, then we'll go on from there," she suggested. There was a deep feeling of approval from the four holding the matrix of minds together, with most of the rest agreeing.

"We all know the fourteen Talents: Healer, Mind Voice, Visionary, Catalyst, Time Walker, Dreamer, Booster, Manipulator, Empath, Inner Sight, Storm Caller, Water Shaper, Flame Shaper and Earth Shaper. Does anyone here have any of the last four? They are the most ancient and rare," Rhodi sent. She'd found out from Maren that Ryes was in truth a Talent of One plus but had no training. This was a chance for her to see these Talents in use, and get an idea for utilizing her own.

"As you know, Rhodi, I do have Storm Caller, but I do not think the people enjoying this fine gather would appreciate my calling in a storm, of any kind," Ossa returned. There was mirth from the rest in response. Shams wondered about these strange women anew. Who were they? It was an unheard-of Talent!

"How about a little cloud to further shade us?" someone sent out, as things quieted. "I've never seen a Storm Caller work."

"Is it possible to keep it small?" Ryes sent, as there was a general agreement with this idea. Excitement ran through the Talents at the thought of witnessing an ancient Talent brought to life.

"Yes, I can do that. But it has been such a lovely, sunny morning," Ossa replied, then felt Rhodi urge her to open her Talent and demonstrate the fine control she had over the air and clouds. She finally agreed and opened her Talent fully. She'd need it wide open to use it in such a finite manner.

Ryes watched, intently absorbed in this demonstration. As she saw her calling the small wisps of clouds, she opened her eyes to view the sky overhead. The others in the link were amazed, not having this great a control over their own Talents, to be able to operate on both levels at once. As the clouds came into view overhead, there was an inner wash of pride and approval for Ossa. She was taken aback, having never had such adamant support for any use of her Talent in such a long time. She made them form fanciful shapes for a bit to entertain everyone, then let go of the thin clouds, letting them drift as they would.

"You're very good," Ryes told her. "And have every right to be proud of your Talent and accomplishments!"

"Excellent, Ossa," Rhodi added, noting the way Ryes had paid her demonstration strict attention. "Is there anyone else?" she asked.

"I'm a Water Shaper," a woman voiced, "but, not very strong," she added in admission.

"Please show us," Maren urged, smiling to himself. Ryes opened her eyes, once more, spying a tub of wash water nearby.

"Can you do something with that?" she questioned. They felt her hesitant response, then she opened her Talent and reached out to the sitting tub. She was trying to get the water to swirl about, then arch up into the air, but her concentration slipped, and it collapsed back into the tub. Ryes added her own Water Shaper Talent to hers as well as her Booster, which scaled up her power level, privately urging her to try once more. Startled, she went from her thinking herself a failure, to making the attempt again. With the two of them, they managed to get the water to become a tall column, which danced about in a lazy dance, before releasing it to rest in its tub, once more.

"We did it!" she declared, amazed at what the two of them were able to accomplish. "My name's Eyan from Atinas Hold. I hope we'll get another chance to practice together, Ryes."

"I could use the practice," she admitted. "I'm still learning this Talent."

"I didn't know you could shape water," Shams commented. "You have Mind Voice, Empath, Healing, Manipulator, Catalyst and now Water Shaping? You almost have all fourteen!"

"My mother was very Talented," she sent him in response. "I'm merely following in her footsteps. And my father was the Healer and Booster," she added, "Maren's just like him."

"Ah, I forgot to add Booster," he agreed, humor coloring his mental tones.

"Does anyone have Earth Shaper or Fire Shaper?" Mitt sent out, not wanting what else Ryes could do made public. She knew she was a Talent of One plus, outdoing her mother, but didn't want that knowledge let out too casually. Something made the tiny hairs on the back of her neck prickle at the thought. Maren caught it from her, his heart in full agreement. Then they both saw Rhodi was of like in heart. There were some things you didn't let get out without good reason. There were no respondents to Mitt's request.

"How about if you merely take us up on one of your Empath voyages?" Shams pressed, wanting to see more of the world through her senses.

"If you could?" Lissel pressed, "I still need the exposure to what you are doing, to better understand how to extend my own Talent further." There was instant interest from the other Empaths in the link-up.

"Yes! Do it, Mom!" Sayer added, hoping to get her to try.

"Could you, please, little Ryes?" Dastin urged, wanting to see it, too.

"Alright," she gave in, mentally sighing in defeat. She took control of the link, then opened her Empath and Booster Talents fully. Her Booster startled all but a very few, in the link.

Which one... which one? He considered the little ones as they sat on the grass, as a whole group, enjoying the pitiful performance several of the plainsmen and other villagers put on for entertainment. But Murin realized he was here to work, not judge these others. He had a job to do, and it was just waiting for his opportunity and making his best choice.

Two white-haired cubs, both female... White hair was far too rare, and too hard to hide. But the other female had a light-brown colored hair, with reddish highlights in the sunlight. She wasn't exactly as he'd been ordered to find but would do. At least her appearance was far more common and easier to hide in such a large gathering.

"They're enjoying themselves," Squeaker whispered to his employer.

"Not long now," he returned, "be ready for the signal."

"As always," he replied, smiling as he thought of the ease this one looked to be. Both parents were busy with their own concerns and the two main cub-sitters were reduced to one. It was perfect.

"The first two groups were far and away the best," Denas commented with a sigh.

"Well, at least the last one was funny, even if I don't think they meant to be," Ardis returned, smiling. "We're going to have to organize some of our own performances for the next gather. I hear they have an annual competition in the fall. One for the best singers, one for the best play, one for the best performance of a play, and one for the best musicians."

"That's what we can do," George agreed. He was still astounded at the number of the people here in this place. The variety and differences among them made him realize how tiny a world Booda had been. He wished his sister had come out to see the singers, but she was with the Talents doing their practice. She and Nesa took it far too serious for his tastes! "I haven't tried to sing in several months, but if we all tried, I bet we couldn't do any worse than most of those people."

"George, you've got a point. If I could find my old harmonica, I'm sure we could come up with something entertaining!" Shawn replied, smiling as he thought on the idea.

"What's a harmonica?" he returned, curiosity in his eyes. Shawn and Monty laughed at this, understanding the question.

"Hey, hey. Now you're waking up the cubs," Ardis scolded, seeing Adris and Jann starting to fuss at the sound of their voices. She bent down to scoop up her son, as Raby quickly picked up Jann. Denas took over the handle of Raby's stroller, letting her hold the infant, trying to comfort her. Katas was still pushing the one with Dale still sleeping peacefully.

"Sorry, we didn't mean to wake them," Monty apologized, smiling as he met Shawn's eyes. He nodded his head in agreement.

"The question merely took us by surprise. We're going to have to work at culturing our newest immigrants," Shawn replied. "We didn't mean to awaken the little ones. Sorry, Ardis."

"It's all right," she returned, nodding her head to the men in understanding. Suddenly, as they resumed walking toward the market area, a man ran up and shoved Shawn and George forcefully, down into the dirt, practically trampling them both.

"Animals!" he yelled out, then dashed off laughing.

"What was that about?" Dodi questioned, not recognizing any distinguishing features about neither him, nor his dress. She couldn't tell where he'd come from. As they looked in the direction he ran off, another man ran up. He punched Raby with full force in the face, knocking her down upon the ground, then grabbed the now crying Jann as she fell, and ran off in another direction. Monty gave chase, pulling out his stunner as he ran, but lost him in the thick crowd. He couldn't spot him anywhere, nor hear her crying above the din! He quickly returned to the others, seeing Shawn comforting a crying Raby, as the rest looked absolutely furious, being protective of the remaining cubs. Seeing this was serious indeed, he stopped and called up his Mind Voice, knowing there was only one person who could locate Jann now.

Ryes was showing the whole group a view of the stars and planets, briefly touching the deserted colony upon Booda, which delighted Nesa and Abbra. Suddenly, she heard her named called out, in an urgent manner. She was ready to pull them back, anyway,

so did so more quickly than she was usually wont. It was a good
thing Maren, Raya, Rhodi and Mitt still held the group together,
managing to get them more of a sense of themselves, once more.

"Who is it and what do you need?" Ryes questioned, knowing
the others could hear this exchange.

"Jann! Some man punched Raby and stole her! I tried to
chase him down, but with the crowd," Monty sent, feeling responsible
for her loss, and frustrated, as well as angry. He knew he should've
been more alert for something like this to happen! Instant rage ran
its course through her being. Someone dared to steal one of her
cubs? Monty clearly caught the backlash of it and cringed, as Denas
joined her husband in contact with her.

"It's all right, Monty. You did the best you could, under the
circumstances. I'll find her. Get the others back to our camp and sit
tight," Ryes ordered, finally finding some control over her temper.
She'd never meant to hurt Monty!

"It was so unexpected. First one man shoved Shawn and
George to the ground, then as we were puzzling him out, the second
one punched Raby in the face and grabbed Jann. I apologize. I
should have had my Mind Voice up, to be aware in case of danger.
This place only seemed so much safer, than what it used to be, long
ago," Denas admitted, taking part of the blame, herself.

"It's all right. I never would've thought of it happening,
either," Ryes assured her. "Go take care of Raby and the other cubs.
I'll return with Jann, soon." She let go of her and Monty, letting them
take care of what she charged them to do.

"Are you sure you'll be able to find her?" one of the others in
the link questioned.

"I'll find her," Ryes assured him. Then she extended her
Empath, quickly locating her missing daughter. "I'm going to go
confront these two triumphant thieves," she told her friends holding
the matrix together. "But I don't know if I can extend my Talents for
your use, while I'm away from the circle."

"Then it'll be another experiment," Maren told her, "Go!"

With this, Ryes opened her eyes, handed Sayer's hand to
Mitt's, then stood up then carefully stepped over the gap between
them. She left her Talents and contact with the others open, as she
strode through the various encampments, until she arrived at one
which seemed a motley mix of men and women from no particular
place. It seemed out of place in this gathering yet was just the type
of event to attract such rootless others. She walked straight up to the

newest, best-looking tent of the whole group. A large man stood with a naked sword in his hand, blocking her way.

"You're not allowed in here," he ordered waving it threateningly in her face.

"I've come for my daughter," she replied in a voice dripping ice. He made as if to swing at her, but she merely used Manipulator and shoved him. He flew off, out of her immediate sight, smashing into the top of a tall tree, nearby. There was the sound of some scuffling within the tent as a second man appeared in the doorway. She knew he was giving another man the opportunity to escape with her daughter. She merely flung the tent aside, ripping it apart in the process, revealing the two women and two other men who'd been about to sneak out the back slit. Shock was in their eyes as they saw a lone woman standing before them.

"You!" one of the men whispered, his color drained from his face. Ryes extended her Talent, recognizing him from the brief flash Denas gave her, and suspended him in the air. She yanked Jann from the arms of a woman, who screamed out in terror.

"You're stealing my baby!" she called out, fear in her eyes of Ryes, but also in her thoughts, if she didn't play out her role fully. Ryes reached within her mind, revealing to the others what she knew of this whole scheme.

"I'll hold him for you," Mitt volunteered, as she extended herself to utilize her sister-in-law's Talent, so she could concentrate upon other things. A half-dozen men were charging her with their swords and spears. Ryes called up a wall of flying dust, using her Storm Caller Talent, driving them back and away from her. She floated Jann to her arms, her loud cries turning to laughter, as she was back in her mother's arms again.

"If she's yours, then why does my daughter know me?" Ryes returned. She tore off the course wrap they'd put over her clothes, revealing her wearing a tiny T-shirt with the Winterhaven Phoenix stitched upon it, just like the one painted on the front of her own T-shirt. "And funny how she has green eyes like mine and is dressed like me, too." With this she dropped the wrap upon the ground in front of her. "If you ever come near any of my children again, you'll end up like this!" With this, she extended her Fire Shaper Talent, as she'd seen Garth do, and instantly torched the blanket to ashes in seconds. It got a little out of hand, but the spectacular burst and small explosion impressed the remaining onlookers, who now back away and left her alone.

"Let me go! I had nothing to do with it!" the man twisting in the air called out. Ryes smiled, ice in her eyes.

"I know better, and so do the other Talents here at the gather," she told him, then searched his mind, finding the truth about much she would've never believed, if she'd been told. How could people like him, and those who worked for him, be so cold and callous toward all others? It deeply troubled her and in her ice-cold anger, she was sorely tempted to torch him for what he'd done to her and the others. Then an image of Doran's mad face was suddenly in her mind, and she knew she couldn't deal with him as she wanted, because it led to the dark path which that witch had tread. She saw the fear in the eyes of the rest of the witnesses and recalled the Laws set forth. She couldn't murder him in cold blood, no matter that he well deserved it! With this, she walked back to the rest of the circle, taking the lead criminal with her, leaving him to twist and struggle helplessly, as he was suspended in the air.

"Ma'am," Monty said, as he caught up to her and fell in beside her, providing her escort. She glanced over and saw Raby was with him, with deep anger in her eyes. This troubled her, for she would take the pain from her, if she could. She reached over and extended Healing to her, repairing what damage this one carelessly did to her oldest daughter, wishing in her heart that she could heal her inner pain as easily.

"Will Raby be all right?" Dodi questioned, as they arrived back at their own encampment. Torr met them, hearing from the watch that they all looked upset about something.

"What's wrong with Raby and, where is she?" he asked, troubled as he saw they weren't all fine. Dodi quietly sobbed as she wrapped her arms about him, seeking comfort. He held her, genuinely worried now.

"Jann was stolen. Ryes went to get her back, and Raby and Monty went to catch up with her," Denas explained. He noted there were only four cubs in the stroller, after all.

"We'd better secure the camp and make sure all the cubs are accounted for," Ardis suggested. Torr gave her a nod of his head, as he activated his headset, issuing the orders.

"I think we had better make sure everyone is accounted for. Back in the old days, people were nabbed when there were political issues at stake. They were used as leverage to help sway opinions, or votes," Denas explained, as she made sure the rest of the cubs were still all right. They were awake and watching her intently, as if they knew what happened. It unnerved her a little, but then she recalled their mother's strength of Talent. They might be sensitive to her. If so, then it was a good sign that their missing sibling was safe again. She was almost afraid to extend her Mind Voice to see what Ryes had done to the cub-nabber!

"How could anyone do such a thing?" Ardis questioned, shocked at hearing it. "How would anyone ever feel safe in such a world?"

"It used to happen from time-to-time back on Earth, too," Shawn told them, nodding his head to Denas. "There're always ruthless people who'll have their ways, no matter what the cost, in their quest for power, and they usually avoid getting caught, themselves."

"Well, it won't happen again to Winterhaveners," Torr declared, his honey-colored eyes were now the color of steel.

"I pray so," Denas agreed, as she pushed the stroller over to the play enclosure Minn had set up here, for them to use outdoors. Ardis and Dodi joined her, while Katas stood about, just short of tears. It upset Torr to see the fear in her eyes. He wished he could erase it.

"Why are all the children being counted?" Dotti questioned, coming up to the group with Maren's three younger siblings accompanying her. There was a hint of fear in her eyes, as if she suspected the reason.

"Jann was taken," Ardis explained. Dotti stopped in her tracks, her eyes wide as she saw there did, indeed, exist cause. She threw her arms about Rowis, picking her up and holding her tight.

"Is she?" she couldn't even voice the rest of her question.

"Ryes went to go get her. I only feel sorry for the cub-nabber," Denas replied, smiling tightly. She was now checking the young ones, to see if they needed changing.

"Of course, Jann," Dotti breathed, stepping closer. Ardis looked up to her sharply, surprise written in her eyes.

"Why? What do you mean?" she demanded, needing to understand, since it could be important.

"Shyla and Shaysa are too distinctive," she pointed out, "Jann was the only one who looked more normal," she finished. "Unless it was merely something of opportunity."

"At any rate, we'll keep a sharp eye to anyone who comes near our children!" Torr replied. Tars looked up to him, smiling as she nodded her head in agreement.

"I'll help watch my little cousins," she volunteered. Torr chuckled at this, nodding his head.

"And we'll watch out for you too, Sweetling," he assured her, putting an arm around both her and Katas, hoping they could keep them all safe.

The Curse of Murin

Chapter 28

Ryes finally calmed a little, as the others in the link now held this lowly creature's will for her, so she could decide his punishment as she walked back to join them. She had to find something that would prevent him from doing this ever again! Mitt sensed her brother's presence nearby, approaching.

"Stay out of this, Garth!" she sent to both him and Sabin in warning, as they stepped into the ring of bystanders, curiosity upon their faces. Her warning took them aback, for they had no idea what was happening to attract this crowd. Ryes strode back to the circle, to its center as she floated Jann over to Raby's arms, still holding her nabber aloft in the air. "He took Jann intending to sell her to another man, who wanted a child of Talent. It's a good thing Ryes has enough goodness in her heart to not have torched him on the spot."

"Should we see what they intend to do with him?" Sabin questioned aloud. Dyan's eyes were wide with fright, seeing the man twisting in the air, helpless, for no apparent reason. There was a grimness in Rowan and Darman's eyes, as they wondered what Ryes would do with this stranger? They had no idea why she was holding him aloft. And there was no one who could ever stop her, except Garth. He looked curious about things, not ready to interfere.

"What's going on here?" Dyan demanded loudly, seeing everyone around them looking upset over what they were witnessing.

"We'll put our trust in Ryes. She knows the Laws and will abide by them, even if she'd rather not," Garth assured Sabin, Darman, Dyan and the other nearby elders. Ethan stood frozen in place, as he saw what was happening here at the caravaner's main campfire. He had no idea why this man was being held in such a callous manner, but he trusted Ryes, just as Garth did.

Ryes now closed her eyes, trying to think of a way to stop this man's madness - for good. She opened up to the rest of the link, what she'd found in his mind and heart. Maren, Raya, Mitt and Rhodi only knowing it besides her, up until now.

The children he took were merely animals, used to bring him comfort and money, from those for whom they were stolen. There was no mercy, nor compassion in his heart, and he saw no reason for not doing as he pleased, no matter what it did to others, nor what became of the children, themselves. This revelation reviled the rest in the link, as they bent to examine him themselves, to verify what she'd already seen. After several long moments, there was a strong tide of emotion, an urge to end his life and the pain he brought others, once and for all. But Ryes resisted, having finally come up with another idea.

She released her Empath Talent fully, reaching down deep into Tayna's life pulse. She bent her will, becoming one in the harmony of the dance of life of this great world of her birth. In her mind she sought the whereabouts of the children he'd taken, and all else that she could glean of him, and of the families of these lost ones. Immediately, the spirit of Tayna reacted, reaching out to Ryes and the others who sat in their great circle, enveloping them in a welcoming warmth. They were each of part of this world, as she was a part of them, whether, or not, they were originally born here.

But Ryes resisted falling blissfully into this harmony, seeking instead what she needed to know...were any of the cubs he'd taken still alive? If so, where were they? And what of their families? Where were they? Suddenly, she knew more about each and every one of them, than she thought possible. The pain, anguish, and suffering of both the children and their families came blazingly, clearly through. It almost threw her out of contact, but she held on resolutely until she had all the things she'd come to know. She gently released the spirit, feeling the final release from her own anger as she did so. She couldn't murder him, but she wouldn't let him get away without being punished, as he had in the past. He'd escaped prisons before.

"Murin, I've decided your punishment," she announced to both him and the others gathered around them in the link, as she opened her eyes again.

"You can't do anything to me without suffering the consequences, too. Winterhaven will be burned to the ground, and everyone one there will be taken and sold as slaves by my friends, if you try to have me killed!" he declared shouting, so everyone could hear him. He wanted witnesses! Yet, he noted, no one spoke up against her, nor moved to stop her.

"Who said I needed to kill you? That would be too quick and simple an ending," she replied, shouting in kind, she met his eyes directly. He saw coldness in their emerald depths and knew there were far worse things than death, after all. And she was a very strong Talent. Words failed him as he realized he was doomed.

Ryes wanted vengeance, but also wanted the witnesses to know others had been deeply hurt by this man's actions, too. She first reached out to a mother of a cub, who was now living with a wealthy family in Cootain. Her mother was here at this gather and she let her know the fate of her daughter, and who'd done the deed, those who helped him, and why. Then her eyes focused upon Murin, again.

Ryes reached out to his mind, the others in the meld were watching her closely. She gave him what the spirit of Tayna showed her: all the pain, suffering, death, and grief which both the children and their families had suffered through the years. She let him know that Tayna knew what he did, and was ever watchful, even if the spirit let him act by his own will. She saw tears flowing from his eyes, as she let him back down to the ground, outside of their circle. He curled himself up into a ball, as he cried out his heart uncontrollably. The link dissolved as Rhodi, Raya, Mitt and Maren released them, to watch things unfold with their own eyes.

"I still think he deserved to die," Maren commented, under his breath, even if he did understand why Ryes did what she'd done. It was more than his punishment; it was her own sanity at stake in such a deep matter.

"What've you done to him?" Darman questioned Ryes, as he stepped forward. There was anger in his heart, as he confronted her. She looked up at him with a deep pain in her own eyes.

"What I had to do. Do you think Jann's the only cub he's taken through the years? You wouldn't ever believe what he's done to both the cubs and their families, so he can live comfortably for his own, personal gain," she replied, tears glistening in her eyes.

"But what did you do?" Garth questioned, joining them, needing to know.

"Mom gave him all the pain he's done to others back to him, so he can know what they went through," Sayer explained, stepping up next to Ryes, throwing her arm around her in support. "She said she couldn't kill him because she didn't want to end up like some ol' witch named Doran."

"He was going to sell Jann, because she's the daughter of two Talents," Rhodi loudly informed the gathering crowd. Ryes nodded her head at this, still worried for her children. How could such things as holding a child hostage over the outcome of a peace treaty, ever be permitted? She realized she had to tell all of what Rhodi revealed to her, privately, to Garth later.

"So, when will he stop crying?" Dyan demanded.

"When the pain he caused the children and their families has ceased," Shams told him, smiling. "I thought it's a far more fitting punishment, than merely putting him to death would be. The Curse of Murin."

     "WHERE IS MY DAUGHTER?" a woman loudly demanded, as she now stood in the center of the impromptu gathering. Two men and three women were with her, adding their support.

     "She's in Cootain, right now," Ryes explained, stepping forward. "This man took her and sold her to a woman there, who needed an heir for her estate. She was the last of her line and paid him a lot of money for her, because she resembled the last girl cub she lost in some kind of accident. Your cub's not the only one he's taken. There have been too many others."

     "Why's he lying on the ground crying that way?" one of the men with her questioned.

     "He's been given all the pain the cubs and their families suffered, to keep as his own," Shams explained. The smile was gone as he recognized these people. They were regular customers of his and he recalled the story of how her daughter had disappeared a few years ago. Now he knew the truth of the matter, directly from the fiend's mind. "We'll get her back, Andus, I swear," he vowed. She pulled her eyes up, away from this pitiful excuse for a man, meeting his. She saw Shams meant it. She gave him a nod of her head, seeing whatever had happened here, had the elders and the rest of the crowd greatly upset.

     "Show me what you saw," Garth urged his wife in a low voice. She gave him a nod of her head as she closed her eyes to do so. Sayer was already doing the same for Raby because she asked it, too. Darman, Ethan, Rowan and Sabin quickly grabbed onto Ryes, needing to see what she was going to be showing him. After a few minutes, they all opened their eyes, full in the knowledge of what truly happened, and why. Raby was crying as she clutched Jann tightly to her chest, startling the cub into crying with her. Ryes saw she was upset, so stepped over to the girls and wrapped her arms around Sayer, Raby and Jann, giving them all her love and support, from within.

     "It's all right. This one can't hurt any others and we now know of the ones who helped him, and those who do things like him. They'll never catch us off guard, again," she vowed, giving each of the two older girls a kiss on their foreheads. She used Manipulator to gently clear the last of the dry blood from Raby's face. "Let's go back to our camp and put Jann down for her nap."

     "I'll never let it happen again, Mom," Raby stated through her tears. Ryes realized Raby's own inner core of steel had just crystalized and knew she'd come into her own, in due time. She gave her a nod and one more hug. Jann quieted at this, sucking on her fist now as she cuddled against Raby's chest. Raby crooned over her for a moment before passing her over to Ryes. Ryes smiled and took her little one back, so relieved they were both fine, once more.

"I'll join you, soon," Garth told her, having come over to check on the girls, himself. It was a scary situation for an adult, he could only hope that Raby wasn't traumatized by the whole thing. He gave each of the girls a kiss, then another one for his wife, and let them go, knowing they were all exhausted. They then turned for their own camp, ready to go. Maren, Mitt, Monty and Shams followed in their wake. Rhodi and the rest of the Winterhaven Talents stepped over to him.

"She showed everyone that even if she does have the greater power, she has a heart and the wisdom to not abuse others cruelly, even if she could do so very easily," she told him in a clear voice. Sabin and the elders heard her, too. "What she has done is the best justice which could be administered, under the circumstances." No one noted Squeaker moving off, headed for his own camp, and the news he now bore.

"I understand, now," he assured her. "I need to borrow Dunn and Raya for a while. We want to make sure all the elders fully understand what this man did, and how he viewed his victims and their families." He got nods of assent from the two women. The rest of the Talents turned as a group, heading back for the Winterhaven campsite. Then, the caravaner, plainsmen, village and mountaineer Talents followed them, still feeling the need to stay together.

"If in no other way, at least all our Talents are united in mind and heart now," Darman observed, commenting to Ethan and Rowan. Sabin turned and nodded his head to this.

"Why not? There're no barriers within, when you're in commune," he stated, a hint of a smile upon his lips. Raya and Dunn were grinning, too. They knew and agreed with him, fully.

"Let's gather the rest of the elders and relay the story of this man's trade," Garth suggested, wanting this duty discharged. Ryes had given them a brief sketch of what Rhodi revealed of the practices of old… that children were taken as hostages to add leverage to any bargains made. It deeply disturbed him, and he, and the rest of his own team had to come up with a way to not only dissuade this type of behavior but stop it before it ever began. "And we'll need to get a party of armed men to remove what's left of that camp of thieves." Darman nodded, a fell look in his eyes. He knew their faces now!

"Do we just leave him this way?" Dyan asked, uncomfortable with seeing his pain and crying.

"Yes. As long as his victims suffer, so shall he," Sabin said, then glanced up to see the woman, who'd charged into the middle of the camp, turn to follow their Talents back to their own camp. He wondered if another trip back east was going to be shortly in the works?

The shuttle hovered in the air, in the dark of the night, after bright Shaysa had set, leaving only orange Menna in her last quarter and small Porr in his half-moon phase. It was unlikely anyone would note its presence here over one of the larger estates on the outskirts of great Cootain. A hatch opened as a young child ran out into the well-kept garden, in the back of the estate. She looked upwards, curiosity in her bright eyes. Suddenly, she began to float up into the air, being pulled up to the strangely shaped "ship" above her. She giggled merrily and spread out her arms, as if they were wings, pretending to fly by her own will. She dropped her doll, accidently, but instead of it falling to the ground far below, it remained aloft with her, floating upon the breezes. She reached the odd ship far too soon, to her mind.

"Aron!" Andus cried, once Ryes had sealed both hatches and given Sabin the go ahead to return to the gather. The child in her arms looked at her mother with curiosity in her eyes.

"First, Maren, could you please check her life pulse, to make sure I'm correct," Ryes said, noting Sabin didn't use Mitt's high-powered ascents. Maren was ready, knowing she'd want to be sure.

"I'd know my own daughter," Andus stated, almost insulted by such an idea. It was Aron! Tears were starting to come forth, frustrating her further. Still, these people had helped her find her, when she thought of her as dead, all these long years!

"A child will always know her mother, but I need to be absolutely sure. A few moments won't truly matter," she gently scolded in response. Andus finally relaxed and nodded her head. Maren offered her his hand, so she gave him a smile as she placed one of hers in his. Then he took one of the child's hands. She smiled with dimples in her cheeks as she allowed it. He closed his eyes, opening his Talent, fully. After a few minutes, he opened them again, smiling as he gave Ryes a nod of his head.

"This is Andus' daughter," he assured them all. "I also took the liberty of clearing your system of a budding infection, too," he told the western villager. Andus smiled, nodding her head.

"My thanks to you, Healer," she replied, then took the young girl from Ryes' arms, her eyes tearing once more. Maren gestured Ryes to sit in the seat next his own, feeling the family needed some time alone, now. Reluctantly, Ryes sat down.

"Why are you crying?" the young girl questioned, feeling this woman was familiar, even if she couldn't remember her.

"Because I finally have you back, my dear little Aron," she told her, as she sat in the offered chair. "I've missed you so much and prayed you were still alive. I'm your real mother."

"But, Aunt Ahnn said you died a long time ago," she replied.

"She lied to you. I've been looking for you all this time. A mean man stole you from me," she explained. "He sold you to this Aunt Ahnn. Now you can come home, where you belong."

"Aunt Ahnn would never lie to me! She loves me," she denied, tears starting to run down her own cheeks. Andus wrapped her arms around her and hugged her to her, until Aron struggled to sit back up. Ryes stood back up, unsure if she should help, or not.

"Let me show you what truly happened," Shams offered, seeing the child's distress. She twisted to look at him, across the small aisle.

"You're a Talent, too?" she questioned, tears still in her eyes as she sniffed. He smiled for her, nodding his head.

"Yes, I am. Let me show you the truth, so you will know it," he enticed. She finally smiled a little, nodding her head in agreement. Ryes sat down again but was still unsure.

"He does already know both her mother and family," Maren sent to Ryes as their arms touched, having called up his Talent, so he could consciously tap hers to do so. She smiled at him, nodding her head to this.

"I just worry about how much truth a seven-year-old can stand," she sent in return, sighing aloud. "But you're right. I'll trust Shams to know some of how to handle this one."

"What is it with him?" he suddenly questioned, knowing his constant presence sometimes upset her, and he knew his interest in Ryes didn't make Garth very happy, either. Still Garth hung back, leaving it in Ryes' hands.

"I don't think he even knows," she replied. "I only hope he finds his own lady. After all, I'm already taken and have no intention of ever leaving Garth, true-mate vows aside." She turned to meet his eyes. "Have I ever thanked you for making that motley bunch go out hunting with me that day? Garth told me you were the one who insisted on it and wouldn't let the idea go. You badgered them into asking for my help." There was humor in Maren's thoughts as he recalled that day, too well, even now.

"No, but I'll accept it," he returned merrily, "but if I hadn't, I would've never found my Dotti."

"I still believe it was all fated and shame on Sabin for not seeing it all ahead of time," she teased in response.

"I'll tell him you said that. He has been keeping his Visions too close to his heart, lately. I don't think he tells anyone anything, except Garth. What was that one you two were arguing about? You still haven't shown me," he pressed.

"Garth sided with Sabin and ordered me not to show it to anyone else, so I can't," she admitted sadly. "If it's truly as they think, that it'll never be, then how can my showing it to you, or Mitt, change that? I still think what I saw will be the truth and they're afraid that I'm right. How can it hurt to show you?"

"I've no Idea," he admitted, sighing as he saw the little girl suddenly clinging to her mother, crying. Shams must've released the deep memories she held of her mother, her nabbing, and the truth of the people she lived with. He wondered how long it'd take for her to heal deep inside, in her heart?

"It shouldn't take too long. I took care to be gentle and made sure to link in Andus' mind, spirit and heart, so she'd know her mother still cared about her deeply," Shams informed them in sending, having to resist eavesdropping in on their mentally-projected conversation, while he was helping Aron through this ordeal. Ryes blushed as she nodded her head. She kept forgetting he had Mind Voice and no sense of when he shouldn't listen in, or not. She wondered about the way he'd been brought up with his Talent? He was at least two years older than herself, as was Garth, yet the differences were like night and day.

"That's a relief," Maren projected, knowing he'd hear him clearly.

"Who cares what Garth thinks of this Vision you forced? If you want to show it to Maren, or Mitt, you should be able to show them," Shams scolded Ryes, having overheard that part, at least.
"He usually has his reasons, and until he's made it clear to me, either way, I'll honor his wishes in this, whether or not he's my

husband," she replied. She suddenly dropped the link and shut him out of her mind. She didn't want him snooping into her thoughts, uninvited. Maren was shocked at her action, even if he could understand why she did it. He was only concerned that she shut him out, too. As if Shams could get to her, through him... He wondered if he could?

"So, as it stands now, we have about half of what we were hoping to push through, with most of the larger issues settled, and those who were left in that thieves' camp have been punished by a council of elders," Garth informed the Winterhaveners, as they grouped near the central fire to hear him on the last night of their presence at the Gather.

"How about the Laws?" Torr questioned. There were nods and murmurs of agreement to this one by most of those gathered.

"They're now officially reestablished with the Caravaners, most of the Mountain tribes and several of the western and northern regional villages and shires. The plains tribes were no surprise, as they still practice many things the rest of us find primitive. It's felt they'll come around in time, with most of the younger men understanding the importance of establishing these laws all across Tayna," he admitted. "Only time will tell. They have a copy of them, at least, but refuse to allow us to plant a pillar next to the Elder's Gathering hut here, to display them for all to see. Of course, that's not going to stop us from having one within our own campsite." This was met with laughter and shouts of agreement.

"Can most of their tribesmen even read?" a voice questioned, out of the back. There was a smattering of laughter at this, causing Garth to smile in return.

"Only those of linage can, as far as I've determined," he responded. "But there're always exceptions, such as our Raya," he pointed out, as she blushed a dark gold.

"Dyan's my uncle," she informed him, grinning merrily. "I fought to learn and had my way before. But, yes, you speak the truth."

"And we have to thank our elders for buying up almost every man, woman and child put up for auction by the plainsmen and others," Kovin called out, teasing them. Ethan, Rowan, Darman, and Metta laughed as they stood and took bows for the deed.

"Yes," Garth agreed, chuckling as he smiled merrily. "We have more new citizens for Winterhaven, thanks to our elders. It's a creative solution, at least for now. We'll have to house them in shelters, as our Boodans. If nothing else, we can enlist some of them to help build their own, new homes," he said. There was laughter and agreement from the crowd.

"We've got to expand our vision, far more quickly than we ever imagined last winter. We've got to start thinking on a global scale, so Winterhaven will be going through some dramatic changes, far sooner than we originally wanted. I'll be asking more out of each and every one of you as we reach outwards, to strive to bring this world together as one. I know we can do it. We have the fire of Tayna's awakening to kindle and only those of the Phoenix, the fiery bird of rebirth, can do it!" Garth assured them, with pride in his voice.

There were cheers and shouts of support from most, as others were quiet and thoughtful of what he finally, publicly admitted. There was more at stake here than just their own comfort and lives. The small group of Boodans were wondering what they'd committed themselves to, in settling in with these people. They weren't worried about the next crop's harvest, nor how good the hunts were going, nor how fat their birds were in their cages, they meant to conquer this whole world and unite all the peoples.

"He has ambitions," Shams commented in a low voice to Lissel, as he sat between her and Maren. She gave him a sidewise glance as she smiled.

"Yes, but they are noble ones," she replied, in a low voice. He chuckled as he nodded his head in agreement.

"We're being pulled into a new world and are having to scramble to catch up, already," Maren said, in a low voice. Ethan was now addressing the crowd.

"Did the humans start all this?" Shams questioned, wondering about it. Maren chuckled, trying to keep it low, seeing Dotti's interest, as she sat at his other side.

"No. Ryes began it all, literally. She dragged us off to Hailys with her, then brought down the human starship from out of the sky. Things have kind of progressed on their own, and Garth's merely helping to move along what she started," he assured him, seeing the Sleepers were all paying heed to him.

"Did Korman finally drive her to leave Matlowe, in the first place?" Shams asked. Maren's eyes were suddenly shadowed, as the smile melted from his face.

"Yes. My father wouldn't leave Ryes alone. She didn't want Garth hurt, so decided to leave. We went with her, and in the end found Winterhaven. That's why all challenges are banned in Winterhaven, because of the way my father held Matlowe in his claws, for so many years," he explained. Shams nodded his head, understanding it all much better.

"I'd heard the stories through the years, of what Korman did to Ryes' mother and father. I think it was why I wasn't in a pressing hurry to journey there, myself. My grandfather wanted me to come meet her, but I didn't want to have to face off someone like he's reputed to be."

"Maren, how can you be so kind and gentle with such a father?" Lissel asked, amazed to hear what she thought she was hearing from these two men. She'd heard Rowan relate the story but had forgotten that these events were still very fresh. Nesa leaned forward, wanting to hear more, too.

"I saw what he did to others. People feared him, which made Korman happy, and decided I wasn't ever going to be that way," he replied, smiling once more. "Garth, Torr and Sabin helped me let go of my anger when I was younger, and to turn my mind to other things which were far more important. Ryes helped me through what he's done in the last year. And my dear Dotti made me realize that I have much to live for and look forward to," he admitted, noting the intense interest around them. "We'll all be back home, soon. So, if anyone wants to hear the full tale, we'll have to arrange a storytelling day and have everyone relate what events have shaped their lives, to each other," he suggested, giving Nesa a wink. She looked surprised, then smiled as she laughed lightly.

"Yes, we wouldn't want to upset the elders by not paying them attention, right now," she replied, keeping her voice low. There were a few chuckles of agreement from the others, as they turned back to hear the rest of the speeches. She realized she felt at home, now. She was included and a part of things.

"I'll go check to see if it's already outside, Mom," Sayer told Ryes, as she was searching for the horde's groundcover sheet. They were trying to get everything packed, with the things they used most often, packed separately. As she ran out of the shelter, she almost ran into a tall man. She stopped short, looking up in surprise, but her apologies died upon her lips, as her eyes widened in shock, recognizing him instantly.

"I came to see how you fare, Sayer," Shins said, surprised to find his little sister practically running into him. He hoped to see her before they left.

"I'm fine," she told him, curtly. "I have a new family and am going to school, and I have lots of new friends."

"But I worry that you have so much to do with caring for their cubs," he replied, his brow furrowed with concern. She did look healthier and was wearing new clothes, but he wanted to be sure in his heart. He was surprised to hear that she now held Talent! Their grandfather, Dyan, wanted more news about this, after hearing what the other plains Talents had related a few days ago.

"They're now my little brothers and sisters, and I spend most of the day in school, learning how to read, write, our history and to cipher," she retorted, growing angry now. "What would you really care? You sold me!" she shouted. He sighed, noting Ryes standing in the shadow of the door to her shelter, watching them quietly.

"I thought they were men of good heart, or I would've never sold you to them," he returned, meeting her eyes. "I only want you happy."

"Do you really?" she demanded, frowning, "or are you just looking for a reason to take me back, so you can use my Talent, and breed me to whomever you want, later?" She'd caught a little of this from his surface thoughts and it made her blood run cold. She couldn't believe it of her own older brother! Ryes stepped forward, having seen and heard enough.

"Are you all right, Sayer?" she asked in a low voice. She turned, saw her, then ran to her, throwing her arms about her as tears came to her eyes. Ryes had her arms instantly around her, murmuring her reassurances in a quiet voice, as she held her tightly.

"I came to see if she was truly happy," Shins told Ryes. "I didn't mean to upset her so much."

"Yes! I'm happy! Now go away!" Sayer turned and shouted at him, now knowing better. She held onto Ryes tightly, determined to face him down, knowing she had Ryes' full support.

"She's always been given the choice to return to the Moondance Tribe if she wanted to, but she's been happy with us. I've adopted her formally into my family and she's my daughter now. She has a house name and is now Sayer Mada of House Li," Ryes replied, a little more civilized than her daughter. Sayer had directly let her see what she'd seen in Shins' mind, but it wasn't as unexpected for her, as it'd been for her daughter. "And I don't allow any of my children to be poorly used."

"Then I'll go," Shins responded, blushing as he realized why Sayer might be so deeply upset, now. He wondered if she could read minds? "May I come see her, when I can, in Winterhaven? I'd like to see how she's living," he requested.

"Yes, that should be all right," Ryes agreed, smiling as she saw Garth approaching them. Shins gave her a nod of his head, then almost bumped into Garth, as he turned to leave.

"Shins! Glad to see you're well," he told him, chuckling as he saw the plainsman almost stumble in surprise.

"I feel the same, Garth. I'd better leave. I've upset Sayer, when I hadn't meant to," he explained, doing a shallow bow as he spoke. He quickly left, hearing Garth's low chuckle as he did so.

"What was that all about?" he asked his wife and daughter.

"He was looking for reasons, or a way, to take Sayer back. She has value now that her Talent's awakened," Ryes informed him in English. The smile melted from his lips as he gave her a nod at this.

"Let's get you ladies and the horde aboard the shuttle. You're getting the quick trip home, after all," he decided. Sayer let Ryes go to throw her arms about Garth, sighing in happiness.

"Thanks, Dad!" she told him, smiling through her tears. He chuckled merrily at this, as Ryes gave him a smile and nod of her head. She felt better about this arrangement, too.

"So, do I get my next piloting lesson today?" she teased. He looked surprised for a moment, then threw back his head and laughed heartily.

"Not yet," he told her with a big grin lighting up his eyes. "We want to get home in one piece and not terrify everyone else onboard." She blushed and playfully swatted at him, then turned back to her packing with a laugh.

"You!" he heard from within their shelter. Sayer laughed with him.

Revelation

Chapter 29

"So, what do you say?" Riss questioned Sayer, as they were walking out of the classroom and back into the bright afternoon sunshine.

"Nah. I promised Mom I'd go riding with her after class. Do you want to go riding?" she asked in return as they stopped to chat. He wrinkled up his nose at this, shaking his head no.

"The windracers still scare me," he admitted, shuffling one of his feet. "How about the day after tomorrow? It'll be our weekend."

"I'll see what my parents have scheduled," she hedged, "after that last gather, I have to clear almost everything now," she admitted, unhappy with being so leashed.

"What's it like to ride a windracer?" Casta asked, after he trotted to catch up to the pair. Sayer turned and flashed him a smile, having noted his interest in her the last few days. He was one of the crosses from Booda and his appearance intrigued her. Would her tiny cousin, whom Dotti was still carrying, look something like him when she's born, she wondered? He had a face which looked more human than her own. He had practically no body hair, and his ears were shaped like, and as large as hers, but were hairless. At least his upper lip had a split, so she imagined kissing him might feel normal.

"Like riding the wind," she described, smiling. "You can come with us, too," she invited. Riss looked unhappy with this invitation.

"I'd like that. You're sure your mother won't mind?" he asked, a little nervous as he recalled who her parents were.

"She won't," she assured him, laughing. "Just go on and dump off your books and meet us over at the corral."

"Alright," he hedged, smiling nervously, then gave her a nod and turned for his home. He hoped he could sneak out, before his father found some chores for him to do.

"I heard there was a fishing trip planned for this weekend," Riss commented, as she turned back to meet his eyes. She looked surprised but gave him a nod. "I'll see you later," he promised with a nod, then turned for home.

Riss' mother should be back from work by now. Missa had come with them from this last gather, but he was now spending time during the day in Matlowe Village several days a week, running a small shop, selling some of the things they sold at the gather in their booths, for Sabin. He still wasn't sure what he thought of him, but knew his mother enjoyed his company a lot. And with a new sister on the way... There were so many changes still ahead! Missa treated him very well and was teaching him caravaner skills in trading and evaluating. It was curiously interesting most times.

"Casta, this is my mother, Ryes," Sayer introduced them, as Ryes smiled, giving him a nod of her head. He bowed to her, not knowing if he had the courage to speak in her presence.

"It's all right. I don't bite," she gently teased, chuckling to see him so nervous. "Let's pick our mounts," she suggested, turning to see Honey trotting up to her at the gate. She sighed, knowing she couldn't ride her now. She was pregnant, reportedly by Pacer, and she should've known that she was finally reaching the age where it'd happen. She reached out a hand to gently scratch her dear friend.

"Mom, you're not riding her," Sayer scolded, frowning with concern. Ryes laughed lightly at this, shaking her head no.

"She's going to be upset with me, but you're right, I can't. I'll ride Pacer, since Katas will be riding Spur," she told her, seeing Katas and Raby coming to join them.

"You like Spur that much? But Pacer's Dad's windracer," she replied, amazed at her stated choice.

"Spur's faster than Pacer, but since both your father and Sabin neglect the poor things, it's up to us to let them know they're still loved."

"Blaze!" Sayer called out, seeing her own mare nearby. She was glad, because then she wouldn't have to ask her mother to call her in, using Empath Talent. The windracer picked up her ears and trotted for the gate. Spur, Pacer and three of the others joined her. Ryes turned to see Casta utterly entranced by the animals, as they nosed their way closer, so each could get their share of scratching and treats.

"Casta, this one's Honey. She's mine but is pregnant so I can't ride her for a while. That's Pacer, Spur, Blaze, Sweet Girl, Brownie, and Prince. You're welcome to ride either Sweet Girl or

Prince. Brownie's Raby's mount," she told him. He met her eyes amazed and afraid. "Here, offer your hand to them this way," she invited, showing him how. He did and Prince stepped over to nuzzle his hand, looking for a treat.

"Now give him a scratch behind his ears and along his jaw," Sayer encouraged, laughing merrily as Blaze nudged her, impatient to be off. "I'll go get our gear," she added, stepping away from the railing.

"I'll help," Katas offered, as she and Raby arrived. The two girls left for the shed.

"Where're we going today, Mom?" Raby questioned, noting Casta's rapt attention to Prince, and the windracer's enjoyment of the attention.

"Out to our fishing spot. I thought it'd make a nice, comfortable ride that's not too far away," she replied, seeing Shams and Jim approaching. "And I'm sure our escort would appreciate the slower pace." Raby turned and saw who was heading their direction, then grinned as she nodded her agreement to her mother's comment.

"You'll never escape them, now," she told her in a low voice. Casta saw the two men approaching, wondering if he was in trouble for being out here with the women. Ryes put a comforting hand atop his shoulder to stay his flight. He still had much to learn, now that he was away from Booda!

"It's all right. I always have to have an escort whenever I'm outside of Winterhaven, proper," she informed him, in a low voice. He turned as saw her smile, then relaxed a little. The girls returned with saddles, headstalls, reins, and blankets. They managed to find the men two suitable mounts. Ryes got them organized, then saddled up. She wasn't going to risk Jim, Casta, Katas nor Raby, by making them only ride with a blanket beneath them. She, Sayer, and Shams were already experienced riders. They mounted up and headed out, leaving a disappointed Honey behind. With the windracers, they were able to take a more direct route, than the one the vehicles used, and quickly arrived at the fishing cove.

"This is my favorite place around here," Jim commented, sighing as they dismounted. The fresh cool air revived his senses. Ryes chuckled, nodding her head in agreement.

"It's the perfect weather for swimming, too," she replied, teasing him. He chuckled, nodding his head.

"If I'd known, I would've brought my fishing rod," he told her, then tied up his mount with theirs, near some fresh, green grasses and started a quick survey of the surrounding area; his drones flying above and ahead of him.

"It's a beautiful spot," Shams agreed, staying near the women, doing his duty as their protector, too.

"Just stay away from that area," she warned both him and Casta, indicating where the group usually set their chairs when they came here to spend a day fishing. "They've now lost almost a half dozen hooks and I don't want anyone finding them the hard way." The girls were already stripping down to their swimsuits, heading for the inviting water.

"If I'd known, I would've brought something suitable to wear," Shams protested. Ryes laughed merrily at that, nodding her head in agreement.

"You can always strip down to your undergarment. It's what we do, when we forget," she informed him, seeing Sayer already telling Casta to do just that. She turned and threw her blouse across Pacer's blanket, having already taken it off him. She was wearing her swimsuit beneath her clothes, too. She kicked off her boots, and unbuttoned and unzipped her jeans, throwing them into a small pile, atop the blanket. She took off her socks, and turned to see Shams stripping down, too.

"Come on, Mom! The water's perfect!" Sayer called out to her, as the others were already in the water. Jim joined them again, nodding his head to her.

"Looks good, but you're the expert on that, after all," he reminded her. She smiled as she extended her Empath, double checking him. After a few moments, she gave him a nod of her head, focusing in on his face, once more; having kept her eyes open while she did her check.

"All clear," she agreed, smiling. "We're only going to be here about an hour and a half, today. So, you two can decide who's going to be first in the water, or what," she told the men. There was mischief in her eyes as she turned and ran for the cool water of the Yuri.

"Since you're already ready, you get the first forty-five minutes and I'll take the last forty-five," Jim told Shams, grinning. "She's a handful to keep an eye on, no matter how it seems otherwise," he warned. Shams nodded his head to this, still grinning.

"I'll keep my eyes open," he assured him. Jim pointed out to the river, past him. He turned to see Ryes swimming out to a rock formation in the middle of the river. She was almost to it, already!

"You'd better hurry," he returned, chuckling. Shams began to run for the water's edge, wondering at how fast Ryes was in the water. Nothing seemed to slow her down!

"Well, I found out Casta has Talent," Ryes told Garth, as they sat at dinner later. "I'm going to have to start testing all our Boodans, to see who has Talent and who doesn't." He grinned at this, nodding his head in agreement.

"I would've thought you'd already done so," he teased in response. "You should take care of it soon," he advised.

"I will," she returned, smiling. "How about tomorrow, after that storytelling circle Maren and Nesa organized? We're supposed to have everyone there to hear, or tell, their tales."

"What're you planning on doing after the storytelling?" Maren questioned, joining them with his siblings in tow, at the table.

"Checking all our new people for Talent. Earlier today, I discovered Casta has Talent and am reminded I'm not fulfilling my duties as a Catalyst. I haven't checked our the Boodans, the new humans, nor the people we purchased at the gather."

"Oh, that's a good idea. What Talent does Casta have?" he questioned, as he was getting everyone organized. It seemed a good day to keep Karis and Rowis away from each other, so he sat them one to each side of him. They were mad at each other for some small reason they'd probably forgotten already. Still, they were trying to hit each other this evening – every chance they got. It was frustrating when they acted this way, he realized he hadn't been any better when he was little, remembering some of the things he and Tennan did, too.

"He has Empath, but it's pretty weak. He never even suspected he had Talent, but I felt it as we were taking a quick Empath journey, checking out the animals around us," she explained as Raby, Sayer and Katas appeared out of the kitchen, giggling among themselves about something. She turned to deal with the horde, still getting them fed.

"How do you feel about a trip to Hailys in a few days?" Garth asked, baiting his wife before he lost his resolve.

"Oh yeah, we do have that tree harvesting scheduled," she replied, glancing back to see something more in his eyes. "What?" she added, puzzled.

"You wanted to make an attempt to rescue your great aunt," he began, not even wanting to encourage this, but wanting it either accomplished quickly, or put off for a few years. He could guess where her heart lay in this matter. Her eyes held shock as she turned to face him fully, her disbelief plain as she fully realized what he'd said.

"Why now?" she sharply questioned, frowning, still not quite sure she heard him correctly. She noted Maren was barely breathing as he looked to him, too. So, she must've heard it right! She set down the spoon she was using to fill the cubs' bowls; having given them each their own spoons this evening and bowls that fastened to their highchair trays. She found her mind had gone numb.

"Actually, I'm basing this on that Vision you two shared," he informed them. "If you're both all right to face off whatever attacks you in that Vision, then it means that either you'll find a way to save your great aunt without having to bring her forward into our time, or that if you must bring her into our time, you'll both make it through the experience - sane and whole," he explained, proud of his reasoning. Questions danced in Ryes' eyes.

"Find another way, without having to bring her forward?" Maren questioned, thinking as he settled back in his chair. "Like help her tunnel her way up to the surface?"

"That's an option, provided there isn't a firestorm to kill them as they reach it," Garth agreed. "We have several factors on our side to take into account. We have the circle of Talents to draw upon, to help control things. We have you, Saree and Ryes as Boosters, and Rhin to help provide focus, then we have the Windrose Stone to give everyone added power. Phil has the Stone's cradle ready for it, but I thought we should make our attempt before it's raised aloft, under its small dome, over the Phoenix fountain. I don't think we should move it around too much. There's a danger that it'll fracture, or crack, if we accidently mishandle it."

"So, while the crew's out to harvest the wood we need for our new buildings and furnishings, we'll be out making our one attempt to save my Aunt Adina," Ryes said, her eyes held her doubts and fears. His eyes held hers for several long moments, then she finally sighed and relaxed, again.

"You can do it," he encouraged her, smiling his confidence.

"I believe I can," she finally returned, smiling for him, but still not quite feeling the courage within, yet. She hoped they could pull it off, in spite of the risk such a venture like this carried. She wasn't sure if she was ready, but fully trusted his reasoning. She turned back to her fussing cubs.

"Yes! We CAN do it!" Maren agreed, encouraging her. He saw his cousin still had doubts in her eyes. "We can't leave them like that," he reminded her, as Dotti joined them, a puzzled look in her eyes. "I'll tell everyone about what you saw the last two times you went time walking in Hailys, tomorrow," he warned, grinning. She turned to him, shaking her head.

"You're mean," she protested, then her eyes took on a pensive look. "Perhaps not. It might still be too much for our Lady Sleepers," she hinted. Saree looked over to her, puzzled.

"What do you mean?" she questioned, frowning delicately.

"I've no idea if anyone else had family here upon Tayna, who might've died during the Hailys attack. It wouldn't be right to remind them of all they've lost, again. Denas truly had a hard time coping with it, when she finally saw the truth," she explained.

"I see," she replied, thinking about it, now. "I know Lissel, Minya and Denas had family here, but I am unsure of anyone else," she added.

"I'll ask Poli and Rhodi. I wouldn't want anyone included in our circle, if it'll only hurt them to experience what happened then."

"That's a good idea," Garth agreed, wiping at Shyla's chin as she dribbled out some of her food, playfully, as he'd taken over the cubs now. She grinned up at him and screeched happily as her tiny fist pounded her tray. He had to smile in return. She was always such a happy baby! "So, what're you planning with this storytelling of yours?" he asked Maren, as Ryes decided to start in on her dinner, while she had the chance.

"You'll see," he teased, smiling as Dotti sat down next to Rowis. She returned his smile, nodding her head. They didn't need to know everything.

"This world's so vast, with so many things to learn. I don't truly know where to begin," Nesa told the assembly, feeling nervous to have to stand at the microphone, up on the small platform they raised for this gathering. But this get-together had been partly her own idea! There was laughter and shouts of approval from the others, most understanding her far too well. Even the Matlowe Villagers were just realizing how much of Tayna they were still discovering. It made her feel much better, as she found the challenge of the changes were exciting her, and she was finding out new things about herself and what she could do now!

"How about right here? Let the world come to you!" Ardis shouted out in suggestion. There was scattered laughter at this, as many realized she might be right.

"There's that," she replied, having heard her clearly. "Is there anyone else who wishes to share his, or her, tale?" She knew Maren had a few things to relate, but he said he wanted to wait until everyone was more relaxed.

"There are a few things I could tell of the world, as it was before," Denas said, standing up. Doubt played in Monty's eyes, but he smiled his encouragement and gave her a nod of his head when she glanced back to him.

"Let me say it, instead. I am now the last of the true Foresters," Lissel spoke up, also getting to her feet.

"How about the both of you tell us what you know of Tayna," Nesa suggested, smiling. There was still a lot about these women which she didn't understand at all. Who were they, truly?

"That's an idea," Ryes agreed, smiling as she waved both women to take the platform. Denas smiled and gave her a small bow, as Lissel laughed lightly, quickly moving to comply. Nesa stepped down, surrendering the mic gratefully. Denas trailed her, waiting her turn.

"My name's Lissel and I am the daughter of Lissa and Nees. My parents were Foresters and worked to conserve the animals and their habitats, while enforcing the Law upon Tayna. We lived in a small village named Ronam, on the Southern Continent of Singas. There were two large reception centers near there for newly arrived animals from off-world, and for those who were either being relocated, or were sick and needed treatment. I loved the forest and the quiet and would've been very happy spending the rest of my life there, except one day my Empath Talent awoke. I was sent away to a special school, to be trained in how to use my Talent," she explained. She saw the surprise and the intent curiosity in Ryes' eyes. Her grandfather had mentioned before that she loved the woods and spent most of her days there, until she left Matlowe for good. She wondered about it, now.

"So, how did you end up in Doran's Valley?" Raya questioned, intrigued with her tale. They protected and managed the animals? Why? Lissel smiled at this, nodding her head.

"While in school, I was courted by a man who was of a House. I wasn't, as my mother surrendered her House to become a Forester. I didn't want his attention because I wanted to return and help my parents with their work. But this young man had a strong, opinionated father, who decided if I was the one his son wanted, I had no choice. He was a man of power and bought favors wherever he needed them. My parents were far away and had no money, nor power to stop him, so I ran away. I ran back home, of course. I hid out in small villages, once I managed to get back to Tayna, keeping on the move as he had hired trackers to search for me. Finally, realizing there was no other way, I journeyed to the Valley of the Sleeping Goddess. It was a cursed place, but I had run out of friends and family to hide out among, and I didn't want anyone else hurt. I went before the High Priestess, who took pity upon my case, and they encased me to sleep with the Goddess and her Chosen Ones, since my mother was originally of a noble House, and I carried her Talent."

"How did you escape?" Traci Kruggins, one of the new human women from the past, questioned, intrigued with her tale. Abbra wanted to ask the same thing, giving a nod of agreement. Lissel laughed, as did the other Sleepers. Ryes, and those who'd been a part of the party to take the Windrose Stone, were laughing with them, knowing the answer too well.

"I actually went from bad to worse. I was in a frozen sleep for several hundred years, while Doran sank deeper into madness, constantly trying to make the rest of us as miserable as she, or worse. I never actually escaped on my own. Maren and Ryes offered a chance of freedom to myself and the others who were imprisoned with me, and I took it. I hoped the world was at least no worse than they showed me and have been delightfully surprised to find they were wrong. It's been far better than I could've ever hoped." There was laughter at this and shouts of agreement from the gathering.

"I promised to make a return trip to the Valley to free the rest of the Lady Sleepers," Maren stated, standing up to address the ladies, who already lived among them. "And if any of you wish to go with me to convince them that life out in the sunlight is far better, then you're free to do so."

"Yes, I'd love to go with you, Maren," Lissel replied, smiling. "I only hope we can convince the others that this is far better than sleeping away eternity in the cold and darkness. Such an existence is pointless," she added. Denas stepped closer to the mic. Lissel surrendered it, smiling as she gave her a nod of her head.

"I agree. I will come, too," Denas stated. Maren bowed to them, then the other Sleepers, as each of them spoke up with their statements of support and concurrence.

"Only if you feel you're ready to face the Temple, once again. I wouldn't want this trip to burden your hearts, anymore," he stressed, hoping the ones who would accompany him won't be reminded of their endless years of torture.

"I will be fine. I have my little one, yet to be born, to remind me of how much promise life still holds for me," Denas told him, smiling merrily as she placed a hand to her stomach. "Like Lissel, I was on the run from a man," she added, launching into her tale. Maren gave her a nod of his head as he sat back down, grinning. "Only my mother and grandmother were living in Hailys, the city of my birth. I fled to Tayna from the Academy, where I was training to be a communications technician. He turned up, after several months of my thinking I was safe. Hailys was a great city with an endless restlessness, which I thought would continue on into eternity," she said, her eyes misting as she recalled the busy, protected, underground shops and homes. "I always felt safe and alive in our great, underground city. At any time of the day, or night, there were a hundred things to do, or places to go... I never thought he would ever find me!"

"Since I had left the Academy without proper notice, I could not go before the authorities to have my pursuer restrained. So, my grandmother bid me to seek out the Sleeping Goddess; that she would protect me from him. I found her handmaidens in a small temple, in a bad part of the city. They immediately transported me out to the Valley of Doran. They encased me in a suspension chamber before I even knew what was happening. But I was not like the others. I was only seeking shelter for a short time, not for hundreds of years. I wanted more of the world, not less. I finally withdrew from their games and gossip, practically curling up within my own soul. First Ryes' call, then later Maren's, drew me out. I realized there was a way out and took it immediately. And even if the city I knew no longer exists, and my family is now long gone, I bless the people here for granting me my freedom. And I bless my dear husband for being so sweet and loving," she finished, smiling through her tears. There was clapping and cheers as Minya stood up, approaching her friends on the platform. Denas smiled as she surrendered the mic to her, as she joined them.

"I have a confession to make and an apology to extend," she told Denas and the others, keeping her eyes to her friends, next to her, so she could keep her courage to speak. She saw she had her attention. "I rushed your season forward, as I was deeply afraid we were going to lose you, after you saw what our old home had become. I knew you wanted cubs of your own, but never thought you would choose Monty to father them," she teased, smiling through her own tears. "I know it was wrong, but thought it was what you needed most."

"It was what was already in my heart. You did not do anything wrong in this," Denas assured her with a huge smile, still crying as she put a hand to her stomach. "And I have come to know that Monty was the best choice of a husband, I could ever make!" There was clapping as people were shouting for him to stand and take a bow. He did, his face a beet-red, as Denas stepped down, heading straight for him. The other two stepped down, too. Knowing there were others who wanted to speak.

"The mystery's solved," Ryes commented to Maren.

"But it was against the Laws," Garth said, also keeping his voice low.

"Denas just admitted it was something she wanted, after all. How could it ever be judged against Minya?" Maren questioned, a frown alighting his brow.

"I'll issue an official opinion, letting everyone know that to willfully abuse others with a Talent won't be tolerated and that it will be prosecuted," he replied, a set look to his eyes.

"As long as this once you let it go," Ryes ordered him. He met her eyes, then saw it was pointless to go against her on this issue. He sighed, then gave her a nod of his head.

"This once is it," he agreed. She smiled, granting him a nod of her head, too.

"Ryes! Tell everyone about the events which lead up to our finding Winterhaven," Maren loudly urged as a diversion, smiling. No one else was inclined to take the mic immediately after the women had their say. She smiled at him, shaking her head, but was suddenly thrown over Garth's shoulder, as he physically took her up to the platform amid the cheers and shouts of laughter.

"Ryes has a short tale to tell," he said into the mic, then set her on her feet. She was laughing merrily as her bright eyes met his.

"Since I was so cordially asked to step up here, I believe I'll tell everyone about our journey from Matlowe Village to this place we now call Winterhaven," she said, grinning to see the interest in both the Sleepers and the Boodans. Even Shams looked sharply interested. She took in a deep breath and began her tale.

Plans

Chapter 30

"And don't forget we do have the Field Ball Match to play against the Matlowe Villagers tomorrow afternoon. The game should start about two o'clock," Maren reminded everyone, before stepping off the platform. "The Firebirds will win!" A loud cheer went up as the eight players and their four backup team members stood up and took a bow. Leon was their coach and he stood and signaled the players over to him.

"And as a final request, Ryes and Denas need to see our latest newcomers; the Boodans, the new people from the Star Quest, and the people who returned with us from the Great Spring Gather." He noted some puzzled looks, but everyone else took this request in stride, so it was accepted by the people called. They knew by now that the Winterhaveners had their ways of doing things, and it was simplest to follow directions, especially with Ryes being mentioned specifically. Maren turned off the mic and stepped off the platform to join them, too. The gathering started to break up, as a good number of people started to gather around Ryes and her cousin.

"Why would you need to see us?" Abbra asked, puzzled.

"We need to double check everyone for Talent," Ryes explained, smiling as she noted almost everyone had gathered near them, as requested.

"But you already know I have a Talent," she protested, frowning at a wasteful check for something already known.

"Ah, but you may have more than one," Denas told her. "We need to be sure, my dear." Ryes was getting everyone calmed down, so Denas sat down, gesturing Abbra to join her. She did and waited while she called up her Catalyst Talent. Denas took her hand as she opened her senses to her. After a few moments, she lightly touched her tiny daughter, in her arms. "You are correct. You only have Mind Voice, but your daughter carries Talent, also. We will not know what it is until she is old enough for it to manifest, but it seems very strong to my senses," she informed her, smiling as she saw the shock in Abbra's eyes.

"You can tell if a child carries Talent?" she pressed, thinking this was unheard of before. Denas gave her a nod of her head.

"Yes, Ryes showed me how to look without disturbing a sleeping Talent. If it were to awaken before she is ready, it could cause her to sink into madness, so we are very careful to only note whether or not it exists," she explained, smiling her assurance. Abbra gave her a nod of her head, clearly recalling that mad night when her own Talent awakened within her. It was a struggle, but she finally realized she had to control her Talent, herself. She recalled Crazy Benas, who was a mad, old starwoman, who had to be constantly cared for until she died last year. Had she been that way because she'd lost a battle with her Talent? With the large group here, she knew her own child would never have to face it all alone. Not in Winterhaven where there were many strong Talents available to help.

"Thank you," she replied. "We'll see what Misti's Talent will be when she's older. And I have a different question," she hesitantly began. When she got a curious nod from Denas, she paused. Took in a breath, then asked, "the fresh clothes and undergarments... we can use a new set each day?" She got a warm smile from Denas which lit up her rich honey-colored eyes.

"Yes, and please make sure to cycle your used clothes in the laundry chute. They will be returned to you later in the same day all fresh for your next use," she advised, understanding. Abbra gave her a relieved nod in return and smiled as she stood up.

"Thank you, Lady Denas," she said, then turned around.   She saw her brother ready to take her place. He had a big grin upon his face, as he gave her a wink, then sat down. Denas laughed lightly as she closed her eyes and took his extended hand.

Abbra worried about him since he and Nesa had taken to free mating the last few days. Previously, she knew Nesa had free mated to one of her hunters, Hogan, but she rebuffed his attempts to re-establish their relationship. That she turned to George, and he was quite willing was the surprise. She wasn't sure to be happy for them, or not, but at least there were several mixed couples here in Winterhaven, so their being together was widely accepted by others.

"Misti has a Talent," she whispered to Nesa, then gave her a kiss on the cheek and smile, as she was standing behind George, ready to be next. Her eyes grew wide in wonder.

"She's a miracle," she replied, giving the infant a kiss, then kissed her back, too. Her happiness shone in her eyes, so Abbra let her worries go, as she stepped back to wait for them both.

"Do I have to do this?" Shams questioned Ryes, smiling with a mischievous light in his eyes as they both sat in chairs now. "We both know I have a Talent."

"Yes, you do. I want to be sure Mind Voice is your only Talent," she returned, then closed her eyes and put a hand to his chest as she called up her Catalyst Talent. After a very few seconds, she realized he had a second Talent.

"Ha! I'm right," she sent to him. "Be ready," she added, in caution. She released it, allowing it to fill his being. Shams struggled for a few moments, in utter shock that he did, indeed, have a second Talent. He quickly conquered it, joyous over this unexpected discovery.

"I'm a Dreamer?" he sent her in question, unsure if he was getting this right.

"Yes, you are and if you need help understand your new Talent more, please ask any of our Lady Sleepers for advice," she returned, happiness coloring her mental tones. "Now, I must see to the rest," she urged, letting go of their inner commune. She opened her eyes to see the joy in his own. He suddenly threw his arms about her and soundly kissed her, startling her. Maren laughed at his display, shaking his head.

"Okay, break it up," he said. "Guess you must have more than one Talent?" he asked. Ryes' eyes met his, grateful for his presence, as Shams released her.

"Yes! I never knew," he admitted, laughing happily. He bowed to them both, then stood and left, with his heart still singing.

"Any more gratitude like that and I'm going to need an armed escort," Ryes commented to Maren, noting the interest in the faces of the others around them. He chuckled as he nodded his head.

"That's why I'm here - to protect you," he assured her. She shook her head at this but gave him a bright smile. Then she turned to deal with the next person in line, glad he was beside her after all.

The two teams came into the now spacious dining hall to celebrate after their game. Minn had headed up the crew that enlarged the room to accommodate the now-larger population in Winterhaven, using several blocks of unused bunk rooms, as the facility had originally been designed to house several thousand researchers. They also used the empty rooms to create the larger fitness facility and pool. The team expanded the kitchen to Chuck and Raya's specifications. Even if they were going to be pouring the foundation for the new Community Hall soon, they knew they needed this now.

The Hunters, Matlowe's team, were still singing and laughing about their victory, as they ate a special dinner prepared for them by Chuck and Raya. At least the Healers made sure none of the players suffered any aftereffects from their sport. And the rest of the Matlowe villagers, who'd come with the team to cheer on their victory, were amazed with Winterhaven. Most fully enjoyed the comforts offered and being able to visit with friends and family. Metta was in his element, playing guide and host.

"I still can't believe we lost! Twenty-three to twenty-one! So close!" Mitt groaned out, sitting down with her tray. Garth chuckled, nodding his head.

"I'm glad I was too busy to get put on the team. Next game will be different," he promised.

"Leon did pretty well, considering the amount of time we had to prepare, and the other things happening around here," Ryes said. "The Firebirds will be better prepared for the next game."

"So, when should we schedule it?" Ted questioned, as he paused by their table, overhearing what they were saying.

"Let's give them a month. Maybe we should have more than one team? So, there's more of a mix of games. Do you think the Boodans would want to form their own team? They're getting stronger and looked like they wanted to play today, too," Sabin asked, looking up to meet Ted's eyes. He gave him a nod of his head in response. The excitement of the game still had them all charged.

"They might be ready. We'll see. And a month sounds good," he agreed, then went on to his own table, thinking on the idea of more teams to add to their new league.

"We could challenge Wicker Village or see if the Moondance tribe would be interested in playing," Mitt suggested, smiling as she thought on the idea of more teams. She'd played her best but knew she could still do better. Still, she and Axel were truly busy now and didn't know if she'd get the time.

"Or how about a team made up of caravaners?" Shams returned, getting into the spirit of the idea. "Why don't we start some informal games between established teams at the gathers?"

"It'd be a safer way to compete for villages in dispute," Ryes agreed, as Maren shook his head no. And Sonta, who had stepped over to talk with the group had heard the exchange, shook his head no, also.

"It'd be best to leave politics out of it. Keep it just for the love of the game," Sonta denied her. She laughed as she nodded her head in agreement. "It was a lot of fun to watch, and I know the players enjoyed themselves. So, adding in more teams to play against would provide more of a challenge for all of them." Sabin nodded his agreement.

"Hello Elder Sonta! We'll see what we can stir up," Sabin assured them all, meeting Garth's eyes, briefly. He saw the smile upon his lips and knew the idea held promise. They'd get the chance to talk about it later. Sonta sat down next to Rowan and Ethan.

"Do you think you're ready for Hailys tomorrow?" Garth prompted the rest of group, amused as he saw the surprise register in their eyes. Sonta's held curiosity.

"It's a good thing field ball doesn't require Talent," Mitt commented, smiling. "I'll be ready, but it sure sets back some maintenance I planned for tomorrow."

"I already had you cleared with Axel," Garth assured her.

"I'm as ready as I'll ever be," Ryes told him, meeting his eyes. Sayer and Raby were feeding the horde tonight, taking turns with them, as Sayer looked up, puzzled.

"You're taking Rhin with you, but why not me, Mom?" she questioned, hurt at being left out of the operation.

"I'd never risk Rhin, if I didn't have to," she replied, meeting her eyes as she did so, "and I won't risk you, either. Since Rhin's along to help with focus and control, I have to bring him, but since you're still building your Talent and aren't up to your full potential, I'm having you stay here. Someone needs to look after things at home, after all."

"But, Mom," she protested, then noted the look in Garth's eyes. There was pain, but he wasn't going to let her go against them in this decision. She nodded her head in surrender, turning back to the cubs quickly, to hide the tears which were starting up in the corners of her eyes.

"What's happening in Hailys?" Sonta asked, wondering as he was trying to puzzle out their conversation.

"We're going to try to rescue my Great Aunt Adina from out of the past, using my Time Walking Talent. We've actually pulled people out of the past before, having rescued seven humans off the Star Quest right before she took off. This one is harder since it's at least going back three hundred years," Ryes explained to him, feeling she could trust him.

"And Rhin is?" he pressed, glad to get some answers that sounded true to his ears, and wanting to know more about it, now. She blushed and nodded.

"He's our younger son. He's a Booster and we think has some other Talent leaking through that seems to help provide focus for using other Talents. Once he's grown, and his Talents come out, he'll learn to use them himself and I think will be amazing," Garth explained, pointing out his son to him. Sonta's eyes were filled with wonder.

"And my father knows?" he asked, surprised, then Metta put a hand upon his shoulder, startling him. He chuckled merrily.

"For some time now, son," he told him directly. "We don't normally talk about such things too freely – even here. The unique Talents here are very precious," he added. "I don't need to tell you that this is all in confidence, do I?" he asked, knowing he'd understand.

"That's the truth," he agreed with a nod. Metta sat down next to him, and they began to talk in low voices.

"This is the one and only chance I'm granting you to do this," Garth warned his wife, unnecessarily. "If we fail, we fail."

"I thought Sabin had a Vision," she returned, smiling.

"I only saw a part of the operation," Sabin admitted with a sigh as he looked from Ardis to Ryes. "Not the conclusion."

"I could try to see," she started, but saw the instant ice in his eyes and merely gave him a smile and nod of her head. "Or not..." she added, surrendering.

"Oh yeah," Mitt spoke up, looking to her brother. "If what Ryes saw before in her driven Vision won't come true, why can't she show it to Maren, or me?" she pressed, needing to understand. It was always better in front of plenty of witnesses.

"We don't want to accidently direct our actions to make it come into being, possibly deviating from our correct course of actions, otherwise," Garth told her. "It's better if only Sabin, myself and Ryes have seen, what she thought she saw."

"Then, what about the one where she, Dotti and Maren might get hurt? You've doubled her escort now, each time she leaves Winterhaven," she added. "Isn't that deviating from your normal course, too? What good is a Vision if you can't heed its warning and prepare?"

"I didn't know I was going to be injured, too," Dotti said, speaking up, now understanding why Maren and Ryes both refused to show her what they saw. It also explained why they rarely went out together anymore.

"But everything will be fine. I had one, which I didn't drive, nor expected yesterday, where I saw Maren delivering your daughter," Ryes assured her, smiling. Maren looked surprised at this, wondering now about the truth of Visions.

"Still, for now, Ryes isn't allowed to show you what she saw involving our great-great granddaughter," Garth ordered.

"Ah, so you at least admit she will exist," Ryes teased, smiling merrily. He chuckled at this, nodding his head.

"She was here. I saw her with my own eyes and heard what she told you. So, there'll be Time Walkers in the family. I shouldn't be surprised, after all I've been through with you," he admitted. She laughed at this, blushing. Ryes turned her eyes back to her cubs, trying to figure out whom Gram most resembled.

"Please share this Vison you and Maren had with me?" Dotti requested, as Ryes turned back to eat. She met her eyes and saw her pain and understood it so very clearly. Maren shook his head, not wanting her to see it.

"No," he asserted as gently and firmly as he could.

"Why not?" Ethan asked, curious. "It might help her to prepare for the event, if she can," he asserted. He saw the agony in Maren's eyes and knew he didn't ever want her hurt.

"Dotti does have the right," Ryes told Maren, knowing his heart in this matter. "I'll show you, if you truly want to view it," she offered, coming from her heart. Maren was shaking his head no, and now Dotti appeared to be considering it.

"I know you both have to be prepared for tomorrow, so after your great aunt is rescued, perhaps I'll be ready to see it, too," she replied, feeling it'd give her time to really know her own heart. If she's hurt, did she really want to know it? How do you prepare for something like that?

"I'll be ready, whenever you are," she promised, smiling for her. Maren appeared relieved and gave her a nod in understanding.

"So early tomorrow morning we'll have the rovers start out and the one large chopper will fly out shortly thereafter to meet them and set up where they'll be harvesting the trees and whatever fruits and nuts are ripe in the area we designated," Sabin stated, getting nods from the rest, who didn't see anything wrong with this plan.

"And then, shortly thereafter we'll fly out in the remaining large choppers to where we'll try to make a rescue of Ryes' aunt," Garth added, giving Sabin a nod. "We've already made sure everyone's ready?"

"We will be ready," Denas agreed, while Saree gave him a nod. Monty gave him a nod, too.

"What can I do to help?" Metta asked, knowing he should have a role in these operations, too.

"It depends upon where you'd like to be. I could use someone to supervise the gathering and harvesting operations, or to take care of anything that happens here in Winterhaven. I haven't heard from any of the three of you about what you each prefer," Garth responded, addressing the elders. Ethan smiled as both Rowan and Metta each gave him a nod.

"We were discussing it earlier," he admitted, "but weren't entirely sure what you needed for our part in these events. We decided that Rowan would go with the harvesters, since he's more familiar with a forest setting." Garth nodded, seeing their clear logic in this choice.

"And?" he encouraged, smiling.

"I'll remain here to keep operations running smoothly, while Metta will be going to assist Dotti with recording the rescue event and offering any direction, or assistance, which might be needed," he finished. Garth appeared surprised, but thought for a few moments, then gave them another nod, smiling again.

"All good, solid decisions," he replied, seeing their reasoning, once again, and feeling they were gently teaching him how to be a better leader, too. "And I agree it's a fair division of your talents." He'd come to realize for some time now, Metta had become an active part of Winterhaven as if he were in truth one of their elders. They each gave him a nod of agreement, smiling as they turned back to each other, since the final decision was made. Sonta appeared surprised, but upon looking at his father, he realized he appeared far younger and more fit and energetic than he was, himself, now.

Rescue

Chapter 31

Three large choppers sat down upon the grassland, near the edge of the crater, which was originally Tayna's starport. One smaller chopper sat down in front of them. Security teams swept out immediately thereafter, checking the area for any real dangers. After a long wait, the all clear was given and the crews of all four aircraft emerged into the bright, morning sunlight. Part of the security group scrambled to set up an area near the crater for the participants to use. They spread out groundcovers, then large foam-filled mats, for them to sit upon. A field medical treatment facility was set up near the groundcovers, under a protective canopy by other assistants. Finally, the Talents were allowed to approach the site.

"This looks promising! It's such a beautiful morning," Ryes commented, grinning up at her husband. He was still not amused and had been grumpy all morning long, even if this trip had been his own idea. She sighed, feeling burdened, but stooped down and plucked up a pink flower which she put into her hair, above one of her braids. This got a chuckle out of Maren as he recognized her reasons. There was a warm breeze blowing, which brought smells of different flowers to them, and Ryes realized this was where she wanted to explore next for some plant gathering. Garth passed Rhin to her for a few moments, having taken him from her when exiting the chopper, and strode purposely toward the mats.

"Be careful with that," Phil directed the team carrying the Windrose Stone, which was set in a heavy-duty sling, over to the cradle they made for it to occupy. It was bright to look upon, even with the sunlight shining around them. The men carrying its sling were wearing goggles that totally covered their eyes, as was Phil. The cradle had been made partly of the metal of the door from Matlowe. Phil had tapped Ryes and her Talents to shape it, so it would protect the stone, yet deny scanners' ability to analyzing it, and being Ryes, she made it so it would appear artfully crafted, too. They would do the final install into its rightful place in the plaza soon. Until then, he didn't think it was wise for the Stone to travel in it. He wanted to add in some more protective padding first.

Minya strode past them, heading toward the lip of the crater. She was determined to see it with her own eyes! She'd been frustrated in the chopper, being purposefully sat so she couldn't see out the windows before now. She was born and grew up in Hailys, as

Denas, and still couldn't conceive of it being totally wiped from existence. It was too great a city! She stopped at the edge as she realized she was seeing bright metal beams sticking up through the soil and profuse plant life. She recognized it all, even if it was well gone to ruin and covered with a thick blanket of green plants. There were vague memories of what the city had been like before, then the shadow dreams given to her by her Dreamer Talent, while she'd been encased and a prisoner of Doran. She had denied the shadows of Hailys' destruction for too many years! Her heart twisted within her breast, and she was panting for several long moments as she came to grips with this deep loss of all she held so dear. She hung her head as she calmed down, with acceptance and vengeance now waring within.

"Are you all right?" Poli questioned, having trailed Minya. She was concerned how she would take the demise of this city. Even after showing them all photos on a computer screen, being here made it more personal. Ryes hung back, letting her handle it, knowing they were closer friends, then continued to their set-up area. Other Sleepers stepped up behind the two by the crater's lip. Minya's hands were balled into fists, and it appeared she was practically shaking, but after several long moments, Minya turned back to face them all. Her eyes were filled with tears, but there was a steely look in them, as her determination came to the fore, which Poli had never seen before in her mild-mannered friend.

"I will be fine, but those Snagospin will pay for what they have done to Hailys," she snarled out, as she swiped at her eyes. Poli gave her a nod of her head in understanding. Minya realized for the first time in her life she was truly free and had access to almost limitless power in Ryes. She would make them regret this conquest!

"Let us see if we can save a few souls today, at least," Poli urged, as she resisted peeking into her mind. Minya gave her a nod, then walked back to the large, open-ended circle, which was now being formed on the mats. The rest followed in her wake.

"Everyone get settled, and as comfortable as possible," Ryes urged, glad to see Minya's determination. She was afraid she would've gone the way Denas had, after her discovery of the ruins of Hailys and what it meant to her. Now, Ryes stayed out of the joining of hands of the open-ended circle, remaining in the middle, next to the Windrose Stone. Denas sat next to Monty, holding his hand, and looked to have taken spirit from Minya's pay-back attitude. A new unwavering set came to her eyes, too. Ryes gave her a nod in understanding. For the two of them, this war with the Snagospin was personal!

Dotti had the recording drones up and set to best advantage, so there'd be a record of this historic day. She even had Ryes wearing a remote recording device, so she could really see what the past was like, if not during the operation, it would be recorded for later viewing. She appeared as ready as she could be, with Metta standing at her side and his intent interest in everything happening. It wasn't often he got to participate in such an event. Phil was on her other side, as they were all out of the way, but ready in case of need, as well as their assist team. The medical team had their area set up and ready to help, too.

Garth now held Rhin in his arms, trying to get him to snuggle down upon his lap. He kicked his feet, smiling up at his father, which finally broke Garth's unusually gloomy mood, as he smiled back at him. It was a good thing Rhin was getting used to being a part of their practice sessions. The cub settled quickly, as it was almost his nap time anyway. Maren, Raya, Sabin, Mitt and Rhodi began to form up the inner linkage, as Ryes stay on her feet near the Stone, trying her best to relax, as it felt like a bunch of flutter-wings were loose in her stomach. She'd done everything she could to help ensure the success of this attempt. Now all she could do was pray, thinking Aletagga would be amused with her daring, at least.

"We're ready," she "heard" Raya tell her. She closed her eyes and extended herself into the link; Raya catching her in quickly with love and humor in her heart. The others welcomed her warmly, excitement now running through the commune. She opened her Pool of Power for the others to freely tap, as well as all her Talents, holding nothing back from her team. There was surprise from some as they realized her full range of available Talents. This prompted the rest to now open their own Talents to add in for others to use, too.

"First off, we've never practiced with the Windrose Stone during one of our regular sessions, so only those who've used it before are allowed to call its energy to themselves," she cautioned. "If you find you've accidently done it, remember to let the energy flow through you, uninterrupted, then see if you can release it back to its natural flow. If you try to resist it, you'll be seriously hurt, and I've been told it can burn out your Talent. If everyone's ready, we'll begin," she stated, getting nods from the others around her as they closed their eyes. She felt amusement ripple through from within, and smiled to herself, her tension evaporating. She felt Garth's warmth, at last. She had to leave her eyes open for this venture.

She reached out and called some of the Stone's energy to herself. Three beams instantly obeyed her will. It seared as she let it flow through her being, noting their Sleepers, as well as Raya, Mitt, Garth, Sabin, and Maren were calling individual beams, too. Monty did it, too, and using the examples around him, letting the energy sear through, holding on through the pain, which finally lessened and found he was more powerful than he could ever dream. The alarm at this unanticipated action of his using a beam from Denas and Ryes, soon lessened as everyone saw he was managing it. They left him alone.

Ryes waited for them all to calm down and stabilize before she began. She focused upon her Talents with Rhin's help, then unleashed Time Walking fully, concentrating on how she last saw her Aunt. The wrenching sensation wasn't quite as bad with the added boost from the Stone's energies and her deeper Talent focus. A huge golden halo of light surrounded her, and the minds of the others gathered with her, but still didn't fully counter the inner wrenching. When it lifted, she was standing and watching the small group of survivors striving to dig their way up to the surface.

Smoke filled the air, making it hard to see very far, as flames burned unchecked in a corridor nearby. The light panels built into the walls were flickering, with many having burned out. The ground beneath seemed to be shaking and bucking at times, as great forces fought each other in reshaping and rending the structures. The people appeared haggard and desperate, hoping for a way to save their lives and escape the horrific destruction happening all around them.

"It is too far and there is not enough time! We need out now," Adina commented loudly, as Ryes willed herself to be visible to them all. Her aunt appeared exhausted, and as if her courage was finally failing.

"There goes the idea of helping them tunnel their way topside," Maren sent to Garth. Others heard it and they agreed with him whole-heartedly. Many were shocked at witnessing this unimaginable destruction happening all around Ryes, and now understood her desperation in finding a way to rescue her aunt and as many as she could.

"This is what was," Rhodi emphasized to the link which brought overall calm, once again, realizing they were far from the flames and destruction.

"We're all going to die!" a woman cried out, huddling close to an injured man as they sat upon the floor near Ryes. He put an arm about her, trying to comfort her.

"Lady Ryes," Hadu called out, pointing her out to Adina. Adina's head snapped up as she turned to face her niece.

"I hope you bring us some good news, dear niece of mine," she pleaded, appearing to hope in her heart that it was true.

"Yes. I'm going to try to pull everyone to the future. We tried it on a shorter time journey and succeeded, so I believe we can do it.

Are you ready?" she asked, inwardly quaking as she thought of physically stepping out into this terrible past, as she'd stepped out onto the deck of the Star Quest before. The walls and floors were shaking, as the city was still being bombed. She stepped up close to everyone as she spoke.

"It sounds impossible, but I am as ready, as I can be," Adina replied, then she turned to the others as they paused in their efforts. There was something strange about the sudden appearance of this young woman; she wasn't dirty, nor coughing, nor in panic as they were now. "Is everyone ready to attempt a journey into the future, to escape certain death here? This is not without risk, so only step forward if you feel you truly wish to make the attempt," she urged, seeing new hope dawning in their eyes.

"What do we need to do?" the sobbing woman asked, standing up and helping the injured man to stand.

"Take my hand," Ryes told her, smiling as she extended it. They hobbled to her, and the woman reached out to take the ghostly-looking hand. Suddenly, it was real, as their hands clasped one another. "Here, I'm going to hand you back to the people in my own time. It'll feel terrible for a few moments, but they'll help you arrive safely," she explained as she passed them back, as she'd done before on the Star Quest, feeling the surprise and delight of the rest of the link, as it looked like this was working as well as their previous operation. Monty had opened his eyes to confirm their arrival for the commune and Ryes.

Suddenly, in the spot where Ryes had stood, was the couple she had sent to the future. Ted stepped forward, through the open end of the circle and urged them to join him away from the spot Ryes was standing in. He helped take the weight of the injured man, giving the woman a smile.

"You're safe now," he assured her. She looked around, amazed.

"But where is the city?" she asked, feeling out of place in this grassy land with trees growing all around them, but willingly moving in the direction he led. She was coughing now with the fresh air to breathe.

"The city lies below our feet, beneath the plants," Metta assured her with a nod. He helped Ted support the man out of the circle of Talents and get him settled on a stretcher, so he could exam him. They were both coughing from the smoke they inhaled before. Phil helped the woman to their treatment area and clear the people sitting, without disturbing them. He fetched a bottle of water for her after he sat her in a chair. She appeared bewildered.

"We should have some people to help keep them away from Ryes' spot," Metta ordered, sure of this need, at the very least. Jim nodded as he and Anders stepped up to assist, along with four others, all ready to lend helping hands.

"They just disappeared!" another man declared, sounding astonished while stepping closer. Ryes laughed, then started coughing as a thick plume of smoke drifted her way. Maren pulled up her Healing to help, while Ossa used Ryes' Air Shaper to change the course of that fouled air current, all without disrupting her Time Walking Talent.

"Yes, they're in the time where I, my family and friends all live," she assured him. "I don't have the strength to keep this up for long. Are you coming, or not? Do you want to live?" she insisted, as she extended her hand. Another two men ran up and took her offered hand, quickly disappearing as she passed them back to her time. A line started up as hope dawned in everyone's eyes. Quickly, Ryes sent them to her teams, as her great aunt now stood beside her, beaming merrily. She was glad she had the Windrose Stone to draw upon to boost her Talent immensely, or she wouldn't be able to last so long. And Rhin, whatever his new Talent was, it helped her focus her own abilities to a crystal clarity.

The people staggering up to her were giving her thanks, while she smiled and nodded, afraid to take too deep of breaths to keep from coughing uncontrollably and breaking her focus. She was grateful for Maren and Ossa's help and let them know it. Her Aunt Adina was so proud of her as she stood next to her. She barely knew her but felt the kinship strongly now.

Ryes' sense of family suddenly inspired Monty. He wanted to do something to help Denas heal fully. Her family had to be here somewhere! Seeing how little Ryes wasn't using her full range of Talents, he "borrowed" her Empath and Healing searching, getting a feel from his intimacy with Denas, for her life-pulse. Perhaps her mother and grandmother could be saved, too? He had to try! He stretched out searching, using her Talents, as he'd worked with her before while in playing with then. After several long moments, he finally found them and was devastated to find they were already dead. But there were two young boys nearby that "felt" related, so he pulled up a small part of her Manipulator and started threading a way through the collapsing city. It was an impossible, shifting maze! Denas finally noted what he was doing and was horrified at seeing it all so personal and close-up through Monty. Then she recognized these two young boys as her younger brothers.

Feeling desperate, Monty dug in deeper into the range of Ryes' Talents, looking for a solution that would speed things up, yet keep them safe. Finally, he found something Denas' Catalyst Talent said was a Translocation Talent, but before he could act, she seized it and moved her brothers over near Ryes. Denas realized she'd used it as Ryes would have, with her Catalyst Talent showing her the basic use of the new Talent. He felt the singing in her heart at having done this one small feat herself.

Then Minya joined them, now seeking her own family through the wreckage of their home city. Not finding them, she was puzzled, so took over the Empath and did a broader search, only to discover her family was in the southern continent. They seemed safe, so she turned her attention upwards, to the Snagospin ships. She used Ryes' Molecular Manipulator and Inner Sight to destroy vital parts in over two dozen invading starships, preventing parties of Snagospin from landing craft to help finish off the fleeing population. All this Talent borrowing partly distracted Ryes, as she was trying to save the trapped people. Rhodi and Maren pulled the extra Talents away from Minya, in case they needed them for the rescue, knowing Ryes did have limits.

After Ryes handed back at least thirty people into the future, there was a horrific booming noise and the "floor" beneath their feet began bucking and shifting; tearing open an endlessly deep trench starting in a nearby corridor, as if the deck beneath their feet was made of tissue-paper! Ryes screamed as another fissure in the floor opened right behind her, with the floor tilting to drop her down into it, causing her to lose her balance and tumble back. She fell, scrabbling for something to grab, catching hold of a cable dangling from the ruined ceiling above. Luckily, it was a no longer powered data link cable. She was trying not to get stuck between layers of the floor and its substructure, but with the shaking and jostling of the floors, she slipped down into the jagged opening in it. Her body was being crushed, ground, and stabbed by the ragged pieces of floor's support materials, and the movement from the building's collapse.

Ryes' mind was racing, as she realized she could actually die here in Tayna's past! She refused and held on, as her stubbornness came to the fore, but there was no one who could reach her to save her! Hadu had snatched Adina away from the immediate danger and appeared uncertain on how to save her too. Despair filled her as her body was being torn apart! She was still holding tightly to her Time Walking connection and the power streams from the Windrose Stone; so afraid to let that slip – even now! And with the others tapping her other Talents, in her terror she felt herself fumbling to pull up any of her Talents herself, even to save herself! She was being ripped open and could barely breathe! Still, she scrabbled for purchase as the cable was now loose and slipping from her fingers, trying to find anything she could grasp to help pull herself out of her dire dilemma, but the floor had been slick and smooth. Ryes closed her eyes for a moment, as she felt overwhelmed and so very lost! What could she do? She couldn't pull herself back to her own time, as she didn't think she'd survive the transition, as torn up as she thought her body was right now. But she didn't want to die!

Garth struggled to reach her, to let her know he believed in her and knew she could do this. The others in their circle were in a panic over how to reach Ryes to save her. Her despair and charged emotions were blocking them from reaching her and hindering their ability to tap her Talents now. It was like almost all her Talents had shut down!

"Ryes! Ryes!" Maren, Mitt, Raya, and others in the commune were calling out to her to get her attention away from the moment she was mired in, before she actually died! Her highly strung emotions were blocking them, now. And her body being torn apart was as horrific for them, as well as her!

....

Then, another consciousness in the commune noticed what was happening. And Rhin, who had almost as deep a link to his mother, as his father's, started to let her know he was deeply upset.

...

He did the mental equivalent of a loud, unhappy, wailing cry, throwing all his small being into expressing his own despair.

...

Their bond ran deep, and Ryes realized how much he loved her, and how terrified he was at seeing her this way, and not understanding what was happening, nor why.

...

And somehow, he tapped her Talents and pulled in his siblings. The remaining four infants, with Sayer and Raby; suddenly they knew it all! Their deep, joined cries and terror reverberated through her very soul! It shattered her inward focus and Ryes suddenly knew what she had to do!

...

Ryes' eyes snapped open, she frowned, and forced herself to push aside her deep depression and despair, as she poured out to Rhin, Garth, all their other children, and the others in the original link all the love in her heart. Her Talents were fully open once more, as she strove to shield her cubs from her pain and anguish. She would never surrender her life so easily and hurt them this way! She looked up to her Aunt Adina to see the horror on her face, as Hadu carefully stepped over to her side, daring the crazy tilt to the floor, where she was trapped. The distress in his silvery eyes showed her how dire her situation was now!

As Hadu grabbed her arms to pull her out, Mitt took full control of Ryes' Manipulator and Molecular Manipulator, with Almas and others in their circle adding in their experience and control, as she was still barely learning these Talents. Together they dissolved the molecules of the floor plates around her and pulled Ryes free and back on her feet, moving her and Hadu closer to the remaining survivors. Maren and the Healers quickly had her body repaired, while Rhodi, Raya and Denas kept her links solid with her Talents, the Windrose Stone, and themselves. Garth was beside himself; feeling so helpless, but saw there was a little he could do by extinguishing the flames that raged nearby and threatening to kill them.

"Ryes!" Adina cried as she wanted to hold her and protect her, as she ran to be next to her, again. Hadu steadied her and while there were still tears streaming down her face, she gave him a nod and a brave smile for her aunt.

"Hurry, come forward!" Ryes shouted before another bout of coughing hit her again. Desperate people came from all around the area. Mitt had found more people, as Lissel and Poli had employed Ryes' Empath and with Almas' help, pulled them over to Ryes; they had been on floors above and below and it'd been no easy task to gather them all here, without any further harm, until Denas showed them how to use the Translocator Talent. Dunn and Sabin had to calm down everyone and let them know how to escape, once they were near Ryes. And Mitt had to help Lissel and Poli distance themselves within, as the death around the people they were rescuing, almost overwhelmed them. They were not used to the broad extent of Ryes' Empath. Saree kept Ryes' Booster open for all to use, with her own added in to help, and she saw how much more easily everything was accomplished with Rhin's Focus Talent in full operation. Ossa combined her Storm Caller with Garth's Fire Shaper to eliminate the fire storms and give the people a chance to retreat away from the city. Her cleansing winds kept the air fresh for them. Adina found herself momentarily drawn into their link, and with Ryes' Pool of Power, used her Earth Shaper to keep the ceiling from crashing down upon them and strengthened the floor. It was something that would've been a struggle before and was incredibly easy now!

People that had been pulled into the area, as well as those originally trapped with Adina and Hadu, crowded near all three of them, gathering as close as possible, so that Ryes could take their hands and pass them onward to her own time. Their vanishing from the here and now, while noted, wasn't questioned as they were in terror of their world literally crashing down around them. Men, women, children of the starmen and other peoples were handed forward.

"How is this happening?" a woman demanded with tears in her eyes, as she clutched her youngest daughter tightly. The cub was crying hysterically, now.

"It is an attack upon Hailys, and Ryes is pulling us all to safety in the future! Hurry," Adina urged, fear in her eyes now, even if she was just so proud of her wondrous niece. She grasped Ryes' hand and she and her daughter vanished. Those who knew, rushed over to Ryes, and eagerly took her hand now. The ones from below seemed to quickly figure it out and joined them in this seemingly impossible passage of escape. After a few moments of still searching with Empath and feeling the intensity of thousands of people dying just nearby, Mitt was practically reeling and sick to her stomach. Rhodi broke her connection to Ryes' Empath, while Minya healed her body back to normal, to keep her steady and supporting the full link with the other stronger Mind Voice Talents, once more.

"I wish Mada was here to meet you," Adina told Ryes as she handed back another woman. Ryes smiled; her eyes merry once more at hearing it. "Not that I would want her here for this disaster, but I believe she would cherish knowing you, Ryes." Finally, it was down to her and Hadu.

"It's time," Ryes told her, extending her hand to them. "I can't keep this up, anymore. I'm utterly worn through," she admitted, feeling a little "thin" now. Adina nodded to this, still amazed at how powerful her Time Walking Talent truly was! Hadu suddenly wrapped an arm around her, pulling her tightly into his arms, then took Ryes' offered hand. She laughed as she pulled them both back through time with her, the wrenching sensation hitting her hard, as her exhaustion and damage to her body caused her to lose control over the energy beams. She settled back into herself; glad it was finally over! She saw the sun overhead and felt Adina and Hadu's weight against her body before she lost consciousness. Hadu managed to catch her before she fell to the ground.

Adina saw bright morning sunlight all around her, as she realized they truly were somewhere – some when - else. Hadu released her, as he supported Ryes in his other arm. Adina was glad her stomach quickly settled after that horrid wrenching feeling but was still coughing. Then noticed Ryes was unconscious.

"I'll take her," a strange man urged, stepping over to them. Hadu handed her over, only because he was unsure whom to call to help in this strange land. "Thank you," Ted said, then turned to carry her straight over to Maren. He noted the icy coldness of her skin, and he couldn't tell if she was breathing, or not. Still, he remained calm as he bent and waited for Maren to open his eyes. It wasn't long before he did and readily released the other hands he held, to take his cousin and focus his Healing. Ted stepped back to help care for the others they rescued, knowing she was in the best hands possible.

"A Stone of Power? It is the largest I have ever seen," Adina questioned as she turned to see it sitting next to them. She was still coughing but knew the fresh air around them would quickly help that. The group gathered in the open circle were now opening their eyes and letting go of each other. The people who'd been trapped were still standing around, gawking at the empty grasslands around them; most having been moved outside their circle. The three large and one small machines nearby were a new curiosity to their eyes, too.

"Let me help him," Tennan offered, standing to take care of an injured man, who'd been one of the first to take Ryes' offer. "I'm a Healer."

"Will the one who saved us be all right?" the woman who was with him asked, hoping, seeing she'd collapsed.

"My brother will take care of her," she replied with assurance, "He's the most powerful Healer we have." Tennan bent to see to her partner's wounds, closing her eyes. Minya, Ruan, Sadie and Torr all stepped up to help others, who'd been injured, too. Adina turned to note Ryes was now being held by a young man, who was still sitting upon the soft matting. She and Hadu walked over, noting another man held a young cub in his arms. He looked more anxious than the rest and she guessed he was Ryes' husband.

"Here, can Rhin help you any?" he questioned as he held the child in his arms. A woman with gray eyes and brown hair shifted closer to help provide the bridge with Mind Voice. She gripped Maren's arm while the husband extended his hand to the Healer's shoulder, gripping it lightly. A woman, who had lavender eyes, stepped over, knelt, and closed her eyes, putting her hand upon the Healer's other shoulder.

"Will Ryes be all right?" Adina questioned a woman, who sat near the others, with deep concern in her eyes.

"I do not know," Rhodi admitted. "I cannot believe what it was like back then. I have never felt so much death before."

"I cannot believe Ryes succeeded and we are now in the future. How far are we from the starport?" she questioned, not seeing any signs of civilization around. Rhodi stood up, smiling, as she gave her a graceful nod of her head.

"My name is Rhodi of House Klark, and we are only a few dozen feet from the starport. It lies right over there," she informed her, pointing to where the great crater lay.

"I am Adina of House Li, and this is my protector, Hadu-ramashan," she introduced herself, smiling to see manners had not gone out of vogue through the years. Hadu quickly bowed to her, then went to see it for himself, striding through the grass quickly, with his long stride. "Hadu will see it for me and report," she explained. Rhodi laughed lightly at this, giving her a nod of her head. She turned her attention back to Ryes, as the others gathered here began to collect nearby, too. Maren was taking a very long time with his treatment. Finally, Garth opened his eyes, as Saree relaxed back, sitting upon her heels, and Dunn let go Maren's arm and gave Garth a nod.

"She's going to make it," he told the gathering. "But it was a tough fight." Maren opened his eyes, looking down at his cousin, sighing in relief, even with all the blood now drying on her clothing.

"Thank goodness we had the Windrose Stone," he commented, "And we already knew how to tap it."

"Garth, we're going to have to make sure everyone understands English, as none of the ones we rescued understood a word you two just spoke," Mitt teased in Dolbith, with a merry laugh. She was relieved that Ryes had made it through.

"You're right," he agreed, deliberately using English, getting to his feet. He handed Rhin to Denas, seeing the panic still in her eyes. He'd be something for her to focus upon after the destruction she witnessed through Ryes' Talents. Mitt, Lissel and Poli's view through Ryes' Empath had sickened the whole link, as so many people were trapped and dying in Hailys. All of them had been shocked at seeing what it was like, with her physical presence in Hailys of the past. He then took Ryes from Maren's arms, allowing him to stand. Maren quietly touched Adina, easing the damage to her lungs from the fires and chemical-laden smoke. She momentarily smiled her thanks at him.

"You must be Ryes' Aunt Adina," Garth said, smiling as he gave her a small bow, recognizing her from his earlier time journey. He cradled his wife close to his chest, not caring one bit about her drying blood transferring to his clothes. She was still out, but was in a deep, healing sleep now. "I apologize, as we usually speak a mixture of both the human's English and Dolbith in Winterhaven. Our stronger Mind Voice Talents can give each of you an understanding of English.

I'm Garth of House Ledearis, Ryes' husband. This is our youngest
son, Rhin. Her second cousin Denas of House Clenons, my sister Mitt,
Ryes' cousin Maren," he began in introduction, indicating the others
around them, as he did so. She gave each of them a nod in
acknowledgement, then when he was done, she turned back to
Denas.

"House Clenons? Do you know of Tair?" she asked Denas, a
look of delighted curiosity in her eyes. She looked up from Rhin, who
was squealing in delight now, to meet her eyes. She was surprised to
meet someone who knew her cousin.

"He is my cousin!" she told her. "I apologize if we have met
and I do not recall," she voiced, blushing. Adina gave her a nod in
understanding.

"Perhaps at Mada and Tair's announcement ceremony? But I
am given to understand that it was now some time ago. I am Adina
of House Li," she introduced herself.

"They were another pair, who seemed so truly meant for each
other," Denas commented. Adina smiled in surprise and nodded her
head. Then a teen-aged boy and a younger cub ran over to her,
recognizing Denas. They threw their arms around her and were
crying and laughing at the same time. "Tekkan! Bonat! You made it!"
The others around them were merry at this unexpected family
reunion, while she was being careful of Rhin, who was still in her
arms. Adina wondered at their manners now, as no one gave them
any space, nor privacy, then saw a face she knew.

"Sabin, I finally get to meet you in person!" she delightfully
declared, smiling as she recognized him. She noted Hadu had
returned to hear these quick introductions, but was holding back what
he needed to say, until she was ready to listen. Sabin bowed to her,
laughing as he stepped closer now.

"I'm glad to see we succeeded, and you and Hadu are well,"
he replied. Hadu gave him a short bow in acknowledgment.

"And what have you seen, Hadu?" Adina questioned, giving
him her full attention, beginning to feel as if this were an impromptu
carnival. The other survivors gathered near now, too. She just then
realized there were over fifty other survivors from Hailys. It was quite
the crowd and yet just a pitiful handful from such a huge city.

"The starport is no more," he informed her. She frowned as
she tried to wrap her mind about such a concept. She saw many of
the others from out of the past were shocked at hearing this news.

"What happened to it?" a woman questioned, not believing, even if it came from a Demmias.

"It was completely destroyed over three hundred years ago, along with the entire city of Hailys," Garth informed them. He raised an arm to indicate where the crater lay. "You may all see it for yourselves, but if it might be too much for you now, we do have plenty of images of what Hailys appears like today."

"And what of Kahmarr?" Adina pressed, needing to know. His eyes held pain as he gazed steadily into hers.

"At the last report from Prince Callas, the Snagospin were close to a full invasion of Kahmarr. Since we've heard nothing through the years, and after seeing the remains of Hailys, we believe it no longer exists. Right now the human's homeworld, Earth, is under siege by the same dark enemy and we're making plans to break through the blockade to free Earth and her inner system colonies," he explained.

"Then, why do you not go save what may be left of Kahmarr?" a man demanded, upset with the thought of his home destroyed.

"It's been hundreds of years since there was any communication with Kahmarr. Ryes pulled all of you out of our past, up through time. We don't even know where Kahmarr lies," Sabin told them, seeing shock in their eyes from hearing his words. There was a murmur of agreement from their own people, who were gathered around them.

"Let's get everyone back to Winterhaven and we'll catch you all up to date about what's happening on and around Tayna. We even have a copy of the last message Prince Callas left us, as a part of an archive, for you to see," Garth added, motioning for the teams to start gathering their things and packing it away. There'd just be room for all their latest newcomers in the choppers, glad they'd flown the two in almost empty.

"Where is this Winterhaven?" Adina questioned, as the crowd began to break up. She moved a loose lock of hair from Ryes' face, seeing how much she looked like Tyra. Then she took off the wreath of flowers from her head and put it back upon Ryes with a smile upon her lips. Garth chuckled at this, realizing they were related in many ways.

"It lies quite a few miles to the south, and is a couple of hours' travel by rover, if Ryes is driving. It's a couple of hours' flight by our choppers, our aircraft parked over there. We've been using the human's system of measurement, as it's more standardized than the one we were using before, when we were simple villagers. We're just

learning of the systems of measurement used by the old Alliance,"
Garth explained.

"She is so much like her mother," she stated, after a few
moments of silence, as she digested what he was telling her. "How
long ago did Tyra die?"

"Shortly after Ryes was born. Rowan, her father's father,
raised her mostly by himself. During the winter months, he had help
from some of the caravaner women, but he's been the only parent
she's known. And she's just as stubborn as he is, most times," he
replied, smiling as he looked down to her in his arms. She was very
precious to him, and it'd scared him at how close they came to losing
her today. "It's too bad she'll also be our best defense against the
Snagospin, or Darkens, as the humans call them. I don't want to use
her that way, but I don't think I'll truly have a choice in the matter."

"Are they the ones who destroyed Hailys? When are you
planning upon going against them?" she pressed, with myriad
questions plaguing her mind, now.

"Yes, they are one and the same destroyers. And we'll go
when we have starships capable of taking them on," he replied,
smiling. "It may be a few years, yet."

"Can you recover any of the ships here?" she asked, sweeping
out an arm to indicate the once-starport lying nearby.

"It's one of the things I was going to have Ryes and Mitt try,
now that we've rescued you. She's been worried about this attempt.
It's too bad she's not even awake to enjoy it," he returned, chuckling
as they walked back to the choppers, walking behind the team
carrying the Windrose Stone. His own people around him were paying
their conversation strict attention.

"We will have plenty of time to get to know each other, now.
And time enough for your other projects. Is your sister an Earth
Shaper?" Adina questioned, wondering. Mitt, who'd been walking
beside Garth started to chuckle at this, as she shook her head no.

"I have Inner Sight and Mind Voice," she informed her, "Ryes
has Earth Shaper and can use the practice."

"And do you have Talent, Garth?"

"Yes. Fire Shaper and Empath, but my Empath is not to the
degree of Ryes' own Talent," he admitted.

"My goodness, she is Talented," she returned in comment as
they stepped up to the chopper.

400

"She's even more Talented than her mother, and she got the power from her father," he told her, meeting her eyes, sure that she'd understand why he worded it the way he had.

"Astounding," she returned, seeing what he meant. Hadu nodded his head to this, grasping his implications. It wasn't a matter easily let out to just anyone, after all!

"Let's go ahead and get you folks aboard," Mitt suggested. "Then Maren can do a thorough check on everyone back in Winterhaven. Afterwards, Raya, Dunn and I can grant each of you an understanding of English, so you won't feel so left out of things."

"My dear, I have Mind Voice, also," Adina stated flatly, as Mitt held open the passenger's door. She noted they were loading the Stone of Power into the cargo area in the back of this smaller machine.

"Then we could always use the added help," she quipped back with a light laugh. Adina smiled in return, not quite sure what to think, as she climbed into the strange machine. She now had a new future ahead and no idea what to expect, but it was good to be alive with possible hopes, once again.

The End of Book Five

For more books, please check my website:
www.mariedaley.com

Whatever It Takes

And a small treat... a peek at book 6 of the Adventures of Ryes and Garth

Arrival

"You do not have to constantly keep your eyes to the scan screens when on duty. You will develop a way to keep them in your sight peripherally," Corsley of House Muratha gently chided Julie Larson, who was sitting at the main scanner board on Flutter-wing. She looked up to him a little round-eyed but gave him a nod.

"This is my first time being wholly responsible for my own board. I'll figure it out," she admitted as she blushed. Corsley loved the blend of her features, knowing she was a starman-human cross from Booda. She appeared an artful balance between the two peoples.

"What did you do before?" he asked to draw her out and get her to relax; she seemed young, not in years, but in life experiences, as he resisted using his Mind Voice to get answers directly.

"In Winterhaven? Or where I came from?" she asked, puzzled, as he was studying her face. It was often the way others acted and she was past letting such behavior get to her, by now.

"Both?" he asked as he took the empty second's chair beside her. "We are going to be working here together and I am curious," he admitted as he smiled encouragement. She drew in a breath and gave him a nod.

"In Winterhaven, Max trained me to help in the control room and he seemed very happy with my work, so recommended me to move up to Flutter-wing," she told him, smiling now, seeing he was genuinely curious about her past. He gave her a nod in understanding. They were short on skilled people in Winterhaven, but this was an important post, too.

"If Max thinks you should be here, then that is a high recommendation. And you have been doing a good job, from what I have seen," he assured her, as he smiled again. She smiled in return, her blue eyes lighting up from within at his compliment. "And what did you do before that?" he pressed, wanting to be sure, loving the bright spirit awaking in her eyes.

"I was born on Booda, the third moon of Tyssen. All I did was help my parents with the garden when I was younger, then helped to care for the young crosses, when I got older. It was heartbreaking at times, since not many lived long, but I was there to provide comfort and care as long, as possible. Not much, when compared to what I can do - all by myself - now," she finished, appearing more confident. "And you? You seem amazingly comfortable with this space station, as if you've lived here all your life." He chuckled in response, giving her a nod. It was a fair question.

"I was brought out of the fires of Hailys destruction by Ryes and our strong Talent team. I used to work in Central Control for Hailys but had been at Nazaneen Starport to see my brother and his wife off to Kisteela for a family vacation. They never made it; I saw them crushed in an instant, before my eyes," he related, his mind was immersed in the horror of that day for a few moments, the memories still horrific. Julie was saddened, unable to imagine it all.

"Corsley, we have an alert update from the Challenger," Briel stated flatly, not as curious about the new scan tech. She recalled he asked about her past, too, when they were first brought up to the empty spaceport. He gave her a nod as he snapped back to the present and stood to return to his post, being he was the Station Chief for Starport Flutter-wing. He put on the primitive headset, returned to his station, and tuned in. Maren had removed his neural net when they were processed at Winterhaven, and it frustrated him at times.

"Flutter-wing here, Corsley speaking," he commed.

"Hi Corsley, it's Axel. We have an update for you on those inbound Earth ships. It's confirmed they're due to arrive an hour before lunch today," he informed him on the vid.

"And what are the standing orders?" he pressed, wanting to be sure. He used to work in the command center for Hailys, so this small station was in no way as complex. Still, he wasn't completely comfortable with so few defenses set up for the station; they were vulnerable. Phil assured him better defensive capabilities were in the plans for Flutter-wing's next expansion; he only hoped it'd be soon.

"We'll invite them to dock up there for a while, so be ready for company. We don't know how they'll behave, so keep an eye to protecting the secure areas and the people there. Shawn will be arriving shortly with some added security to lend you a hand, and the staff and supplies you'll need for the larger population," he informed him. Corsley gave him a nod in relief.

"We will take care of it," he confidently assured him.

"Have their officers assist in policing their own people, too. That'll help give you a breather. See if you can come up with some good do's and don'ts to advise them about. We're leaving it up to you if you want to lease any rooms for the crew to use, or not. Remember, it's our station, not theirs! And don't hesitate to call for help, or advice, if needed. We're all here for you," Axel offered.

"I will handle it, but appreciate the back-up," Corsley stated with confidence and a nod. A smile finally showed on his face. "After hosting a diplomatic party of Vastins, this will be easy," he bragged. Axel laughed and gave him a nod, with unvoiced questions in his eyes.

"It's why we thought you were the best one to head up this command," he replied. "Call us or Winterhaven if you need anything."

"Your confidence is very appreciated. We will be ready to receive our guests. Anything else we should know?" he pressed.

"Ryes is concerned that their Talents may not be very polite, so feel free to intervene, as needed," Axel added. Corsley nodded with another smile.

"My specialty! It will be fine. We will do whatever it takes!"

"Thanks! Anything you need from us right now?" He shook his head in response. Axel nodded. "Then over and out. Challenger on standby," he responded and cut the communication.

"What's a Vastin?" Julie asked with a frown, as she'd swiveled to face him. Corsley laughed, as did Briel, but it wasn't derisive laughter.

"They are a belligerent people, who smell horrible and think the whole universe owes them whatever they take to fancy. They were good warriors though, and a good people to have at your side in a fight," Briel explained with a merry light in her eyes. Julie smiled in response and gave them a nod.

"Sounds like we could use a few with us now," she replied.

"Truly, we could," Corsley agreed.

"Incoming shuttle from Winterhaven," Julie chimed, seeing the tell-tale, and recognizing it. "Shawn's almost here."

"Good man; good pilot," Corsley assured her. She smiled and gave him a nod. "Now to get the station buttoned down for this friendly visit by potential allies. We will all be on the alert and take nothing for granted," he ordered. He turned for his own board and set to work. The others here in the control center would handle the mundane tasks, for which he was grateful. Still, he stole a glance at Julie as she focused upon her console once again. He smiled as he thought of getting to know her better during their next free time together.

www.ingramcontent.com/pod-product-compliance
Lightning Source LLC
Chambersburg PA
CBHW011147190726

48288CB00010B/3213